"McMyne's debut is a reinv[...] luscious origin story from the witch's point of view.... McMyne melds folklore with actual historical figures and cleverly bookends the narrative with opening and closing chapters set in the twenty-first century." —*Booklist* (starred review)

"This is the fairy-tale retelling I never knew I needed. Rooted in history, *The Book of Gothel* highlights the relationships between women and the ways in which we both help and hinder each other in the name of love and loyalty. Haelewise will be in my heart for a very long time."

—Genevieve Gornichec, author of *The Witch's Heart*

"An inventive retelling of a classic tale that pulls you deep into the wild woods of medieval Germany. *The Book of Gothel* is a spellbinding debut." —Signe Pike, author of *The Forgotten Kingdom*

"Fable and history rhyme in McMyne's captivating vision of a medieval past steeped in women's magic and bound by women's love."

—Jordanna Max Brodsky, author of
The Wolf in the Whale

"Heartfelt and vividly imagined, this intriguing backstory to a classic fairy tale lifts the curtain on a medieval world where women battle to keep magic alive."

—Emily Croy Barker, author of *The Thinking Woman's Guide to Real Magic*

By Mary McMyne

The Book of Gothel
A Rose by Any Other Name

A ROSE BY ANY OTHER NAME

MARY McMYNE

REDHOOK

Copyright © 2024 by Mary McMyne
Excerpt from *The Book of Gothel* copyright © 2022 by Mary McMyne

Cover design by Lisa Marie Pompilio
Cover photographs by Blake Morrow
Cover copyright © 2024 by Hachette Book Group, Inc.
Author photograph by David S. Bennett

Redhook Books/Orbit
Hachette Book Group
1290 Avenue of the Americas
New York, NY 10104
hachettebookgroup.com

First Edition: July 2024
Simultaneously published in Great Britain by Orbit

Redhook is an imprint of Orbit, a division of Hachette Book Group.
The Redhook name and logo are registered trademarks of Hachette Book Group, Inc.

The publisher is not responsible for websites (or their content) that are not owned by the publisher.

The Hachette Speakers Bureau provides a wide range of authors for speaking events. To find out more, go to hachettespeakersbureau.com or email HachetteSpeakers@hbgusa.com.

Redhook books may be purchased in bulk for business, educational, or promotional use. For information, please contact your local bookseller or the Hachette Book Group Special Markets Department at special.markets@hbgusa.com.

Library of Congress Cataloging-in-Publication Data
Names: McMyne, Mary, author.
Title: A Rose by any other name / Mary McMyne.
Description: First edition. | New York, NY : Redhook, 2024.
Identifiers: LCCN 2023057225 | ISBN 9780316393515 (trade paperback) | ISBN 9780316393614 (e-book)
Subjects: LCSH: Shakespeare, William, 1564–1616—Fiction. | LCGFT: Biographical fiction. | Romance fiction. | Novels.
Classification: LCC PS3613.C58557 R67 2024 | DDC 813/.6—dc23/eng/20231218
LC record available at https://lccn.loc.gov/2023057225

ISBNs: 9780316393515 (trade paperback), 9780316393614 (ebook)

Printed in the United States of America

LSC-C

Printing 1, 2024

To the only begetter of these ensuing chapters, Mr. D.B.

PROLOGUE

My name has only been whispered, heretofore, so that is where
I'll start. *Rose*, my mother christened me, for the thorny
blooms in her garden. *Rose Rushe*. Her name for me was prescient.
I grew to be much like those flowers: petaled, prickly, blood dark.
Delightful to look at from a distance but like to make you bleed if
touched.

Let no man fault the barbs in my disposition. I came of age during the latter years of Queen Elizabeth on the southeast coast of
England, a time and place where women like me were especially
scorned. I was the daughter of an ill-starred astrologer and a witch
who refused to hide her Catholicism. A flower that grows in such a
garden needs thorns.

Though my identity be hidden, much has been written of my
character. It is true I am a wanton woman, no virgin, no goddess.
It is true I broke my bed-vow; I loved my friend too much, my
husband too little. I stand accused of using my wiles, or worse,
some hellish power, to plague a certain poet with lust.

The truth is, that poet—a pox on it, I'll say his name—Will
Shakespeare, pursued me freely, of his own choosing. And the sonnets he wrote of our encounters, the bitter spew of a jealous lover,
nearly ruined me.

1

No doubt it was a fault in my stars that made me what I am: a wild, unruly wench. Venus was enjoying Aries while my mother laboured to bring me forth, and Mercury was conjunct with Jupiter in Aquarius. I have always been bold, contrary. Not the sort of girl who dreams a man would woo her, wed her, and carry her off to a farmhouse to raise his children. Given the choice, in truth, I would have chosen a case of dropsy over a husband.

I do not shun all womanly pursuits. I can embroider a delicate handkerchief, make an excellent mead. I love to wear a fine gown, and I have mastered the art of being alluring. But I am also a lover of astrology and poetry, music and merriment. The sort of girl whose mother had to lock the cellar where she kept the mead, who kissed five different youths before she turned fifteen, who convinced boys to take her to plays at the innyard.

Mother scolded me harshly, claiming my fame would make me unmarriageable, but that was suitable to me. I did not wish to marry any of the youths with whom she caught me "venturing." I saw them as they saw me: sport and little more. What else was there to do in our sleepy village?

From a young age, I dreamed of escape. I wanted to wander the bustling streets of London, watch plays in famous theatres, see the notorious houses of ill repute. I wanted to hear performances by great musicians, attend masques and decadent feasts.

To live in London, I thought I might have to find my mother's family, Italian immigrants of whom she refused to speak. Or that I might take a position as a servant in the house of an astrologer.

But the escape plan that appealed to me most, my dream, was to become a court musician.

I have always loved how music moves the spirit, awakening instincts that would otherwise lie dormant—like the lute string that vibrates when another of its consort plays its note. There were no women in my father's music company, but women sang in the streets and performed in masques at noble houses. I didn't see why the queen's court need be different.

If there were no female musicians at court already, I could be first. I was blessed with a singular talent. When I sang hymns in church, other women stopped singing to stare. Father's musician friends said my voice was like a siren's.

As I approached marrying age, my father encouraged me to prac-tise my music because he thought it might help me attract a hus-band. Mother warned me to be chaste and modest in my playing so I didn't further damage my name. Their matchmaking attempts were going nowhere. No one wanted a woman like me for a wife, no matter how beautifully I bedecked my hair or brightened my cheeks.

Garlands and ribbons cannot repair a reputation.

I listened when Father, a spinet player, advised me on my music. I practised during every spare moment. By twenty-one, I was uncommon skilled with the virginal—my favourite instrument—and adept with the psaltery, viol, and lute. I knew I was good enough to play at court. The question was how to get there.

Near the end of August that year, when Father and his music company were in town, they heard me singing my little brother to sleep and called me downstairs to perform. I put on one of my mother's old dresses, a rich rose-coloured damask gown from her trunk full of the fine clothes she owned from before she met Father. I checked my appearance in my mirror, coiled my hair into a net, and carried the psaltery into the garden, slipping a rose behind my ear.

It was almost twilight. The horizon looked as if it were on fire. The sky was a sea of lilac, perfectly clear. Mother's garden glowed with a reddish golden hue. The bees whose wax she used for candles buzzed as they returned to their hives. The air was heavy with the scent of blooms.

Roses, of course, whose petals my mother used in love charms. Lavender to soothe jealousy. Dianthus, rosemary, rue. Beautiful, but they reminded me of what I wasn't. I had no trace of the occult gifts my mother said ran in her family. I seemed to have access only to star charts and the world of the senses.

I placed the psaltery on my lap, remembering the song I'd written for my friend Cecely, inspired by our dreams of escaping to London. Father's friends gathered around me, dressed in faded summer attire, sipping mead from cheap pewter goblets. I pretended I was playing for an audience of rank, a visiting earl or duchess. The silver tune filled the garden.

I met the men's eyes as I played, watching their inner recalcitrance awaken. Mother frowned from the back door, her black hair pulled into a severe bun. She disapproved of me playing secular music, but I loved the way playing it made me feel—seductive, powerful.

When I finished, the men applauded, wildly appreciative of my performance. Mother rolled her eyes and went inside. Father ignored her, rewarding my efforts with a goblet of mead. I savoured the honeyed taste; it was like drinking sunlight.

The violist said my song was extraordinary, that he'd never heard anything like it. The elderly lutenist announced that a boy as skilled as I could play at court. "Though boy she clearly is *not*," he said, raising a lecherous eyebrow and drawing a chuckle from all but my father.

I raised my own brow, pressing the psaltery to my chest, smiling prettily. "I'll be sure to tell your wife you noticed."

The lutenist went pale. Father and the others howled with

laughter. I drained my goblet and bade them good night, counting the evening a success.

I had been waiting for the right moment to tell Father about my musical ambitions, and the lutenist had raised the subject for me. Normally I am blunt of speech—perhaps too blunt—but the stakes were too high to be careless about this subject. I checked my ephemeris to ensure that the stars were favourable. Mercury was still in Leo, an auspicious time for persuasion.

I waited for my father's guests to depart, my heart tripping like a child playing hop-egg at Easter. When the last guest was gone, I found Father in the kitchen, draining the last bit of mead from the jug. He seemed to be in good spirits, his brown eyes merry behind his spectacles. "You're still awake?"

"I had difficulty sleeping. All the excitement."

"You distinguished yourself in both music and wit tonight." He laughed, shaking his head. He was proud of my skill with rhetoric. "That whitebeard deserved that barb."

I righted a goblet that lay sideways on the table. "Mother says your latest matchmaking attempt failed?"

Father set down the mead jug, puzzled at the change of subject. His cheeks were bright red, his eyes slightly crossed as they always were when he was in his cups. A smirk pulled at his lips. "You haven't exactly made things easy, Rose."

"Perhaps marriage isn't as foregone a conclusion for women as it once was. A new era is dawning. There's an unmarried woman on the throne. The queen employs female dancers, a female painter."

"What are you getting at?"

"Do you think Underhill would ask the Master of Revels to audition me as a court musician, if you offered him a wager?"

Father blinked at me—once, twice—looking both shocked and impressed by my proposal. Our old friend Master Underhill, an alchemist with connections at court, had visited last spring with his son Richard. When he bragged about how close he'd become to the Master of Revels, I had seen an opportunity. Underhill was fond of me, and he had a terrible weakness for gambling.

Father didn't laugh. I'll give him that. Suddenly he looked completely sober. He drew a deep breath, closing his eyes. The moment stretched out. "Where would you live?" he asked finally.

"I could use my salary to rent a room from Underhill."

Father opened his mouth, but I continued.

"This is highly irregular, I know. There are a dozen problems to solve if it works. But I'm good enough to play at court, Father. You know it. Let me audition, and I'll prove myself."

Father shook his head, the corners of his mouth turning downward in an indulgent smirk. "What am I to do with you?"

Master Underhill visited with his son Richard the next week on their way back from Bohemia. I waited until my mother had gone upstairs to bring up my idea. Underhill was always in better spirits when she wasn't around. He was in particularly good spirits this trip, chattering about a breakthrough in his alchemical experiments as soon as he hung his tall hat at the door. He was so excited, his hands shook, and his fingertips were still stained red with cinnabar.

He listened with interest as I proposed the wager my father suggested: If I was hired, Underhill would rent me a room. If I wasn't, Father would give Underhill his astrologer's ring, which he admired each time he visited. I had been surprised when Father offered to gamble the ring. Father had always said it was lucky, the reason he was so good at casting horoscopes. But Underhill was fascinated with the ring, and Father told me: *It isn't much of a risk, Rose. I believe in you.*

Underhill looked at my father, his kind green eyes wide with surprise. His gaze fell, eager, upon the ring, which glinted in the candlelight. Underhill set down his goblet and pushed back his silvery hair. "The Master of Revels will think you a novelty," he said finally, his eyes crinkling with amusement.

A rush of affection for him filled me. "I owe you a debt."

He shook his head. "This will be my pleasure."

That night, while I was beating his son Richard mercilessly at our favourite card game, triumph, I asked him to tell me what it would be like to live in London. Richard, never shy about talking, was happy to oblige. He told me about the Queen Elizabeth's Day festivities that took place each November—the elaborate musical performances that would echo through the tiltyards, the massive horned effigy of the pope that the Basketweavers would burn—his eyes gleaming with a Protestant sense of reprisal. Perhaps my audition would coincide with the holiday.

He told me about Underhill House. Although the Underhills came to visit us twice a year or so, I'd never been to their home. It was three stories, he said, finely arrayed with rich furnishings. They had a great library with shelves that stretched from floor to ceiling, hundreds of books on astrology and alchemy, over two dozen servants, a talented cook. I *ached* to live in a place like that, where the chairs didn't have wobbly legs and the tapestries on the walls weren't a hundred years out of fashion. I would be able to see plays, attend balls and feasts, spend my days playing music.

The only part of my plan I had left to reason out was how to take Cecely with me.

Unfortunately, by the time Underhill wrote back with good news, my father had fallen ill. We thought it was an ague at first, but my mother's most potent healing charm did nothing, and the smelling herbs the physician prescribed only made his cough worse.

As the weeks passed, I tried to tell myself that Father was getting older, that his healing would simply take more time. But Mother cast her healing charm so many times she became weak, and Father only grew sicker.

The week before we were supposed to go to London, Mother

bought a nostrum from Cecely's parents, mountebanks who had just returned from one of their medicine-selling tours. Their remedies were supposed to be of dubious quality, but nothing else was working.

When Mother offered Father the red nostrum, he made a jest about whether she was trying to kill him or cure him. Mother reminded him of the brevity of the lifeline on his right palm. "It's the only thing we haven't tried, Secundus," she said, her expression mirthless. "This illness could be what kills you."

A few nights later, Father called me to his room. It was late. The moon was new. The chamber was dark except for the small circle of light my candle cast.

As I approached the bed, I noticed my father's laboured breathing. His black sheepdog, Hughe, lay on the floor beside him, his muzzle pressed to the ground, his eyes mournful.

Something knitted my stomach. Fear, perhaps, or dread.

"Rose?" my father said in a gravelly voice. "Is that you?"

I closed my eyes, struggling to master the tightness in my chest. *Tranquilla sum*, I thought. *Tranquilla ero.* I have always found Latin soothing.

I drew the bedcurtains, holding out my candle so I could see my father. His brown eyes, enlarged by his spectacles, wandered up to meet mine. He was only forty, but his hair, once as red as the queen's, had gone white. He'd lost two or three stone in as many months.

"I'll be plain." He sighed, shaking his head. His eyes were shadowed. "My death will leave your mother and brother vulnerable. We must reconsider our plans for your future."

My heart dropped. His death? *Will leave,* future tense, as if he were certain. "Don't speak that way, Father. You get an ague each summer. You're frightening me."

His gaze was steady. *This is not an ague,* his eyes said, *and you know it.*

"Mother's predictions don't always come true. Palm reading is notoriously unreliable—"

He sighed. "I know my body, Rose. It's failing."

A cold sensation travelled through my chest as I allowed myself to consider for the first time what my life would be like without him: the chill of a house ruled by my mother.

"Your uncle Primus is going to try to take back the farm. If you marry, we can arrange for your husband to take in your mother and brother."

Marry? The word called up a sorry image of myself in my night-gown, wild hair frizzing from a braid, a babe nursing at my breast. A much older man in bed behind me, moustached, a widower who wouldn't be bothered by my reputation. The image fought with the future self I'd imagined in London—performing at a royal feast dressed in finery, hair carefully arranged. My chest went tight.

"Why wouldn't Uncle Primus let Mother stay here? Aunt Margery stayed in Uncle Tertius's house after he died. They're still there, all these years later."

"Your uncle plays favourites." Father turned his astrologer's ring anxiously, his eyes sad. "Perhaps your husband will let you sing with the choir here."

My throat constricted. Half the local choir's members couldn't carry a tune. "With my reputation, I would be lucky if my husband let me out of his sight."

Father laughed, but it quickly devolved into coughing. "I cannot change the past, Rose. Or set the future."

He removed his ring—an easy feat, it had grown loose—and held it out. "Keep this safe. Don't let your mother have it, no matter how hard things get. It's too valuable. You know how she is. I want you and Edmund to have something to remember me by."

I stared at the ring, uneasy. Under ordinary circumstances, I would've jumped to take it. But now, I felt as if accepting the ring would mean accepting what he was saying.

"Go on," he prodded. "Take it."

The ring was heavier than it looked. The candlelight was too dim to read the outer ring's inscription, but I knew it by heart: *SUPERIORA DE INFERIORIBUS, INFERIORA DE SUPERIORIBUS.* Father said it referred to the connection between the heavens and the world below. The ring was of excellent artisanship. Stacked beneath the outer band were several concealed inner hoops that fanned out into a miniature model of the heavens.

I rubbed my finger along the cold metal, feeling the grooves of the inscription, unsettled. "Couldn't Mother take Edmund to live with her family?"

"Your mother's family—" Father said. He opened his mouth as if he were going to say more, then shook his head. "That's not an option. I'll speak to my brother."

"Why must he be involved?"

"Don't be obtuse, Rose. Where else would we get the dowry?" My father's voice was resigned. "Go to the Queen Elizabeth's Day festivities in town tomorrow. Bless the Protestant martyrs. This will be easier if you make it clear where your loyalties lie."

He waited for me to signal agreement. *Yes, Father. With all my heart. Even so.* But he was so sure of himself, and I was so sure he was wrong.

I wanted to throw the ring at him.

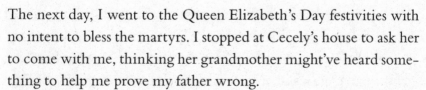

The next day, I went to the Queen Elizabeth's Day festivities with no intent to bless the martyrs. I stopped at Cecely's house to ask her to come with me, thinking her grandmother might've heard something to help me prove my father wrong.

Mother had forbidden me to see Cecely because she was "common," but I've never been particularly concerned with her edicts. Cecely and I had become close three years ago when her parents stopped taking her on medicine-selling tours and sent her to live with her grandmother.

Apart from my father and Edmund, she was my favourite person. A Libra sun, charming and airy, and a Taurus moon with a taste for fine things, unfortunate given her family's poverty. But her Mercury was in Gemini, so she was singular clever. She had a wicked sense of humour.

Her grandmother lived in a tiny ramshackle cottage with barely enough room for the two of them. The straw roof was in need of repair. Three trees clustered around the house: A hawthorn, whose haws made a syrup that went into her father's nostrums. A blackthorn, whose berries were always too sour, but which her grandmother wouldn't cut down for fear of bad luck. And a service-tree, which they had planted beside the house to protect its inhabitants.

The hawthorn was skeletal now, having been picked clean of its red haws a few weeks before. The blackthorn berries glowed bright blue, covered in a thin layer of frost. The service-tree shivered as I approached, as if it were trying to decide if I was a threat. Cecely always nodded at it. She said if you acknowledged the tree's presence, the shivering stopped. Her grandmother answered my knock.

Cecely called down that she would accompany me to the festivities but needed to change first. When she came out, she was wearing the scarlet brocade bodice with the low, square collar I had outgrown and given her a few weeks before. The scarlet fabric brought out the russet in her golden hair; the plunging neckline accentuated the milky curve of her neck. She had brightened her cheeks with fucus, coloured her lips to match her bodice, and pinned her coppery hair back into a golden net. She was breaking the sumptuary laws in at least three ways for her family's income, but she was grievous beautiful.

It gave me a thrill to see her in my clothes.

"You look *splendid*," I breathed, then worried my enthusiasm would make her uncomfortable. Her beauty was a theme to which my thoughts returned too often.

"I try," she said with a coy smile. She tugged on her bodice, straightening the way it sat on her hips, then smoothed its fabric over her chest. "*There*. It suits me, doesn't it?"

"Very well."

Cecely had become an expert on costuming herself from performing in her father's street show. Her mother played the fiddle, and she danced. I had been envious of their freedom to perform in public until Cecely confided how difficult their travels were. She said the reason she stopped touring with her parents was that they were run out of Southwark.

I started to tell her what my father had told me as we set off, but I couldn't bring myself to mention it. She was as invested in our dream of moving to London as I was, although she had always been more sceptical of our chances.

"Have you heard anything about the Rushes?" I made myself ask.

She looked at me, her eyes watchful, just this side of suspicious. "Why?"

"My father thinks they'll try to take back the farm. If he dies, he wants me to—" My throat felt suddenly dry. "He thinks—"

"What?"

I knew I had to tell her. "He wants me to marry to protect Mother and Edmund."

She searched my face, her black eyes large. Her sigh deflated me utterly. When she spoke next, her voice was hard. "I'll ask my grandmother if she's heard anything."

I made myself meet her gaze, ready to say more, but she shook her head, an unspoken entreaty to lay the subject to rest.

Feeling defeated, I turned my attention to the square, where the Basketweavers were preparing to burn a small straw simulacrum of the pope. Several of the men stopped working to gawk at Cecely, who rolled her eyes, accustomed to the attention. At the sight of the tiny trio of town musicians setting up on the rickety stage, I felt a wave of bitterness. How I longed to hear the grand musical production Richard had said would take place in London.

I rarely pray, but the urge struck me then, the prayer so self-seeking it bordered on blasphemy. The words rushed from my mind before I thought better. *Lord, please let Father recover so we can still go to London, please and thank you.* Immediately feeling guilty, I raised my eyes to the heavens and begged forgiveness.

When the musicians began their warm-ups, Cecely and I exchanged a pained glance. The fiddler hadn't fully tuned his instrument; every time he slid the bow over the bottom string, the note was slightly false. As we neared the platform, he noticed the out-of-tune string and fixed it.

Finally, Cecely mouthed.

I stopped beside her, watching her with faint anticipation. Sometimes when we stumbled across street musicians, Cecely moved in a mesmerising way—closing her eyes and doing a subtle version of the brawle—as if she were remembering her part in her parents' show. I loved watching her.

The noise on the platform stilled, and the musicians looked at one another, ready to start. The fiddler counted, and the three of them leapt into motion at once. As they conjured a bright and dizzy tune, Cecely began her subtle dance, touching my arm to try to entice me to dance with her. I shook my head. "*Cecely*," I protested, laughing. "You know I cannot dance."

She grinned. Her skirt shivered around her hips, and the coins in the pocket she kept hidden in her petticoats jingled. The bodice truly did suit her.

"Hot codlings!" a passing peddler called.

"Ripe chestnuts, ripe!" shouted another.

"Hip, hip," someone cheered. "God bless the queen!"

Then we heard it, in the distance. My little brother's tiny voice above the din. "*Rose!*" he was shouting. "*Rose!*" Edmund was snaking his way through the square toward us, his little brown flat cap bobbing up and down as the crowd parted.

I felt a familiar rush of affection at the sight of him. His freckled face, the rounded cheeks that made him look younger than his five years. Then I saw the fear in his eyes, and my stomach dropped. I bent and held out my arms, knowing what he would say before he spoke.

"*It's Father*—" he sobbed in a small high voice, pressing his face against my chest. "He's dead—"

It took every ounce of my restraint not to break into sobs right then, but I swallowed my feelings and hugged him until his chest stopped heaving. Then I looked him in the eye. "Good now," I told him. "Let's get you back home."

He climbed up into my arms and the three of us rushed out of town.

The road home seemed traitorously pretty; the leaves were turning on all the trees. Madder-red and marmalade-orange, they fell, hither and thither, going about the business of autumn as if nothing was wrong. My thoughts scattered like a flock of rooks. Flapping about, filling my head with a noisome dread. This had happened so fast.

Once home and upstairs, we found my mother sitting beside my father in bed. The bedcurtains drawn, his body still. From where I stood, he could have been asleep. Hughe lay at the foot of the bed, shoulders slumped, his sad eyes fixed on my father's body.

Cecely curtsied to my mother, lowering her eyes. "Madam Katarina."

Mother looked up, frowning when she saw who had spoken. She met my gaze, ignoring my friend's greeting. "*Dio lo riposi,*" she said to me, betraying her feelings only with the Italian she used when she was upset. She was never one to make a show of emotion.

I hung back, struck with the thought that entering the room would make this real.

Edmund stared at our father's body, his breath starting to hitch. Mother scooped him up, her thick black braid swinging behind her back. "Shhh. We must be glad, Edmund. Your father is with God."

She met my eyes. "He started coughing up blood and couldn't stop."

I moved past them. On the bed, my father's eyes were closed. His expression was oddly composed, the sort of expression a man wears to trial or the gallows. Hughe whimpered.

"The soul lingers," Mother said, crossing herself. She carried my brother to the doorway. "Why don't you bid him farewell?"

As she stepped into the hall to give me privacy, Cecely leaned in and touched my hand. "I'm so sorry, Rose," she whispered, her voice choked, meeting my eyes. The sympathy in her expression was almost too much for me to bear.

I nodded, not trusting myself to speak. She squeezed my hand and followed my mother out.

Turning to my father on the bed, I found myself doubting the accuracy of my mother's statement. I sensed no spirit, no ghost. Nothing but my own sadness. I swallowed the sob that was rising in my throat, making myself take his hand, trying to summon the necessary self-control to tell him goodbye. A moment passed, two.

I couldn't bring myself to do it.

The floor creaked, interrupting my thoughts. Behind me, Edmund stood, sucking his thumb. His resemblance to my father struck me: his big brown eyes, his coppery hair. Both he and the first Edmund, who'd died seven years earlier, were like tiny copies of my father.

"I sent Cecely home." Mother's voice was tight. I could feel her disapproval. "She said she'd tell the Rushes and fetch the parson."

My grandmother and Uncle Primus came by later that afternoon, but they didn't offer their condolences. It was as if they didn't see Mother holding the door open, as if she didn't exist. In my father's chamber, my grandmother went to the bed first, approaching his body with a distraught expression. My uncle showed no emotion, preoccupied with something he saw on my father's dressing table.

I peered over his shoulder to see what it was. My mother's spell book, open to the healing spell she'd been trying to use to cure Father. I froze. In her shock over his death, Mother had forgotten to put it up. Two circles darkened the top of the page, her code for fortnight spells that worked best when the moon was waxing. The incantation was the usual jumble of Latin and nonsense, a harmless prayer to banish sickness—except for the invocation, which was addressed to a decidedly un-Protestant subject, *Regina Caeli*, the "queen of heaven":

●○

For ague
Ring a candle with blossoms of herb of the fourth star,
one cluster each night until the moon is full. Speak this
following prayer by candlelight while laying hands:
O Regina Caeli, roudos—
fugite, mali
fugite, febres.
Fiat fiat

Reading it, Uncle Primus blinked, once, twice. "Mother," he said, gesturing for my grandmother to look. The two of them exchanged a glance.

Without another word, Uncle Primus tore out the page and started downstairs. My grandmother looked at the bed one last time and followed him out.

"Primus!" my mother called in a plaintive voice, but the only answer was the front door slamming behind them.

After the funeral, everyone followed us home. Everyone except the Rushes, that is, whose failure to turn down our lane raised more than a few eyebrows. When Aunt Margery's carriage passed us, following the rest of the family toward their homes, she mouthed an apology. My mother paled with fury. She had watched Aunt Margery's babies while Uncle Tertius was sick.

The Underhills were already waiting outside our farmhouse when we arrived, having come in their coach. They stood at the door, their London finery far surpassing that of the other funeral-goers. Richard's black hair shone as it always did, no matter how far he had travelled. He wore a black brocade doublet with velvet sleeves and Venetian breeches.

Master Underhill was similarly caparisoned, though he looked deeply unwell. There were dark circles under his kind eyes, and his expression was devastated.

As I let them in, my mother hurried to put out funeral cakes and ale.

Edmund, maddened by all the excitement, began running circles through the parlour like a hen with her head cut off. He was being a terror, but I was too exhausted to correct him—that is, until he knocked Master Underhill over as the old man hung his tall hat beside the door.

"*Edmund!* Look where you're going!"

My brother looked up at me, his eyes wide. So startled, I flinched, wishing I hadn't raised my voice.

When he saw my expression, he fell into a fit of the knavish laughter that is so regrettably common in five-year-old boys.

"Are you hurt?" I asked Underhill.

Our friend shook his head, a thin smile beneath his silver beard.

"Forgive him. He's as wild as a woodland creature, or perhaps an imp."

"As it should be," he said, holding up a hand. "For a boy his age."

"Mistress Rose," Richard said, his green eyes soft.

We moved aside, so the other guests who were now arriving could come in. "Master Richard."

"How are you?"

I knew he spoke in kindness, but his question irritated me regardless. *How do you expect me to be?* I wanted to reply. *Most terrible. Fouler than foul. Father is dead, and his last wish was for me to marry.* But Mother was watching from the corner. From her raised eyebrows and strained expression, I could tell she was reading our lips. "Not well."

"Of course," Richard said. "Of course. This is a great loss. God rest your father."

I nodded.

"I was saddened when Father told me of your father's passing. Of course, he is in a better place now, but—"

"When we received your mother's letter, we took the first wherry to Gravesend," Master Underhill said. "I was disappointed to hear you changed your mind about your audition."

"Changed my mind?"

"In her letter, your mother explained that you've decided to marry," Underhill said, searching my face.

My throat tightened. Fury lashed through me. How dare she tell them this was my decision—without a word to me, before Father was even in the ground? At least *he* had the courtesy to tell me what he planned.

"I told the Master of Revels. The bastard said he should've known a woman couldn't be counted on."

I blinked at him wordlessly, vaguely aware that I was shaking.

Richard's brow furrowed. He touched my arm. "Rose? Are you unwell? Should I get you a drink?"

Suddenly my mother was standing beside us. "That would be *lovely*, Richard," she said, her voice tinkling with gratitude. "There's ale in the kitchen."

As Richard went off in search of ale, Mother pulled me aside, her grip fierce. She gave me a warning look. "Let it be," she whispered. "I have my reasons for saying what I did."

"How could you?" I hissed, yanking my arm back, but it wasn't a serious question. She had ever been like this. Since I was a girl, she'd neglected my feelings. I could remember passing the first Edmund's door at eight or nine years old, watching her ruffle his hair and wondering why she never showed me affection. I had told myself that he was small, that he needed more attention than I did. But after his death, her neglect toward me only worsened. The only time she paid me any attention was when she needed something.

"Madam Rushe," Master Underhill said in the formal, clipped voice he always used to address her.

Mother turned, smiling stiffly. "Master Underhill."

Father had warned her to act like a Church of England woman in Master Underhill's presence because he was so connected at court. Although Mother submitted to his wishes, she seethed with petty resentment whenever he visited, avoiding his eyes, going to bed early. Underhill, too astute not to notice her disdain, didn't care for her either.

Richard returned with our tankards. "Here's that ale, Rose. Shall we have a seat?"

I allowed him to lead me to the draw table near the window. The sky outside was overcast, the sort of smoky grey that presages a storm. It suited my mood.

Richard handed me my ale. It was watery with hints of biscuit and sweetness. Mid-sip, I realised how thirsty I was, how hungry. I hadn't eaten that morning, and I had no appetite the day before. It occurred to me that I should eat soon, or I'd say something ill-advised. From across the room, I could see Mother watching us. My temper flared. How could she expect me to lie about this?

"Better?" Richard asked.

"Ale cannot fix what ails me," I said morosely.

"He's in a better place, Rose. Remember that."

I forced a smile, irritated by what I thought was a faint note of condescension in his tone. In that moment I wanted nothing more than to correct the lie my mother had told him. "Richard," I began, turning my face so my mother couldn't read my lips. "I wasn't the one who had a change of heart."

He cocked his head. "No?"

"The Rushes have turned against us." I sighed, meeting Richard's eyes, my voice so low he had to lean in. "Before he died, Father ordered me to marry. Mother cancelled my audition without my knowledge."

Richard searched my face, his only acknowledgement of what I said a slight lift of his eyebrows. "Marriage might be an easier life," he said at last, his voice catching with subtle emotion. "Godlier."

"But not the life I want." I took another ill-advised draught of ale, annoyed by his piety. Over the rim of my tankard, I could see him watching me, eyebrows raised in what looked like pity.

"Did your father have someone in mind?"

His tone irked me. He sounded almost hopeful, as if there were a choice of husband that would please me after all. "Does it matter?"

"Rose—" Master Underhill called out in a doddering voice. "I apologise, but we must be on our way. We have a vital audience with Lord Burghley this afternoon. Please do not take our early departure personally, my dear. I'm afraid I would've left my own wife's funeral for this appointment."

I smiled, grateful for a reprieve from Richard's marriage-mongering. "It was kind of you to come at all."

Richard bowed. "Nonsense. Forgive us for leaving early."

Following them out, I ushered Edmund into the meadow to expend some of his restless energy. The midday sun had briefly come out from behind the clouds, setting the pond ablaze with a wintry light. The geese clamoured toward us, honking, expecting scraps. Edmund chased them, flapping his arms. For a moment I was grateful to be alone. Then my grief came rushing back, followed quickly by a terrible regret. I hadn't been able to bring myself to tell my father goodbye at the graveyard either.

"There you are," Cecely called.

I froze, reluctant to let her see me so upset. I drew a deep breath and made myself turn. She was hurrying toward me, her fair hair glinting in the impossible light. "*Rose,*" she said, her voice breaking, wringing her dark wool skirt with her hands.

I breathed deep, dreading what I had to tell her.

"My grandmother heard a rumour from the cobbler's wife that your mother hexed your father, but the cobbler's wife wouldn't tell her where she heard it."

My breath caught. I could feel the dam that held back my fury and sadness shuddering under the weight. "From my grandmother, most like," I whispered. "When the Rushes came to pay their respects, they took a page from my mother's spell book."

Cecely's eyes widened. She understood what damage such evidence could do to a woman at trial. She blinked, took a deep breath, and met my gaze. "Your father was right, then."

The dam inside me broke. I could hold back no longer. Blinking back tears, I told her what my mother had done.

Cecely usually guarded her feelings closely, but that day, she was unable to maintain her composure. She closed her eyes, pressing her lips together so tight they turned the colour of lavender blossoms. A long moment passed before she met my gaze, her eyes blacker than I'd ever seen them.

"Perhaps it's for the best," she said bitterly, her voice ringing with false cheer. "London wouldn't have known what to do with us."

That night, my mother and I had difficulty getting Edmund to sleep. Mother recited prayers with him. I sang lullabies. But he kept running into our rooms, asking for his father.

When he finally fell asleep, I found my mother downstairs with a lantern, hairbrush on the table beside her, black hair loose. She was holding her rosary, but she didn't seem to be praying. The dark wooden beads hung from her fist, forgotten. She stared at the wall, deep in thought, sipping ale from her tankard. Her expression resembled the one she wore when she played chess. She's calculating her next move, I realised, but the game this time is find-Rose-a-husband. Rose the difficult, Rose the shrewish. Rose the lustful.

"Why did you tell Underhill I wanted to marry?" I asked from the doorway, my voice as tight as a fiddle string.

Mother looked up. It took her a moment to make sense of what I'd said. She sighed, pushing her finger into the cut of an ave bead. "You know nothing of men's hearts."

As a child I had loved that rosary, its beautiful myrtlewood, the small beads carved into the shape of roses. Now I wanted to strangle her with it. "I'm no innocent."

"I'm well aware of your experience, Rose. I'm not referring to the sort of knowledge you've collected."

I rolled my eyes. Her condescension was infuriating, but I was used to it. She had been berating me for my desire for sensual entertainments since the first time she caught me kissing a boy behind the church.

"Cecely heard a rumour that you hexed Father. No doubt my grandmother is behind it."

Mother shook her head, as if it didn't surprise her. "Your father had an idea about a match for you that might benefit the Rushes. He was going to talk to Uncle Primus about it. But now, of course—"

The urge to strangle her with her beads grew stronger. "Why can't we go to your family?"

"We're better off here," she snapped.

"What in God's name is so terrible about your family that you don't want their help?"

She searched my face, taking a deep breath. When she finally spoke, her voice was quiet. "I grew up in—" She cleared her throat. "A *nunnery*." She emphasized the word, assigning it a peculiar significance. "My mother ran the place."

I thought she meant my grandmother was an abbess, at first. Then I understood. My grandmother ran a brothel.

Suddenly everything made sense. My mother's reluctance to talk about her family, her obsession with modesty and status, the way her affection was so *transactional*.

She watched me, waiting for some indication that I understood.

Cecely had told me stories about the brothels in Southwark. Men going in and out at all hours, drunk and singing. Women hanging out of the windows with holes cut out of their bodices, so their breasts were covered only in translucent silk. I couldn't believe my mother was the product of such a place. My prudish mother. "You grew up *in* the brothel?"

Mother winced at the word she'd avoided saying. She drew a deep breath, her eyes full of a stubborn pride. "A cottage in the woods behind it, but I was in and out of the place."

A mile away, in town, the parson rang the clock bell. I counted eight tolls. I imagined my mother growing up in a brothel. The singing, the merrymaking, the spirits. The sex. Considering the expensive nature of her old clothes, the brothel must've been successful. I had always thought her family was gentry.

"Think this through, Rose. A position as a court musician wouldn't be permanent. The queen will not live forever. And you couldn't stay at Underhill House permanently either. You're in a better position to wed now than you would be from the almshouse, where we'll be if the Rushes take this farm back."

I tore my thoughts from the brothel to consider what she was saying. I hadn't thought that far ahead.

"Marriage isn't a death warrant," she said, frustrated. She pushed a shining lock of black hair out of her eyes. It framed her face, freshly brushed, flowing over her faded wrapping gown. "You might even find this match tolerable. Consider the happiness you'd bring us. The security you'd bring your brother. If your husband provides for Edmund, he'll have a far better life."

I closed my eyes, fighting back bitterness. I loved my brother as much as she did, but for once, I wished she would consider my prospects. "Isn't there a spell you can cast? Something to make Uncle Primus more sympathetic?"

"Who do you think I am, Merlin?" She tittered, dropping her rosary in her pocket, then stood. Her candle sputtered as she made her way toward the stairs. At their foot, she turned, her face just inside the candle's penumbra. The partial shadow made her resemble an ancient sybil, eerie, with dim cheeks and black holes for eyes. "Draw a bath tonight. Wash your hair. Brush off your other black gown. In the morning we go to Rushe House."

My hands were shaking. "After what she said about you?"

"Especially after what she said about me."

I didn't have the will to argue.

Mother nodded. It was settled. I felt rooted to the spot where I stood. The steps creaked as she went upstairs.

I stood there for a long time, turning the situation over in my mind. Horrified at what I would have to do tomorrow. Angry at the Rushes for betraying us.

It felt as though the ground were collapsing beneath my feet.

It took a moment for my eyes to adjust to the dark. My thoughts raced. I loved Mother and Edmund. I didn't want them to be without a home. But there had to be another way.

I opened the shutters, looking out the window into the dark. On the horizon, I imagined I could see the faint impression of smoke and light: a barely perceptible haze of street lanterns, chimney smoke, torches. London, I thought, overwhelmed by an unfamiliar ache. Something like nostalgia, but for a future that was slipping out of reach.

I imagined myself in a gorgeous gown, performing before a royal audience, racking my brain for a way to make it happen. Underhill wouldn't want Mother living under his roof; they hated each other. Perhaps now that I knew the truth, I could find her family and convince them to reconcile. They had money, that was clear, and land. Mother might be too proud to ask their help, but I wasn't.

Mother had always refused to speak of her family, refused even to tell me her maiden name. Finding them would take time. But once I did, I could ask them to let us stay in their cottage. So what if it was near a brothel? It was London! From there, I could send for Cecely and arrange our auditions. I wondered how much court performers made, if our salaries would be enough to rent rooms. With Mother a widow, it wouldn't be unusual for us to live alone.

Through the window, I could see the smallest sliver of waxing moon above the marsh. I shivered, angry at the beginning this new moon had marked. The sun had not yet left Scorpio. I could feel the Scorpion's influence, the urge to sting.

There's a flaw in my mother's plan, I realised. It depends on me behaving like the kind of woman a man would want to marry. I could stall the negotiations considerably if I indulged the tendencies for which I was famed. I laughed at the idea, the sound filling the kitchen.

If there was anything I knew how to do, it was to misbehave.

2

The sun was rising for the last time in Scorpio when Mother woke me to dress for Rushe House. She smoothed the bodice of my coal-black gown, attaching a lace collar high enough for a duchess. She pulled my hair into a subdued black billiment and cheine lace caul, then demanded I let her lighten my skin with spirits of Saturn.

My heart rioted as she worked. It seemed too soon after my father's death to attend to my betrothal. I was still waking up from dreams in which he was alive, having to convince myself all over again that he was gone.

Sitting for her to paint my face was maddening. Although I often added a touch of colour to my cheeks and lips, I hated the false white complexion that was then fashionable. The way it glorified the purity, the *innocence* of the so-called Virgin Queen. Each second my mother took to paint my skin seemed a testament to how foul she thought our darker complexions were. "Be still," she told me repeatedly. "Rose, you're cracking the paste."

It was over an hour before she offered me the hand mirror. My face stared back at me, treacherous pale with bright red cheeks. I looked completely unlike myself. The only features that remained unchanged were those she couldn't alter. Nothing about my brown eyes could be lightened. My black hair shone, thick and smooth, beneath my caul. I handed the mirror back.

"My hair looks pretty," I said dryly.

Mother rolled her eyes. "When we get to Rushe House, Rose, let me do the talking. And God-a-mercy, please, at least *attempt* to act the gentlewoman."

I opened my mouth to snap back at her but stopped myself. Doing so would only give my position away, the way committing the Mad Queen too early in chess could cause losses. I drew a deep breath, then offered what I hoped was a reluctant nod. "As you wish."

Mother's eyes widened. "I expected this to be more difficult. You are usually so obstinate."

I fell silent for a moment, as if considering, then gave her a sad smile. "I suppose I understand what's at stake."

We headed outside to start down the lane toward Rushe House. Edmund fell behind as usual. The weather had turned cold. My breath issued from my mouth in frozen puffs. Tiny snowflakes spun hither and thither, like angels suspended in air.

Beside me was Hughe, who had been shadowing me since the funeral, not leaving my side except to relieve himself. Even now, his eyes were wide and sad, and his head was lowered. He slunk down the lane, stopping here and again to look over his shoulder as if he wished my father would appear behind us. It broke my heart to see him like this. I scratched his ears the way he liked, but his tail wagged only a little.

"Don't touch the dog," Mother said. "You'll get fur on your gown."

I pretended not to hear her. Perhaps she has letters hidden somewhere, I thought, or perhaps I can find her maiden name in the parish records. Once I know that, I can ask Cecely's parents if they know a bawd by that name in London.

When we came to the lane that led to Rushe House, and Edmund saw the pair of yew trees that guarded it like two great beasts, he rushed ahead to climb into one's branches. Higher and higher he went, disappearing into the colourful tapestry of leaves. "All hail Prince Edmund!" he called out in a mock-deep voice.

I suppressed a titter. The night before, I had told him a story in which he was a prince. "Stay," I told Hughe. "Watch Edmund."

Hughe looked up at my brother and back at me. He settled at the base of the tree, pressing his nose to the ground, his eyes fixed on Edmund as if my brother were one of my father's sheep.

I followed Mother, Rushe House growing larger at the end of the lane. A great manor constructed of stone and glass with ivy covering all but the windows. It had stood watch over this lane since before my father was born, unchanged except for the growing maze of a garden that my grandmother was designing behind it.

Mother marched up to the door and knocked, squaring her shoulders, as if she were preparing for battle. Oswyn, the elderly steward, answered the door. "Madam Katarina," he said stiffly. "Mistress Rose. The master of the house is away, but his mother is home." He opened the door reluctantly. "Come in."

The parlour he led us into was three times the size of the one in our home. As a girl, I had been fascinated with the curule chairs with rich fabric, the massive cabinet, the tall armchairs with turned work. The steward gestured for us to sit beside the drawing table as the scullery maid hurried past. "I'll tell her you're here."

As we seated ourselves, he bowed so slightly that it was insulting, then disappeared through the door. In the distance we could hear the creak of his footsteps on the stairs, the cook humming in the kitchen.

My grandmother was talking upstairs, her voice too muffled to comprehend. There were two other voices with her: one male, one female. The feminine voice sounded familiar, but I couldn't place it. "Sit up straight," Mother hissed. "Don't slouch. It's unbecoming."

I rolled my eyes but adjusted my posture. When my mother whispered *good girl* in the same tone she used with Hughe, I groaned.

Upstairs we could hear my grandmother's voice rising, outraged, at the steward. We could make out only a few words of their exchange, but they were enough for us to imagine the rest. "They're here? In the parlour?"

I met my mother's eyes, unable to hide my mirth, a rebellious laugh rising in my throat.

"Rose," my mother snapped. "Her contempt for us is no laughing matter!"

From the staircase we heard a skirmish. A white form half scratched, half slid downstairs. My grandmother's lapdog darted into the parlour, yapping noisily, sniffing the bottom of my dress, standing on his hind legs.

"Good morn, Toby," I whispered. He sat and licked my hand, his eyes occluded by a mop of fur.

"*Toby,*" my grandmother scolded from the doorway, her shoulders squared. The dog scuttled back to her, seating himself obediently at her feet, waiting to be picked up. She did so, meeting our eyes, as severe as ever, her white hair pulled tight from her forehead by a black French hood. "Katarina. Rose. Why have you come uninvited?"

"To discuss my husband's will," Mother said, holding up a hand. "He left me the farm, but I expect you won't honour his wishes considering the recent—and unkind, I might add—rumours about my involvement in his death."

She gave my grandmother a pointed look.

My grandmother blinked at her, ruffled. Mother had just called the rumours she started unkind, but she hadn't accused my grandmother of starting them directly. She couldn't defend her actions without incriminating herself. "Go on," my grandmother said impotently.

Mother offered a tight smile. "Before his death, Secundus told me you wish to give our home to your youngest son. If you help us secure Rose a husband who'll take us in, we'll get out of your way. He suggested you consider Master Valentine Garway. He said it would solve two problems at once."

"How did he . . . ?" She trailed off, searching my mother's face. "He told you?"

"I don't know what you mean," Mother said. I couldn't tell if she was sincere. "He only said that Master Valentine was a problem, and his family might accept a smaller dowry than expected."

My grandmother narrowed her eyes at my mother. Something passed between them that I didn't understand.

Valentine was the eldest son of Sir William Garway. Why his family would even consider marrying him to me was a mystery. He was my age, no widower, handsome. When his father died, he would inherit his father's estate. The only negative thing I'd heard about him was that he had been expelled from the King's School. No one knew why, but Cecely's grandmother guessed that he'd been caught with a schoolmaster's daughter.

My grandmother turned her attention to me. Her eyes lingered on my subdued yet elegant headwear, my painted features, my gown. Perhaps she saw something of my father in me—my nose, perhaps, or my cheekbones—the estranged son for whom she still harboured some trace of maternal love. For a moment, sorrow pulled at her eyes. Then she mastered it, measuring me up like a sow she planned to sell at market. "An interesting idea. I might be able to convince Primus. *Oswyn!*"

The staircase creaked as the steward descended. "Madam?"

"Tell Pleasance and Octavian to come downstairs."

Pleasance? I startled. Pleasance Garway and I had been friends once. Close, in fact. Before Cecely moved back home, we had gone everywhere together. I had worshipped her. Once, she had left a pretty shift at my house and told me to keep it. I wore it often, enthralled by the fact that it had touched her bare skin. Our affection for one another had dwindled when Cuthbert Crane, a squire's son from Gravesend, started courting her.

In a moment she and my twenty-three-year-old uncle Octavian were making their way downstairs. Pleasance was wearing a silver-threaded black gown with a loose bodice like those that pregnant women wore. Seeing me, she smiled politely.

I smiled back, doing my best to hide my surprise, wondering what happened to Cuthbert.

For a moment, neither she nor my uncle spoke, gaping at us like rudesbies. Then Pleasance piped up in a small voice. "Rose," she said. "I am so sorry for your loss. I know you and your father were close."

My grandmother cleared her throat. "Pleasance, dear, tell me. Have your parents found a wife for your brother yet?"

"Valentine, madam?"

"Yes."

"Not that I've heard."

My grandmother beamed at them. "Katarina has come today to offer you two the farm if I can find a match for Rose. Before he died, Secundus suggested your brother. I think it's a brilliant idea."

Pleasance's face brightened. "My parents just acquired a manor on the Isle of Sheppey for Valentine. With a strawberry patch, if I recall correctly. Or was it blackberries?"

"Blackberries," Uncle Octavian said stiffly.

"No matter." Pleasance laughed.

My grandmother cleared her throat. "I'll speak to Primus as soon as he returns. If I can convince him, we'll approach the Garways. We could have everything ready by Easter, before the baby comes! Wouldn't that be wonderful?"

Pleasance nodded, brightening. "What say you, Octavian?"

Octavian sniffed. "I am sure Valentine will be excited."

My mother turned to me with an unsettling optimism. "Well! What say you, Rose?"

Her gaze was pointed, expectant. I remembered my image of myself in a nightgown—black hair wild, nursing an infant—only this time, the man behind me was Valentine Garway. The nightgown was silk with lace on the edges, the curtains of the bed just as fine. It occurred to me morosely that if I had to be locked in a cage, at least that cage would be luxurious.

I sighed, dread filling my stomach. Every bone in my body wanted to refuse. *Pluto and hell*, I wanted to say. *In the devil's name, no!* But I swallowed the oaths, nodding submissively.

I would gain nothing by refusing now.

My mock obedience was a boon. For the first time in my life, my mother trusted me. She stopped asking where I was going when I left the house. She stopped bolting my shutters at night. My uncles went back to greeting us in the market, and my grandmother stopped to speak with us when we met in town. The rumour that Mother hexed Father withered on the vine. Cecely heard a story that my mother had finally converted to the Church of England, a ridiculous claim no one would believe unless my grandmother had made it herself.

Cecely listened with interest when I told her my new plan, but I could tell her scepticism about our chances had increased. Her gaze was flinty and black. She nodded wordlessly, and I understood she was protecting herself from hoping too hard, afraid that she would be disappointed again.

Uncle Primus planned a feast for the Garways to be held on the day after Christmas: a grand show of wealth and prosperity, which would work to correct the impression that we weren't accepted by the family. If everything went as expected, he promised to return the page from my mother's spell book. I was grateful for the time to gather information about my mother's family.

The days grew colder. Advent arrived: the season for fevers and sickness. Every time Mother left the house, I made an excuse not to go with her. I pretended to have a stomachache when she invited me to market, a headache when she made her weekly appearance at church. I ransacked the farmhouse, but I never found any letters from her family. Sagittarius season, supposedly a good time for solving mysteries, was failing me.

All I found was her spell book and the coin purse she kept beneath a loose floorboard in her bedroom. In the coin purse, a royal glinted, tempting me. Parson Uric took bribes. Everyone knew it. I could use the royal to convince him to let me search the parish records for my parents' wedding.

I started looking for opportunities to speak to the curate, but it wasn't that simple. I went by the church several times, but there was always someone there, and I didn't want anyone else to know about my interest in the records.

I didn't notice how busy Cecely had become after the funeral— not in the beginning. The first Sunday she missed our usual walk into town, I shrugged it off. When she didn't answer my knock on her window a few nights later, I thought she was asleep.

It wasn't until the sun was beginning its journey through Capricorn that I finally had the opportunity to see the curate alone. Running errands for my mother, I saw no carriages outside the church. The snow crunched under my boots as I hurried into the graveyard, where I told Hughe to stay until I came back. He was still shadowing me everywhere I went, watching me the way he used to watch my father.

Inside, Parson Uric was lighting candles. He moved slowly from candleholder to candleholder, his back stooped. The pews on the right side of the church glowed with a pale golden light. The rest of the church was dark. No one else was around.

"Mistress Rose? Is that you?" He peered into the shadows. "Or is my addled brain playing tricks?"

"It's me," I said, grinning. It had been so long since I had set foot in church that I was courting a fine. "No trick."

"Spoken like a true illusion." He set down his candle and tottered toward me, his progress grievous slow. He had been parson of the church for almost sixty years, since the beginning of his career as a Catholic priest. "The real Rose has shunned this place for months."

"Prick me and I bleed. Or perhaps I should prick *you* to prove myself."

"That might be more to the point."

I laughed at his pun. For a moment, I felt guilty about my plan to deceive him. But I couldn't very well tell him the truth: *My mother grew up in a brothel, and I want to find it.* "Forgive me for missing services."

His eyes softened. "What can I do for you?"

I held out the royal. It glinted in the candlelight. "A donation for the parish."

He lifted an eyebrow. "What do you want?"

I drew a deep breath, picturing the saddest thing I could conceive. Hughe, looking over his shoulder for a master who wasn't coming. When I spoke, my voice trembled. "The night before Father died, he gave me a letter. He bade me give it to my grandmother without my mother's knowledge, but they were estranged, and she has never even told me her surname. I need to see the records from when you called the banns for their marriage."

The parson frowned. "What year was that?"

"1569."

"Let me see." He made his way to the front of the church and disappeared behind the altar.

I watched the shadows dance in the dark church while I waited, impatient.

He emerged with a heavy book beneath his arm. It took an eternity for him to reach me, set it down, and open its cracked leather cover. "1569, 1569," he muttered, turning page after page of sloping brown ink. He pointed at an entry. "There it—oh dear."

I looked down at the page. It read:

Scnds Rshe m. Katrna Mnl—7 Jan 1569

My heart fell. *Mnl*—? God-a-mercy. What did that mean? My knowledge of Italian surnames was scarce. "Is that Mainoli? Mancinelli?"

He shrugged ruefully. "It was so long ago."

Three letters, I thought. All this trouble, and only three letters.

"Thank you," I made myself say, though it didn't sound terribly convincing. I hurried out of the church before I spoke the slur on the tip of my tongue: *You should keep better records.*

I went immediately to Cecely's house to tell her about what I'd discovered. Hughe, accustomed to my visits to Cecely's cottage, lay down in an area near the service-tree where the sun had melted the snow.

Inside, Cecely's grandmother warned me my friend wasn't feeling well. I found her in bed in her nightclothes, looking wan, but somehow beautiful regardless. Perhaps it was the way her shift hung about her like a shroud—translucent, her curves faintly visible beneath it. Or perhaps it was her resolute expression, as if despite her illness, she was determined to accomplish something. What, I wasn't sure. I hoped it was recovery.

"God-a-mercy, Cecely. What ails you?"

"I think I ate some bad meat," she said, although the lines pulling at the edges of her eyes betrayed that there was more to it.

"Is there anything I can do?"

She shook her head. "What's wrong? You look worried."

She was obviously attempting to change the subject, but I had known her long enough to know that when she didn't want to tell me something, there was no getting it out of her. I told her how little information I had found in the church records. "*M-N-L,* that's all the record book said. The parson uses shorthand."

"That might be enough." She sighed. "I'll ask my parents as soon as they get back."

"Thank you."

After that, she called unusually quickly for her grandmother to usher me out, but I was too distracted to think anything of it.

The next night, I thought I heard a knock on our door—so soft, even Hughe wasn't certain anyone was there. He tensed at my feet, cocking his head at the door. When the knock sounded again, he went on alert, shaggy black hackles raised, looking to see how I would react. "It's all right, boy," I said in a soothing tone, and he relaxed.

Out the window, the marsh glittered in the light of the waxing moon, still and dusted with snow. I couldn't see our visitors, but I could see their footsteps. There were two of them.

Mother hurried downstairs, her candle casting a golden pool of light at her feet. "Who's there?" she called, going to the door.

A hard voice spoke the code words my mother gave out, which had spread by word of mouth among those who sought her help: "We are here by the grace of our holidame."

All my life, whenever Mother heard those words, she opened the door quickly, so our visitors wouldn't be seen by our neighbouring uncles, who thought my mother's work damaged their reputation. Folks came from miles away to get their palms read and purchase her love charms—even though they didn't always work. Mother told her clients that if a spell failed, it must not have been the will of God. She saw farmers' daughters, mothers and grandmothers, widows, farmers and widowers.

"Fetch my trunk," she said to me before she opened the door.

Although her witchcraft was an open secret, she kept her things hidden in case she was ever accused. I pried the stone in the chimney loose and removed the chest.

Outside, to my surprise, were Cecely and her scowling grandmother. Mother pressed her lips tight, her dislike of Cecely clear. My friend shook her head at me, raising her eyes to the ceiling. I understood that she was here by force.

My mother waited for Cecely's grandmother to speak. The draft that blew into the kitchen was cold. I wrapped my shawl tight to ward off the chill. "Madam Katarina," the old woman said, adjusting her flat cap with an irritated nod.

Cecely stood behind her, paler than usual, exhausted. Her fair hair unpinned, curling out of a fine cap I'd given her. *I thought I was ill,* she mouthed. *I swear it.* I raised my eyebrows, a question. What was she talking about?

"Goody Eleanor," Mother said. "Cecely. Come out of the cold."

Cecely followed her grandmother inside. The chill followed them. Mother shut the door and lit the lantern.

The four of us sat at the table, settling into our chairs. Mother nodded, raising her eyebrows, a question. Cecely folded her arms, obviously angry about being here. Her grandmother let out an impatient harrumph.

"Go to, Cecely. Tell them."

My friend's eyes were like embers, furnace-hot, glinting with a barely repressed anger. The candlelight set her face aglow. Her small pink lips, her bright cheeks still flushed from the cold. As she smoothed a wrinkle over the waist of her dress, which looked tighter than it had been the last time I saw her in it, I remembered her anxious expression as she held the chamber pot, and I understood what she meant when she said she thought she was ill.

"You're *with child,*" I blurted, my chest going tight.

She stopped glowering at her grandmother long enough to nod.

"That's not all," her grandmother said. "She won't say who the father is. He made her promise not to."

"I haven't even told him. You haven't given me the chance."

Her grandmother turned to my mother. "I was hoping Rose here would tell me his name. I know Cecely must've told *her.*"

"I haven't told anyone," Cecely said.

"Don't give me the lie!"

Cecely stood up. The legs of her chair clattered against the flagstones. "I told you. I don't need help."

"Tell her his name!" her grandmother said. "She can force him to marry you, so the child won't be a bastard!"

My friend went pale. She looked as if she were going to lose the contents of her stomach.

"Can't you *make* her tell?"

"I can't make anyone do anything against their will, Eleanor. You know that. I'm a wise woman, not a necromancer—"

"Can't or won't?"

"*Can't*," Mother snapped.

She told all her clients that she only cast natural spells. That there had to be at least some small part of a subject that *wanted* a spell before she would cast it on them. But I had seen spells in the back of her book that were intended for reluctant subjects. Love charms to force an unwilling groom into a betrothal, hexes to bring an end to a spouse's affair. I'd never seen her cast one, but I suspected she did so in private.

I shouldn't have said what I said next. Not in front of the others. But I was hurt that Cecely had kept a secret from me. "What is he, a gravedigger?"

Cecely's eyes flashed. "It's Geoffraie," she said in a flat voice. "Geoffraie Coppinger."

Her words hung in the air. Geoffraie was the last person I had in mind: the lord mayor's son, and a known philanderer. She had dallied briefly with him last spring, intrigued that someone of his station would court her attention, but lost interest when he'd developed an unexpected affection for her. *"Geoffraie?"*

"I know, I know," she said. "He's above me. He has a reputation. But honestly, Rose, so do *we*—"

A laugh burst out of me, as uncontrollable as a sneeze, and her grandmother jumped up. So fast, the candle flickered, and her chair almost fell over. She slapped Cecely across the face.

The old woman's whisper was taut with rage. "The lord mayor's son? We'll have to see the apothecary."

"God-a-mercy, let me tell him. He'll marry me. You've all been begging me to find a husband—"

I felt a sudden tightness in my throat. For years, Cecely and I had been dreaming up ways to escape the village, to *avoid* our families'

expectation that we marry. Now she was begging her grandmother
to let her?

"You're mad," her grandmother said, grabbing her arm. "His
father would never let him marry you."

She pulled Cecely outside by the arm, not bothering to say
goodbye as the door slammed behind them.

———

On Christmas night, after we put Edmund to bed, I sneaked to
Cecely's house to check on her. We had long ago perfected the
procedure: I rapped on the shutters of her window and hid behind
the hawthorn tree in case anyone else looked out. Between all
my worries about her and my fear that her parents wouldn't come
home in time for me to escape the betrothal, I was miserable.

Cecely opened the shutters, coppery hair a mess beneath her
nightcap, shift falling from her shoulder. She was lovely as usual,
but her arm was an ugly mess of black and blue where her grandmother had grabbed her. "Are you all right?" I whispered, concern
overwhelming my hurt feelings.

She pulled her shift back up her shoulder so that it covered the
bruise. "Well enough."

I sighed. There was no way that was true. *"Geoffraie Coppinger?"*

She closed her eyes. "He showed up the night of your father's
funeral, begging me to see him. I was so upset your audition had
been cancelled, it seemed like an opportunity."

"He bores you."

"He's a Coppinger, Rose. My feelings are beside the point. I
didn't grow up on a pretty little farm like you. On the road, we
had to worry about whether we would have food or a safe place
to sleep." She met my eyes, her expression steely. "I don't want to
spend the rest of my life worrying about those things."

I nodded, thinking about what she'd said. As a girl, she wasn't around much because she was travelling, but I had seen her from time to time. A tiny little thing, wild-copper-haired, skin the colour of bone. I imagined her bumping along in the back of her parents' carriage, listening to them argue about sales and money. Afraid—

I searched her eyes, sympathising. I had to ask. "You didn't do this on purpose?"

She blanched. "The pregnancy? No. I didn't even want to lie with him. I was drawing things out, biding time until we found out what my parents knew. But he kept pressing."

"Have you told him?"

"Last night. He said he would talk to his father tomorrow after the St. Stephen's Day feast."

My chest felt like it was going to collapse.

"This doesn't mean I won't talk to my parents."

"Just that you're not coming with me."

She bit her lip. "I had to choose."

We stared at one another. Finally, I blurted what I was thinking. "There's even less of a chance that his father will let him marry you than there is that we can find positions at court."

"Geoffraie thinks he can convince him," she sighed, already leaning out to close the shutters. "I'm too tired to explain. I'm barely fighting off sleep. Let's talk tomorrow."

I stood there for a long time, staring at the closed shutters, uneasy, going over our conversation in my head. Her sudden desire to marry Geoffraie confounded me.

The next morning, my mother woke me at dawn to help me put on the green velvet gown my grandmother had procured for me to wear to the feast for the Garways. Skin thick with spirits of Saturn, cheeks mock red, I felt completely unlike myself. My new heels wobbled on the step of the carriage my grandmother had sent to retrieve us.

Mother beamed. She hummed happily all the way to Rushe House, stopping only to periodically shower me in advice.

"Be not shrewd, Rose, nor clever."

"A good bride is chaste, without cunning or lust."

"Keep your eyes down while you sing!"

The last admonition awakened what must've been my last remaining fragment of good cheer. I smirked at the virginal on the seat beside me. When my grandmother asked if I would play something for the Garways, I had thought of a way to sabotage this union without my mother's knowledge.

The Garways' large carriage was already outside when we arrived, the driver standing guard beside it. We could hear the younger Garway children playing noisily behind the manor.

The steward opened the door before we knocked. He made a show of greeting us cordially and loudly before he invited us inside. The difference in his attitude toward us between this time and the last was immense.

Inside, Lady Garway sat in an armchair before the drawing table, her posture stiff, her expression troubled. My grandmother and Pleasance were seated at the opposite end of the room, looking likewise disturbed. Since the last time I saw her, Pleasance's belly had swelled significantly. She looks five or six months along, I thought anxiously.

They sipped brandywine, their expressions pinched. The men were nowhere to be seen. I wondered if they were occupied with some business of which the women disapproved.

"Madam Katarina, *dear* Rose, we thought you'd never come," Pleasance said, smiling. She got up hurriedly to take my hands. Though we had been friends once, her affection seemed outsized until I remembered my uncle's intent to show the Garways we were an accepted part of the family.

"*Oswyn!*" Grandmother shouted.

The steward appeared in the doorway.

"Tell the cook to set out dinner. Summon the men."

"Madam," the steward said with a bow, and disappeared.

In a moment I heard a scuffle followed by the sound of yapping. Toby scuttled into the parlour, a streak of white fur, to my little brother's delight. Edmund rushed toward him, grabbed the little dog's tail, and pulled. I scrambled down onto the floor to stop them from hurting one another. Hughe knew better than to get within my little brother's reach, but Toby, apparently, did not.

The little dog froze, terrified.

Pleasance knelt beside my brother. "We must pet Toby softly, my love. Remember?"

I smothered a laugh, impressed by her play-acting. The Rushes had stopped inviting us over when my grandfather died. Edmund had never met Toby before.

As my little brother and Pleasance played with Toby, the steward appeared in the doorway to summon us into the dining room. Uncle Primus, Valentine, Sir William Garway, and Octavian entered next. The two elder men glowered. Octavian's shoulders slumped. I wondered if the men were angry with him for getting Pleasance pregnant.

Only Valentine seemed untroubled.

My would-be husband was dressed in a fine brown doublet and breeches that matched his dark hair, which was shining, freshly washed. His shoulders were broad, his waist narrow. As he sat, he met my eyes and nodded briefly, unfolding his napkin. His eyes glittered, bright blue. If Mother thought his good looks would make marriage to him tolerable—

I drew a deep breath, annoyed, as I sat across from him, washing my hands with the pitcher of rosemary water a serving-woman brought.

The governess led the rest of the Garway children to the table and seated them. Uncle Primus stood and led the table in an unusually stern blessing. After we all said amen, Sir William thanked my uncle for inviting his family to join them for dinner.

My grandmother smiled and stood. "Thank you for coming today." She nodded at a mousy blond-haired maidservant, who poured her a glass of wine. "Here's to Queen Elizabeth. Let the health go round. In heart."

"In heart," I echoed unenthusiastically.

Uncle Primus caught the maid's eye. She filled a glass for him, which he held up to pledge. "Here's to my beautiful niece," my uncle said, his smile so kind, I started. "To Rose!"

Everyone beamed. "To Rose."

I drank my brandywine, hoping it would alleviate my unsettlement. These were not the Rushes I'd known these last ten years. My uncle never spoke to me, much less called me beautiful.

We passed around delicious marchpanes and tarts, dried suckets and scrumptious wafer cakes. The brandywine was stronger and sweeter than anything my father kept at home. Rather than alleviate my unease, it only made my dreamlike feeling worse. I kept fading in and out, trying to blink away my disbelief, hearing the conversation only in bits and pieces.

"Is this marmalade?" someone said.

"These goodinycakes are glorious!"

When a servant brought around the pork and we were all on our second or third drink, I overheard a fragment of what Uncle Primus was saying to Sir William. "As to the question of the dowry—"

Across the table from me, Valentine blinked. He set down his pork, watching my uncle and his father, his eyes full of resignation. The din had risen too loud for us to hear the rest of the exchange. When he saw I was watching, he arranged his features into a more neutral expression.

Sir William listened intently, nodding at whatever my uncle was saying. As I watched the two of them, irritation spread through me. It rankled me to watch them discussing my future so casually.

As the servants took away the remnants of the final course, my grandmother turned to me. "I see you brought your virginal! Are you ready to perform?"

At last. I nodded, my cheeks hot with the effects of the wine. I lowered my eyes, smothering my glee, and led everyone into the parlour.

The Yule log crackled in the fireplace as I launched into my opening. My fingers tripped over the jacks. The shock on Octavian's, Valentine's, and Sir William's faces delighted me. Sir William's face puckered, as if he'd bitten into a very tart apple. Valentine and Octavian exchanged an amused glance, struggling to contain their laughter.

Although the style of my song was courtly, I had adapted the melody from "A Wanton Trick," the bawdiest street tune I knew, which I'd learned from a particularly debauched former beau. Uncle Primus, the women, and the children wouldn't recognise it. Only Sir William, his son, and my cousin spent enough time in taverns to catch the reference.

I smiled a mock-innocent smile. My song was *just* different enough that I could deny the connection if needed, though the original tune was so ribald, I thought it unlikely that anyone would admit to knowing it.

As I finished the opening, I focused on the wooden keys, smiling in anticipation of what was coming. My lyrics seemed innocent on the surface, but they evoked those of the original and bore a double meaning. I sang, taking care to keep my face straight:

> *If anyone long for a Yuletide song,*
> *Tickled from these jacks,*
> *Gather round the Yuletide log,*
> *And fill your cup with sack.*

> *When the days are filled with winter cheer*
> *And wassail we drink as we must,*
> *The wives, they sing to their kindling kings*
> *And the fire, it burns with great lust . . .*

When I sang the final line and stopped playing with a flourish, I smiled prettily at Sir William. Then I lowered my eyes the way my mother advised, my expression chaste and modest.

My grandmother smiled, passing drunk, eyes closed. "Thank you, Rose. That was *festive!*"

Mother beamed, likewise unaware of what I had done.

Sir William stared at them as if they were mad. "Indeed," he said, clearing his throat, looking uncomfortable. "That was something."

"May they have many children!" Lady Garway said.

Octavian nearly choked on his drink.

My grandmother smiled, echoing the health. Then, pushing out her chair, she asked if anyone would like to take a walk in the winter garden.

"Of course," Lady Garway said.

"It's so charming," said Pleasance.

The maidservant went round, pouring wassail into our tankards. I drained mine, feeling triumphant as I followed my grandmother out. My ruse seemed to be working.

Outside, my grandmother led us into the maze of winter greenery, past a cherub font sparkling with coloured glass. Toby yapped at our heels. Behind us, I noticed that the two men had stopped beside the font. Sir William had pulled Uncle Primus aside, and my uncle's face had gone beet red. When he glowered at me, I knew— I *knew*—what Sir William had told him.

My stomach dropped.

"*Mother!*" my uncle boomed.

Valentine and Octavian glanced at each other and hurried into the maze, speeding up at the sound of my uncle's voice. As my grandmother made her way toward him, my head spun, and the garden seemed to sway.

Overcome with a sudden need to be as far away as possible from them, I hurried into the maze. Pleasance followed me.

When we caught up with the boys, Valentine smirked at me, clapping his hands slowly. "Well done, Rose."

Beside him, Octavian shook his head. "That was admirable. Did you see Sir William's face?"

"I did," I said, uneasy, worrying about the consequences of my misjudgement. Uncle Primus still had the sheet from my mother's spell book.

The boys shrugged and walked ahead, conversing with bowed heads and lowered voices. I stopped to admire a blooming hellebore, one of my favourite flowers. I plucked the bloom, tucking it behind my ear, certain that the Rushes were talking about what I'd done. It occurred to me that it might be advisable for me to stay in this hedge maze forever.

Pleasance shook her head when she saw me with the flower. "Still fascinated with dark things, I see."

I shot her a look. Once, she had shared my fascination with beautiful, poisonous plants. But when she started seeing Cuthbert, she told me she had "outgrown" it.

She rolled her eyes, turning her attention to the path ahead of us. The boys were gone. Their disappearance seemed to nettle her. She cocked her head, trying to puzzle out the source of the distant voices that echoed from the stones. "Octavian!" she shouted. "*Octavian!*"

When my uncle didn't answer, her expression turned dark, and she excused herself, hurrying back to the house. I let her go, heading the way the boys had gone. There was no way I was leaving that maze until I had to.

For a time, I saw nothing, heard nothing but the occasional sound of footsteps ahead. The boys had gone quiet. It wasn't until I approached the centre of the labyrinth that I heard voices. Muffled whispers, difficult to make out, through a yew hedge.

I crouched beside it.

Through the leaves, I could see Valentine and Octavian. So close, I could've touched them through the needles. They were whispering in urgent tones, facing each other. I held my breath so I could hear what they were saying.

"She wants to spoil the match," Valentine said.

"So let her!"

"The Isle of Sheppey isn't far, Tave. It wouldn't be so different from now."

"The thought of you with her," Octavian said, his voice breaking.

My breath caught. Were they—?

"Now you know how I've felt."

Valentine pulled my cousin close, his blue eyes full of an unmistakable ache. Octavian turned his face up to meet Valentine's, letting out a soft moan. When their lips touched, I felt their desire—forbidden, impossible—as keenly as if it had been my own. I gasped.

Valentine and Octavian pulled apart, peering at the hedge, their eyes wide. "Who's there?" Valentine said.

I ran as fast as I could through the maze toward Rushe House, my heart hammering in my throat.

When I emerged into the courtyard, I felt dizzy, as if something deep inside me had been shaken loose. The sunlight seemed too bright, the shadow of the garden wall so deep, it gave me vertigo.

Valentine and Octavian were lovers. There was no question about it. No wonder my uncle and Sir William wanted to separate them. If their relationship was discovered, the penalty, technically, was death. Since both boys were noble, execution was unlikely, but if an enemy of either family found out, it would make them vulnerable.

Pleasance's baby might be Cuthbert's after all.

Mother was waiting for me at the courtyard gate. "*Mannaggia a te*," she hissed, motioning for me to follow her toward the front of the house, clutching Edmund's hand. "What did you do?"

"What do you mean?"

"Your uncle asked us to leave. If you've spoiled this for us, Rose—"

I sighed, too overwhelmed to dream up a response. I *had* spoiled this, no doubt, and she would find out how soon enough.

The horses' hooves clacked against the cobblestone drive that led away from Rushe House. Out the carriage window, the sky was white. Trees drifted past, their branches skeletal, casting an intricate web of shifting shadows. Beautiful, more elegant a dance than any human could perform, but suffused with sadness. I felt as if I was going to cry.

"Rose," my mother said.

It took me a moment to pull my gaze from the trees.

"I know you don't want this. *I know.* But look your brother in the eyes and tell me. Could you live with yourself if your uncle turned him out onto the street?"

Edmund grinned at me, oblivious to the meaning of my mother's question. His nose running, his face reddened with cold, his expression impish.

A lump formed in my throat. "Of course not."

"Then *behave* from now on. Please—"

As the carriage rocked us the rest of the way home, a heavy shame settled over me. I had gone too far. The beginnings of a headache pulled at my temples. I closed my eyes, thinking suddenly of Geoffraie's plans to tell his parents about him and Cecely. He might have already done so. He might be doing so now.

A terrible dread kept me awake that night. My head pounded. I hadn't had a headache this intense in ages. I was certain my uncle would move against us. The only question was how. I don't pray often—music has always seemed a better way to commune with heaven—but the urge was so strong that night, I tried.

Clenching my fists, I pressed my eyes tightly shut. The words *please* and *help* and *God* whirled inside me, too wild to fashion into a sentence. But the failed prayer stirred my grief. I got up, overwhelmed by the urge to find my father's ring.

I pulled it from the pouch where I'd hidden it, fingering the inscription. My heart ached for the man who had given it to me, the man who believed in me, who taught me how to read music and star charts. I unfolded the inner bands, turning the stars around an invisible world.

When I slipped the cold metal band onto my finger, I felt somewhat better, less alone, as if I could finally sense my father's ghost in the room with me. I felt a sudden ache in my rib cage, a hollow where my heart had been. *Goodbye,* I mouthed silently. *I couldn't bring myself to say it before.*

Saying the words lifted a weight I hadn't known was there. I sighed, relaxing into my featherbed. The shadows of my bedchamber seemed louder, deeper somehow. My eyes filled with tears. I couldn't sleep, but I stared at the ceiling for long enough that I fell into a dreamlike state.

On the backs of my eyelids, I saw myself running through my grandmother's hedge maze at night, looking for something. At the centre of the labyrinth, a great bonfire licked the sky. In the distance, I could hear inexplicable waves crashing on a beach, though my grandmother's house was nowhere near the sea.

A rap at our door woke me, loud, insistent. I thought I detected a faint scent, vaguely floral, almost too subtle to perceive. My headache, I presumed. Sometimes I detected the strangest smells with them. I thought I heard a woman's voice through the window: "I am here by the grace of our holidame!"

I remember thinking she must be desperate to call so late.

Mother hurried downstairs. I saw her candle, a bright circle of light, as she left the staircase. Shadows followed her, black and deep. In a moment I heard her speaking in urgent tones. I couldn't make out the words, but her voice was so tense, I crept downstairs. As I was taking the last few steps, our visitor raised her voice. "Everyone knows what you are!"

My mother's response was so quiet, I couldn't hear what she said.

"I know witching when I see it!"

Peering into the kitchen, I saw Mistress Coppinger pointing a finger at my mother, her white sleeves glittering with snow. In her other hand she clutched a sheet of paper. They were so involved in their argument, they didn't notice me.

"I assure you. We had nothing to do with it."

"Don't give me the lie. Primus saw Cecely and her grandmother come here. There's no way my son's love for that girl is natural!"

My skin crawled. I had known Uncle Primus would move against us, but this was even worse than I expected. I thought of Joan Prentice, all the other women who were hanged or imprisoned in Essex. It was absurd that we would be accused of witchcraft in *this* case, the one time we didn't do anything.

I rushed into the kitchen, my voice tremulous. "Mistress Coppinger, please, I beg you. Don't do this."

She rattled the sheet of paper. "You've done this to yourselves. Primus told me you hexed Secundus. This is proof."

Mother peered at the sheet of paper, her face ashen. "I've never seen that before in my life."

"Primus tore it from your spell book. He said he's willing to tell a judge. And you—" She pointed a finger at me. "You've witched half the boys in town, that black dog following you around—"

My chest tightened. We would have no chance at trial against the Rushes and the Coppingers. "He's a sheepdog. We don't have anywhere else to go. Give us time. There's my brother to consider." I remembered Edmund's innocent expression, his runny nose when my mother described this exact circumstance earlier that night.

"Please—" Mother said. "He's only five."

The lord mayor's wife smiled, taking pleasure in watching us squirm. "You should've thought of that before you witched my son."

3

Mistress Coppinger slammed the door shut behind her, leaving our kitchen as still as the frozen marsh. Apart from my mother's candle, the kitchen was black. I blinked, trying to make sense of what had just happened. In a single day, everything had changed. We were in grave danger.

Mother reached into the pocket of her wrapping gown and pulled out her myrtlewood rosary. "*Regina Caeli*," she whispered, then murmured something under her breath.

She stared into the candle flame, eyes narrowed, her expression so cold and furious, she looked as if she might well be in league with the devil. Just outside the candle's penumbra, something drew my eye, a subtle movement. The shadows seemed almost to shiver, rolling around my mother in a ring.

It wasn't the first time that day the shadows had drawn attention to themselves. I shuddered, stricken with a sudden chill. Mother was holding a rosary, and her prayer had addressed the queen of heaven, but those shadows didn't seem holy. Her gaze was less pleading than determined, as if she were staring through the flame into hell or heaven.

The candle flickered, reflected in her pupils—now orange, now red—making her eyes glow. She put the rosary back in her pocket, her expression resigned.

"Pack your portmantle," she said in a cold voice. "We need to be on the first wherry to London tomorrow."

A shiver ran through me. The night seemed to change shape, transforming into a new version of itself. Still dark, but full of confusion, the creeping horror of dreams realised. This was not how I had meant to achieve my goal. *"London?"*

"We're going to Underhill. I see no other choice."

That voice. It chilled me. I should've been happy about the prospect of seeing my father's friend. In other circumstances I would've looked forward to the stories he would tell of my father or the audition he might still help me get. But all I could think about was the look on my mother's face, the shadows that still seemed to be moving slightly around us.

She glared at me, her mouth pinched. This was not the expression of a mother who was giving in to her child's dreams. She was plotting something. I took an unwitting step backward.

"Underhill won't let you stay with him. He hates you—"

"Let me handle that."

"You hate him."

She narrowed her eyes. I took another reluctant step backward, overcome with an eerie certainty that it was *she*—not the Coppingers, not the Rushes—whom I should fear.

I excused myself and went upstairs, trying to convince myself that I had imagined the shadowy energy around her. It was faint, barely perceptible. She's a wise woman, I reminded myself, not a necromancer, but my hands were trembling.

In my room, I lit a candle, relieved to be away from her. I knew I wouldn't be able to sleep, so I started rummaging through my trunk, deciding what I would take to London. As I worked, I thought about what I would do once we got there. I would persuade Underhill to go back to the Master of Revels or find the brothel myself. Once I had secured employment, I would send for Cecely.

As I sat on the portmantle to try to close it, I heard Mother coming upstairs, witching trunk in hand. Then Hughe started barking. Someone else was at the door. The sound woke Edmund, who started crying as he always did when the dog was upset. "Answer it," Mother sighed. "Call if you need me."

I hurried to the door with my candle.

Cecely stood outside, her face ashen. Her eyes were wild, and her hair was a mess. There were black patches all over her shift. Her feet were bare. "The Coppingers came to my house," she sobbed. "Your uncle was there too. I climbed out the window."

Soot, I realised. The black patches—

They had set fire to her cottage.

Shame washed over me, a tidal wave. "Come inside."

She did, tears streaming down her face in black rivulets. As I shut the door, she sobbed, hysterical. "My grandmother—it was her screams that woke me. She slept until the fire was upon her. When I came out, her bed was in flames."

"Is she—?"

Cecely shook her head, her face crumpling.

"Oh no. Cecely—" I made myself reach for her. It was plain to see she needed comforting. "I'm so sorry—"

She let me embrace her, pressing her face into my shoulder. I squeezed her arms, feeling ill at ease, uncertain where I was sup-posed to put my hands. After a moment, her sobs stopped, and her breathing became more regular.

When we pulled apart, I called upstairs. *"Mother!"*

Mother appeared at the top of the staircase. When she saw our faces, she hurried down, protecting her candle with her hand so it wouldn't blow out. I explained what Cecely had told me.

Mother closed her eyes, taking a deep breath, obviously think-ing. It was only a moment before she met Cecely's eyes. "*Santa madre di Dio*," she breathed, already on her way back upstairs. "Fin-ish packing. They'll come for us next."

"Who'll come for us?" My little brother stood at the top of the stairs, watching us with a frightened expression.

A sob leapt from my throat, followed by another terrible wave of shame. "No one," I said with false composure. "We're going on an adventure."

He rubbed his eyes with his fist as Mother picked him up.

My friend sat at the kitchen table, staring at the wall, her expression numb. Soot and tears covered her face. Watching her, I felt her fear, her grief. She had lost so much.

"Cecely," I said quietly.

My friend turned to look at me.

"Come with us. We're going to stay with the Underhills in London. We can audition for positions at court like we always wanted."

She stiffened, expelling a tiny puff of air, as if what I said had hurt her somehow.

I touched her hand. "Mistress Coppinger accused you of witchcraft. The *lord mayor's wife*. If you stay, there'll be a trial at the next assizes, no matter what Geoffraie wants. The judge will believe whatever the Coppingers say. You could be imprisoned or worse."

She coughed, pressing her hand against the swell of her stomach, closing her eyes. "Perhaps I could send for him once we get there."

I made my voice as gentle as possible. "Do you truly think he would disavow his inheritance? How would he support you?"

She rubbed her temples.

"I'm going to try to convince Master Underhill to approach the Master of Revels again. We could get you an audition too."

"Ready?" Mother called in a harried voice as she came downstairs with another portmantle.

Cecely blinked—once, twice—obviously overwhelmed. Her black eyes shone. "Do you have clothes I could change into? Shoes?"

We hurried to finish getting ready. Then the four of us rushed out into the snowy marsh—as much as we could, weighed down by our belongings. Cecely lingered for a moment in the pasture, falling behind us, looking over her shoulder. Then she caught up, the look on her face so dark it scared me.

The plan was to get to the shore and change and wash up before we left for London, but it was slow going. Edmund was heavy, and Cecely's breathing was laboured. She couldn't stop coughing.

I only looked back once from the edge of the woods. Our farm-house was already bright with orange tongues of flame against the night sky.

The bonfire from my dream, I thought, skin prickling with hor-ror. But no. Surely it was a coincidence.

"Is that our house?" Edmund whispered.

No one answered. Cecely's grip on my hand tightened. Hughe, sensing our fear, growled.

"It's our house, isn't it?"

I bit my lip. There was no reason to lie to him. "Yes, but don't worry, there's no one there. We're going somewhere else."

He whimpered, letting out the tiniest of sobs. I closed my eyes tight, furious at everyone who had allowed my brother to be sub-jected to this. Uncle Primus, me, God, the Fates.

"Why would Uncle Primus burn down our house if he wanted Octavian and Pleasance to live in it?" I asked my mother.

"They were going to have to replace the roof anyway. It's a per-formance to show he's cut us off. Let's go, before they see us."

It took the better part of an hour for us to reach the shore. As we approached, I heard the waves crashing against the beach. My dream. I shivered. I had never foreseen anything before outside star charts. It occurred to me with horror that perhaps the sight that ran in my mother's family hadn't skipped over me after all.

Tranquilla sum, I thought. *Tranquilla ero*. Edmund needs you.

I sang him to sleep, rocking him, then walked out to the shore, where Mother handed me half a cake of soap.

Cecely waded into the waist-high water and began to scrub her arms. The sea was freezing. When I approached, she sent me a look implying she wanted to be alone. Beyond her, the water was star-spattered, black. Shivering, I washed my clothes, keeping watch over her, half-worried she would walk into the sea. She kept scrub-bing, as if ridding her body of all traces of the soot could change what happened.

While I was putting my gown back on, Mother approached, dark circles under her eyes. She motioned for me to turn so she could fasten my bodice, then lowered her voice. "If you want Cecely to come with us, see if she will pose as your maidservant."

"She just lost everything." I pulled up my half-fastened bodice, disgusted.

"Underhill isn't likely to let someone of her sort stay in his house except as a servant, and you know it."

I hated to admit it, but she was right. Underhill was an eccentric like my father—given to indulging the women in his family, preoccupied with alchemy and truth—but he was not particularly flexible in his thinking about his station.

"She has until tomorrow evening to decide. It will take that long to get to Underhill House."

"I'll talk to her."

"She'll have to leave once she starts showing."

My temper flared, but I made myself nod, turning for her to finish fastening my clasps.

"I need to cast a spell before we go, but when we get there—Underhill is fond of you. I want you to be the one to talk to him about renting us rooms. Richard is fond of you too. Meet his eyes, awaken whatever love he may have for you..."

She trailed off. Following her gaze, I saw Cecely emerging from the water. Soaking wet, not a drop of soot anywhere on her, her shift wrapped about her like a towel. She made her way to the pallet where Edmund slept and curled up beside him, shivering.

"I want you to play for them," Mother whispered. "Something sweet this time, Rose. Something to inflame his passion—"

I turned to her, incredulous. "You want me to *seduce* him?"

"I want you to help find us a place to stay. Don't play innocent, Rose. The only difference between this and what you've been doing is that you were wasting your talents."

I watched her carry her trunk to the edge of the meadow, sit, and open it. In a moment candlelight outlined her figure. I shivered, sensing the same presence that I thought I'd sensed in the kitchen, but stronger, more difficult to attribute to my imagination. All around her, the shadows seemed to shiver. I thought I detected a faint odour too, a floral scent, though my headache was gone.

What sort of spell was she casting? Why could I sense it?

I thought of the hexes at the back of her book, the shadows, that *presence*, and my chest tightened. Her magic had seemed far more innocuous when I lacked the ability to perceive it.

When the waterman tied the wherry to the dock, we climbed out of the barge into a busy riverside market. Beggars called out for alms. There were street sellers. "Oyst'rs!" one called in a Scottish accent. "Mackerel!" The wind whipped my coat, assaulting me with a thousand smells. Spiced apples, horses, fish. A hurly-burly sea of scents. Tuberose, musk, and jasmine.

Hughe shadowed my brother warily, growling at everyone who came too close to Edmund. The bustle was overwhelming. Beggars, horses, cats. Marketgoers bartering with shop keeps. The clop of horses' hooves as carts stopped for passengers.

We climbed into the back of one with Hughe while Mother climbed up front with the driver, directing him. As soon as the carriage started moving, Edmund's head lolled. Cecely turned to me and spoke in a low, trembling voice. "I never thought the Coppingers would react this way."

"You couldn't have. Don't blame yourself."

She twisted her skirt.

The carriage rocked. I remembered my mother's advice, the problem of getting her into the Underhills' household. It still felt too soon to ask, but we were running out of time. I turned my father's ring, ill at ease, gathering my courage.

"Mother thinks—" I paused. Cecely would probably agree with whatever I suggested, but I didn't want to hurt her. It was difficult to make myself finish the sentence. "She thinks you should pose as my maidservant."

"Of course she does," Cecely said in a resigned voice.

"I'm sorry. It's only temporary."

Cecely sighed, nodding at my mother with a pained expression. "I heard you talking last night. If Underhill lets you rent rooms, how will you convince her to leave Underhill House?"

"I'll figure it out."

The carriage creaked as the horses slowed.

Underhill House was a three-story stone manor with rows of mullioned stained-glass windows. The roof was adorned with a dizzying array of gables and pinnacles, so tall they looked as if they would prick the sky. Between each pair of windows was a small statue of an angel built into the wall. The effect was less uplifting than forbidding, as if I were staring up at the impregnable gates of heaven.

My mother carried her portmantle inside the gate and knocked on the door, unperturbed. I picked mine up and followed her.

A pale man with shoulder-length black hair and an owlish air— the steward, I presumed—answered. His lips were pursed, and a disapproving expression pulled at his eyes, probably at how dirty we were. He wore black breeches and a black tunic; even his stockings were dark.

The only thing he wore that wasn't black was an enamel and gold pendant on a thick chain around his neck, which matched one that Master Underhill used to wear—U-shaped, for his surname— except the alchemist's was set with emeralds. I was so tired, I didn't recognise what the steward's all-black attire meant until I saw the look on my mother's face.

My chest went tight. Who had died?

The steward studied us. He sniffed, then spoke with forced politeness. "Whom should I tell the master of the house is visiting?"

I couldn't help but wonder what master he was referring to. The thought of Richard or his father dying so soon after my father had set me off balance. I felt as if I were going to be sick.

"Secundus Rushe's widow and his children," Mother said piteously, her voice ringing out with more emotion than she'd shown at the funeral. Not for the first time, I wondered if all emotion was performance for her.

The steward told us to wait outside. It was several minutes before he returned, herding us through the centre of the vast anteroom with a warning not to touch anything. He allowed Hughe to follow us with trepidation. The anteroom was in shadow. Perhaps it was a draft or the unwelcoming way the steward treated us, but I felt a chill as he shut the door behind us.

The steward called for servants to light the candles and bring our things inside, then led us into the equally chilly parlour. It was a lofty room with a high ceiling, doors on either side, a grand square spiral staircase at its back, which led to both upper and lower floors. I settled Hughe in an unobtrusive corner.

A middle-aged maid with freckles and a severe yellow bun rushed in to light the candles in the wall sconces. A young servant with rich brown skin hurried into the room behind her, tucking a stray coil of frizzy black hair back into her bonnet. She was pretty with long lashes and a rounded nose, but her eyes looked tired, as if she hadn't slept well in weeks. As she brought our bags into the anteroom, the steward glared at her. "God rest you," she murmured to us, rolling the r.

I went to a curule chair, then noticed that it was stretched with damask and paused, afraid to get it dirty. I chose a wooden bench instead, gesturing for Hughe and Edmund to settle at my feet. Mother sat beside me. When Cecely attempted to join us, Mother shook her head. "You're supposed to be a servant."

We heard a distant sound, footsteps coming up the lower staircase. As I craned my neck to see who was there, I confess, I hoped it would be Master Underhill. When Richard appeared, I felt a little sick. He looked decidedly thinner than he was at the funeral. His forehead was dewy, and he was wearing mourning clothes. A black brocade doublet, velvet-sleeved, and black breeches. On a thick chain beneath his collar was the U-shaped pendant that his father had always worn. My stomach dropped.

"Rose! What happened?"

"It's a long story. Forgive me, but who are you mourning?"

His face turned solemn. "My father."

I felt a physical pain in my chest. First my father, now his. "What happened?"

"His tremors worsened, and he began to have difficulty breathing. The damned physician could do nothing."

A memory surfaced of Underhill and my father teaching us to play triumph in our parlour, laughing. I met Richard's gaze, forcing myself to convey my condolences with my eyes, since my voice had left me.

He nodded, his expression solemn.

"God rest him," Mother said sorrowfully, performing more grief over our friend's death than I knew she felt. "He was such a friend to Secundus."

Richard crossed himself, then shook his head with a quizzical expression. "Where is Rose's fiancé?"

"Still a bachelor," Mother chirped.

Richard blinked. "And she, a maiden?"

Even in my state, I felt a dim amusement at his question. From the corner, Cecely stifled a cough.

"The betrothal was called off," Mother interjected.

"I see. Should I have supper prepared?"

"Please," Mother said. "The last day has tormented us."

"You'll want to get washed up. I hope you'll do me the honour of staying here tonight. It's late."

When Mother nodded, Richard turned to the steward. "See that they are settled in, Graves."

The steward bowed slightly, then turned and called out in a kind voice. "Fraunces?"

A pale woman in an apron with straw-like red hair hurried in, a half-embroidered doily in her hand. "How can I help, sir?" she said in a thick Scottish accent.

"Set the table for five at dinner."

Fraunces slipped her embroidery into her apron and set off for the kitchen.

"*Mary!*" the steward called in a voice so harsh, I winced.

The young maid who had taken our bags returned, still fighting that rebellious coil of black hair that kept escaping her bonnet. "Sir?"

"Clean the dog."

Mary nodded, then scanned the room for such a creature. Seeing Hughe at my feet, she broke into a smile so sudden it was startling. Her dark eyes lit up. Hughe wagged his tail so hard it shook the back of his body, and she grinned, coming over to pet him. "Does he have a name?" she said under her breath, meeting my eyes, a note of sadness creeping into her voice. "We haven't had a dog since Mistress Underhill died."

"Hughe."

When Graves cleared his throat, she straightened, her expression tightening as she led Hughe away. The steward glared at her back.

Another set of footsteps drew my gaze. A man I'd never seen before stood at the top of the cellar stairs. He bore a striking resemblance to Richard but was younger, and the ruff above his black doublet wasn't as fine as Richard's. Something about his eyes seemed troubled. His black beard was distinguished, perfectly groomed. This must be Richard's younger brother, whom Master Underhill had sent away to the country as a boy because the city exacerbated his already saturnine temperament.

"Master Humphrie Underhill," Graves announced.

As the steward introduced us one by one, Richard's brother bowed, his face alight with a sad but welcoming smile, his eyes crinkling. He knelt and smiled at Edmund, straightening his cap. My little brother beamed at the attention. Then he turned to Cecely, examining her with so much interest it rankled me. "And you are...?"

"Cecely Weaver," she said in a strained voice. "Mistress Rose's maidservant."

Richard met my eyes, confused. "I didn't know you had one."

"She's new," Mother and I said in unison.

"The servants' hall is that way," Graves told my friend, pointing at the door Fraunces had left through. "The rest of you, come with me. I'll show you where you can wash up."

I sent her an apologetic look as he led us away from her.

After we washed up, a servant led us into the great hall, a vast echoing room that looked as if it were intended to host revels. I had been awake for long enough that I couldn't be sure what was real. I thought I sensed shadowy shapes in the corners, faint voices that might or might not have been servants in adjacent rooms. The table was arranged with an intricate candelabra at its centre that cast a sad net of shadows over the waiting goblets and napkins.

Richard said grace, a lengthy blessing that expressed gratitude for God's gifts in interminable rhyming couplets. *God have mercy,* I thought, *and bring this interminable grace to its conclusion.*

When he finally said the closing amen, we took the napkins at our places, and the freckled maid brought around a pitcher of rose-water with which to wash our hands. Another servant I hadn't seen before, accompanied by Cecely, brought the dishes from guest to guest. I tried to catch my friend's attention, but she kept her eyes down. Her play-acting resurrected my guilt. *You did this,* a dark bird chirped in my head. *You did this—*

I had turned the corner from exhaustion into madness.

A number of dishes were passed around. Seethed venison sauced with sugar and currants, a grand salat, and lemon custard. All I could bear was a few bites of custard.

I noticed that neither of the brothers was eating much. When Richard raised his cup to pledge a health, the liquid that splashed out looked like water. "To our guests," he said, "with whose presence God has brightened this dark house today."

We raised our glasses and drank. Richard turned to us. "Tell me, please. What happened?"

Mother nodded at me to answer. I opened my mouth to speak, but the horrible bird in my head kept chirping nonsense. *Rose the ruinous*, he twittered, *Rose the reckless*. Seeing my discomfort, Mother set down the slab of venison she was nibbling and wiped her knife with her napkin. Her voice was uncharacteristically full of emotion when she met Richard's eyes and launched into her story.

"We've lost everything."

She told him all we'd endured since the funeral, embellishing to impress her audience as she always did. As she described a torch-bearing mob chasing us out of town, Richard pushed his plate away, horrified.

Expressing relief that we'd escaped, he called for more wine to soothe our nerves. Humphrie raised his glass, pledging a health to his brother. "To Richard Underhill—"

We raised our glasses and echoed the pledge.

Richard held up his glass next. I couldn't help but notice the red tinge to his fingertips. "To the Right Honourable Lord Burghley—"

Mother made the pledge, giving Richard a quizzical look afterward. "Burghley?"

Richard raised his eyebrows with a subtle horrified expression as if it were the queen whose name my mother didn't know. "The Lord High Treasurer. He administers the queen's letters patent. We convinced him today to grant us an extension to fulfil our father's alchemical contract."

"How wonderful!" Mother said.

"Assuming we can complete it," Humphrie said without optimism. "Our father's notebook is cryptic."

"You are *so* melancholic, by the Rood," Richard snapped at his brother, the strain in his voice revealing that he was worried too. "It's only a matter of time before you figure out scrying. The Lord knows you have the temperament for it."

Humphrie shook his head, tight lines pulling at the edges of his eyes, and I felt suddenly sorry for him. Richard was a generally kind person, but he could be insufferable if you disagreed with him. He glared at his brother, lowering his voice to say something I couldn't hear. Their whispered conversation became so animated, I found myself straining to hear it, but I could recognise only two words: *Kelley* and *spirit*.

I was still trying to eavesdrop when the kitchen maids began to clear the table. My mother turned to me, her eyes full of a subtle threat. "We've all had such a difficult time these past few days. Would you play one of your songs for us, Rose? Some music would soothe my spirits immeasurably."

I wanted to say *no*, but I was distracted. The floral scent had returned. It could not be blamed, this time, on my mother's spell-casting, and my head no longer hurt. I blinked, wondering if I'd gone mad.

"What a splendid idea," Richard said, without even waiting for me to answer. He stood and gestured for everyone to gather in the drawing room. The servants led me to the anteroom to retrieve one of my instruments. I stared at my psaltery and virginal, suddenly anxious about playing after the disaster at my grandmother's.

I selected the psaltery, trying to will myself awake. In the mirror, my hair shone, black as night. My face paint was subtle for once, due to the limited time my mother had to apply it. I looked like a stranger, a mysterious noblewoman from my mother's country. Good, I thought. If I want Richard to approach the Master of Revels for me, I need to look like I could play for royalty.

The horrible nightbird chirped at me all the way back to the drawing room. *Wherever you go,* he tittered, *disaster follows—*

The admonition gave me pause, making me question if I should pursue my plan at all, if I should resign myself to what my mother wanted.

Gritting my teeth, I made my way back to the drawing room and sat in a large curule chair with my psaltery, trying to ignore him. The servants had lit all the wall sconces, casting a net of flickering light over the room. I smiled at the dark shapes that were my audience and plucked the psaltery, the opening notes of the song I wrote for Cecely tinkling through the parlour.

Mother smiled, her apprehension fading. She knew this one.

Imagining that my friend could hear me as the servants moved back and forth to clear the hall, I improvised, letting the melody drift. I lost myself, making the tune less reckless, more soothing. I imagined the tune vibrating the sympathetic strings inside her.

When the song ended, Richard straightened, blinking as if he were startled. He stood, cleared his throat, his smile reserved. "That was skilled."

"Thank you."

His brother excused himself, saying he would wait for Richard in their workshop.

"I'll be down in a moment," Richard said, then shook his head, as if an obvious thought had just occurred to him. "You must be exhausted."

At last, I thought. Sleep, sweet sleep.

Richard walked me to the spiral staircase, then leaned in to kiss the hand I was dutifully proffering. He let his lips linger for slightly longer than was necessary, then smiled at me, squeezing my hand with affection. "I am glad you came. I can't imagine what you've endured."

Mother hurried past, smiling her approval.

"Thank you," I said awkwardly. He had not let go of my hand. I cleared my throat, withdrawing it. "Forgive me for the failure of memory, but what was it the Master of Revels told your father? Not to trouble him about me again?"

"I believe so."

"Do you think if you told him there was a misunderstanding, he might agree to let me audition after all?"

There was a reluctance at the edge of his eyes, the same disapproval he had shown after the funeral when he suggested married life would be godlier. "I'm not certain he would even see me."

I wasn't entirely sure I believed him. "Would you be willing to try?"

He hesitated. "I am not as optimistic about your chances as my father was. Court positions go to friends of the court, the queen's relatives. Even if I managed to arrange an audition for you, I doubt anything would come of it."

I felt my cheeks grow hot. Richard knows nothing about music, I told myself. If the Master of Revels hears me play, I'll be hired. I only need to audition soon, before Mother's scheming finds purchase. "I would appreciate you trying. Would you please refrain from sharing this request with my mother?"

He nodded, his expression so lacking in enthusiasm, I didn't know if I could trust him.

He waved for Mary to show me upstairs, lingering at the bottom of the staircase. Mary smiled and gestured for me to follow her, apparently more relaxed around Richard than she was around the steward. As she took the candle from the holder beside the steps, I heard him descending the lower staircase.

Mary lit the candle, causing a pool of light to shiver into being around us as we took the steps. On the floor above, no light shone through the windows of the statuary. One by one, white marble angels emerged from the dark as we passed. They looked displeased that their prayer had been disturbed, their uplifted eyes vacant, surrounded by shadows. "Through here," Mary said, opening a door.

In a corner of the room where we had washed up, something moved. I nearly jumped out of my skin before I realised it was Hughe. The sweet dog had curled up to wait for us. Mary lit the wall sconce with her candle and the antechamber brightened, as Hughe greeted me with a regal kiss on the hand. His curly black fur shone, puffing out as it always did when it was damp. Mary had done an excellent job washing him. I patted his head, and he pressed himself against me, panting happily. Mary patted him as she passed, then showed me the bell to ring if I needed her, and—giving me a knowing look—left the room.

Confused, I wondered what she thought she knew. She hadn't been present to hear my mother's story at dinner.

My room had a small bed curtained with an elaborate embroidered tapestry. As Mother and Edmund settled into their rooms, I drew back the bedcurtains. The blanket was heavy, warm, the sheets beneath it soft. The featherbed was the thickest I had ever seen, nearly two feet deep. Mary had put my portmantle beside the trunk, my virginal atop it. I found my nightgown in the case. As I was pulling it out, Cecely rushed in. She rolled her eyes and spoke in a loud, deferential voice. "Will you need help undressing, miss?"

"We're alone," I whispered. "You don't have to pretend."

"You're never alone in a place like this," she whispered back. "I think the maid suspects..." She trailed off, checking to make sure no one was behind her, then looked pointedly at her stomach.

"Which maid?"

"The one I just passed on the way in."

I looked over my shoulder through the door where Mary had disappeared. As I remembered the maid's knowing look, a pit formed in my stomach. What if she told someone? Would Richard ask Cecely to leave?

"How could she know?"

"I kept getting nauseated in the servants' hall at dinner." She sighed. "Rose, I've been thinking about where I'm going to go."

My chest went tight. "Oh?"

She fiddled with the hem of her skirt where a seam had unravelled, tugging at a loose thread, cinching the material, then straightening it. Her words came out in an apologetic rush. "I can't stay with my aunt, and my parents won't let me travel with them anymore, but—" She met my gaze finally, her eyes black and tired, defeated. "My cousin is a brewer in Norwich. I think she'd let me work for her until—" She paused, frowning. "Until I figure something else out."

Though she was being intentionally vague, I knew what she was implying. She meant to do the same thing she had tried to do back home: find a husband. "You really want to work as a brewer?"

She rolled her eyes. "Not even a little."

"Then why go to *Norwich*? You could stay here."

She shook her head, eyes flashing with an obstinate pride. "I can't live as a servant for long, even pretending. I'm like you. I balk every time someone tells me what to do. It's been two hours, and I already want to murder that steward."

I chuckled. "Restrain yourself."

"He acts like a nobleman. His fine stockings, that ridiculous pendant. He carries a handkerchief embroidered with his initials in goldwork. He corrected my *grammar*, Rose. I used the word 'will' instead of 'shall.'" She raised her chin, emulating the steward's haughty tone, her lips downturned in a pretentious scowl. "'It's shall, not will,' he said. 'Remember that. We speak proper English in this house. Master Underhill went to Oxford.'"

"Pluto and hell. He said that?"

"He's even worse to Mary, finding fault with everything she does. Could you help me find an apothecary tomorrow? I have no options unless I address my condition. Do you think your mother would give us money? It should be simple. I'm not very far along."

I thought about this. I was becoming less and less certain I understood what my mother believed. She summoned shadows. She had grown up in a *brothel*. Perhaps she would be more understanding than I would've expected. "I'll talk to her."

"I need to let my aunt know where I am so my parents can send for me. They always go to Norwich in the spring. With everything that has happened, I think they'll agree to take me with them. Will you help me find a messenger tomorrow too?"

I nodded, reluctant, as she set to unlacing my bodice. Though she was *loosening* the garment, I found it difficult to breathe naturally as she worked, painfully aware of her touch.

By the time I stood in my shift, I was almost dizzy. Cecely pulled off her simpler dress and sat on the truckle bed in her smock, one of the straps falling off her shoulder, her expression disgruntled. She shifted on the hard wood, uncomfortable.

"Would you prefer to sleep up here?"

"God, yes. I think I have a splinter."

She blew out the candles and climbed into the bed. I lay beside her, having second thoughts about my invitation. My uncomfortable consciousness of her proximity was almost unbearable now. She kept shifting under the sheets, her nightgown brushing my leg. I couldn't stop thinking about her body beside me until I reminded myself of what she had been through the night before.

Then the nightbird returned. *Your fault*, it chirped. *Murderer!*

Despite my exhaustion, it took hours for me to drift off. I had just slipped into the shadowy realm between awareness and sleep when I heard my mother's voice at the doorway. I didn't move, pretending to be asleep. I was in no mood to deal with her. I watched her, wondering what she wanted, knowing she wouldn't be able to see me until she was close. The candle she held flickered. "*Rose*," she whispered again. "*Cecely—*"

The floorboards creaked. She was creeping toward the bed. Deeper shadows seemed to rush in with her. Dark, eerily sacrosanct, similar to what I'd sensed the night before in the kitchen. She moved quietly, as if she didn't want to wake us. Was she testing us, calling our names to see if we were awake?

I shut my eyes tight.

I could hear her breathing, shallow and fast, as she hovered over the bed. She didn't move for a long time. Then I heard something, a faint swishing sound near my right ear. What the devil was she doing? I peered out of the corner of my eye.

She was creeping from the bed, candle lighting the way before her. It cast a pale pool of light that shivered with each footstep. Her other hand was at her waist, clutching something I couldn't quite see until she moved the candle.

She had cut off a lock of my hair.

I lay awake for hours after that, unable to sleep, certain now that my mother was witching me. The idea that she was doing so without my permission made my blood boil. It would be a love charm to make me more amenable to her plans for me and Richard, no doubt. That would require a fortnight spell, which meant she'd keep a candle somewhere and tend it. I needed to find it and sabotage it.

She was being so reckless. What if Richard found out? He shared his father's connections to court, and he was suspicious of the occult realms that lay outside alchemy and astrology. The courts in London would not be any kinder than the assizes if he found out what she was doing.

By sunrise, my exhaustion had only worsened. My head pounded. My thoughts were scattered. The horrible nightbird darted about, pulling the strings of my thoughts as if it were settling in to build a nest. *Avventata*, it chirped, *egoista*, berating me in my mother's language. I gave up on sleep and slipped into her room to look for the candle and spell book. Mother was fast asleep beneath a pile of blankets, her bedcurtains open from the last time she'd gone to check on Edmund.

The grey light of dawn was just beginning to show through the windows, ghastly, unsettling. I scanned the room for her trunk.

There were no bulges under the featherbed, the sheets. It wasn't in her portmantle.

When Edmund cried out from the next room, I had to hurry back to bed before my mother got up to soothe him. I slipped into bed next to Cecely, careful not to wake her. She had tossed and turned for much of the night, as if she had nightmares, but for the moment her sleep seemed peaceful.

When I heard my mother passing back into her room, I got up and dressed. I stilled the anger that burned in my breast and knocked on her door, pretending to have just awakened. When I asked her for money to pay the apothecary for Cecely, she went silent. A great sigh escaped her lips. "We shouldn't have taken her with us," she said at last.

"But she's here, Mother."

She closed her eyes. "This is not our problem. She should go to her aunt."

"She can't. Coppingers live next door—"

"Get out," she grumbled, shutting the door once I obliged. There was thumping inside, a clank. Then she opened the door and put some coins in my hand, speaking in a low voice.

"I don't want to hear about this again. While you're out, buy me a pound of beeswax, grapeseed oil, and some dried roses. I want to infuse a candle with rose oil for Richard."

I doubted that was all she wanted to do, but I didn't want her to know that. I put my hands in my pockets so she couldn't see that they were shaking. "Are you entirely certain that's a good idea? Richard might think it devilish."

Her brows knitted. "It's a candle, Rose, a fragrance. A womanly act of kindness. His own *mother* used to keep bees—" She held out the shilling again and I took it. Seeing my father's ring on my finger, she stopped midsentence. "I wondered where that was."

"Father gave it to me before he died."

She frowned. "It's a man's ring, Rose. It looks ridiculous. Let me put it somewhere for safekeeping."

Remembering my father's warning—*it's too valuable, you know how she is*—I shook my head. Mother glared at me, the wrinkles at the edges of her eyes deepening.

Withdrawing to my room, I found Mary straightening my bed-sheets. She met my eyes. "I know a place," she whispered.

My own mouth fell open. "What?"

"There's an apothecary at the north end of Bishopsgate Street. My friend Cornelia works there. Ask for Tessa Montefiore, the apothecary's wife. She'll help."

I stared at her. "Why are you being so kind to us?"

"I—" She checked to see if the door was closed behind us, met my eyes, and lowered her voice. "I sympathise with Cecely."

My first reaction was to wonder why she was being so secretive. Then I realised what she was implying: She, or someone she knew well, had used Tessa's services. "I see," I said, embarrassed to have such personal information. "Whatever the reason, I appreciate it."

Mary nodded, accepting my thanks, then went back to tidying up.

Once Cecely woke, I wrote out the letter she dictated to her aunt explaining what happened—Goody Weaver couldn't read, but she had friends who could—and asking her aunt to send for her when her parents arrived. Swallowing the lump in my throat, I helped her find a post house so the letter could be sent to Gravesend.

We found the apothecary tucked into an alley just inside the city gate beneath a great sign painted with the word MONTEFIORE'S. Inside, a huge ceramic mortar and pestle sat on the floor. At the counter beside it sat Montefiore himself, a bespectacled elderly man with olive skin, a grizzled head of black hair, dark eyes, and a manicured beard. He was reading a huge book with an intricately embellished cover, which he put away as soon as we walked in.

Behind him were rows of beautifully coloured jars on tall shelves that spanned from floor to ceiling. Most were carefully labelled in Latin, another language I didn't recognise, symbols and glyphs. Others were full of herbs and dried leaves.

A girl—fourteen or fifteen—with ebony skin was reshelving bottles on the wall behind him, thick black hair gathered into a simple mesh caul.

As the door fell shut behind us, they both looked up. Montefiore glared at the girl, and she went back to shelving more quickly. Then he turned to me, pushing his spectacles back onto his nose. They were almost as fine as the ones Underhill had brought home from Paris for my father. "How can I help you?" he said in an unfamiliar Italian accent.

I told him what my mother wanted. Montefiore nodded, turning to search a shelf.

While his back was turned, Cecely took a deep breath and blurted, "I need to see your wife. Tessa Montefiore."

The apothecary caught the girl's eye. She bowed deeply, set the broom aside, and hurried into the next room. As she passed, I noticed her sleeves were too short and there were scars at her wrists. A moment later, an elderly woman with greying black hair and the same olive complexion appeared in the doorway. She wore a bright wimple, and her eyes were dark, intelligent. She was beautiful.

Her husband tilted his head at Cecely. "The fair one is here for you."

Tessa Montefiore looked my friend up and down and met her eyes. "Come with me."

Tessa shut the door to the back room, speaking in a low voice to Cecely, while her husband gave me the things I'd asked for. By the time I followed them, Tessa was telling Cecely she could solve her problem with an infusion of juniper, rue, and pennyroyal. The room was windowless, and the table was covered in flickering candles. "Close the door," Tessa reminded me.

Once I did, Tessa went to a cabinet and pulled out a copper mortar and pestle, whose bowl was marked with the symbol for Venus. As she filled the mortar with herbs and began to crush them with the pestle, she bowed her head and murmured something in a language I didn't know. For an instant, the shadows seemed to draw close, and the scent of the herbs—earthy, feminine—almost overpowered me. I thought I smelled a faint floral scent, though she hadn't used any flowers. It was the same scent I smelled when Mother cast the spell at the shore.

"May I ask who you're invoking?"

"St. Afra." She met my eyes, closing the subject.

Mother was fond of St. Afra, a Cypriot girl who was a sacred prostitute at the Temple of Venus before she converted to Christianity. Was *Afra* responsible for the dark energy my mother carried—a saint? Or was Tessa lying?

It took half an hour for her to make the infusion. When she was finished, she poured the liquid into a stoppered bottle and offered us a bag full of things she said we'd need. "For all that and the wax and oil and roses, one shilling."

I handed her one of my mother's coins.

The old woman handed Cecely the bottle. "Drink half tonight. If it hasn't done its work by the morning, drink the rest. This preparation will be strong while the moon is full."

Cecely nodded, gripping the bottle tightly.

When we got home, we hurried upstairs, trying to keep out of view of the servants, who were eyeing us curiously. I made a big fuss about giving my mother the beeswax and roses, tucking away the rest of the items we'd purchased until everyone had gone to bed.

The infusion worked rapidly, as if whatever power blessed Tessa's herbs wanted Cecely's suffering to be as brief as possible. I stayed up with her, giving her the poppy Tessa had put in the bag for pain. Around midnight, Cecely woke shaking, racked with chills and cramps. I lit a candle, giving more poppy and applying the poultice. The house was silent, still, and dark except for the faint sound of a church bell tolling the hours.

Around three or four in the morning, I woke to the sound of Cecely crying. It was too dark to see her face. My first instinct was to pretend I didn't hear and give her privacy. But her breath kept hitching, and I could tell she was working hard to be silent.

"Don't worry about me," I whispered. "I'm awake."

She stopped trying to master herself. "I should've chosen some-one else," she sobbed. "I was foolish to think his parents would let him marry me. My grandmother. This is terrible—"

"Don't blame yourself," I said. "You couldn't have known it would end this badly. Geoffraie's the one who made promises he couldn't deliver, and Uncle Primus wouldn't have told Mistress Coppinger if I hadn't betrayed him."

She didn't respond, her breath catching as she choked back an-other sob. I reached for her hand, swallowing a surge of irrational anxiety. She went silent, and slowly, her breathing became regular.

By morning, the worst of her ordeal seemed to be over. We gave the soiled blankets to Mary to wash. I asked the maid to tell Rich-ard I was ill and ask if we could stay until I recovered.

Richard agreed, sending up a bouquet of pansies and a note inscribed with a short verse:

> *When you look upon these, think of me,*
> *And my thoughts for your recovery.*
> *Your loving friend while I draw breath—*
> *Richard*

The note trembled in my hand, the parchment strange and smooth beneath my fingers. The handwriting was Richard's, sophisticated, the tails of his *y*'s and *g*'s looping and curling with elegance, but the tone felt uncharacteristically intimate. He had always been kind to me—we were old friends—but he was usually more reserved.

I was still standing there, staring at the note, when my mother walked in. She snatched it from my hand and read it, then smiled at me broadly. "Very nice."

I snatched it back, disgusted.

Cecely slept most of that day. I kept her company, my thoughts still scattered and apprehensive. The only time I left Cecely alone was midmorning when Mother left her bedroom to bathe. Mother had complained of a backache at breakfast. I could smell the lavender and willow bark she used to cure those wafting from the red room. I searched for her candle—and spell book, which I wanted to scour for information on the powers her spells invoked—but found nothing.

Cecely woke more often as the hours passed. When she complained of pangs or aches, I sent Mary downstairs for herbs to refill her poultice, asking the maid to pretend she needed them for me. I hoped she was telling the truth when she said she was sympathetic.

Mary brought us supper at the table in the antechamber, where we could watch the sun set over the rooftops. She brought more food than was possible for two people to eat. Apples, olive pie, bread, custard, the cuttings from a chine of pork. All things that were good, she said, for recovery. I wondered if she had told the cook, if we could trust her. Thinking it would be wise to treat her well, I invited her to share our meal, but she looked startled.

"Thank you, miss, but—" She sent me a rueful glance that said more than her words. "I would be missed in the servants' hall."

Remembering how the steward mistreated her, I nodded, understanding. Graves expected her to eat with them, not us.

While we ate, Cecely and I looked out the window over what was left of Mistress Underhill's snowy garden. The sun outlined the chimneys bright pink and set the horizon aglow behind it. Thin wisps of chimney smoke drifted like ghosts.

"Rose," Cecely said, her eyes downcast. I could tell she was searching for the courage to speak with me in earnest. After a moment she raised her eyes up to meet mine. "I know we don't talk about our feelings much, but I want to say this. I'm grateful for everything you have done for me."

I nodded, an uncomfortable affection for her welling up in my throat, which I was too afraid to express. I closed my eyes. "We are friends, Cecely," I said tentatively, unable to keep my voice from catching. "It was nothing."

Several days passed without word from the Master of Revels, without progress on finding my mother's candle or spell book. Graves gave me a tour of the house, methodically taking me into each room, naming the sculptors who made each statue, describing the organization of the books in the library.

The only floor he didn't escort me through was the cellar, which he said had nothing that would interest me. There were only the servants' quarters, the buttery, the pantry, and Master Richard's workshop, which of course was prohibited.

Richard and Humphrie disappeared down the cellar staircase each morning before I even came down to eat breakfast. They never came up for dinner and sometimes stayed downstairs so long they were late for supper. Richard expected me to sit with him each night after we ate. He asked me to play the virginal for him, watching me so closely it made me uncomfortable.

It was almost a week after her ordeal before Cecely began to feel like herself. By then, no one else said anything or seemed suspicious, so I began to trust that Mary hadn't told anyone.

I stopped feigning illness. Richard did not ask us to leave.

On Twelfth Night, when Richard announced that he would go back downstairs to work immediately after supper, I decided it was time to try to find my mother's family. I couldn't bear to sit on my laurels for another moment. Because of the holiday, we could wear masks to reduce the chances of anyone we met recognising us later. I asked Cecely if she wanted to help me find the brothel. She thought for a moment, then nodded. "That sounds like a marvellous distraction."

I remember how I adorned myself that day, since my would-be lover later spoke of it often. Richard had given me access to his late mother's closet. I chose a black bodice with red embroidery and a matching overskirt, its goldwork borders pinned back to reveal the frills of my petticoat. Cecely selected a deep green gown with seed pearls at its neck and a gorgeous ruffled petticoat. When I pulled back her hair in a golden caul, my fingers lingered longer than was necessary.

We didn't use spirits of Saturn, but I painted her cheeks and lips with madder and outlined her eyes with kohl. I could barely sit still as she darkened my eyes. So distracted by her proximity, I stopped her before she could paint my lips or cheeks. "That's enough," I said. "We'll be wearing masks."

Checking the mirror, I saw how darkly she had outlined my eyes. The effect was startling. My expression was perpetually sorrowful, as if I were still in mourning. We put on the masks we had found in the late Mistress Underhill's wardrobe: Mine, feathered black adorned with a single red rose and gold filigree. Hers, rich emerald, painted with leaves.

We hurried downstairs, leaving Hughe with a bone my friend had snatched from the remains of dinner to keep him busy.

Outside, Cecely explained that the brothels were concentrated in the outer wards because of the regulations against them in the city proper. Shoreditch was straight up Bishopsgate Street, so she suggested we start there—it was close enough to walk even in heels.

She led me toward the city wall, in better spirits than I had seen her since Christmas Eve. The street was busy, filled with wassailers and revellers getting into coaches. By the time we passed through the gate, the sun was setting over Bedlam like a pale ball of fire. We could hear madmen swearing and arguing from the other side of the street.

Beyond the hospital, the busy coaching inns of Bishopsgate-within became dim cottages. There were shadowy chickens and vegetable gardens draped in tarps, tenements and almshouses.

The music coming out of the ramshackle taverns and inns was wilder beyond the wall, untutored: fiddles instead of harps and lutes, simple unaccompanied singing. There were gaming houses and houses with promising names like THE STALLION and THE GOOSE. Cecely shook her head as we passed a place called THE HEN HOUSE, laughing. "The connection between harlotry and water-fowl baffles me."

We drifted down the street, looking for places to ask about the brothels' owners' names. There was a theatre with a dim sign advertising a reprise of *Tamburlaine*, a brutal play that I had seen the previous summer in Gravesend.

As we tried to decide whether we should enter a tavern with-out an escort, we saw a masked woman in a gaudy cream gown approach the one across the street. Her bodice was tight, its neck adorned with silvery embroidery, so low it showed the tops of her shapely breasts. Her sleeves were rosy velvet, her skirts damask. Her mask—feathered, pearled, pink—towered over her face. Her hair was dyed a bright golden red. I couldn't tell if she was a duch-ess or a courtesan.

When Cecely nudged me, I had my answer. "*She* might know the place we're looking for."

We followed her into the bustling tavern, where she sat at a brightly lit table with three men in their late twenties. They weren't in festival costume, but we could see only two of their faces. A blond man with tempestuous brown eyes was glaring at a man with shoulder-length brown hair. The brown-haired man's eyes were an unusual hazel, light brown with flecks of gold that made them glow like the eyes of a cat. He was straddling a chair that he'd turned backward, watching the blond man with a complicated expression that appeared to be a mixture of admiration and contempt.

Between them was a scatter of loose papers covered with writing and splotches of wine. The blond man was smoking a pipe; the scent of tobacco filled the air.

The courtesan peered over their shoulders as if she were reading. A jug of wine sat on the table. The serving-woman had given up on keeping their cups filled. They were gentlemen judging by their apparel, or the sons of wealthy merchants at least.

My gaze was drawn to the brown-haired man for reasons I didn't then understand. He was not especially handsome, though his features were pleasing enough. Perhaps it was his insolent posture, the impression he gave of confidence. His eyes were deep-set, and his shoulder-length hair shone in the candlelight. His eyes were the most interesting thing about him: that gold-flecked brown, aloof and intelligent.

"*Enter a messenger, with two heads and a hand,*" the blond man said in a disdainful voice. He had the same accent as the Underhills, as if he'd been to Oxford. He smirked, projecting an air of amusement, but I thought I saw a subtle insult in his eyes. "Is this satire?"

The brown-haired man smiled faintly, his eyes flickering with cold amusement, like a cat that climbs onto a tall shelf to watch the world from above. I expected him to speak in an educated manner like the blond man, but he had the accent of a rustic. "Perhaps it is," he teased, smirking subtly. "Or perhaps not. Who can tell?"

The pull I felt toward him startled me.

"Don't provoke him, Will," the third man said. "And for Christ's sake, Kit, please, content. There are echoes of your work, to be sure, but only because we want *Titus* to rouse theatregoers as *Malta* and *Tamburlaine* did. We want your opinion."

Tamburlaine. Was this Kit the dramatist? He searched the other two men's faces, then shifted in his seat, apparently satisfied with what he'd seen. "Aaron is interesting," he said finally. It took me a moment to realise he was referring to a character. "But unless you intend this to be satire, I don't think you've sufficiently examined his motives."

"*Interesting*," the brown-haired man—Will, I supposed—echoed. His chuckle was forced, and his eyes weren't laughing.

"Indeed." Kit shot him an apologetic smile. "I don't think the script is finished, truth be told. The ending is better than the beginning."

"If we thought it was finished," Will said with a tight smile that barely concealed his displeasure, "we would not have sought your advice."

"Anything else?" the third man asked Kit.

"It's no masterpiece, but it's bloody enough to sell tickets. And it's set in Rome, or at least some vague *approximation* of the place," he said dismissively, "so you won't have trouble with the censors." He lowered his voice and spoke in the tone of someone offering valuable advice. "If you set something in England, be kind to the Tudors until you have a patron."

Before Will could respond, Cecely pulled me toward the table. "Pardon me," she said.

The courtesan gave us an irritated look. "Before you ask, no, I don't know your 'usbands." Her voice was the deepest voice I'd ever heard come out of a woman's mouth, throaty, seductive.

"We're not here to speak of husbands," Cecely laughed, as the men stopped bickering to watch our exchange. "We have a question about a subject in which you may have expertise."

She looked surprised. "Well, then. Out with it."

Cecely turned to me. I cleared my throat. The woman looked me up and down, her eyes lingering on my clothes, her expression shrewd. I met her eyes squarely, removing my mask. "I'm looking for an Italian bawd whose last name might be abbreviated *M-N-L*. Would you happen to know such a woman?"

She stared at me, unblinking. For a moment I thought she

wouldn't answer. Then she dissolved into laughter. "Give me a moment, sweeting," she said, shoulders shaking. "That is not what I expected you to say at all."

Will caught my eye, his lips quivering with amusement. "Nor I. You are full of surprises."

When the courtesan stopped laughing, I addressed her. "Well? Do you know such a woman?"

She shook her head. "But that doesn't mean she don't exist. I keep to Shoreditch. No doubt, you realise, bawds don't exactly advertise their legal names."

I drew a deep breath, disappointment making me shaky. "Do you know anyone who *might* know of her?"

She shook her head. "Try the other districts, love. Smithfield. Southwark. Clerkenwell."

Will stood. For the first time I noticed his apparel. A fitted, dark-buttoned doublet that emphasized his narrow waist. Black breeches, lace-up sleeves, dark hose beneath black knee-high boots. Simple, but he wore it with dignity.

"I am often in those wards. I'm an actor," he said with as much pride as someone might state an aristocratic title. "A gentlewoman like you would no doubt do everything in her power to avoid entering such establishments herself." His eyes danced, as if he were daring me to admit otherwise. "It would be easy for me to visit on your behalf. Tell me where you live, and I'll call if I find your woman."

I considered his offer, trying to see the risks from every angle. Cecely caught my eye, giving a subtle shake of her head. I knew what she meant. We didn't know this man at all. It was foolish to tell him where we lived when he was no doubt trying to extract the information. But something in me wanted to see him again.

"Underhill House, Bishopsgate. Come to the servants' entrance. Ask for Cecely." I nodded at my friend. "I don't want the master of the house to know I was here."

At the mention of a *master of the house*, I thought I saw Will's eyes narrow with—not disappointment, exactly, but interest, as if the possibility that I was with someone else enticed him. "Of course," he said quickly. "It wouldn't be proper for you to be in Shoreditch without your father—or is it husband? Forgive me. I didn't catch your name."

"She didn't give it," the third man said.

"*Signora Irraggiungibile,*" said Kit.

Will rolled his eyes, either hiding his ignorance of Italian or ignoring the implication that I was above him. His reserve had transformed into an amorous defiance, as if he wanted to challenge me to a contest. Something about the way he looked at me—his wantonness, the promise of misrule—made me want to rise to the challenge.

"Mistress Rose Rushe," I replied.

"Not Underhill?"

I shook my head. He waited for me to say more, but I didn't.

"I would've expected *baronessa, duchessa,*" he said. His Italian accent was terrible, but I found his attempt to impress me charming nonetheless. He bowed, pretending to kiss my hand. His movements were graceful, almost elegant. "Will Shakespeare."

Cecely smiled stiffly.

4

The moon waned. The days passed uneasily. The time I spent with Richard grew more and more uncomfortable. Every time I asked him if he'd heard from the Master of Revels, he became irritated, until I was almost certain he hadn't approached him at all. Whether this was because he disapproved of my ambitions or wanted to limit my freedom was irrelevant. I found either possibility infuriating.

My search for my mother's spellbook turned up nothing.

We heard nothing from Will. After a few days, Cecely and I started walking the outer wards while the brothers were downstairs in their workshop. They stayed down there for hours, sending up for food on the rare occasions they ate. We always had explanations ready for our trips into the city. *Out to tour Bedlam,* we would claim, *to see the menagerie, to pray at church—*

Though of course we were looking for the brothel.

On these walks, we talked about how we would persuade my mother to leave Underhill House. I thought the key would be to heal whatever rift she had with her family and remind her that if we lived independently, she could take back up her witching work. At home, it had been the centre of her life, but she could never continue that work while we lived at Underhill House. It could only be something she did for herself here, a secret.

I began to wonder if Cecely was right that I couldn't trust Will. My hope began to falter.

One mid-January day, Richard left his workshop early, storming up the cellar staircase just after dinner, calling my name. "Rose?" he kept saying. "Rose?"

He found me in the library, dejectedly flipping through a beautiful but incomprehensible manuscript on astrology. The language was Latin, but the handwriting was so full of flourishes it was impossible to read. There were gorgeous illuminations of angels, gods, and personifications of zodiac signs. When he walked in, I set the manuscript aside, forcing myself to meet his eyes. Lately he'd been confiding in me about his work, seeking reassurance as a husband might from his wife. It was so out of character that it seemed like confirmation that my mother had cast a spell on him. Though he'd always been happy to brag about his life in London, he had never spoken so freely of his failures without a significant amount of brandy in him.

"My father's notes are indecipherable, Rose. I fear—" His eyes shone, almost feverish, and his forehead was dewy with perspiration. "My confidence is faltering. We know how to activate the elements that are present in metals—Venus in copper, Mars in iron, Saturn in lead—but his contract requires transmuting those metals into gold. We've been trying to conjure an angel to help us, but the ritual my father copied from John Dee's notes doesn't work."

I had to suppress the urge to groan at the mention of the queen's conjurer. Richard never missed an opportunity to mention his famous friend.

"We've tried everything. Fasting, prayer—"

Fasting. That was why he almost never ate, why he'd become so thin.

"The ritual worked for Dee?" I couldn't keep the doubt from my voice. If the stories about John Dee were true, he was a genius at everything: conjuring, summoning spirits, alchemy, astrology, mathematics. But that was the thing. Those stories were like the stories about Merlin: impossible. When people spoke of conversing with angels, I always thought they were listening to voices inside them, whispers from the house of dreams. Why an angel would be moved to help Richard with his alchemical contract was beyond me.

"For Kelley, yes. His scryer."

"Why don't you ask him?"

"He's in Bohemia." He sat beside me, pushing his hair out of his eyes, and took my hand. "I hope you don't mind me confiding in you like this. This is Father's *life's work*. We cannot fail."

I frowned. He plainly wanted comfort, but I didn't want to give it to him. "No alchemist has succeeded in turning base metals into gold," I tried. "At least not in England. Your father will forgive you."

"*Will?*" he said, a vein of hurt running through the word, his eyes narrowing. The transformation from vulnerability to anger was so quick, I felt dizzy. "You assume we'll fail."

"I didn't say that."

"You're thinking it," he snapped. "*You*, a countrywoman with a passing interest in the stars, a guest in my house. Who do you think you are?"

I straightened, working to hide my reaction to his insult. *Countrywoman. A passing interest in the stars.* The words shot through me like lightning, striking this corner of my heart and that. I took a deep breath, reminding myself how dependent we were upon him for food and shelter. I swallowed my pride and shrugged, pretending to be chastened. "Forgive me. I spoke out of turn. You have been to Oxford. I only know what Father taught me."

That seemed to satisfy him. Thinking it would be wise to appease any residual hurt, I made myself ask him what he thought about how the stars worked on metals, a subject I had long been curious about myself. Long ago, I had learned that if your relationship with a man becomes strained, an easy way to fix it is to ask him to teach you something.

Predictably eager to hear himself talk, Richard launched into a lengthy dissertation on the planets and metals, spouting theories I already knew about the seven wandering stars and how their influence was present to varying degrees in the seven metals. I couldn't have gotten a word in edgewise if I wanted to, which gave me time to stew on how he had just treated me. He had always been slightly insufferable, but he had never been this mean to me. Perhaps his anger was a result of my mother's spell. His growing affection for me could've made him more sensitive. Or perhaps I simply hadn't been around him long enough to see this side of him.

As he went on—and on—a paroxysm of indignance began to build inside me. By the time he finished his lecture, I was fully angry.

Richard didn't notice. When I extracted myself from his company at last, he was watching me with fondness, as if he hadn't expected to have such a rewarding—that is, one-sided—conversation with me.

Mother was not in her chamber. I could hear the servants setting up the curtained bathtub in the red room. She had complained of exhaustion again at supper. It occurred to me that I had better find her spell soon and sabotage it; I couldn't bear it if Richard became any more fond of me. I had looked everywhere, but perhaps if I retraced my steps I would find it.

Setting sunlight flooded her room, dim and pink; dust motes spun in the fading light. The side of the room where the bed stood was already dark. The shadows around the bed seemed to ripple, and I thought I sensed a presence, the faint scent of roses and—was that copper? I thought of Venus, suddenly, given my conversation with Richard, but set the thought aside. The floorboards *beneath* the bed, I thought suddenly, the hardest place to get to—

I crept under the bed, inspecting the floorboards closely. Two planks were loose. The nails came up easily. Heart hammering in my chest, I lifted the boards and saw the trunk. Inside was her spell book, one of the roses I bought from the apothecary dried and tucked inside it.

My hands shook. The thorns had been pinched from the rose's stem. Mother had twined two strands of dark hair around it— Richard's and mine, no doubt.

I scanned the page, my throat constricting. The page the rose marked was a fortnight spell, the very last in the book, a spell she had obviously written to encourage a bond between me and Richard:

●○

For reluctant lovers
Take up rose and hair from each lover. Cut one barb
each midnight by beeswax candlelight until stem is bare,
twining hair. Drop oil of sea holly in each lover's drink.
Recite this following prayer each night by the light of
the evening star:
O Regina Caeli, enmortos—
huat haut haut
fugite, odium.
Fiat amor

The page rattled in my hand. I stared at the incantation until the words blurred, becoming strange. Not Latin, not nonsense, but inscrutable glyphs. When I blinked, they were words again. I threw the rose into the flames, furious.

The petals caught, sizzling, releasing a sweet-smelling smoke. I felt the beginnings of a headache, a stab of pain behind my eyes. I massaged my temples, regretting what I had just done. Mother would know I sabotaged her spell if the rose was gone.

I hurried into my room and found the rose I had worn on Twelfth Night, which I had hung upside down to dry from the rafters. I plucked out two hairs from my head and wound them around it, removing its thorns. Then I placed it between the pages of my mother's book, hands shaking, and put everything back.

When Cecely came to bed, I told her what I had found.

"Good Lord," she said, her eyes wide. Then she met my gaze, her shock fading to concern. "Do you feel it working on you?"

"My affection for Richard is no stronger than it was before we came. In fact, it has significantly lessened. But his affection for me…" I trailed off, furiously calculating how long it had been since Mother asked me to buy the roses. About a fortnight, unfortunately, I realised with a sinking sensation. The moon was new. "She's been working on this since we came to Underhill House. I doubt I caught it in time."

Cecely sighed, frustrated. "I wish there were a way to convince your mother to stop scheming."

"I think it would be easier to convince her to stop breathing."

Before he descended the stairs to his workshop the next morning, Richard announced that he would come up early, and he would send up a gift to help me prepare for a special dinner. My stomach roiled as I went upstairs. My mother stood in my chamber, beaming. Her exhaustion seemed to have vanished.

"He has something to *tell* you," she sang ominously.

When I saw the gift Richard had sent, my blood ran cold. On my bed was a gown finer than any my grandmother ever purchased in Gravesend. The bodice was cream, embroidered with deep green thread—the colour of emeralds, the Underhill family crest—and gold lace. The sleeves were green with gold-embroidered cuffs. There was only one kind of news that would make Richard buy me a dress like this.

A river of dread flooded through me, leaden, heavy.

"Try it on," Mother sang, "so there's time for the maid to take it in or out before dinner if needed."

She called in Cecely to help me put it on. As my friend helped me step into the skirt, my mother started chattering about the surprise Richard would tell me about at dinner, and I was overcome by a wave of nausea.

"*Stop*," I said. "Get this off. I'm going to be ill."

Cecely must've thought my behaviour another ruse. She smirked as she began to unlace my bodice. Mother didn't believe me either until I lost the contents of my stomach.

"Why are you so cursed?"

I went to bed and stayed there for the rest of the day, fever-ish, afraid I would faint. I felt truly unwell—my head ached, and everything smelled burnt—but I was grateful for the excuse to put off listening to Richard's announcement.

When Cecely finally came to bed, I was sitting in the dark ante-chamber, staring out the window, eyes burning, my thoughts scat-tered and racing. Most of the glass was coloured, but I could see a moonless semicircle of sky through a clear pane at the bottom.

"What a performance," she said, shaking her head, an admiring gleam in her eye. "If only you could work as an actor. You would be a sensation."

I stood from the window and closed the curtain so the room fell into shadow, wiping my face, not wanting her to see my tears. I felt embarrassingly powerless. "I wasn't acting. I am truly sickened. I have never been this angry, and you know me. That is quite a feat."

"You're in a difficult situation."

"I have one of the worst headaches I've ever had. I keep smelling roses. I hear a bird. It's as if I'm going mad."

I couldn't see her face, but I could hear her sharp intake of breath. When she spoke, she sounded worried. "Maybe you should let Richard send for the physician after all."

I rolled my eyes, remembering the smelling herbs the physi-cian back home prescribed my father, which only made his cough worse. "Physicians are useless," I said, my voice shaking with a sudden fury that made my tone sound harsher than I meant.

For a long moment Cecely didn't respond. A full minute passed, perhaps two. I could hear her moving toward me, soft footsteps, the swish of her skirts. "Rose," she said softly.

Her hand brushed my arm. My skin tingled where she touched me. "There you are," she said, closing her fingers around mine. I froze, a tiny gasp falling from my lips.

The anteroom seemed to shiver with her nearness. My anger faded, leaving only an ache. I never knew what to think when Cecely was physically affectionate. It seemed to come naturally to her, but the only person I had ever hugged with any regularity was Edmund. I stood perfectly still, afraid to breathe, afraid to move, my mind racing with interpretations.

"I hate this," she said softly. "I hate him."

"Who?"

"Richard."

"He's quite hateable."

She squeezed my hand. "Let's go to bed. You need rest. You're exhausted."

We withdrew to our chamber, changed, and climbed into bed. For a long moment I could see nothing, hear nothing except Cecely's breathing beside me. Then my eyes began to adjust to the dark and her figure took shape. A dim form, nothing more, lying on her side next to me. I stayed on my back, staring at the shadows on the ceiling, my whole body tense. "I'm furious," I breathed. "I can't master myself."

She sighed, and the sheets rustled. She made an uncomfortable sound, as if she were reluctant to say what she said next. Her voice was no more than a whisper. "I would be too. What your mother did—"

"It's not only that."

"I know. Neither of us has even had a chance to grieve."

I fell silent. Something yawned in my throat, an ache. I saw a flash of my father on his deathbed, Cecely in her singed night-gown at our door. Everything had gone so wrong. I pressed my lips together, trying to stay in control, but the words tumbled out before I could stop them. "Underhill House would be like a prison. Richard is so condescending, so tiresome. He'll want children—"

I waited for her to comfort me, but the only answer was a slow exhalation of breath, the sound of her shifting uncomfortably beneath the sheets. I peered into the dark, wishing I could see her face. It occurred to me suddenly that my complaints might be difficult for her to hear. I was rejecting the very thing she'd tried to get from Geoffraie, and it was being handed to me on a silver platter.

"You could hire a governess," she said finally, her voice trembling with a false brightness. "You could play music for nobles, and as a gentlewoman, not a hired hand. You could go to masques, throw balls, wear dresses like the one he sent up today every day—"

"I don't want that!" I said. My eyes burned. I was dangerously close to tears again. "I want a position at court, the freedom to choose my own lovers. I want charge of my own house. I want *you* there—" I stopped, embarrassed that I had said too much. "And Edmund, and my mother," I hurried to add. "If we found positions at court—"

"Oh, Rose," Cecely said, her voice full of a quiet intensity I couldn't parse. She paused for a long moment. When she spoke again, her tone was embittered. "It's not what either of us wants, but perhaps—" Her voice caught, and she hesitated. "Perhaps it's the most practical thing. The world is cruel to women who live alone. Even widows, unless they're wealthy. I don't like it either, but gentlemen's wives have power."

The darkness seemed suddenly thick.

"I wish there were another way," she said finally, fumbling for my hand. "But look at us. Me, a maidservant. You, about to become betrothed again. Aren't you tired of fighting it?"

"Yes," I whispered in a voice that sounded too much like a sob for my comfort. I knew that many childhood friendships naturally ran their course as children grew up and married, but the thought that it might happen to us was devastating. We had become much closer since we came to London, sleeping in the same room, confiding in one another. "But the alternative is worse."

Her reply was so low, so soft—so sad—I almost didn't hear it. "Wealth is freedom."

The next morning, Mary knocked on the door. Cecely clambered out of the high bed before we told the maid to come in. My friend sat on the truckle bed, listening blearily as Mary explained that Richard's feast had been rescheduled for dinner. She gave me the rose Richard wanted me to wear in my hair and a vial of rosewater to perfume myself. As I accepted the gifts, I caught Cecely watching, eyes wide, gleaming. When I met her gaze, she turned away, embarrassed.

Mother must've been listening at the door, because she hurried in to work on my face paint. Cecely curtsied and murmured for Mary's benefit that I should ring for her when I was ready to dress. As my friend walked out, I felt a tightness in my chest.

It took Mother hours to paint my face and arrange my hair. She was adamant that I wear spirits of Saturn, but the room felt so hot, it was difficult to sit still. When I reached for my handkerchief to pat the sweat from my brow, Mother caught my wrist. "You'll ruin the makeup," she hissed.

"Let go."

"Rose—"

"If you want me to sit through this dinner, *let go.*"

She released my hand.

"I want to be alone."

She sighed but went to her room. I was nearly finished dressing. All that was left was to de-thorn the rose and slip it behind my ear. As I cut the prickles from the stem, I couldn't help but think of my mother's spell. The words that had shifted and blurred.

By the time we went downstairs, I was deeply irritated. At the foot of the staircase, Mother pulled me aside. *"Arrange your face."*

My spirit rioted. Then I smelled the ghost roses again, admixed with the faintest scent of fire and ash. Her spell. Was that what I was sensing? Or was it only a headache?

I followed her into the dining hall reluctantly. Richard had hired three men—a trio of viol players, bass, tenor, and treble—to play in consort. They were setting up their instruments.

Richard was sitting at the head of the table. For the first time since we'd arrived, he'd cast off his mourning clothes. He wore an emerald green doublet with goldwork and cream breeches made from the same fabric as the gown he'd gifted me. His attire matched mine, and he was watching me eagerly. I wanted to run out of the house screaming.

As I found my seat, Richard stood—his chair scraping the stones of the dining hall floor—reciting the interminable blessing for which he held such a baffling affection. Why he was so attached to it was beyond me. Even God, I thought, would find such doggerel tedious.

As the servants brought food, my stomach turned. There was peacock, custard, a beautiful sugar sculpture of a bird. Although I had once dreamed of sampling such novelties, I couldn't bring myself to eat any of it. Even the musical accompaniment for dinner seemed unpleasant. A brash, almost nasal melody, marching along like a royal parade. Ostentatious, whining. Like my life would be if I stayed here.

I fidgeted with my knife, trying to look like I was eating, watching Edmund marvel at the sugary swan. He wanted to reach out and grab it, I could tell, but Mother had been fighting with him about manners.

Richard leaned close. "Your appetite is usually much stronger. Does this meal not suit your tastes?"

"I haven't fully recovered from my illness. The food is wonderful. The mead, especially, is lovely."

He cleared his throat and waved at a servant girl. "Bring the claret. I would like to pledge a health."

The girl returned with the bottle and poured us each a glass. I felt woozy looking at it, a bloody purplish red.

"To Rose—" Richard raised his glass, not taking his eyes off me. "Most enchanting. May you recover soon."

The constancy of his attention, his near fascination with me, made me uneasy. Clearly my sabotage of the spell hadn't affected him.

"To Rose—" my mother and Humphrie echoed, raising their glasses.

Suddenly dizzied, I couldn't bring myself to take a sip. The claret looked so much like blood.

My head pounded. I thought of the nightbird. The roses. The metallic scent. It occurred to me again that I might be going mad.

Richard's voice faded, echoed, becoming distant. "I spoke to your mother yesterday. I'll be plain." His eyes searched out mine. It was difficult for me to meet his gaze. "I have decided to take you as my wife," he said magnanimously, as if he were offering me charity.

Something clutched at my throat.

Mother smiled as if she was overcome with gratitude. "I could barely keep the secret," she said brightly, but behind her eyes was an asp waiting to strike. "Isn't it wonderful? Richard has agreed to take us all in."

"Master Edmund and Madam Katarina will remain in Humphrie's old chambers. You'll move into the chamber beside mine upstairs," Richard said enthusiastically.

"I'll have a playroom!" Edmund chirped.

"I'm going to replant the pleasure garden. Richard will purchase beehives, so I can go back to making candles."

"It will be so nice to have women overseeing the household again."

The music droned, whining, then fading.

"You're too kind," I made myself say, having difficulty forming the words. My vision blurred. My tongue felt swollen. I felt too hot, flushed, out of balance.

"Rose?" Mother's voice sounded far away.

I blinked at her, realising that my decision to throw the rose into the flames had been foolish. I was the rose. She had tried to remove my thorns. I'd set myself on fire. "I don't feel well."

"Is it yesterday's illness, or something else?"

I closed my eyes, my thoughts racing. What had my mother done? What had *I* done? My hands shook with furious tremors.

"I'll send for the physician," Richard said.

The physician, an ill-tempered old man with thinning white hair, diagnosed me with an excess of yellow bile. He said it was a strange time to develop such an ailment, given that the sun was in Capricorn and it was the dead of winter—until Mother told him about the surfeit of fire and air in my chart.

"Ah," he said. "That explains it."

He advised Mother to have the cook prepare watery foods like cucumber, lettuce, and spinach. He said I should substitute fish for the hotter, drier meats we had been eating. By the time Mother led him out, I was furious with her for meddling with my feelings. When she returned, she shook her head disapprovingly and sat at my bedside.

"Why do I feel like this?" I hissed.

She shut the door, withdrawing her beads from her pocket, and said several Ave Marias, chanting "*Regina Caeli fer aquam*" between prayers.

At supper, the cook followed the physician's advice, sending up bread and salat and spinach tarts, a cut of mackerel in a buttery sauce. I ate as much as I could, but my stomach was uneasy. I gave Hughe half of the bread and mackerel.

That night, when Cecely came to bed, I was flipping through a book on alchemy from Richard's library, feeling foolish. None of the symbols in it looked anything like the glyphs I thought I'd seen. I was almost certain I was going mad.

Cecely beamed at me, opening her mouth to tell me something, then saw what I was reading. "What's that?"

"Nothing," I said, putting it away. I told her what I had learned at dinner: how foolish my decision to burn the rose had been. The physician's recommendations. But instead of concern, she gazed at me with an irritating optimism. "Do you feel better now?"

I nodded, confused. "I think so."

Her eyes danced. She lowered her voice, but she was so excited, the words came out in a rush. "Just now, when I was leaving the servants' quarters in the cellar, I heard chanting. Richard and Humphrie had left the door to the workshop open a crack. Of course I had to look inside, since I've been told a dozen times not to go near it. When I peered in, I saw Humphrie leaning over a crystal ball, which had been placed in the centre of a table on an intricate seal. There was a great book open on the table between them. Humphrie was chanting in Latin."

I leaned in toward her, curious despite what a terrible day I'd had. "Then what happened?"

She grinned. "The ritual didn't work. They just sat there, waiting, until Humphrie started arguing with Richard. He wants them to go see someone named Kelley—in Bohemia—so Kelley can teach him how to scry." She beamed at me, happier than I'd seen her in weeks. "He said they would need to leave soon if they want to fulfil their father's contract."

I blinked at her, once, twice. I could scarcely breathe, my heart filled so suddenly with hope. A trip to Bohemia would take months. "What did Richard say?"

"That he hadn't arranged for the parson to call the banns yet, and that process could take weeks. Humphrie said you would be here when they return. Richard said he would pray on it."

"God-a-mercy," I breathed, wishing with a sudden fervour that his god would indeed have mercy on me.

"*Rose*," she said in a trembling voice, taking my hand. Her black eyes shone. "This would give us the time we need."

Late the next morning, Richard informed my mother and me that he'd arranged for our marriage banns to be called at St. Helen's. He said it would be a while before they were finished, but he thought we could hold the wedding as soon as Lent ended in March. I forced a smile, devastated that he wasn't mentioning their trip to Bohemia.

As the day wore on, my disordered thoughts and headache abated. The scent of roses faded. The nightbird fell silent. But that night, I lay awake beside Cecely, unable to sleep, tormented by another voice. All the whispers from my house of dreams said the same thing: Run your fingers through her hair, hold her hand. It was getting more difficult to ignore them.

The next day, we resumed our search of the outer wards, but no one had heard of our bawd. Cecely nudged me as we were walking through Southwark. "Look," she said, nodding at a building with a brightly painted sign that said CARDINAL'S CAP. Beside the words was a bright red painting of the clergyman's headwear, which was conspicuously phallic.

Waiting outside the door was a familiar figure in a fine black tightly fitted doublet, black stockings, and a simple white ruff. His shoulder-length brown hair shone in the late-afternoon sun. *Will.* As a woman opened the door for him, I smiled.

Cecely rolled her eyes. "*Rose!* You don't actually think he's there on your behalf. The owner is the least likely candidate for your grandmother in London, an Englishman named John Raven!"

I cringed. "Maybe he doesn't know?"

"Go ahead and tell yourself that, sweeting. That place is famous."

But the following day, Graves came to our chamber. "Good Cecely," he said haughtily, his eyes narrowed with barely disguised disapproval. "Someone by the name of Shakes-beard is here to see you."

Cecely straightened. My spirits soared.

"I'll be down in a moment."

The steward nodded.

As soon as he shut the door, she looked at me and breathed, "He actually found her."

She hurried downstairs. Hughe sensed my cheer and came to me, kissing my hand. I patted his head.

A quarter of an hour passed. It felt like an eternity.

Finally, I heard footsteps in the statuary. Cecely shut the door behind her, checking to make sure my mother's and Edmund's doors were closed. "*M-N-L* stands for Minola," she whispered. "Will said a woman called Black Luce runs a stew in Clerkenwell called the Abbey. Last night, he met the Italian woman who runs the place with her. Lisabetta Minola. He offered to meet us at Aldersgate tonight and escort us, but he would *undo* you, Rose. I can see it in your eyes. We can just tell a carriage driver to take us there."

I bit my lip. The devil in me wanted to see Will again, but I didn't want to argue with her. "Do you think we'll encounter trouble if we go alone?"

Her eyes sparkled with mischief. "Not if we dress the part."

For the rest of the day, I was cautiously hopeful, happier than I had been in weeks. The prospect of posing with Cecely as women of commerce delighted me. By supper, my spirits had recovered enough that I could keep food down.

"It's good to see you eating again," Richard said.

"It is," said Mother.

I cleared my throat, concerned that perhaps I'd been too open about my good cheer. "It's good to feel better."

When dinner was over, I tried to excuse myself, but Richard pulled me aside. "Rose," he said, touching my hand, his green eyes filled with affection and something else I couldn't quite categorize.

"Richard," I said, drawing a deep breath, forcing a somewhat cold smile that promised nothing. I was doing my best not to lead him on. The candles on the table and in the sconces flickered. A servant passed, carrying goblets and leftover bread back to the kitchen.

"I know you came under dark circumstances. Neither of us has had a good year. That said—" He paused, searching for the right words, that emotion I couldn't identify growing stronger. Greed, perhaps. "It seems as if these horrible events conspired to bring us together, as if there is some incomprehensible divine logic underlying all this tragedy. I've wanted to take you as my wife since I was ten."

I stared at him, unsettled by his word choice again—*take*—not to mention the implication that God had killed our fathers so we could be together. I tried to recall any signs that he'd wanted to marry me that young, but all I could remember from that period was beating him mercilessly at triumph. Was he telling the truth, or was this simply what my mother's spell had deluded him into believing? He had such a reserved character, it was possible he would hide such a thing. "I had no idea."

He met my eyes hopefully.

Pluto and hell, I thought, he wants to kiss me. I cleared my throat and lowered my eyes, pretending to be flustered by his attention. "I should go," I murmured softly, hurrying away as fast as I could without betraying my horror. On my way upstairs, it occurred to me that I should be grateful he'd become such a fool for me, or he would realise how unlike me it was to behave demurely.

As I waited for Cecely to come to bed, I paced, feeling trapped—no, caged—by Richard's growing affection for me. I tried to console myself that we would leave soon, but my skin crawled at the way he looked at me.

When Cecely came to our chamber, my spirits lifted. Soon we were searching the wardrobe for the gaudiest clothes we could find, laughing over which styles were the most scandalous. I chose a shining black gown with a plunging neckline and silver-embroidered sleeves. Cecely chose a cream gown with a similarly low-cut bodice. We held them up, checking our appearances in the mirror.

My fingers trembled as I laced her bodice as she had done for me so many times. It took everything I had to still my fingers enough to fasten it.

Soon we were ready to go, bodices tightened, cheeks pink with fucus, lips painted a bright cerise. Our hair almost completely visible, coiled loosely into thick braids and curls. Ready to squeeze the life we wanted, against all odds, from our difficult circumstances. We checked to make sure my mother and Edmund were asleep, stuffed pillows beneath our blankets, drew the bedcurtains, and settled Hughe in a corner with a bone.

The clock bell was tolling midnight as we crept downstairs, costumes hidden beneath our cloaks. The house was dark, the steward and all the rest of the servants abed. We used no candle as we crept down the square spiral staircase. No light shone through the front windows.

Cecely opened the door, letting in a rush of wintry air. We hurried out, shoes clicking against the cobblestones, meeting one another's eyes and taking pleasure in our transgression. When I told the carriage driver to take us to the Abbey, he raised his eyebrows but said nothing. Imagining what he thought—that we were leaving some gentleman's home after showing him a decadent evening—I laughed. Our costumes were effective.

A grim determination filled me as we passed through Aldersgate. Clerkenwell descended quickly from city to country. Close to the wall, there were inns and churches, a hospital. But soon our carriage was passing gardens and pastures. The Abbey was farther out than I expected. Disembarking, we saw a crumbling stone façade that looked as if it had been home to actual nuns before they were expelled from England.

I paid the driver, then motioned for Cecely to follow me around the back. There we saw an unkempt garden, a pitch-black pasture, and a shadowy wood that might hide the cottage my mother described. Unable to resist, I hurried into the trees to look for the cottage, but I saw no path, and the ground was covered in briars, so I made my way back, discouraged. As we approached the door, two gentlemen stumbled out, laughing and drinking from tankards. They tipped their hats at us, obviously intoxicated.

Beyond the anteroom was a dark hall scattered with candlelit tables. From this distance, the flames seemed to twinkle like stars. The tables were sat with men and scandalously dressed women whose voices drowned out the soft strains of music. The women's faces were painted boldly. Skin brightened with spirits of Saturn, lips darkened red, cheeks ablush. There were blond twins in matching crimson gowns holding tiny white dogs that reminded me of Toby, a gorgeous dark-haired woman with a Spanish accent, a woman who looked like she was from the East. Two men sat at a corner table, one leaning toward the other, his hand on the other's knee.

As we made our way inside, the scent of sea holly and roses overwhelmed me. I thought of the spell my mother had cast on me. Both sea holly and roses were components. There was another odour too, earthy and feminine, so faint it was barely perceptible. The dark, the candles, and the fragrance made it a far more pleasing place than I'd expected. The rafters were wreathed with garlands.

In the corners, shadows shifted. For an instant, I thought I sensed the same dark presence my mother sometimes carried with her—but no, it wasn't the same. It was softer, sweeter, soothing. Then it was gone, and I was left wondering if it had been there in the first place.

The hall looked like it must've been a chapel once. I wondered which saint it had been dedicated to. On the dais, three women with red hair played a sweet, seductive song. They were so alike, I thought they were sisters, dressed in the most sensual garb I'd ever seen, white silk barely covering their breasts, gaudy necklaces glittering in the candlelight.

The tallest of the three, I realised, was the courtesan I'd seen with Will. She was playing the virginal and singing in a voice more beautiful than that of any woman I'd heard. She caught me watching her and winked. I blinked at her, wondering if I'd imagined the flirtation. My cheeks grew hot. Anytime a woman caught me looking at her before now, she'd ignored it.

Cecely rolled her eyes. "*Rose.* We're here for your grandmother. Focus."

Behind the bar I saw a strikingly handsome woman who must be Luce. Her skin was a rich brown, and the candlelight brought out a bronze glow in her unpainted cheeks. She was listening to the customer across from her with a barely concealed bored expression. Her sable hair was short, pulled back tight beneath her hat. She was dressed less like a courtesan than a merchant in a broad-brimmed men's hat, a form-fitting grey doublet, and a thick wool skirt.

She was running her finger over the rim of a goblet, expertly making it sing. She moved like Cecely—back straight, fluid gestures. The man in front of her watched her finger circle the glass, enthralled. I couldn't stop watching her either.

Noticing us, the woman stopped, set the cup aside, and rolled her eyes when the man wasn't looking.

Cecely and I exchanged a bemused glance and approached. The man leered at us but stalked off when I glared at him. As soon as he was out of sight, the woman's shoulders shook with laughter. "If you're here for a job, sweet, you'll need to master your face."

I smiled. "That may well be impossible."

"Happily," Cecely said, "we have other reasons for coming."

"To chase out all my patrons, so I can catch up on my sleep?"

"You are the—abbess, then?"

She cleared her throat. "Who's asking?"

"I'm Rose Rushe. Katarina Minola's daughter."

She straightened, falling silent for a long moment, before she said quietly, "I'm Luce. Some refer to me as Black Luce." Her lip quivered with a scornful amusement. Then she turned and shouted into the doorway behind her. "*Betta!*"

Her tone was so urgent that everyone nearby stopped talking. My breath caught, and I felt suddenly anxious. Even the musicians slowed their playing, the redheaded singer's low voice trailing off. Luce rolled her eyes, waving her hand in a dismissive gesture. "Proceed, proceed. There's no reason to stop the revel."

The singer picked up where she'd left off. The buzz of conversation slowly returned to the room.

"Do you dance?" Cecely asked.

The corners of Luce's mouth curved downward with the pleasure of being recognised. "I used to," she said. "For the queen. It feels like a lifetime ago. You too?"

Cecely nodded. "How did you get the position?"

"The same way I lost it." She smirked. "Luck."

An Italian woman emerged from the cellar with a jug of ale. From her thick black braid to her dark eyes and tawny skin, she was obviously my mother's sister. She froze at the sight of me. "Who are you?"

I stepped forward. "Katarina's daughter. I'm here to see my grandmother."

My aunt's mouth fell open. Luce put a calming hand on her shoulder.

Lisabetta Minola took a deep breath, obviously shaken. She eyed me suspiciously. Whatever dispute my mother had with her family, my aunt was still angry with her. "Your grandmother is dead, as your mother well knows. What does Katarina want?"

I blinked, unable to believe what I had just heard. *Dead?* I pushed down the uncomfortable sorrow that was rising in me, surprised at how upset I was over the death of someone I had never met.

Focus, I thought, mastering myself. Lisabetta was the one I needed to convince, then. Her eyes were hard, narrowed. This would be difficult.

I summarized the events that led us to London. Sadness tugged at my aunt's eyes when I mentioned my father's death, and I wondered if she knew him. She didn't react to the rest of the story at all, her face as stony and calculating as my mother's usually was. "Mother doesn't know we're here," I finished. "She took us to a family friend's house. She's bewitched him."

Cecely met the women's eyes pointedly. "To marry Rose."

"And give you all a place to live?" my aunt asked.

I nodded.

"That sounds like Katarina." She met my eyes, a touch less warily than before. "What do you want?"

"Mother said there was a cottage in those woods. We're in desperate need of a place for the four of us to stay while Cecely and I find work." I looked at Luce hopefully. "We'll pay rent. I'll do anything I can to avoid this marriage."

Luce caught my aunt's eye, a question. My aunt tucked a black curl back into her braid, watching me, taking my measure. Her expression was pensive, sympathetic. I thought she was going to say yes, until she shuddered and turned away. "No," she said finally. "I want nothing to do with her."

My chest went tight. "Lisabetta, aunt, please. We have nowhere else to go. They can't stay with Richard once I leave. He's going to be furious."

"Betta," Luce interjected. "She's trying to escape a marriage. That cottage is far enough from the brothel that you wouldn't even have to see your sister. We aren't using it."

My aunt shot Luce a warning look, so sharp it could've cut through stone. "No more. I have said."

Luce fell silent.

Lisabetta met my gaze. "I sympathise with your plight, Rose, but as much as I would like to help, I cannot allow your mother to live here."

"Please. I beg you." My voice trembled. "We have nowhere else to turn."

"Let me give you some money." She fumbled in her pouch, then held out a sovereign, her eyes full of a maddening pity.

"I need a *salary*. A place to stay while I find work."

Lisabetta's eyes were stony. "If I ever see your mother again, I'll kill her."

Kill her? A desperate laugh bubbled up in my throat. Of course, my mother had managed to ruin this too. Everywhere I turned, every option I thought I had, there she stood in my way. I would never abandon my brother, but if I had a chance to leave her, I would take it in a second.

I rushed outside before I could start crying. My heels clacked against the cobblestones. My cloak slipped from my shoulders. I felt ridiculous, suddenly, my face so brightly painted, wearing such a gaudy black gown. I sped up, wanting to put as much distance as I could between myself and the brothel. I hated the glee with which I'd dressed earlier. I had pinned my last hopes on this sorry place, and now it had come to nothing.

The street was dark except for a distant lantern.

"Rose—" Cecely called in a voice so hopeful, it rankled. I could hear her heels clicking on the street behind me.

When she touched my shoulder, I stopped, a shiver running through me. My breath caught, and my eyes burned. I whirled on her. *"What?"* The word came out angrier than I intended.

She watched me carefully, her expression suddenly hesitant.

"How can you be so calm? This is a disaster."

She blinked, her expression so quizzical, I found myself wondering what she had seen that I missed. She pressed her lips together, waiting for my anger to fade. There was a light in her eyes, a mixture of mischief and hope, as she showed me what she held in her hand. The sovereign. When she spoke, her voice trembled with an inexplicable excitement. "Didn't you hear what Luce said? She used to dance for the queen. She might know the Master of Revels."

"What does it matter? They said no."

"Your mother's spell worked so well on Richard because he was already fond of you. There is plainly at least some small part of your aunt that wants to help you. She was considering, despite how much she hates your mother. We can cast a sympathy spell to tip the balance in our direction." She held up the coin. "She gave us this. It's the perfect symbol of her sympathy."

Her words hung in the air. I felt unsteady, stretched thin. She was right. Lisabetta had considered. We might be able to open her heart further—that is, if I had any ability whatsoever with magic. "I have never cast a spell that worked. Even my mother's spells aren't completely reliable."

Her eyes shone. "You don't even want to try?"

My eyes burned. I wanted to say yes, yes, a thousand times yes, but my heart was full of doubt. I remembered the flames eating the roof of our farmhouse, Mistress Coppinger's accusations of witchcraft—and that had all happened when we were innocent. The truth was, we were vulnerable to such accusations no matter what we did. There would be no reward for not trying. If there was even a chance—if we did nothing, we might never escape Underhill House. A sympathy spell would bring the pillory or at worst a brief stay in prison. For a witch to be hanged, she had to cause someone's death.

There was no malice in this.

I closed my eyes, hope blooming in my heart like a poisonous flower. Then I drew myself up, meeting Cecely's gaze. Her dark eyes were earnest. The naked feeling she was showing me summoned a lump in my throat. I nodded. "It might work. We could adapt a spell from Mother's book."

She bit her lips, her eyes bright with joy. "We have to try."

Mary was waiting in the parlour when we crept back into Underhill House, a candle on the table beside her chair. She jumped at our footsteps; she must've fallen asleep. Her bonnet had slipped off her head, setting her cloudlike black hair free. She reached up to adjust the bonnet as a shadow at her feet moved, changing shape. Hughe hurried toward us, tail wagging, toenails clicking against the marble floor. He leapt up to kiss my face when I reached down to pet him, joyful at our reunion.

"He was whining," Mary explained with a yawn. "He got bored with the bone you gave him. Graves hates animals. I was afraid he would whip him."

My heart dropped. "Did they notice we were gone?"

"No, miss."

Her expression was troubled. I got the sense that she was trying to impress me, that she needed something, but I had no idea what. I set the thought aside for later. "Thank you, Mary," I said, and motioned for Hughe to follow us.

We hurried upstairs as fast as we could without waking anyone, stepping softly to make sure the stairs didn't complain. Then we crept toward the door to my mother's room. Hughe tried to follow us, whimpering when I motioned for him to wait in the corner. The only light was our candle, partially covered by Cecely's palm. When we opened the door, it creaked. I held my breath, waiting to see if Mother roused. The chamber was dark.

I tiptoed in and slowly climbed beneath the bed to remove the floorboard. As I slid the witching trunk out, the covers rustled. I froze. When she stilled, I crept out with the trunk. We climbed into our bed, drew the curtains, lit the candle, and opened the book. "We need to hurry," I said. "Her sleeping was fitful."

Flipping to the back of the book, I found a spell to increase an unwilling subject's sympathy and cure their hatred. It was a double-fortnight spell, but the wedding wasn't supposed to be until after Lent, and it was one of the few spells that could be started at any time of the moon's cycle. We would have plenty of time to convince Lisabetta after the spell was complete. As I read the incantation, the letters blurred and I thought I saw glyphs again. Frustrated, I forced my eyes to focus. I needed to make sure I understood how to pronounce the chant, and part of it was nonsense as usual.

"What?" Cecely asked.

"It invokes *Regina Caeli*, the 'queen of heaven,' like many of her spells. I always thought that was St. Mary, but the spell uses wolfsbane. Poison. I keep seeing symbols behind the words."

Cecely touched the page, her expression so hopeful it hurt to look at her. "Are you sure you don't have your mother's gift?"

I swallowed my doubt, memorised the incantation, and taught it to her, then pried up a floorboard in the antechamber where we could leave the candle undisturbed. We knelt on either side of the candle, pressed the coin into the wax, and lit it, hurrying to finish before anyone woke.

The flame brightened the room just enough for me to see Cecely bending her face over the candle. Its pale light set her cheeks aglow. The candle guttered as I pulled out the pouch of wolfsbane from the trunk. "*Regina Caeli, roudos—*" I chanted, working hard to hide my self-doubt. "*Huat haut haut fugite, odium.*"

The wolfsbane was difficult to handle; even dried, it could only be touched with gloves, which made my fingers clumsy. I pinched half of a foreboding purple petal into the flame. I thought I felt something as the petals blackened, giving off a thin smoke. Something dark. A sizzling hatred in the air. My throat constricted. I wanted this to work so badly. When the smoke dissipated, I put the first shred of lemon balm leaf down to ring the candle.

"*Nox enmortos—*" we whispered. Our voices rose, stirring something within me, subtle but undeniably real. My voice trembled as I repeated the last line of the spell. "*Roudos, roudos. Fiat sympathia.*" Beneath the scent of wolfsbane and lemon balm, I thought I could smell roses. Not the ghost scent like before, but sweet and true and dark. And beneath that, so faint I couldn't be certain it was there, the faintest whiff of copper again. I couldn't help but think of Venus, but the glyphs weren't Latin or even Greek.

Across from me, Cecely knelt in her cream bodice, its fabric barely distinguishable from her skin. I became painfully aware of her plunging neckline, the shadowy curves of her breasts. My body hummed, the desire I had been working so hard to smother suddenly impossible to refuse. The aura of roses lingered between us, intoxicating. I couldn't tell if it was coming from within me or without, but it was real. The spell was working.

I breathed it in, shivering, all my senses heightened. "Do you sense that?"

She nodded. "The queen of heaven."

Her pupils were wide, expectant, as if the spell had stirred her desire for me too. My breath caught. Was I imagining it? I wanted to touch her. To gently cup her shoulder, trail my fingers over her clavicle to her neck. I wanted to kiss her there and there and there—

In that moment I didn't care *who* saw us.

"We should go to bed. It's almost dawn. Let me help you out of your bodice."

"Please," she said. I thought I heard an eager note in her voice, but I couldn't tell if it was anything more than desire to get out of her uncomfortable clothes. The sun had not yet risen, and the candle cast only a thin circle of light on the floor. We stood.

I had to fumble with her bodice. Its intricate series of clasps and hooks cooperated, clicking apart. When I finished, I held up the candle so I could look at her.

Her undergarments hung about her in complicated layers: her shift, her petticoat, endless ruffles and string and buttons. I reached up to unpin her hair, letting it fall. She shivered when it hit her shoulders.

I met her eyes, moving so she could reach my hooks. The candle flickered. My hand was shaking. "Your turn."

She smiled. I thought I sensed anticipation in the slight quick-ening of her breath, the nervous way her fingers fiddled with the clasps. Each click of a hook coming undone was torture.

When I was undressed to my own undergarments, I caught her hand and pulled her toward me. She gave a barely perceptible gasp. Her pupils were as large as my father's when he was in his cups. There was no mistaking it. She wanted me too. I was so relieved, I laughed.

"What?" Her eyes glinted with insult.

I had seduced a dozen men, played cat and mouse, discarded them like toys. I had spoken boldly, performed, pretended to be someone I wasn't. But it took every bit of my courage to tell her why I was laughing. "I'm laughing at myself. I've never—"

Her eyes softened. "You haven't? I always thought—"

I lowered my voice. "You've done this before?"

"There was a girl in Norwich. One in Essex. It happens."

"Why didn't you tell me?"

"I didn't think you were interested. I didn't want to ruin things."

"How did you find them?"

She laughed. "I was a dancer in a medicine show, Rose. They found me. That was the real reason my parents stopped taking me with them."

I gasped. Why in the world had she hidden this from me? I was probably one of the least judgemental people in England.

"Now I've found you."

A slow smile spread over her face.

I opened the bedcurtains, set the candle in its holder, and ges-tured for her to climb in. "After you."

The candle flickered. She clambered past, smiling at me in an utterly new way: a devastating combination of playful and invit-ing. I was normally so sure of myself in bed, but suddenly I felt utterly unnerved. Her shift—white ruffles over pink skin, lace—had slipped from her shoulder.

I wanted her so much, it hurt. I could hear my heartbeat in my ears. I told myself it was because it had been so long since I had lain with anyone. I slipped my hand behind her head, lacing my fingers into her hair, meeting her eyes.

She shivered with pleasure as I kissed her. The scent of roses grew stronger. She kissed me back, her hand in my hair, pulling it softly. I have never wanted anyone so much.

I lost the ability to think coherent thoughts by the time we tumbled together onto the featherbed. I felt like I was melting, losing my sense of where I ended and she began. It was bewildering, how different this encounter felt from any other. She was like an alchemist, reducing me down to my purest essence: a softness I had never shown anyone.

5

I cannot say how long we were together before we heard a sound from the next room. The rustle of sheets, a thump, and a clank. Mother, fumbling for the chamber pot. We pulled apart. Blinking, as if we were awakening from a shared dream. The rose aura clung to us, faint but undeniably present. The darkness shivered, as if it were made up of tiny grains of sand, which shifted and played in the wind off some metaphysical sea. I wanted to know what those grains were, what they had to do with the queen of heaven.

Through a crack in the bedcurtains, I could see dim grey light just beginning to glow from the anteroom. I had been so caught up in my desire, I forgot to close the door. After all my vows to be cautious, the only veil between us and the rest of Underhill House all night had been our bedcurtains. Cecely straightened. "We should try to sleep."

I nodded reluctantly. She was right, of course. If Mother saw us up at this hour, she'd be suspicious, and way too much had happened last night for us to risk that. I took a deep breath, straightening my shift.

Cecely had no trouble drifting off. As the bedchamber brightened, the grainy darkness fell away, and my dreamy state of mind went with it. I wanted to turn back time, to slip back into the timeless shivering world we'd created.

Instead, I watched her sleep. Her expression soft, untroubled, her lip colour faded from our kisses. I should've been as tired as she was, but my body was tense, like a lute string whose peg had been wound too tight.

When I went at last to the dining chamber for breakfast, starving, the table was set elaborately. Mary brought out pancakes, cheese, bread, cream, and roasted pears filled with custard. She hurried upstairs to retrieve Richard from his study.

I blinked at the massive spread of food, daunted by the performance this meal would require, suddenly nauseous. I knew my part: the devoted bride-to-be who *hadn't* spent the night enjoying her best friend, but I questioned my ability to perform it. Richard was so sanctimonious. I knew what he would think if he knew what I had done. That I had fallen victim to the overwhelming desire that Eve's sin awakened in all women.

The breakfast table was bright with candles. Dozens of tiny lights, dazzling.

Footsteps on the staircase. Richard appeared in the doorway. When he smiled at me, I felt ill at ease. The last time we took an elaborate meal together, he had announced plans to marry me. Since then, his attitude toward me had become more entitled. But the gap between the woman he thought I was and my true self was widening. I sent up a clumsy prayer to the queen of heaven—whoever she was—that I could stop deceiving him soon.

"Any news from the Master of Revels?" I said, forcing myself to smile back.

He shook his head as he sat across from me and threw his napkin over his shoulder. "You've risen late," he said with a hint of irritation.

I picked up a tartlet, more to busy my hands than from any desire to eat. "I had difficulty sleeping."

"I have good news," he said, raising his eyebrows, biting into a chine of pork. His green eyes met mine. "Would you like to guess what?"

"Forgive me. I'm not in the mood for games."

"Well," he said sullenly. "Perhaps this will cheer you. The parson has agreed to allow us to marry before Lent, after only two cries of the banns."

The tartlet crumbled between my fingers. My smile was so full of artifice, it hurt. *"How lovely."*

Anyone else would've been suspicious of that smile, but Richard Underhill believed me. "He suggested the first of February. We'll have a small ceremony in the great hall. Your family and mine, the servants, my closest friends from church."

I closed my eyes, realising what he was doing. Moving the wedding up so we could marry *before* his trip. I would have to see my aunt before the spell was complete or marry him first.

"Rose?"

I brought my hand to my mouth. "Forgive me. A piece of tartlet is stuck in my throat."

Richard turned to the serving-girl. "More ale—"

"No," I said, pretending to cough. February was less than two weeks away. I needed to stop this. Perhaps I could convince him that the season was ill-boding, that the wedding *shouldn't* take place before he left. "Are you certain about that date? Perhaps we should wait until the sun leaves Aquarius." My voice came out too thin, as if it were about to crack. "Mercury will be with the Water-Bearer then as well. It's too much rebellion."

"But that sounds perfect for us!"

I pressed my eyes shut, baffled that he could think himself rebellious in any way. I felt as if a passage to hell were opening beneath my feet. Perhaps I should embrace it, I thought. I might be happier there. Maybe the devil would let me take Cecely with me.

"How wonderful," I heard myself say.

"I'll see that you have a new dress for the occasion. Humphrie and I must travel to Bohemia the day after the wedding. I want you to come with us. It will be the first of many journeys together as husband and wife. We'll be travelling for two and a half months, until mid-April. We'll stare out at the North Sea, see Bohemia. I shall introduce you to Dee's old scryer, Kelley."

No, I thought. No—

I racked my brain for an excuse. "I get seasick. I would be a hindrance. Your work must come first."

His eyes flashed. "My priorities are not your concern."

I blinked, startled at his sudden anger. I summoned the full force of my charms, pretending to be the timid woman he expected me to be. "I'm sorry, Richard," I said, letting my voice catch with anxiety. "I would love to go with you, but I would be miserable at sea. I've been so ill."

"As my wife," he said through clenched teeth, "shouldn't you go where I go?"

I lowered my eyes, several considerations racing through my mind. My need for Richard to leave. My family's need to stay at Underhill House. I made myself meet his eyes, continuing to emphasize my supposed weakness. "Forgive me, Richard. Please do not take what I am about to say as defiance. It pains me to refuse you, in truth. But I pray you to recall that I have not been well. A journey now would hinder my recovery."

His eyes were troubled. I could see his emotions warring on his face. Pity and chivalry, remorse that he had lost his temper. A sense that a man should be able to take his wife with him wherever he pleased, humiliation that I was standing up to him. He looked so conflicted that I thought one more bit of persuasion might sway him. "Please don't make me go," I whispered. "I beg you. I am not well."

The words seemed to tip the balance toward pity. He drew a deep breath and closed his eyes, his shoulders drooping. He pushed away his plate, wiped his hands on his napkin, and stared for a long moment at the wall before him. Finally, he met my gaze. "If you insist," he said, his voice maddeningly gentle, "I will allow you to stay behind, but it is plain your mind is restless. I suspect you will regret it."

Graves called Cecely away to run errands before I could tell her the bad news. Part of me was grateful. Her parents would send for her soon. She would go to them straightaway if she thought my marriage—and thus her position as a maid—would be permanent.

She was gone all morning. I sat in the library, dejectedly flipping through an illuminated book on mythology, lingering over a miniature depicting Venus naked on a bed of roses. There was so much evidence pointing to the idea that she was the queen of heaven—the ghost roses, the copper scent—but that didn't explain the shadows my mother summoned or the glyphs. If they were even real—

Giving up on the book, I asked Mary to draw me a bath suffused with lavender oil, but even that didn't relax me. I was miserable for the rest of the day. I couldn't sleep. I couldn't eat. I couldn't even play music. I kept thinking about how little time there was left before the wedding. Twelve wretched days. Nowhere near enough time to do everything I needed to do.

Late that afternoon, I gave up trying to do anything but think and went outside to sit in the courtyard with Hughe. A chill crept inside my cloak. I pulled it tight about my shoulders, sitting on the bench in the corner. Hughe dropped a ball at my feet. I threw it for him.

Soon, the square of sky above the courtyard began to fade to a ghoulish pink. I dreaded going to bed and telling Cecely the bad news. A single snowflake fluttered, hurly-burly, to the stones. I watched it, thinking about the choices before me. I saw three: Tell Richard the truth. Marry him, then leave him. Or beg Lisabetta before the spell was complete.

Telling him the truth would be the kindest choice. He obviously disapproved when I told him at my father's funeral that I didn't want to marry, but he had expressed it relatively placidly. Of course, that was before he asked me to marry him. I could already hear my mother scolding me—

Don't be childish.

Cecely's voice—

The world is cruel to women . . .

I knew what my mother would tell me to do. Marrying Richard might be the safest choice, but it was also the cruellest, and it might be dangerous. Richard would be furious if I married and left him, and furious people did unpredictable things. I thought of Uncle Primus, my grandmother, the Coppingers, the way they had taken matters into their own hands to retake what they saw as theirs. Would Richard do something like that?

If I disappeared before he came back, how could he?

I couldn't approach Lisabetta before the spell was complete. If she said no, I would be out of options.

Hughe whimpered. I looked down. He had dropped the ball at my feet again.

Cecely returned from her errands while I was playing with Hughe. She must have seen me through the window. "It's freezing. The sun is setting. Why the devil are you outside?" she asked, sitting beside me.

I took the ball from Hughe's mouth and threw it hard, swallowing the sob that had risen in my throat. Hughe ignored it, pressing his muzzle into my hand and kissing it. I patted him half-heartedly.

"Rose?"

"Richard convinced the parson to move up the wedding."

She blinked at me, startled. "Before we finish the spell?"

I nodded. "Over two weeks before. To the first of February."

She bit her lip.

"I'm tempted to see my aunt first so we could leave before the ceremony, but I'm afraid to risk it."

She searched my face. The moment stretched out. I heard the faint sound of children playing on Bishopsgate Street, carriage wheels. "You're thinking of marrying him."

"The only other option is to tell him the truth."

"That's a terrible idea! You could end up in the almshouse. My cousin in Norwich won't have room for all of us..."

Norwich. I hated the word. Didn't she say she had a girl there once? Was that why she wanted to go? I closed my eyes, willing myself to focus. "It might be cruel to go through with the wedding when I don't plan to stay, but he'll be gone the next day." I didn't want to say what I was thinking. That the marriage might have to last even longer if our spell didn't work. I drew a deep breath.

She met my gaze, her eyes focused, bright, as if she were waiting for me to say more. A snowflake fell from the sky, zigzagging down to the bench between us.

"What?"

"I—" She shook her head, took a deep breath. She rubbed her temples, pressing her lips together tight. She was quiet for so long I wondered if she would ever finish the thought. When she finally opened her eyes, the light that had brightened them the night before was gone. "I can't argue with that. You'd have a permanent place to live if you need one."

I couldn't help but notice she had gone back to saying *you*, not *we*, the way she had started doing the night before. I turned from her, a lump in my throat. We sat there a long time, avoiding one another's gaze.

"Cecely," I said finally in a voice that came out so piteous I cut myself off. I blinked, surprised at my sudden, embarrassing urge to tell her how much she meant to me. She might misunderstand, given what we had done. I steadied my voice. "You don't have to go," I said as casually as if I were talking about a simple trip to the market. "Even if I'm trapped here, you could stay."

Her eyes flashed. "I'm leaving as soon as my parents send for me."

I felt a sudden numbness, a hollow in my heart. A long silence fell over the garden. Cecely excused herself, upset with me for pressing. I threw the ball for Hughe angrily a few more times before I stood to go upstairs.

Underhill House seemed darker than it should have been at sunset. The shadows seemed preternaturally close. I stopped on the first-floor landing, stricken with the sudden sense that they were surrounding me. Deep and dark, caressing me, pulling me down. I thought I smelled roses.

The banister was cold and smooth beneath my palm. I gripped it tight, afraid I would fall, closing my eyes, trying to gather my wits. When I recovered, I looked down and saw veins in my hands. I was wearing a blood red velvet gown and holding a glass of claret. In the distance I heard children playing. *My* children. I felt a doubleness, the sense that I would experience this moment later unless I did something to stop it.

I blinked, recoiling from the image as if it were a goblet of poison. The gown and claret vanished. The house went silent.

That was not my imagination, I thought. It was a warning. Suddenly the walls seemed too close, the square spiral staircase with its carved balustrades and gilded portraits nothing more than a gorgeous cage.

I pressed my eyes shut so tight, bright lights flashed on the backs my eyelids, and I felt the beginnings of a headache. This will not come to pass, I thought. I cannot let it. My heels tapped the steps as I hurried the rest of the way upstairs. After the wedding, I thought, I'll orchestrate our independence. I'll have two months, more than enough time to figure something out. I'll leave Richard a note with some horrifying excuse for leaving. I'll convince everyone at Underhill House that I'm dead—

In the antechamber Cecely stood at the window in her shift, back turned. Coppery hair falling down her back, the pink of her hips just visible through the fabric. Behind her, the setting sun had just disappeared beneath the rooftops. She looked like a woman in a painting.

I couldn't bring myself to tell her what I had seen, the future I was fighting, though it was all I could think of. She was already so discouraged. Instead, I took her hand—a silent apology.

We waited for the other residents of Underhill House to go to sleep before we cast the spell: burning the wolfsbane, ringing the candle with lemon balm. The wicked smoke drifted to the ceiling—releasing my aunt's anger, I hoped. The minty odour of lemon balm and roses enveloped us. Our voices were solemn. Though many would condemn our ritual, it felt sacred to me. Reverent, like prayers whispered in an empty church, or the names of the dead etched on gravestones.

After we cast the spell, we shared memories of our adventures back home. *Remember the time we convinced the Harwood boys to take us to see Queen Elizabeth's Men?* The younger one was hopelessly smitten with you. *Remember the time we walked all the way to Gravesend to buy perry?* It was just as good as we thought it would be. *Remember—*

Although we didn't speak of it, a sadness haunted our words, the knowledge that we only might make a few memories yet. As the night grew late, the sadness overwhelmed the happy memories. When we lay together, Cecely seemed distracted and strange. There was no laughter or teasing. We fumbled in the dark, our desire dampened with anticipation of our parting.

The next morning, Richard sent up a strange bouquet: a red rose surrounded by rue. Love and regret—or disdain, or grace, or vision. Rue was ambiguous. There was a note: *For my bride, whose spirit will ever be intertwined with mine, though our bodies may be parted.* I could not help but think—with a sudden chill—of the hair Mother had twined around the rose.

I made myself thank him at breakfast, wondering—if everything went wrong—how the devil I would resign myself to being his wife. The image of myself on the staircase had been apt. To be Mistress Underhill, I would have to drink *copious* amounts of claret.

After breakfast, I approached my mother in her room to complain about the intensity of his affection. She was sitting in the corner, embroidering an elaborate design onto a sweet bag.

"Richard is maddened by his love for me. Could you do something to lessen his passion?"

"Why in the world would I do that?"

"Out of kindness?"

She snorted. "I already witched him. He seems to have been fonder of you than I knew to begin with, so the spell was potent. He is too enraptured by you now to try to swing him back in the opposite direction. When you send... *intent* into someone's temperament, there must be at least faint sympathy for it, or the spell causes too much conflict. The more unwilling the subject, the higher the risk of madness."

I blinked at her, thinking about how disordered my thoughts had been since we left home. That must be why. There was no receptacle in me to receive a love for Richard.

I cleared my throat, putting on a puzzled face, pretending that I had just thought of the question for the first time. "Whom did the spell you cast on him invoke?"

"The queen of heaven."

She said it naturally, as if the words should have been no revelation, but the sympathy spell had the same invocation, and I couldn't believe the presence it summoned was St. Mary. It was sensual, aphrodisiac. "Not the Virgin?"

"I grew up in a brothel," she said with a condescending laugh. "Don't be naïve."

"Who, then?"

She smirked, setting her embroidery in her lap. "You learn things growing up in a brothel. Rituals to soothe common sources of anguish, powers that are sympathetic to women. There are saints who work in this vein, of course—St. Afra, St. Mary—but there are other powers too. Powers as old as the heavens."

I thought of the glyphs. Perhaps they *were* real. "Like your queen."

Mother nodded. "She was popular with the women in the brothel. She rules over the sensual world—sex, death, dreams. Love spells are most powerful when they invoke her beneath the evening star."

"But she isn't Venus."

"She's no single star. She's the space between them, the stars' influence itself. The mistress of the night. Her presence awakens a person's true nature, their deepest desires. Everyone perceives her differently."

I thought of the ghost roses, the shadows I had seen dancing around my mother, the way the darkness granulated when Cecely and I touched. Maybe that was how I perceived her influence. The idea comforted me, filling me with an eerie sense of connection and belonging. I wanted to know what she was called. "How can you invoke a power without knowing her name?"

"Names are illusory. They change. They separate and confine what always has been and will be."

"But what is she?" Mother's gaze was black, inscrutable as ever. "A goddess? An angel? A daemon? A spirit?"

A smile played at her lips. "If the spells work, does it matter? It's best not to think too deeply about ideas you can hang for."

That night, when I heard the muffled sound of my mother pulling her bedcurtains shut in the next room, I put my hand on Cecely's arm as she helped me undress. "Mother and I talked about the queen of heaven today," I said in a low voice.

She stopped unlacing my bodice. "What did she say?"

"That different people perceive her differently. When we cast the spell, what do you smell? Apart from wolfsbane and lemon balm."

She looked at me quizzically. "Nothing. What do *you* smell?"

"Roses, a faint hint of copper. Why did you say you sensed the queen of heaven?"

"That first night?" When I nodded, she bit her lips, smiling. Her eyes danced. "My body hummed."

I couldn't help but smile back. "Mine did, as well. But I smelled roses when Mother was witching me too. And I heard that bird—"

She went back to unlacing my bodice. "Are you still hearing it?"

"Not since I sabotaged the spell."

Cecely stiffened, pulling harder on my laces than before. "Your mother doesn't *have* to meddle anymore," she said in a brittle voice. "She got what she wanted."

The thought was like a storm cloud descending over the room. By the time she finished unlacing my bodice, there was no light left. We cast the spell, then went to bed without talking further.

The air in our chamber was stifling. I couldn't sleep. My chest was tight. I got up and opened the bedcurtains, then the door to the antechamber and the courtyard window. The January air was freezing, but the air moved and the room brightened a shade. Slightly more tolerable.

I slept little that night, and less the nights that followed. Cecely always fell asleep as soon as we cast the spell, exhausted by whatever work she'd been enlisted to help with. But I wasn't terribly concerned with my fatigue, since it assisted with my charade that I was still not well enough to travel.

The night before the wedding, I couldn't sleep at all. By midnight, my pulse was racing so fast I got out of bed, resigning myself to consciousness. Cecely's shift had slipped down one arm as it often did when she slept, showing her shoulder. The white fabric was so thin I could see the shape of her breast, her pink skin beneath it. The curve of her waist, the swell of her hips. The sight of her conjured up a desire in me so strong, I couldn't bear it.

I watched her sleep, tormented by the idea that the next night

Richard would expect me in his chamber. I had been working out a deception that would hopefully prevent much from happening, but at the very least I would have to look him in the eyes and kiss him. The notion was torture.

I don't know how long I stood there before Cecely stirred, opening her eyes, eyebrows raised with pity. "I can't sleep," I muttered, a twist in my throat.

She sat up, eyes shining. "I'll stay up with you."

I climbed into bed beside her, pulling the bedcurtains shut behind us. I could breathe now, but I would have difficulty speaking from the heart if she could see me. Once darkness surrounded us, perfectly black, I spoke, unable to stop my voice from trembling. "I don't know if I can do this."

"Come," she whispered, pulling my hand.

I moved closer. She kissed my forehead, then ran her hands through my hair in a gesture so maternal, all my defences collapsed. It was as if I were a fortress and someone had thrown down the drawbridge. My shoulders shook, and all the feelings I kept walled up in my breast came running out like prisoners escaping. Her touch was tender. No one had ever touched me like that before. Not even my mother.

I pushed her away, shaking. "Don't."

She dropped her hands. "*Rose*—"

"Enough," I said, swallowing my sobs. My desire was so strong, I thought I might choke on it. "God-a-mercy, I want you."

She made a sound so soft it was barely audible, but I could hear the echo of my longing in it. It was all the permission I needed. I knelt, put my hands on her shoulders, and guided her onto the pillows. Her breath hitched. "Rose," she murmured. "*Rose*—"

I have never felt a desire so unruly, so all-consuming. When I kissed her, I was conscious of nothing but the sounds she made— her gasps, her sighs—the way her body responded to my touch. *Stay with me*, I begged her, the only way I knew how, with my hands, my lips. *Stay with me.*

The morning of the wedding, Cecely's side of the bed was empty, the bedcurtains open. I lay in bed for an hour at least, anxious that my plan wouldn't work. When I finally went downstairs to eat breakfast, Underhill House was bustling with activity, servants hurrying this way and that with candles and flowers and ribbons.

I saw Cecely only once: on the staircase as I made my way back up to my room to dress. She was making her way downstairs with a handful of candlesticks to polish. Her eyes hollow, shadowed with dark circles. Our gazes met, and she looked away with such a pained expression that I felt an unbearable stab of guilt.

She hurried past me—a white bonnet, a flutter of dark linen, the rhythm of footsteps on the stairs behind me—and I mastered myself.

I found Mother in my room in an excellent mood. She flitted about, delighted, chattering incessantly. Mary had laid the gown Richard purchased for me atop the drawing table, and Mother couldn't stop talking about how perfect it was. Its fabric was rich black brocade, embroidered with roses and goldwork. Atop it was a traditional hawthorn crown dotted with blood red berries, symbolizing the sacred love of the marriage union.

It was too much. Staring at it, I was overwhelmed by a desire to escape. I was only vaguely aware of Mary standing beside me, holding out a folded sheet of parchment. "Miss," she said in a soft voice. "He left this."

I blinked, took the note, and broke the wax seal with the Underhill crest. Unfolding it, I found a missive Richard had written in a calligraphic hand. *For my bride*, it began, the letters so carefully formed I thought he expected me to save it as a keepsake. The extreme care he had taken with it infuriated me. I wanted to shred it to pieces.

I scanned the rest of the letter. It continued in the traditional fashion, filled with the sort of sweet nothings lovers recite in plays. The gown was *not half as beautiful and sweet* as I was, a less powerful claim than perhaps he thought. The hawthorn berries were *the colour of the love that pulsed in his heart*, a somewhat tortured metaphor, but the overall effect was unsettling. There was something twisted, too sweet, clinging about his affection. He had signed it: *Richard Underhill, no longer friend, but husband Eternal*, capitalising the word in emphasis.

"Are you ready to dress, miss?"

I nodded, my throat constricting.

Mary helped me into my petticoat and gown, then hurried out of the room to find my mother. Mother spent hours painting my face, assaulting me with a useless barrage of advice that I did not want or need about the night to come. If all went to plan, the wedding night would be cut short before any of it mattered. At the end of it all, she held out her hand.

"Your father's ring. Richard will want you to wear the wedding ring around your *vena amoris*."

I stiffened. "I'll put it on the other side."

"It's a man's ring, Rose. At your wedding?"

I turned to Mary and handed it to her, forcing a smile. "Could you keep this until after the ceremony?"

"Yes, miss. Of course."

Mother glowered.

The ceremony was scheduled for three o'clock. The windows in the statuary and library let in little light; the sky was gloomy with a coming storm. When it was time, Mary lit a candle so we wouldn't trip on the staircase. As we processed downstairs, I fidgeted with my hawthorn crown and skirt. I caught my reflection in the mirror in the anteroom. I looked like a stranger, bodice glittering, eyes black and mournful. My long black hair hung loose beneath the bridal crown.

I wanted to fling it into the fire.

Regina Caeli, I thought wickedly as I entered the hall, curse this union.

The candles flickered as if there had been a sudden gust of wind. Through the windows, a pale grey light hung over the courtyard. Richard stood before them with the parson. Gathered around were Humphrie and the servants. The only guests who weren't currently living at Underhill House were Humphrie and a few guests Richard had invited from church. I thanked the stars for that. The more people who met me as Richard's wife, the harder it would be for me to disappear later.

Cecely was resplendent even in maid's clothes: that black and white linen dress, the white petticoat and bonnet, her golden red hair tumbling out of its sides. Her back was straight, her chin high.

When she saw me, she did not smile.

As I stepped into the room, rain began to slick the windows, slapping the glass hard, as if my presence had summoned the storm. A moment later, lightning split the clouds. Mother startled, and I knew what she was thinking. It was an ill omen. I must confess I was pleased at the thought that the heavens might be on my side. Mary went to stand beside my friend, whispering something in her ear and squeezing her shoulder.

When I arrived at Richard's side, he met my eyes, blinking, as if my beauty awed him. The parson, a tall grey man with a grizzled beard and a grave face, began the ceremony in the same booming voice he used at church. I wondered if some holy instinct had taught him to disapprove of me. Was heresy something a parson could scent out like a hound?

The ceremony was short. Richard spoke his vows solemnly. I lowered my voice as I repeated my lines—that was how I thought of them, *lines*—my throat tight. The marriage rings were engraved with a promise of loyalty and chastity. Conjugii firmi et casti sum pignus amoris.

I wanted to disappear inside myself.

Mother beamed, bopping Edmund at her hip.

I will never forget what happened after the parson announced us man and wife. When we turned to process toward the table for dinner, I saw my friend watching me, black eyes wide. She was struggling to blink back tears.

When she saw me watching, she turned and hurried from the hall. I desperately wanted to go after her, but of course I couldn't.

Her expression haunted me for the rest of the day. I kept seeing her—in my mind's eye, on the backs of my eyelids, reflected on the rain-slicked windows. As the festivities reached their conclusion, my stomach churned.

When Richard offered his arm to lead me upstairs, I wanted to refuse him, though my plan called for me to go with him. Think of Edmund, I told myself. You can play the part of wife for an hour or two.

"Rose?"

I forced a smile, fiddled with my shoe. "Forgive me. My heel."

He smiled indulgently and walked me upstairs to his chambers. Out the window, the sun was setting: a slow-dying blush over the rooftops. Sitting with me on the bench along the opposite wall, he squeezed my hand. "I have waited too long for this day. I cannot believe that after tonight I shall have to wait two months before we are together again."

Something about his tone irked me. Beneath the simple longing, I thought I detected a hint of resentment.

I tried to console myself with the fact that he would soon be waiting forever. I cleared my throat, forcing a smile. "It is unfortunate."

I was failing to project the appropriate demeanour for a bride on her wedding night so utterly that Richard noticed. He searched my face, his eyes clouding with hurt. "You don't sound like you mean it."

I panicked, searching for an excuse for the tangle of bad feelings that I had apparently been unable to hide. It was too early to tell him what I planned to say. "I miss my father," I said as soon as I thought of it, letting a wave of genuine sorrow wash over me. "I wish he could've attended the ceremony."

The hurt faded from his face. "By the Rood, I have never seen grief look so beautiful."

I made myself thank him. For an hour, I sat with him. Play-acting the bride, feigning interest in our conversation. As the sky turned black, Richard took my hand, massaging my fingers. I wanted to pull it away, but my plan depended on him thinking I bore him goodwill, that I loved him.

I have thought about what I did next many times. If I made the right choice, if there was some other path I could've taken. Mind you, I did not enjoy deceiving him. The dependence of women upon men for income turns us all into actors.

Before you judge me, understand, I saw no other choice. I am not the cruel mistress, though I would later be called such. *Stop*, I wanted to say. *I'm going to be ill.* But I doubted a reprise of that performance would be believable, and it would only cause Richard to put off his trip.

I had to let him kiss me.

When he had half undressed me, I stopped him, beginning the speech I had planned. "Richard," I whispered in a heavy voice. "I have something to confess."

He stopped, his green eyes narrowing. "Yes?"

I lowered my eyes. I would have to be careful in how I phrased what I said next. "My betrothal went further than my mother led you to believe. She forbade me to tell you before now. I have not exactly been chaste."

He cleared his throat, taken aback. "I see."

"There's more," I said uneasily. This would be the most delicate part. I hung my head, pretending shame. "My courses have not come since my indiscretion."

His face froze. He blinked several times, straightening in his seat, as shocked as I'd expected. He opened his mouth to speak but no words came out.

"I don't know if I'm with child," I whispered, "but I thought I should tell you. I fear it may be why I've had so much trouble eating, why I've been so ill."

He drew a deep breath, emotions warring on his face. Jealousy, hurt, betrayal, that unnatural anger. But none of it was a match for his inborn sense of propriety. "I cannot—we cannot—"

I pressed my lips together tight, eyes still lowered, doing my best to hide my elation. My falsehood was working just as I had expected. It was eliminating the need for me to lie with him tonight, which would have the added benefit of making it easier for him to annul the marriage when I disappeared. *Tranquilla sum*, I told myself. *Tranquilla ero.*

"When were you last together?"

I was prepared for this question. "Just before Christmas."

He stood, his features subtly contorted, as if he were trying but failing to summon the restraint he had possessed before my mother meddled. He went to the window and stared out, his posture rigid.

In a moment the clock bell tolled. Eight o'clock.

"I must know the truth," he said in a voice so cold, it filled me with alarm. He turned to meet my gaze, his hands clenching into fists, his eyes full of a tortured regret. "I couldn't bear to have the evidence of your indiscretion living in my house. I cannot have a wife who—" His hand went to his throat, his eyes animal and panicked. He coughed, apparently unable to finish the sentence. I couldn't help but wonder if my mother's spell prevented it. It took him a moment to gather his wits. "This is a terrible blow, Rose. I care for you more than you know. Sleep in your old room. I'll send for the physician in the morning."

Fear rushed through me. The physician. Could he tell that I wasn't pregnant—that I had my courses just two weeks ago?

No, I thought, no. As soon as his footsteps receded, I slipped out of his chamber, terrified. I wanted to find Cecely, apologise for what I had put her through, talk to her about what happened.

Our bedchamber was empty, the sheets neatly arranged. Had she gone to stay in the servants' quarters? I crept downstairs with a candlestick into the pantry and buttery, searching for the staircase that led down to the servants' quarters in the cellar.

The stairwell was black, my bare feet cold on its stones. There was no light in the cellar but my candle. I slipped from room to room—heart tripping in my breast, wrapping gown trailing behind me like a ghost—checking the beds. There was the scullery maid, fast asleep in a white cotton shift, the kitchen maid. A single groomsman, snoring loudly. Beyond them, the errand boy was curled around the turnspit dog.

I couldn't find Cecely anywhere.

6

I woke the next morning in my own bed, bleary-eyed, blinking at the pale sun that was shining through a crack in the bedcurtains. I could hear the muffled sound of Richard and Mary talking, too low to make out the words. I had lain awake for most of the night, dreading the physician's visit, waiting for dawn to come so I could ask Graves or Mary where Cecely had gone. I hadn't meant to fall asleep. "Mistress Rose," Mary called through the bedcurtains in such a formal voice I knew Richard was still in the room. "Are you awake?"

I blinked away the light. "What time is it?"

"Eight o'clock," Richard interrupted, his voice tight. "Get out of bed. The physician is here."

I wrapped my sleeping gown tight and sat up, preparing myself for the examination, cursing the particular untruth I'd chosen to tell. If the physician confirmed that I *wasn't* pregnant, Richard might expect me to lie with him before he left. If he thought I *was* pregnant, he might put us out on the street. I hadn't thought through my deception fully.

When Mary drew the curtain, Richard towered over the bed, his eyes full of a tightly controlled fury. He looked as if he hadn't slept. There were dark circles beneath his eyes.

He let the physician inside and excused himself. The old man eyed me, squinting in what I thought was judgement. I felt a surge of defiance that I had to work very hard to suppress. "Remove your wrapping gown," he said. "I need to examine your breasts and stomach."

I untied the gown, wondering what Richard had told him, my heart pounding. The old man examined my breasts. His hands were freezing cold. When his fingers pressed my groin, I flinched, praying desperately to whatever god was listening that he couldn't tell there was nothing inside it. He inspected the area methodically, his fingers moving from hip to hip. Finally, he met my eyes. "How long has it been since you . . . ?"

"Christmas."

"Mmm." His rheumy blue eyes clouded. Then he nodded. "Cover yourself."

Gladly, I thought, wrapping my gown tight.

"Master Underhill?"

Richard opened the door immediately. "Well?"

The physician left my bedside to speak with him privately. Their voices were too low for me to hear, but Richard looked as if the old man had struck him. My throat constricted. There was no reason for Richard to look so mad, unless the physician had told him I was pregnant. I could feel a sob rising in my throat. My whole plan depended upon my condition being ambiguous. Where would we go if Richard put us out? The spell wasn't complete. I had no income. I hadn't even talked to Mother—

"Are you *certain*?" Richard snapped, his voice rising loud enough for me to hear. He looked simultaneously furious and crestfallen.

The physician bowed, his expression apologetic. His lips moved, his voice too low to hear.

Richard glared at him. "Come back in a month."

The physician nodded.

Relief poured through me. I closed my eyes, allowing myself to express every bit of it. It would make sense for me to be glad my pregnancy wasn't confirmed. In fact—I crossed myself, closed my eyes, and pretended to say a prayer of gratitude. Whatever happened, it would be wise for me to make Richard think I wanted to remain his wife.

By the time I opened my eyes, the physician was gone. Only Richard remained in the room.

He stood at the window, staring out. His posture straight, the muscles at the back of his neck tense. After a moment, he turned, searching my eyes. I tried to look repentant. "Our coach is outside," he said finally. "Kelley is at Emperor Rudolf's court in Prague. Humphrie and I will return in mid-April. In the meantime, you must pray on what you've done, try to purify yourself, expel the sins from your body. Attend church as often as possible. I've instructed the doctor to return in one month. He should be able to ascertain your condition then. Graves will keep me abreast of the results."

I blinked at him, puzzled by how soon the physician would return. What evidence could he find when I wasn't even three months along? I made myself nod.

"If you aren't with child, perhaps this marriage can be salvaged. But if you are, Rose, I cannot—I will not—I—" His hand went to his throat again, and he coughed with the same unnatural panic as before twisting his features. He pressed his lips tight, struggling to make sense of it, though I suspected I knew exactly what was happening. "Your indiscretion complicates things."

I closed my eyes, irritated by his moral conflict. His expectations of me were directly at odds with my mother's spell, it seemed. The fact that he supposedly was fond of me *before* Mother meddled made little sense. We were a complete mismatch.

Richard stood to go, his velvet breeches making a swishing sound. Knowing it would behoove me to seem dutiful, I followed him downstairs, wrapping my nightgown around me, meeting Mary's eyes wearily on the way out. The maidservant nodded, sympathetic.

Downstairs, it was cold. Last night's fire had turned to ash. Through a parlour window, I watched Graves carry the last of Richard's things to the coach. Humphrie was already inside, looking out the window, his expression dark, full of self-loathing.

As soon as the coach pulled away, the steward came inside. I stopped him. "Graves—"

"Yes, miss."

"I must speak with my maid. Do you know where she is?"

He sniffed, reaching for his handkerchief. "I thought she was with you upstairs."

"Not Mary. I mean Cecely."

"Oh," he said, his owlish eyes irritated. "Something happened. I forget what. A death in the family, perhaps? She asked for a leave of absence yesterday."

The look I had seen on her face at the wedding. No one had actually died, had they?

I hurried upstairs. I found Mary packing up my room, preparing to move my things to my new chamber. I paused at the door, puzzled that Richard still wanted me to move into the chamber beside his upstairs. I wondered if he simply forgot to change his instructions before he left. When she saw me, Mary straightened her bonnet and pulled her sleeves down over her brown skin. "Miss," she said in greeting, with a nod.

"Mary." I nodded back. "Did Cecely tell you where she went?"

"Gravesend, miss."

"Why?"

She hesitated, long enough that I knew the death was a lie.

"Come now. Let there be no secrets between us."

She averted her gaze. "Her parents sent for her over a week ago."

I blinked at her, struggling to believe what she was saying. If that was true, then why would Cecely wait until yesterday to leave? I remembered her face during the ceremony, her black eyes shining with tears. A thought—uncertain, hesitant—struggled to emerge from deep inside me like the memory of a dream. My breath caught. "Does she plan to return?"

"She took all her things."

"Call me a carriage."

Mary bit her lip. The moment stretched out. She bowed her head, her voice soft and apologetic. "I think you should know. Richard asked me to tell Graves if you leave Underhill House except to go to church. I'm supposed to go with you and report back."

I closed my eyes, pressing my lips together so tight, it hurt. Of course Richard would have his staff spy on me.

"Where do you want me to tell him we're going?"

I met Mary's gaze. Her dark eyes were wide, sympathetic. She was willing to lie for me. A rush of gratitude poured through me as I searched for a deception that wouldn't arouse suspicion. I settled on something close to the truth. "To see an old friend. Tell him I need comforting."

It took half an hour for the carriage to pull up outside. The day was ridiculously cold, but Bishopsgate Street was bustling. There were men departing coaching inns, laughing and talking. Determined-looking women carrying baskets full of milk and bread and cheese, red-faced children scurrying around them, clutching at their skirts. I nearly slipped on the icy street in my hurry to step aside.

The driver helped us inside the carriage. Settling in, I pulled my cape tight about me. As the carriage rocked into motion, I thought about how strange it was that Cecely had ignored her parents' summons until the day before Richard went abroad. Had she delayed her departure so she could spend more time with me? Why hadn't she told me?

The wind whipped my cape as we boarded the wherry, a small boat with a single oarsman and only six seats. On the river, the cold wind burned my cheeks. White clouds chuffed through a grey sky overhead. The grass on the banks was withered and white with frost.

Watching the rapids, I agonized over everything that had happened, wishing that I had asked my father about an audition earlier, warned Cecely about the Coppingers before they set fire to her house. If only, I thought. If only, if only—

The fear that Cecely would already be gone or might refuse to come back with me plagued me. As the wherry rocked, I tried to think further about what I would tell her, becoming sick with doubt and self-hatred.

When we docked at Gravesend, we hurried to Cecely's aunt's house, a simple cottage with a pitched roof near the docks. "There's no reason to be anxious, miss," Mary said. "Cecely has a great affection for you."

I nodded, my chest tightening. I could hear my heart beating in my ears as I knocked on the door. My hand trembled.

Still, when Cecely's aunt answered the door, my throat went tight. "Is Cecely here?"

Goody Weaver stared at me, vague recognition spreading over her face. We had met only once, the day Cecely and I walked to Gravesend to buy perry. She looked like she hadn't slept in a month. But of course she wouldn't have, I realised, feeling terrible that I hadn't thought of this before. That was about how long it would've been since she received Cecely's message that her mother had died.

"God rest your mother's soul."

"You're Rose," she said suddenly. "The girl that Cecely was staying with in London."

"Yes."

She narrowed her eyes. "Cecely isn't seein' visitors."

"I've come all this way."

Goody Weaver frowned. I couldn't tell if she was ill-disposed toward me because she knew I'd upset Cecely, or because she knew my friend's proclivities and disapproved of women visitors in general.

"I bring a message from London. From a gentleman," I added hastily.

Goody Weaver raised her eyebrows. *"Cecely!"*

As we waited, my thoughts scattered like frightened mice. The door opened and my friend peered out. Her face was red, and she looked uncharacteristically frazzled, her coppery hair coming loose from her braid. When she saw me, she panicked. "Come inside. The Coppingers will see you!"

I hurried into the tiny kitchen. Cecely's aunt glared at me and left the room. I took a deep breath, my heart pounding. Finally, I lowered my voice. "You left without saying goodbye."

She rolled her eyes. "You were otherwise occupied."

"I saw you crying."

She met my gaze, searching my eyes for so long, it felt awkward. "The wedding was difficult to watch."

"Mary said your parents sent for you over a week ago. Why didn't you tell me?"

She glared at me, obviously frustrated. "I want what you want," she whispered. "An income, a home. If I go to Norwich, I'll have none of that. I'll only be biding time, unless—" She paused, her voice bitter, apparently hesitant to finish the thought aloud, though we both knew what she meant: unless she married. "I thought with Richard gone, I might be able to bear Underhill House for a time and help you find income, so we could move elsewhere—" She met my eyes, her voice breaking. "But I don't think I can."

"You won't have to pose as a servant for long. Richard is gone. The spell will be complete on the sixteenth."

She drew a deep breath, meeting my gaze, her eyes glittering and hard. I knew that expression. I had perturbed her somehow. She stared at me so long, I felt exposed. I was the one who looked away.

"Rose," she said firmly. I had to force myself to look at her. Her eyes were narrowed, her gaze penetrating. "I can't nurse this hope any longer. I'm going to Norwich. Whatever we were doing, it's over."

Whatever we were doing. Her words summoned a sharp ache in my rib cage. My whole body clenched—my heart, my fists. It hurt that she was rejecting me, insinuating that my plan would fail. I met her eyes, swallowing the fury that was rising in my throat. "Whatever we were doing?" My voice trembled.

She glared at me, smiling tightly. "I'm sorry. Does that phrasing offend you? Is there something else you'd prefer me to call it, *Mistress Underhill?*"

"Don't call me that."

"At Underhill House, I would need to call you that every second of every day. They were moving your things *upstairs*. Richard asked the servants to spy on you, so Graves can keep him apprised of what is happening. Mary probably had to report this trip to Graves before you left."

"She already told me. She's loyal."

Cecely rolled her eyes. "One loyal servant in thirty. Impressive."

I could feel a sob rising in my throat. I hadn't considered how difficult I had made things for us. It occurred to me that perhaps I should've said nothing and lain with Richard, no matter how sick it would have made me, how cruel it would've been to him. This deception had caused too much trouble.

I drew a deep breath, meeting her eyes. "I—" I bit my lip, searching again for the right words to express how much our friendship meant without making her think I wanted too much—a delicate balance. "I don't know if I can do this without you," I said finally.

She watched me, her expression turning sad, almost expectant, her eyes full of a sudden tenderness. "Do what?"

"Everything we planned. Set myself up. Get an audition."

She pressed her lips together tight, her eyes clouding with hurt. When she spoke, her voice was brittle. "So you just need me there to support you."

"Cecely, that's not what I meant."

"It's what you said." Her eyes flashed. "I am my own person," she said, her voice rising. "I want my own house, my own life. I've deluded myself long enough. You want the world to be something it isn't."

Deluded. The word echoed in my ears. My voice pitched higher, louder than I had meant for it to. "The world is what we make it."

"What arrogance, to think you can remake the world. Even the queen must entertain marriage proposals."

Her words hurt, not least because I feared she was right. I tried to master myself, but I was too bitter. "I hope you have a *marvellous* time in Norwich, brewing beer, birthing children," I said in a tight voice. "I am sure you'll be *even more happy* than you would have been with Geoffraie."

She stared at me for a long moment before she said in a very quiet voice, "Go your ways. You are as cruel as your mother."

A righteous anger poured through me as I hurried out of the cottage. By the time my wherry departed Gravesend, a song was thrumming in my head, as wild as the whipping wind that burned my cheeks, the most vicious melody I had ever heard. I stared at the Thames, wallowing in the violence of its torrents.

The ride was long, and my heart pounded in my chest. I couldn't believe that Cecely had well and truly abandoned our dream, leaving me to pursue it alone.

The stars rippled in the black water, fractured and indecipherable. I remembered my vision of myself, drowning my sorrows in claret, the square spiral staircase surrounding me like a cage. I couldn't accept it. I wouldn't.

The refusal braced me, awakening a furious resolve. It started small, then built, coursing through me like molten iron. I could not let that be my life. I would convince my aunt to let us live with them, perform, start a business. Whatever it took to fill my purse with enough coins to buy our freedom.

I would prove Cecely wrong.

When we got home, I cast the spell alone. Too tired and upset,

I assumed, to feel it working. I was anxious, in need of sleep. The shadows were still, the scent of roses conspicuously absent.

As I made my way upstairs to my new chamber, I felt the hairs on the back of my neck rise, the way they do when you can tell someone is watching you. Turning, I thought I saw a shadowy figure in the doorway behind me—Graves, I thought—but as I drew closer, he disappeared, so quiet I wondered if I'd imagined him.

The servants had moved my things into the chamber opposite Richard's. It had a fireplace, a bathtub all its own, and an ornately carved bed with black bedcurtains embroidered with an irritating rose-themed pattern.

I slept for a day, not getting out of bed except to cast the spell. I didn't feel it working that second night either. I thought Cecely's absence must be making it weaker. When I finally woke the next day, I lay in bed for a long time, worried it wouldn't work, strategizing about what to tell Luce and Lisabetta.

The days crept by. I went to church as Richard had instructed, reluctant to violate the rules of Underhill House until I had somewhere else to go. The sunny, cold weather irritated me. It was as if the heavens were mocking me, making the city shine. Icy puddles cracked beneath my boots. Hughe kept stopping to chew on shards, which sparkled like instruments of torture.

Late one night, I remembered my father's ring. I had never asked Mary for it back. I jumped out of bed, lit a candle, and ransacked both my old room and my new, but I couldn't find it. I assumed Mary would know where it was, but she was already asleep in the truckle bed.

The next day, I asked her about it, and she looked sheepish. "I knew you didn't want your mother to find it. I hid it at the bottom of your trunk, but—" She bowed her head, that rebellious coil of black hair slipping out from her bonnet again. "It seems to have been misplaced during the move."

"*Misplaced.* I doubt that very seriously."

Mary's mouth fell open, and she looked like she was going to cry. "I would never, madam, I swear—"

It took me a moment to realise what she thought I meant. "No, no, no. I know you wouldn't. My mother wanted it badly."

Of course, when I confronted Mother, she denied it. She admitted she *wanted* the ring, that she *would've* taken it if she could've, but she claimed she hadn't been able to find where Mary hid it.

"Don't play innocent!" I snapped.

"Perhaps it was a servant. Have you spoken to your girl? Upon my oath, I didn't take it."

"She would never. I can't believe you've taken the only thing Father left me. He warned me you would try to do this."

I said it to hurt her, and it worked. She glared at me, for once speechless. We didn't speak for days after that. I searched her room several times, but I couldn't find the ring anywhere. Every time I saw her—at dinner, on the way to my room—I cursed her, certain she had sold it like Father implied that she would.

All the anxiety, the ire, made my mind restless. By the time the spell was complete in mid-February, I had turned the song I had written on the way home from Gravesend into a symphony.

With Mary's help, I concocted a plan to slip down the staircase the servants used that night without being seen. All I had to do was get outside. Graves had too much of a sense of propriety to come looking for me in my rooms.

The hours passed slowly. That afternoon, a thunderstorm settled over the city, and my irritability worsened. Hughe, picking up on my choleric mood, started digging in the corner of my new room—a bad habit he'd acquired after Cecely left.

I asked Mary to bring up my supper, too frantic to see my mother or Edmund. By then, it was almost sunset and my body was as tightly coiled as a spring. I was able to tolerate only a few bites. Mary kept asking me if I wanted her to bring me some ginger biscuits; I kept having to tell her no.

After I washed up, I asked her if she would help me dress. She raised her eyebrows but nodded dutifully. I had chosen a black bodice sewn with gaudy glass beads, square-necked, off the shoulder, with matching sleeves and skirt; at my breast, a pendant with glittering black jewels.

Once I was dressed, she offered to paint my face, saying she was good at it; Mistress Underhill had taught her the art. I agreed, asking her to paint my face even brighter than one might for a court revel.

While she worked, I thought on what I was about to do. It bothered me more than I wanted to admit that I was going back to the brothel without Cecely. When Mary brought the mirror for me to survey her handiwork, I shook my head, more irritated than I should've been. Mistress Underhill had taught her well. Anyone else would've thought she had done an excellent job. "It's too subtle," I said in a tight voice. "It needs to be brighter."

Mary raised her eyebrows again, too polite to argue, but obviously disagreeing with my judgement. I instructed her to add more colour, but she added only a touch.

"Give it here," I said, reaching for the cerise. "I'll do it myself." A moment later, I inspected my face in the mirror, then set the face paints down. "*There.* How do I look?"

"Beautiful, madam," she said, but her voice wavered.

I could tell she thought I had put on too much, that she was worried about what people would think. Her disapproval, the disapproval of what seemed like everyone in England, rankled me. A flush of heat warmed my face and neck. So many terrible things had happened in the last weeks. Some dark impulse in me wanted to set the whole world on fire. "I still think I look too plain," I said through gritted teeth, baiting her. I thought no such thing.

Her eyes widened. "No, madam. You already look as if—" She stopped herself. "As if—"

"What?"

She bit her lip, obviously struggling to find a polite answer. "As if you've put on too much."

My temper flared. "I'm going to a brothel."

She froze, mouthing the word. *A brothel?*

I sighed, already regretting my impetuousness. Now I would have to worry about whether she would tell anyone. "My aunt lives there. She and another woman own the place," I explained, searching for a way to ensure that she kept my secret. "Come with me."

Mary pressed her lips together tight, unable to disguise her horror.

"I shouldn't have to go alone," I snapped, feeling affronted.

A long moment passed in which she said nothing. She closed her eyes, then met my gaze, her expression resolute. "Forgive me for speaking plainly, miss. I have been in England only ten years, working toward being christened for five. I am not sure you understand how tenuous my position is. I am an obvious stranger to this country due to the colour of my skin. I cannot go to the market without being stared at with mistrust or fascination." She met my gaze, drawing a deep breath. Her eyes gleamed with frustration. "If it became known that I went to a brothel, Graves would dismiss me. The pastor at St. Helen's would deny my request to be christened."

I thought about what she was saying, embarrassed at my outburst. I had been so absorbed by my own troubles that I hadn't given thought to how unreasonable my request was. I should've known. I was well aware of the antipathy Englishmen held for strangers. Mother's Italian ancestry had drawn suspicion. Mary would suffer far worse. As an English noblewoman, no matter how minor, I had freedoms that she didn't.

"Forgive me," I said. "I had no idea. There is no need for you to take such a risk."

She closed her eyes, biting her lip. The moment stretched out. It occurred to me that I knew almost nothing about her.

"Where were you before England, Mary?"

"Spain, miss."

That explained her rolling accent. "And before that?"

"You would call it Barbary."

"Do you have any family in London?"

"Only my younger brother, but he's bound to a judge at the Old Bailey, so I don't see him often."

I closed my eyes, deeply embarrassed at my inconsideration, a swarm of remorse buzzing in my chest. I should never have asked her to do something that would be so dangerous for her. This must be one of the reasons she had been so kind to us. She needed our protection. I cleared my throat, wishing I had never asked. "Never mind. I'll take Hughe. Dressed like this, no one will question my travelling alone."

———

No one saw me leaving—at least not that I knew. The servants' staircase was black at that hour, and I didn't want to light a candle. I gripped the rail, carefully making my way down the steps in my stockinged feet, thankful that Hughe was on his best behaviour. I put on my heels and rain cape in the kitchen, then slipped out the servants' entrance.

It was strange to leave Underhill House with only Hughe by my side and none of the pleasure I had previously felt at leaving. I should've been excited. The spell was finally complete. The time for action had come. But as I slipped out into the dark, wet street, the only emotion I felt was a dull resentment. That Cecely had rejected me, that I'd been forced to marry, that Richard had instructed his staff to watch over me as if I were a child.

The cold wind whipped my cape, but I pulled it tight around my face, trying to protect Mary's handiwork from the intermittent gusts of rain. Above, clouds obscured the stars, making the

night heavy and black, oppressive. I wondered about the power
that ruled over the heavens behind them, which somehow summoned both desire and a sacrosanct horror.

I had felt neither since Cecely left.

I scanned the street for a carriage. The only lights were occasional flashes of firelight in windows. Hughe scanned the street
too, mirroring me, his expression wary.

At the sound of carriage wheels ahead, I called out. My heels
clicked on the cobblestones. I was right. The driver didn't bat an
eye at a woman dressed like me and her dog travelling at night. I
watched the city go by listlessly. Aldersgate was dark apart from a
few lanterns.

Getting out at the brothel, I reached for the sachet of lemon balm
I had secreted in my pocket. "*Regina Caeli*," I whispered, "bless this
errand." Only then did I take a deep breath and go inside.

The brothel was emptier than it had been last time, shadowy. A
scattering of men and women in the corners. Candles flickering on
empty tables. Luce stood behind the counter alone. When she saw
me, she looked around surreptitiously—for Lisabetta, I supposed—
but my aunt was nowhere to be seen. I cracked my knuckles, determined to make this exchange go the way I needed it to.

"Mistress Rose," she said in a low voice. "You've returned.
Would you like a drink?"

"Mead, if you have it."

As Luce poured me a cup, Hughe trotted up behind me. "Do
you mind if he comes inside?" I asked.

"He's not the first dog in this establishment," she said with a
humorous lift of her brow. "And he's better behaved than most."

I laughed, lowering my voice. "I would speak to my aunt again,
if she'll see me."

She handed me a cup of mead. "You weren't able to avoid the
wedding, I take it?"

"I was not, but I don't plan to act the wife if I can help it."

"I have a husband myself. I haven't seen him in years, but the appearance of marriage can be helpful in legal matters." Luce nodded to her right. "Here she comes—"

Out of the corner of my eye, I saw my aunt approaching, a mess of curly black hair, a wide skirt. I took a deep breath, steeling myself. I finished the rest of my mead and handed the empty cup to Luce. She lowered her voice. "Betta is upset about something your mother did years ago. You'll have more luck if you don't mention her at all. She'll never permit you all to stay with us."

My chest tightened. What little determination I had faltered. It would take much longer to earn enough money to afford to rent lodging from a stranger.

Lisabetta's mouth was drawn into a scowl so tight, her cheeks must've hurt. My heart sank. In that moment I feared the spell had accomplished nothing. "What are you doing here?"

"Good Lisabetta," I said in an obsequious voice that I realised suddenly I'd learned from my mother. "I apologise for bothering you, but I have nowhere else to turn. I was unable to avoid my wedding, but my husband has gone overseas. I'm looking for a way to support my family so we can leave his household."

A fleeting expression of sympathy crossed her face, but her impassive expression returned quickly. "I want nothing to do with Katarina. That has not altered. Nor will it ever."

Luce put her hand on Lisabetta's shoulder. My aunt relaxed slightly under Luce's touch. There was something intimate about the gesture, something familiar. Six months ago, I would've dismissed it. Now I wondered if they were lovers. Did the brothel give them that freedom?

I shook the thoughts from my head. "I understand how difficult my mother can be. I'm not asking to stay here."

Lisabetta stopped, her brow furrowed. "What *do* you want?"

I turned to Luce. "You used to dance for the queen. Do you know the Master of Revels? Could you set up an audition for me?"

Luce looked at my aunt, her expression hesitant. "Betta."

My aunt met her eyes, her expression tight.

"It's a small thing. She cannot help what Katarina did before she was born."

My aunt shook her head, her eyes resigned. "Go ahead."

Relief rushed through me. I let out a deep sigh, sending up a quick prayer of gratitude.

Luce smiled at me. "What do you play?"

"Virginal, psaltery, viol, lute. I sing." I met their eyes, a cautious hope swelling in my heart. "I'm good."

Luce smiled. "Let's see what you can do."

"Now?"

She nodded at the dais where I had seen the women playing before. A lantern burned on the table beside the virginal, casting a fickle web of shadow. Tears welled in my eyes, surprising me, reminding me how badly I wanted this. I swallowed my feelings—an old habit—then realised that was probably counterproductive.

I sought out my aunt's eyes. "Thank you," I said in a trembling voice, every bit of my gratitude genuine.

The virginal was of fine quality, more so than I would've expected in a brothel. Its legs were intricately carved, its poplar case royal red, overlaid with golden filigree. The inside case was painted with a mural, but the lanternlight was too flickering to see what it depicted. As I tried to think of the right song to play for this occasion, Hughe settled at my feet. Luce brought two candles, setting their holders near the instrument to light the keys. The light revealed the subject of the mural: a nude woman, golden-haired, walking out of the sea. Venus.

It was too perfect to be a coincidence.

I closed my eyes, fingering the lemon balm in my pocket. *Regina Caeli*, I thought desperately, inspire me. When I opened my eyes, I thought I saw the shadows in the corner of the room moving, but it was only the shadows of customers glancing up from their tables.

I made myself smile at them. Then I heard it, a melody I had never heard before surfacing from deep within me. Dark and seductive, teasing, coquettish. The tune echoed between my ears, leaping and springing with a seductive power. Whether it was my own inspiration or the queen of heaven's influence, I revelled in it.

I began to play the virginal with my right hand, fingers tickling the keys, improvising a bold harmony with my left. The tune caught my imagination, making me forget everything but the notes and the soft shadows of men's faces as they watched. Remembering the lyrics I had written for the ill-fated feast, I altered the words to suit this metre:

> *No cupid, Adonis, no lad nor lady,*
> *Infects my spirit as melody;*

> *This poplar with her saucy jacks*
> *Kisses the Venus inside me—*

A series of gasps whispered through the hall. I smiled, proud of myself for scandalizing the audience at a brothel.

When I finished, the room was silent. Both men and courtesans stared. Luce blinked repeatedly, as if she were trying to rouse herself from a stupor. "Who *is* she?" a man at a front table breathed. "Does she work upstairs too?"

I laughed inwardly, feeling powerful, defiant. My performances had always impressed but never this much. I knew I had performed well enough to convince Luce to arrange an audition for me, and I was certain that if she succeeded, the Master of Revels would hire me.

Applause as I left the dais. I approached Luce and Lisabetta to make the arrangements for my audition. "Was that sufficient?"

Luce filled my goblet. "You know it was."

"I can play court music too, but I didn't want to bore your customers."

"I can see your training, sweet. My grandmother came to England with Catherine of Aragon. As a child, I danced at the court of Henry VIII."

"You are nothing like your mother," Lisabetta said.

"Thank you," I said, and meant it. "When do you think you will have the opportunity to see the Master of Revels?"

"It's not him I'll see, but a friend of mine who is still in his favour. I'll go tomorrow."

"So soon?"

She smiled. We were discussing the details—the days of the week, the name I would use onstage, Ravenna Notte, I decided, a defiant reference to the nightbird—when I heard a man's voice behind me.

"Mistress Rushe."

Luce shook her head. "An admirer already."

I turned, saw the catlike eyes. The shoulder-length brown hair, the black velvet doublet and white lace collar, the golden flash of earring.

Will Shakespeare.

———

"That was marvellous," he said in an awed tone as Luce turned to go. His voice was more melodic than I remembered, a honeyed tenor. The way he was looking at me made me feel beautiful, powerful, like the baroness, the *contessa* he saw in me before. His expression was liquid, determined, full of desire, but I could also detect something else in the slight pout of his lips, the lines pulling at the edges of his eyes. A darkness, a barely perceptible hurt, which betrayed how vexed he was that I had failed to meet him when I was supposed to.

After my argument with Cecely, it felt good that I mattered to someone. Not to mention the fact that he seemed taken with my performance. He was an actor who worked with London musicians, a professional. His approval meant something. *See?* I wanted to tell Cecely. *I am good enough.*

"Thank you," I said with more feeling than I meant to show.

"Sit with me," he said with an expansive smile, nodding at a corner table where a candle was melting into a pool of wax.

When I nodded, he took my hand. The nearest man narrowed his eyes at us as Will led me toward the table, obviously jealous.

Hughe trotted after us, his eyes watchful.

Walking beside Will, I noticed the cut of his doublet, the material from which his netherstocks were made. Silk. His ensemble fit so well, emphasizing the taper of his waist. It was so much finer than what he was wearing when I first met him, I wondered if he had received some sort of inheritance.

When we reached the table, he turned a chair around, then sat in it backward, turning his attention to my face. He studied me without blinking—his golden eyes curious, cold—with an intensity that would make most women uncomfortable. Between us, the candle flickered madly.

I met his gaze, curious about what he would say. My mother had taught me that people reveal themselves when they speak to fill a silence.

"You are a contradiction," he said at last. The country accent I'd noticed last time we met was gone. Later I would discover he masked it. It only came out when he was in his cups.

"I could say the same of you."

He smirked. "From what power do you draw your musical talent? I fear you've bewitched me."

"The devil," I said brightly. "Hughe here is my familiar."

He glanced at the dog. Hughe was still on alert. "Egregious. What sort of commands does he give you?"

I grinned. His awe had so completely vanished that I wondered if I'd imagined it. "To sing you all to ruin."

"A siren *and* a witch." He laughed. "What does that make me?"

"The sailor, tied to the mast."

He moved the candle aside, then studied me, his eyes glowing. "You are far too talented to play in a brothel. It's a surprise to see you here tonight." He arched an eyebrow, his meaning clear: *And not the night I was supposed to escort you.* He touched my hand. I shivered, a thrill travelling up my arm as he interlaced our fingers. With a sudden flip of the wrist, he trapped my hand beneath his, pressing it to the table. "I waited hours for you at Aldersgate. Why didn't you come?"

"My friend didn't like you. But she's not here now."

He blinked, startled by my bluntness, then smiled. "Why have you come here tonight?"

"Why have *you*?"

"I'm looking for a friend of my own."

"Really. Does 'your friend' come here often?"

He held up his hands. "I speak truth. My cousin George is in love with a woman who works here, whom he met at a performance of our play."

His expression was so exasperated that I believed him. Now I wonder if he was telling the truth. He was an actor, after all, a writer of many parts. Later, folks would say he became so consumed by the roles he invented that he inhabited them for weeks at a time. Petruchio, though that was not much of a stretch. Richard III. *Husband.* It was what made him such a good dramatist.

"It was produced already?"

"To a small house. At Grey's."

"How did it go?"

"Very well. There are some changes I want to make to the script before we perform it again, but the Earl of Southampton liked it so much, his mother commissioned me to write a series of sonnets convincing him to marry."

There it is, I thought. The money he came into.

"Your turn. Why are you here?"

I cleared my throat. "Luce has promised to help me get a position as a musician. She knows someone in the queen's court. My performance just now was an audition."

"Does the master of your house know you're here?"

"He's abroad."

He pressed my hand again, his brown eyes flickering with amusement. "If I didn't know better, I would say you seem pleased to be rid of him."

"I married unwilling."

"A forgivable offence."

Our eyes met. Neither of us looked away. His were full of the teasing defiance I'd seen in him before. The threat of misrule.

I felt a familiar desire to push back, to rule him. He would be a challenge.

"Marry, Rose," he said in a gruff voice, squeezing my hand. "Are you finished here?"

I nodded. I still hadn't looked away.

"I have a room just north of Shoreditch. Come home with me."

My breath caught. I searched my heart and found only desire, the mercenary sense that I deserved a distraction.

He was watching me with a sly expression, waiting to see what I would say. I finished my mead, teetering on the edge of agreement. Cecely's opinion of Will no longer mattered. No man had ever undone me. I would like to see him try.

Reckless, the nightbird had called me, *ruinous*, and here I was, ready to throw caution to the wind again. Adultery was a serious offence for women. If Richard found out before I managed to leave him, he would be within his rights to beat me. But he didn't have to know.

I met Will's eyes and nodded. To hell with being coy.

A slow smile spread across his face: solemn, intense, sly. He rose and reached out to help me from my chair. "Mistress," he said with a faint lift of his eyebrows.

I raised my goblet to my lips and finished my mead, then let him pull me out of the brothel. Too caught up to concern myself with how tightly he gripped my hand, his smug smile as he led me out.

Outside, a thousand stars pricked the sky, a chaos of impulses. This night is mine, I thought, mine alone. The street echoed with the sounds of carousing: a song here, a shout there.

Will pulled me toward a carriage, negotiating with the driver. Then he bowed and helped me inside. Hughe clambered in after us, letting out a small whimper as he settled at my feet, his large brown eyes focused on Will. He doesn't trust him, I thought, and a small voice inside me said I probably shouldn't either.

As the carriage rocked into motion, Will put his hand on my knee, gripping it tight, but I brushed it away, teasing him. I smiled at him prettily, running a finger in a slow figure eight over the back of his right hand.

He watched what I was doing for a long moment, then caught my hand in his. He held it tight. "*Rose*. Stop that and kiss me."

I did, forgetting everything but him for the rest of the ride. When the carriage finally stopped, it was beside a boardinghouse. A straightforward place, not exactly common, but not exactly respectable either. As we approached the door, I startled at the sight of a drunk man sleeping in the alley. Hughe growled, hackles rising on his back. The man woke and started mumbling about St. Jeronimy, shouting at us for disturbing his dream.

"That's just Christopher," Will groaned, hurrying to let us inside. "Ignore him. He keeps getting kicked out of the tavern across the street."

Inside, the stairs creaked as Will led us upstairs. He closed the outer door of his rooms, and I settled Hughe in a corner. The dog obeyed reluctantly. When I patted his back, his hackles were still raised.

On the other side of the room, Will lit a candle, which cast a pale circle of light over a desk scattered with books and papers.

The rest of his bedchamber was bare, a ragged place. Four walls, a bed, no window. The sort of place a man would write and dream and little else. In the gloom of the candle's penumbra, he watched me silently, his gaze penetrating. I returned it, heart fluttering, delighted at how intense this encounter was becoming.

He pulled me close and kissed me. He began to unlace my bodice—rather expertly, I noticed. The observation brought a shiver of anticipation. I understood that I was being reckless, reacting to my many recent disappointments, but I didn't care. Soon my bodice had come away in his hands. I swivelled back to face him, holding it to my breast.

"Sit," he said, nodding at the bed.

The candle flickered. The bed was forgiving beneath my thighs, soft. Despite the lack of luxury elsewhere in the room, he slept on a featherbed soft enough for a duke.

He knelt in front of me, removing my left heel, sliding his palm up the back of my leg, his hand lingering at the garter that fastened my stocking to my thigh. As he unhooked it, I gasped involuntarily, a soft and animal sound. I could think of nothing but my desire for his hand to go higher.

"Be patient," he teased.

He shifted, removed my other heel, then slid his hand up the back of my other leg. As he unfastened my stocking from its garter and slid his hand up farther, I felt a delicious defiance.

He unhooked my overskirt, my petticoats. When he had removed my shift, he gazed at me for a long moment, taking me in, a feverish look in his eyes. "Lie down," he said. I did. He glided his hand slowly up my thigh. My whole body shivered. He slid onto his side next to me, pressing my wrist to the bed with one hand, touching me, teasing me with the other. "Don't move."

I lay as still as I could manage given what he was doing.

He brought me to the brink, then stopped, stood, and began to remove his breeches. By that point I wanted him so much, I couldn't bear it. Soon he was moving inside me, and I was in a sort of ecstasy. By the time he finished, I felt the way I did when I drank poppy. Tingling, entranced, my mind blessedly blank.

He rolled over, and I admired him, the slender muscles of his back, his tapered waist above the sheets tangled around his hips. I couldn't help but think about how intense our encounter had been, how good it had felt to let him take the lead. He was a delicious combination of controlling and attentive. Then the candle guttered, and the dark came flooding back over the bed, surrounding us.

I must've slept, for the next thing I remember is startling awake. For a moment I had no idea where I was. Then I heard Will breathing beside me: soft, regular, surprisingly childlike. My memories of the night returned. Something yawned in the back of my throat, a faint regret, the sense that I had made a mistake—the way you feel when you eat something delicious that unsettles your stomach.

I wondered what Cecely was doing now. How long it would take her to travel to Norwich, if she would see that girl until she found a husband, perhaps even after. The thought of her with another woman—another man—made me want to scream into my pillow.

Will stirred beside me, mumbling something in his sleep. I started, afraid he would wake and see me upset. I slipped out of bed and dressed as best as I could alone, stricken with a sudden urge to be anywhere but beside him.

7

It was almost dawn by the time I arrived back at Underhill House. I hurried inside through the servants' entrance so I wouldn't be seen, since Graves typically woke up early to sit at his desk. The house was still as I hurried upstairs to scrub the paint from my face. Then I undressed down to my shift and slipped into bed, falling almost immediately into a dreamless sleep.

As soon as I woke, my complicated feelings about the previous night returned. Satisfaction, defiance, and that faint but bothersome regret. I tried to ignore it, but it was much harder than usual.

When I finally rose, the church bells at nearby St. Helen's were ringing three o'clock. I had slept for most of the day. It was already dinnertime. I asked Graves if he could tell the new cook to bring a more elaborate meal than usual. Our best mead, sugar for sweets, cheese, all my favourite things. The steward raised an eyebrow, likely wondering if my drowsiness and hunger were meaningful. Good, I thought, let him. I was eating when the scullery maid came to tell me there was someone at the door, a girl with a private message for me.

Luce. I hurried to find Mary to help me dress. Something simple, I decided. Downstairs I went, heels clicking on the staircase, heart fluttering with hope. Mary followed behind me, hurrying to finish fastening the ties of my sleeves.

Graves was already interrogating the messenger, an older freckled girl with bright red braids snaking out from her bonnet. "Mistress Rose?"

"She won't say who sent her."

"I'm not supposed t' tell anyone but 'er my business."

I met the steward's eyes. "I've been corresponding with the friend I visited a while ago." I cleared my throat. "About *women's things.*"

"Oh," Graves said, instantly ill at ease.

"If you'll excuse us—" I motioned for the girl to follow me into the drawing room. When we were alone, the door shut carefully behind us, I lowered my voice. "What news do you bring?"

"Not good, madam," she said. "The Master of Revels said he is not willing to audition a woman."

I felt a sickening surge of anger at my mother. Her letter to Master Underhill was to blame for this policy. I knew it. Massaging my temples, I thought about how long it would be until the physician returned: a month from the wedding, so the first or second of March. How in the world would I find employment by then? Or even by April, if I could manage to confound the doctor on his second visit? Especially with Graves spying on me, expecting Mary to report my every move—

My throat constricted. When I looked up, the messenger girl was watching me, her bright brown eyes concerned. I closed my eyes, fighting back an annoying rash of tears.

"Forgive me, madam. Did you hear me?"

I shook my head.

"She offered to hire you herself but cautioned that she cannot pay enough for that to be your only employment."

My heart leapt. Here was an idea. If I found enough work, I might be able to support all of us. "I'll do it," I said in an embarrassingly shaky voice. "Tell her I'll come by to discuss the terms. I couldn't be more grateful."

She smiled a roguish smile. "Gladly, madam."

I stood in the drawing room for several moments after she left, fighting back tears. Closing my eyes, I tried to focus. *Regina Caeli*, I thought, let me have this.

I drew a deep breath, trying to decide how to go about accomplishing what I wanted to do next. I dreaded the idea of reconciling with my mother now after everything she had done—she didn't deserve it—but I had to plant the seed that we were leaving sometime. We had been avoiding one another since our argument, but the longer I waited, the more trouble she'd make for me when she found out what I was planning.

I found her sitting in the courtyard, watching Edmund run amok, his winter cape flying behind him. He had broken off a stick from one of the dead trees and was using it to conduct a swordfight with some imaginary foe. Hughe was watching from a corner, his nose pressed to the ground as if my mother had scolded him.

"Nay, my good lord!" Edmund shouted at his invisible opponent.

When she saw me, she stiffened. I sat beside her, working hard to still the anger in my breast. The only thing I wanted to talk to her about were the wrongs she had committed against me, but I made myself choose a safer subject. "He seems to be having fun."

She looked at me askance. "He knocked one of the paintings in his room from the wall and tore down the curtain. He's accustomed to roaming the countryside."

I took a deep breath. I knew I should settle things between us before I brought up what I wanted to say, but it was too perfect an opening. "A place in the country would agree better with all of us."

"*What?*"

I scanned the courtyard to make sure we were alone. "I have a confession to make, Mother. Cecely and I went to plays, a few times, in the outer wards. I met someone who has offered to help me find work as a musician."

Her expression darkened.

"Once we have our own place, you could take back up your witching work. Discreetly, of course. Don't you miss it?"

"Yes," she whispered, "but we don't need our own place.

Underhill House is ours already, and I doubt Richard would approve of you working."

"Ours?" I laughed. I couldn't help it. "Don't be naïve. It's Richard's."

Mother blinked, then straightened, a furious look creeping into her eyes. I could feel her anger coming off her in waves. "*Traditrice*," she said in a trembling, cold voice. "You'd throw away everything I worked so hard to get us?"

"Keep your voice low," I whispered. "I'm leaving, one way or another. You can either be part of planning it or not."

"You'd put your brother in jeopardy?"

"Of course not. I'm being careful."

Mother glared at me for so long, I wanted to look away, but neither of us wanted to be the one to relent.

"Nay, answer me!" Edmund chirped, his voice echoing from the courtyard's walls. "I won't stand for this!"

"Think on it," I whispered finally, turning to go in.

At the door, I saw a shadowy figure at the window. Tall, with dark hair and clothes. Graves.

"Good day, madam," he said as I passed him on the way inside, putting away his handkerchief, fluttering his fingers in a condescending wave.

My throat constricted. I couldn't tell by his expression whether he had heard anything.

That evening, when Graves came to inform me that supper was ready, he was cold, his expression far more suspicious of me than usual. As I ate, I couldn't stop thinking about his behaviour that afternoon, trying to ascertain how much he'd heard of my conversation with my mother. The only statement either of us had made loudly was when she accused me of throwing away everything she'd worked for. That seemed ambiguous enough, but what if Graves could read lips? The question haunted me, but there was nothing I could do about it. Frustrated, I commented loudly about how exhausted I was, how eager I was to withdraw to my chamber. Mother rolled her eyes but said nothing.

I waited as long as I could before I left that night, asking Mary to scour the house for Graves, to make sure I wouldn't stumble into him on my way out. That would be a disaster.

When she reported back that he was in bed, I put on my cloak and crept down the servants' staircase, eager to accept Luce's offer. I planned to see Will afterward. Though I was conflicted about seeing him again, I had some propositions for him.

Hughe bounded down Bishopsgate Street, gleeful to be outside. As soon as we were out of sight of Underhill House, I flagged down a carriage, and he sighed—a breathy *woof*—slinking in after me.

As I settled in for the ride, he pressed his head on my lap in the clearest expression of canine disappointment I've ever seen. It occurred to me that he must miss the country too: There was nowhere here for him to run. I scratched his head, whispering an apology as we bounced toward Aldersgate.

The brothel was nearly empty so early in the night. Luce wasn't around, but my aunt was wiping the bar counter, her face freshly painted.

I smiled at her, approaching gingerly. "Lisabetta."

Looking up, my aunt smiled—more of a welcome than she had ever given me. "I was sorry to hear about your news."

I nodded, thinking carefully about what to say. I didn't want to disturb this fragile equilibrium. "Luce sent word that she might be able to offer me a position as a musician here?"

My aunt nodded. "I don't want to see Katarina, but I don't mind if you perform.

"Luce!" Lisabetta called. "Rose is here."

Luce appeared a few moments later, motioning for me to sit so that we could discuss the terms of my employment. She wanted me to perform on the nights the sisters didn't. Since my first performance, there had been several inquiries about my return.

I thanked Luce, agreeing to start the next night as long as I could arrive late after everyone at Underhill House was asleep. Then I hurried out, hoping to catch Will at his lodging before he went out for the evening.

The moon was setting by the time I reached Will's building, casting a thin, silvery glow over the street. The alley across the street from the tavern was empty, but Hughe's hackles rose anyway. As I approached the door to knock, my pulse fluttered, and I felt slightly out of control, as if I were doing something I might regret later.

Reckless, the nightbird tittered ominously, *ruinous*.

I was so shocked to hear its voice, my hand went to my throat. Was my mother witching me again already? I had told her only that day about what I was planning.

My pulse raced. I checked the street, worried suddenly that someone was following me. Graves, or one of the groomsmen under his command. There was nothing in either direction but cobblestones and the faint echo of someone singing.

I told myself it was my imagination, but it took me a moment to collect myself and knock. A woman answered the door, flickering candle in hand. Middle-aged, thick with greying hair, she lifted her eyebrows at the sight of me. Looking down at my clothes, I realised why. I was dressed like a gentlewoman. When I asked for Will, she seemed even more confused, but she agreed to get him.

"Sit," I whispered as Hughe followed me in. He sat obediently.

The landlady vanished up the staircase. In a moment I heard muffled conversation. Will appeared on the landing with his own candle, thanking her for letting him know I had come in a tone that clearly said *Please go, good woman. I'll take this from here.*

He was wearing another fine white shirt with a wide lace collar beneath a waist-length black velvet doublet, tight-fitting enough that it drew my eye to his waist. His breeches matched the doublet, also more form-fitting than most, and he wore black silk nether-stocks beneath.

As Will descended the staircase, running his hand lazily along the railing, Hughe's body tensed. I wondered why Hughe didn't like Will, if perhaps the dog had picked up on Cecely's mistrust of him. "Mistress Rose," he said with a subtle lift of his brow. "To what do I owe this pleasure?"

"Take me upstairs and I'll tell you."

His eyes danced with cautious amusement. He took my hand and kissed it. Then his grip tightened, tighter than was necessary given that I was the one who asked him to go upstairs. He led me to the second floor. Hughe followed behind us, slinking, making a whining sound. "*Hush, boy*," I whispered, and he obeyed, though his ears flattened. "It's all right."

Will's candle flickered as we made our way up the last flight of stairs. I stepped carefully, noticing the slender curve of his leg muscles beneath his netherstocks. The muscles were tight. *Taut* was the word that came to me. He led me inside his room, closing the door, placing the candle in its holder on the desk. It flickered, lighting a quill, a bottle of ink, several stacks of books, a mess of papers.

"I wasn't sure you would come back," Will said, leaning against the desk with an offhand smile. "Usually, when a woman vanishes—"

"She stays gone?" I settled Hughe in a corner.

Will nodded, a smile pulling at his lips. "But, perhaps, you had dark rites to attend to."

"It *was* the Sabbath."

Suddenly he was kissing me. In a moment my bodice was unfastened, hanging from my torso like a collar.

Meeting his eyes, I pressed my bodice to my chest. With the other hand, I reached up to free my hair from my snood, meeting his eyes coyly. My hair fell to my shoulders. I let the bodice slip to reveal more of my breasts, glancing down at my skirts, looking up at him through my eyelashes. "How long until your next play is produced?"

His eyes narrowed quizzically. "We start rehearsals in a few days if I can finish the script in time. Why?"

"Have you hired anyone to write the music?"

"Ah," he said slowly, understanding coming over his face. "You are looking for employment. Look no further."

Relief washed through me. "Thank you," I said. "Help me with this. There are so many buttons."

He nodded, moving quickly. My overskirt fell to my feet in a rush of silk, and I stood in a pool of shining black brocade. I let my bodice fall so I could unbutton my petticoat. He watched me, rapt, as the white linen slipped down atop my overskirt. He smiled in that aloof way he had, intrigued by the show I was putting on for him. I walked slowly to him and unbuttoned his doublet, his breeches.

In a moment I was straddling him.

His aloofness melted away as I took the lead, his eyes following my every move, the eager youth, the same awe with which he'd greeted me after my performance widening his eyes. His expression was so surprised that, for a moment, I felt as powerful as I did when I played. Then something shifted within him, and a strange expression crossed his face. Not anger, not quite, but a deep frustration. Perhaps he remembered how much older than me he was, or the roles that are proscribed for men and women.

"You wanton," he whispered mock-playfully, but his eyes weren't laughing. He moved out from under me, grabbing my hands, trapping them beneath his on the bed. "Who do you think you are?"

Puttana, the nightbird twittered.

I ignored it, too thrilled by the intensity of our encounter to care what it said. I wanted Will to take me, to make me forget the wreck of my life, to love me so hard I could think of nothing else. "Your undoing," I answered, hoping that this would have the desired effect.

He never could resist me taunting him.

Afterward, we curled around one another like cats. He ran his hand in slow circles over my hip, watching me react to his touch. This was mesmerising; my body was tingling all over. The darkness beyond the candlelight was complete. I thought of Cecely, the way being with her made the darkness shiver, the way the boundaries between our selves blurred. This was nothing like that. Will and I were separate.

"Will," I said, sitting up, cupping my breasts. Fully aware of the way my long black hair was falling about my shoulders. Hoping this was the right time to bring up my other idea, I lowered my eyes, looking up at him through my lashes. On the holder beside the bed, the candle flickered, guttering, creating the perfect atmosphere for what I would say next. "I have something to tell you."

"What?"

I met his eyes solemnly. "All my jests about witchcraft. There's truth to them."

He scoffed. I had suspected from his irreverent approach to the subject that he was a sceptic. He watched me, concern wrinkling the edges of his hazel eyes, still supporting his head with his hand. "Pardon?"

"I'm an astrologer. I cast horoscopes and read them."

He snorted. "You believe the stars hold sway over men's hearts."

I smiled mysteriously. "Doesn't the moon sway the tide?"

"There is no ocean in me," he said, his lips curving downward in condescension and amusement.

His outright disbelief surprised me. I had never met anyone so sceptical of the stars' influence. Farmers consulted almanacs. Every physician I had ever met consulted an ephemeris.

I let my hands fall from my breasts, knowing he wouldn't be able to resist a glance. He took a deep breath, raised his eyes back up to meet mine, his body reacting to the sight before him.

"If the countess is looking for a way to ensure that her son marries, perhaps she would commission an astrologer to help her arrange it."

"Astromancy?"

"Yes," I said. "Introduce me to her."

He cleared his throat. The candle on the headboard flickered, casting a rippling net of light over the room. When he spoke, his voice was husky with desire, almost gruff. "The countess invited me to a masque at Southampton House about six weeks from now, just after Easter. If you like, I could take you and introduce you as an astrologer." He smiled slyly. "But you will owe me."

The next night when I arrived at the brothel, Will was already seated at the closest table near the stage. I had promised to see him after I played. He hurried to meet me as soon as I finished perform-ing, as if he feared I would go home with someone else if he was late. Luce shook her head disapprovingly when she saw me leave with him, though I wouldn't find out why until later. Apparently, she hated *Titus*.

I've still never seen it.

After we lay together, we talked about the script he was finish-ing, how his writing was going. He invited me to attend the first rehearsal so that I could write the music for a single scene. If he approved of what I wrote, he would introduce me to the theatre owner who would make the final decision about whether to hire me. As payment, Will promised to give me a percentage of his share of the commissions he'd receive if the play was performed beyond the first night. I said yes, hoping the play was good enough for that to happen.

We talked late into the night. He confided his fears that he wouldn't finish in time, that the play would be censored—and he imprisoned—because of the way it portrayed royals. He lamented his troubles reconciling characters with legend. Occasionally, I said something insightful—usually about the duchess or the portrayal of magic—and he got up to make notes.

He told me about Lord Southampton, the beautiful, self-absorbed youth whom I would meet at the masque. Will had begun meeting him twice a week to gather material for his sonnets. When I asked about his character, Will said he was so rich, so well connected, that he could say or do anything he pleased. He was a Cambridge man, critical, brilliant, charming. Someone had dedicated a poem about Narcissus to him, and he'd received it with great delight. "That is all you need to know," Will said. "The poet meant it as satire, but Henry only laughed. 'I'm flattered,' he said. 'Narcissus is beautiful. Why shouldn't he love himself?'"

Will showed me the sonnets he was working on, half-formed verses about Henry's self-love and beauty, entreating him to pity the world and make a copy. When he asked me what I thought, I told him the truth: The lines were clumsy with too many feet. His eyes flashed with insult, and he became sullen and withdrawn.

But he must've taken the critique to heart, because the next night, he read them to me again, and he had smoothed their metre. His desire to improve his work far surpassed his discomfort at receiving criticism.

On the day of the first rehearsal, I told Mary to report back to Graves that I was going to get fitted for new bodices because my old ones were growing tight. The deception seemed to work; Graves only pursed his lips and nodded as we passed him on the way out. Mary went to the market, and I went to the theatre in

Southwark for the first rehearsal. I hired a carriage instead of using Richard's, so no one from Underhill House would know where we were going. But the carriage driver, a towheaded man with a grizzled beard and a large belly, looked suspicious as I told him where to take us.

I wasn't terribly adept at recognising faces, but I thought I'd seen him before. *He's a spy*, the nightbird said. *Graves bribed him*— though it didn't make sense that he would know which carriage I would choose. For the entirety of the ride to the playhouse, I felt on edge, angry at my mother for making it impossible to trust my own thoughts.

The rehearsal was a cold reading of the Henry script, which Will had given a title so lengthy that the company simply called it *Harry VI*. Will watched, marking up the master script and prompting the players to read their individual parts as needed. They did so with feeling, even though it was their first time reading it. He was becoming something of a celebrity in theatre circles because of the fame of *Titus*, though he'd paused all productions while he reworked the script. He'd paid a minstrel to go about singing a ballad from Titus's perspective, and everyone was talking about it. I'm sure his commission from the countess and his fine clothes didn't hurt either, nor the money he spent on drinks and food for his fellow actors during intermission. The actors seemed excited about his newest effort.

The play was difficult to follow at first. My father had told me stories about the wars between Lancaster and York, but there were so many characters, I found it hard to keep track. It didn't help that no one was familiar with their parts. But I felt instantly sorry for Henry VI, the gentle child king who had absolutely no aptitude for politics.

As soon as I saw the scene where the duchess has the conjurer raise the spirit, I knew it was the scene I would choose. Thunder and lightning, the script said. *Deep night, dark night . . . the time when screech-owls cry and ban-dogs howl.* The furious song I had invented on the way back from Gravesend would be perfect to set the mood for the spirit rising.

Afterward, I told Will how caught up I had gotten in the ending. I still remember the boyish pleasure on his face, the puffed-up pride in his eyes. He asked me to come home with him, but I had already been gone long enough to arouse suspicion.

Back home, I hurried upstairs, picking up my psaltery and adapting the melody. I adapted the song to play before the scene— wordless, strange, a furious and unnatural melody—then adapted a few of its strains to play at key moments within the scene. I hadn't seen anyone do that before, but I thought it would better transmit the feelings that the dialogue was written to engender. I lost myself in the act of composition, embellishing the melody.

When I was happy with it, I called for ink and quill and scribbled the notes at my desk, adding the drums and hautboys at the beginning and the end to evoke the thunder and lightning. It was the middle of the night before I finished.

The next night, I was so excited to show Will what I had written, I sneaked out earlier than I should have. I didn't bother to knock at the front door of the boardinghouse. The landlady waved me in, no longer surprised by my comings and goings.

Will was startled when I knocked on his door. His hair was mussed, and he was only half-dressed, his tunic barely tucked into his breeches. He startled when he saw me at the door, his eyes flashing with a complicated mixture of anger and hurt. I realised that he was miffed that I hadn't come home with him the day before.

I followed him inside, watching his face, thinking about his constant need for reassurance. There was spilled ink, loose papers on the desk, crumpled pages on the floor, and so many books stacked around the desk that it took me some time to move them. He had been writing.

"I wrote the music last night. Do you want to read the scene aloud together, so you can see where everything fits?"

He nodded, fumbling through the papers in a satchel beside the bed. "Good, and walk me through it."

I sat at the desk, putting my psaltery on my lap, explaining how my music would fit into the scene. The song for the scene change, the ominous sennet at the beginning, not like the other fanfares. I hummed it for him. Hautboys—a low, cold note, out of tune— before the medium spoke her invocation. Then psaltery. I played the melody I had written for the moment the spirit was summoned. His expression was serious at first, then pleased, then excited.

"I've never seen this done before," he said, shaking his head. There was a reluctant respect for me in his eyes, even stronger than the first time he saw me perform. He looked back over the scene, making a few quick notes. "I'll talk to the theatre owner tomorrow. If he agrees, you can sit in on a few rehearsals to take notes."

The theatre owner agreed, so I attended the next rehearsal, making sure to behave professionally with Will. I'm sure some of the actors in his company suspected our relationship, but no one said anything—at least to my face—and I turned over my score to the musicians without incident.

I saw Will for several nights in a row. For the first time in the history of my relationships with men, I showed no signs of losing interest. Perhaps this was partially because the nightbird kept telling me not to see him, but it was also because our time together was so delicious. I couldn't stop wondering whom I would meet in bed each night: the aloof dramatist or the awed youth. Our encounters were like a dance in which both partners fought over who would lead.

When he finished making his revisions to the master script, he told me that the countess had invited him to the Wriothesleys' country house to work on the sonnets. He was eager to go, saying it would give him the inspiration he needed to finish the commission and earn the rest of his payment.

He was gone for almost a week. Those nights were long. Spending so much time alone in Underhill House, I was painfully aware of the passage of time. The masquerade was too close to Richard's return for comfort. I would only have a couple of days afterward to find a place and move out, and my plan depended almost entirely on the countess's generosity.

As the physician's visit drew closer, I consulted an herbal from Richard's library, hoping that a change to my diet would keep my condition ambiguous. My mother could've advised me on what to eat, but I hadn't told her about the risk I'd taken on my wedding night. She thought the doctor's visit the morning after was to confirm that my humours were back in balance.

I ordered special food from the kitchen—boiled lentils, barley bread, candied horseradish, and oatcakes—but it didn't accomplish as much as I'd hoped. My stomach was tight and my limbs were somewhat swollen, but no more than what happened at a certain time of the month. Thankfully, *that* wouldn't coincide with the doctor's visit.

The nights crept by. I spent many sleepless hours in bed, staring into the dark. *Not enough time*, the nightbird chittered. *Not enough.* I knew it was my mother's devil, but the knowledge was not enough to silence it.

I missed Will: his wit, his presence, the way he made me forget my troubles. As the nights passed, the feeling of missing *him* became larger, wider, transforming into a more general ache. Inevitably, my thoughts wandered to Cecely. I was still upset with her for abandoning me, but the fury I'd brought home from Gravesend had dulled to sadness. I tried to ignore it, pushing it down, but without Will to distract me, I couldn't.

The night before the physician was supposed to come, I lay in bed, unable to sleep, overcome by dread and a devastating sense of how much I had lost. My home, my best friend, my father. My grief over his death crashed through me with surprising strength, filling me with a furious ache. I longed for the days he spent teaching me music and how to cast horoscopes. I reached down to touch his ring, but of course my finger was naked. My throat constricted, and a furious sob leapt into my throat.

I couldn't shake the sense that I had lost everything.

The next morning, when I heard men's voices outside my chamber, my whole body tensed. I was exhausted, and the nightbird had been whispering to me all night. *It's useless*, it had twittered. *Graves knows.*

"How are you feeling?" the physician asked as he walked in, his rheumy eyes concerned.

Graves loomed, narrow-eyed, behind him, the look on his face far more sceptical than usual. The doctor nodded; the steward closed the door.

"Swollen," I answered. "Stomach-qualmed."

He raised his brows, the wrinkles on his forehead growing deeper. He nodded for me to remove my gown.

I held my breath as he examined me, fingers just as cold as before. His hands lingered longer this time on my breasts and stomach, making none of the thoughtful sounds he'd made before. I looked up at him, trying to read his expression, but it was inscrutable. *Regina Caeli*, I thought, help me, whoever you are.

"What do you think?" I asked when he nodded for me to put back on my gown.

"Your stomach is distended," he said in a puzzled voice, "but I observe no other symptoms. I still cannot be sure."

I drew a deep breath, trying to hide how pleased I was that my plan had worked. But the relief was only temporary, as I considered what the doctor's next step might be. "When will you be able to tell for certain?"

"Mid-April. I'll come back then."

I had to work hard to hide the relief flooding through me. By then, I planned to be gone.

Will wasn't due back to London until the day the Henry play would be performed. We had plans to meet at the theatre. This time, I had told Mary to report that I was going to see the friend I'd sought comfort from before. I told her she could take the day off if she brought Hughe with her, and she made plans to try to see her brother.

At the playhouse, I saw Will before he saw me. He was speaking with the nobleman in the box beside his in his usual offhanded way, but there was a strain at the edge of his eyes and his hand gripped his goblet too tightly. Another goblet sat on the table behind him, full and frosty in the early March air. When he turned and saw me, his smile reached his eyes. "There you are," he said, excusing himself from his companion and reaching out to clasp my hands.

He pulled me to sit beside him, then squeezed my knee beneath the table, a bold thing for him to do in public. I slapped it away, though a shiver crept up my thigh. I wanted to find some dark corner of the theatre and have my way with him. "Later," I whispered.

I could hear the musicians warming up beneath the buzz of conversation, strange tittering melodies, scales and chords, frenzied and dissonant. Drummers, hautboyists, trumpetists, not a single instrument out of tune, a psalterist practising a line of the furious melody *I had written*. I grinned at Will, who beamed, similarly caught up in the moment. There was an expectant energy in the air like there always is before a play in a packed house. All eyes on the stage, anticipating the experience.

This was everything I ever wanted. Not the way I thought I would get it, but just as thrilling.

Then the musicians played the first sennet, a pompous fanfare of trumpets. Innocent Henry and his men appeared on one side, treacherous Margaret and her attendants on the other. The play had been much improved from the early rehearsals; Will had extensively revised. There were new lines, characters' roles were more distinguished. When the music that introduced the summoning scene played, a hush fell over the audience.

Will looked around, noticing the effect of the music. Every single audience member in our gallery leaned forward, as if their spirits had been infected by my melody. He squeezed my hand, grinning like a schoolboy.

My favourite line was not one I had heard in the original rehearsal. The queen to the duchess after she slapped her:

> *Could I come near your beauty with my nails,*
> *I'd set my ten commandments in your face.*

The boy playing Margaret spoke the lines with a wonderful venom. I caught Will's eyes and lifted my eyebrows, impressed, and he sent me back an arrogant smile. He always knew when he wrote something brilliant.

The play was so much improved, I didn't notice its length. There was so much blood, I wondered how many pigs had died to supply the performance. When York and Warwick announced their plan to go after the king, and the final ominous notes announced the end of the play, the audience clapped and groaned their displeasure that the performance had ended.

"That was marvellous good," the nobleman Will had been talking to before told him, draining his drink.

"Indeed, it was excellent," his wife said.

I had never seen Will beam with so much pleasure.

As everyone began making their way out, the stagehands hurried to clean up the blood and gore before the theatre emptied enough for the kites to set upon it. Will beamed, his eyes crinkling. We grinned at one another like children.

I don't remember leaving with him. I have no idea if we went by foot or carriage.

As soon as he closed the door to his room, he pulled me in for a kiss. "This is it," he whispered. "A second night. Maybe even a third. They'll *beg* for a sequel!"

I smiled, genuinely happy for him but also relieved. If what he was saying was true, my share of his commission would be a pretty penny. "The play was good before, but the changes you and the company made were astounding."

He beamed. "Thank you. I put everything I had into it."

"You'll let me write the music for the sequel?"

"Absolutely!"

He was eager as he undressed me. His aloof persona melted. There was only the earnest country boy, searching out my eyes with real affection. As he kissed me, tears filled his eyes. His voice was husky when he said, "I've missed you."

"And I you," I said, caught up, but an uncomfortable feeling was choking my throat. My own eyes were watering.

As soon as I realised what was happening, I pulled away, pressing my eyes tightly shut to stop the tears from falling. When I opened my eyes, he was searching my face, his brow subtly furrowed. "What's wrong?"

"Stop staring at me that way," I said, embarrassed. "What are you looking for, my soul? I told you, I gave it to the devil."

He blinked, his expression startled. He studied me with those damned hazel eyes as if I hadn't just asked him *not* to. After a moment, the edges of his lips turned downward into a disbelieving chuckle. "Oh, Rose," he said, his pitch falling on my name like a blow.

"What?"

"You're afraid," he said, smirking.

"Of what?"

"Of intimacy."

The word hung in the air.

It was dark, my face in shadow. I was lying in a windowless room with a single man by the light of a single candle. But those two words made me feel as if I were being pilloried before a crowd in broad daylight. I thought of my nativity, the Aquarian influence. I could feel the blood rushing to my face. "No, no, no. I don't..." I trailed off, realising with no little horror that he was right. My embarrassment was proof.

I wanted to rush out of the building.

I thought about what I could lose if I stopped seeing him: the pleasure of our encounters, the potential for music and astrology work, my ability to earn a living. I needed to be kind, but I was too unsettled by his insight. "I didn't come here for you to analyse my character," I snapped.

His eyes glittered with insult, followed by a cold amusement. His aloofness returned, his overdeveloped dignity, his guard. The traits that attracted me to him. "Rose, Rose, Rose. What a name for one so..."

"Sweet?" I said, mocking him.

"I was going to say prickly. No matter." His smile was crooked. "Now that I know what you want. Or, rather, what you *don't*—"

He met my gaze. This time there was nothing in it but desire, pure and simple.

I sighed with relief. He understood. He would meet me in the world of the senses. Knowing that, I wanted him, again, as many times as I could have him, *yes, please, and thank you.*

He took my hand, pulling me to him, saying my name in that gruff voice he used when he was overcome. "*Rose.* Let me prick you. No more of the other. I promise."

8

"Make me look like a baroness, an astromancer," I told Mary on the evening of the masquerade. It was Aries season by then, and I was feeling bold. I asked her not to bother with spirits of Saturn—my mask was designed to cover my face—but I sat long enough for her to ring my eyes with kohl and dust my neck and décolletage with a bronze powder. The mask had a mouth hole through which could be seen my lips, which she painted coral.

My bodice was brocade: rich magenta fabric threaded with black and white. The plunging neckline was embroidered with gold-work. The mask matched, shimmering satin—as red as claret and as dark—adorned with a single black star.

Mary braided my hair and piled it atop my head into a serpentine coil adorned with rose petals. When we were finished, I checked my reflection in a mirror. I looked mysterious, regal, like an astrol-oger for nobles should look.

Mother came in as I was putting the mirror away, surveying me critically. "Where are you going?"

Sighing, I told her.

"You're married, Rose. If Richard finds out—"

I rolled my eyes. "He's in Bohemia."

"People talk."

I had often ignored those words from her, but that evening, they gave me pause. Perhaps it was the way she looked at me, her impe-rious tone. Or perhaps it was my own apprehension.

Stomach sinking, I realised she was right: I needed to be careful.

Then I remembered the nightbird was back, that she was up to her old manipulations. She was probably witching me to stay at Underhill House forever, to become Richard's adoring wife. My fists clenched. I couldn't help but notice that her gloves were new. They looked more expensive than the sort the steward's allowances would let her buy.

I suspected I knew where she got the money.

"I'm going, Mother," I said, defiance making my voice tremble. "Don't try to convince me otherwise. If you ruin this for me, I'll make sure you regret it."

She glared at me, but for once, she didn't argue.

As she withdrew, I asked Mary to make sure the way to the servants' entrance was clear. During the last several weeks, I had been careful not to be seen coming or going on my way to perform or see Will. This would be the least opportune night to be caught.

When Mary nodded that the hallway was empty, I hurried to the door, mask in hand, eager to be on my way. As I was leaving, Hughe tried to follow me out, whimpering. His posture slumped, and he lowered his muzzle. I scratched his ears, guilt rising in my throat. "I'm sorry, boy, but you can't come tonight."

The nightbird chittered as I hurried out of the servants' entrance—*puttana, traditrice*—but I bade it go to hell, peering ahead to look for Will's carriage. He had promised to wait for me around the corner just after sunset. When I arrived, the carriage was already sitting there. Inside, Will was wearing a handsome but simple costume. A black brocade doublet with a white lace ruff, a black feathered mask in his lap. He smiled at me roguishly, and I kissed him.

Twilight was falling by the time we arrived at the mansion. For mansion it was, a giant former monastery converted into a great house that had been expanded upon with modern turrets and stained-glass windows. There were at least a dozen carriages in the drive, letting intricately costumed revellers out. A cadre of servants lined the walkway. As we stepped out of our carriage, my stomach tightened.

How many people were here? Could I be recognised as Richard's wife? I had better not remove my mask at all.

What if someone who knew Richard heard Will call me by my first name and made the connection? "Use my stage name when you introduce me."

He met my eyes and nodded. "Understood."

A steward let us in, wearing attire fine enough for a knight. He led us to a great hall that had been set up for feasting and dancing. I couldn't help but marvel at the lavish décor. Candles glittered along the walls, and lanterns. The ceiling was festooned with garlands and ribbons. On one side of the hall, a long table flickering with candles was set with what looked like a hundred places.

On the other side, a dazzling wall of glass windows faced a dark garden, reflecting the light of the torches blazing in sconces along the wall. A broken consort of violists, lutenists, and drummers played in a corner, a sprightly tune. Revellers stood in a circle around a couple in rich velvet and lace costumes who were dancing a galliard. Being among so many people felt dangerous.

Servants buzzed, greeting us, bowing, offering drinks. I took one but drank none of it, since doing so would require me to pull my mask from my face.

Will scanned the hall. After a moment he nodded and held out his arm. I took it, drawing a deep breath, walking beside him to a circle of *very* well-dressed people in a corner. There was a brown-haired middle-aged woman with dark, shrewd eyes and a coral and white gown with a pearled lace collar. A small mask hung around her neck, simple, white, but set with a hundred pearls.

Beside her stood a beautiful young man of about eighteen or nineteen years with long, curling golden hair. Broad-shouldered, with the slender build of a young man who has only just reached his full height. He carried himself with striking self-possession. He was wearing the frilliest collar I'd ever seen, a dark blue silk doublet, matching mask, and voluminous sleeves and breeches. The attire seemed curiously ornate to my eyes, but this *was* a masquerade, after all, and I'd never met an earl.

For that must be who this was. Henry Wriothesley, 3rd Earl of Southampton, the subject of Will's sonnets. He was carrying something, but I couldn't see what. His puffy sleeves obscured it. It wasn't until we drew close that I realised it was a cat. Or rather, an overgrown kitten. She had shining black and white fur and pale green eyes that glowed in the candlelight. He was stroking her indulgently, whispering to her with such a roguish grin that I suspected he was mocking the revel.

I liked him at once.

Beside him stood a young woman of sixteen or seventeen years with clever dark eyes and thick auburn hair piled atop her head. Her smile, as she watched Henry with the cat, was forced. This must be Elizabeth, the girl they wanted Henry to marry. Of course. The revel was an attempt to ensure that the betrothal went forward.

A white-bearded man stood beside her, his sharp grey eyes troubled, lips turned downward with disapproval. He wore a dignified doublet and breeches like Will with only a black feathered mask to distinguish it for the occasion. I couldn't tell if his displeasure resulted from the earl's focus on the cat or something else. What I could tell from the way he carried himself—imperious gaze, squared shoulders—was that he was powerful.

Lord Burghley, I realised with horror, Henry's guardian and the Lord High Treasurer, the man who administered Richard's alchemical contract. My throat constricted.

I shook my head at Will and stepped behind him to remove myself from Burghley's line of sight.

As soon as the earl saw Will, he set down the cat, who scampered out of the hall. Henry excused himself from his companions and approached, smiling broadly. "*Will!*" he said, his eyes lighting up, the single word communicating a surprising amount of affection. "You're here! Now begins the *real* revel!"

Will had been spending more time with Henry since he returned from their trip, but I hadn't realised how friendly they had become. It was rare for an earl to speak to a merchant's son in such familiar tones, almost scandalous. Will didn't return his familiar tone, bowing obsequiously. "Your lordship."

Henry clapped his hands, looking about for a servant to pour drinks as we approached. Everything about him was larger than life, expansive. His eyes, his voice, his gestures. He smiled, flashing the palest blue eyes I had ever seen, like a thin veil of ice over a frozen lake. They sparkled with anticipation. I couldn't help but wonder what mischief these two had gotten into on Will's trip to his house in the country.

Will took Henry's arm and steered him in my direction. When he saw me, he looked at Will with a quizzical expression. "Who is she?"

Will laughed. "Mistress Ravenna Notte, your lordship, the astromancer. The woman who wrote the music for my last play. Remember? I told you I would introduce her to your mother, so she could advise her on how to proceed with your match with Elizabeth."

"Did you?" Henry asked fretfully.

Will nodded. I got the impression the earl wasn't terribly adept at listening.

Henry turned to me with a strained smile. "A woman astromancer, by the Rood."

Up close, I was startled by the icy blue of his irises, the cut of his jaw, his long fingers. He had broad hands and the muscled arms of someone who enjoyed archery or fencing. What Will hadn't mentioned was that he was passing beautiful, the sort of youth I would have pursued relentlessly back home. I smiled at him. "My father taught me."

Will cleared his throat. "She's very good. Renowned, overseas."

He spoke the lie so naturally, I almost believed it myself. I forgot for a moment he was talking about me. Then I realised what he had said, and I had to stop myself from laughing. I have never met a better liar, and that means something from my mother's daughter.

Henry fell for it completely. "To hell with advising my mother. I want her to advise *me*," he said in the way of noblemen who are accustomed to getting what they want. "Dee's interpretation of my birth chart was horrid. Marriage, imprisonment, death of a fever."

Will looked at me, his eyes flashing with disapproval and—I was almost certain—jealousy.

I pretended not to notice. "It would be an honour to advise your lordship."

Beside me, Will stiffened.

"Tonight, then. After the masque." He nodded at the group he'd been conversing with, then lowered his voice. "I'm eager to be away from that nonsense. All they speak of is marriage. Even Elizabeth grows tired of it. She wants our union less than I do."

I followed his gaze to his intended, who was watching us with a mildly curious expression. I wasn't so certain she didn't *want* the coupling as much as I was certain she knew she wouldn't *get* it. She looked like she was waiting for everyone else to figure that out. I could see why. It was difficult for me to imagine the earl marrying anyone in the next five years or even ten. It was easier to imagine him galloping off to war or flying into the sun like Icarus.

"It's a good match, Henry," Will said under his breath.

Henry shook his head, exasperated, and sighed, his mood turning abruptly dark. He had been effusive enough thus far that his sudden melancholy was startling. "You must understand. I have so much I want to *do*," he said, his voice tight with longing.

The music stopped. Lord Burghley's voice rang out, inviting everyone to be seated. Across the room, Elizabeth, who had been watching us, turned away.

"After the masque, we'll withdraw to my chambers," Henry

whispered as we made our way to our seats. "Cast my birth chart, then advise me on how to shuttle off this alliance. I'll pay you more than my mother ever could."

Relief rushed through me. Henry's words were as magic as any a magician ever uttered. *Abracadabra. Fiat fiat.* A slow smile spread over my face. "It would be my honour."

Will shot me a look, the corners of his eyes tight with lines that revealed he was perturbed. But of course he would be: Henry had just invited me to advise him how to *stop* the wedding, against Will's efforts on behalf of his mother. Will claimed not to believe in the influence of the planets, but perhaps he was less certain about that than I thought—or perhaps he was simply irritated that he would have to sit through a horoscope.

I knew I was being reckless as usual, but I was already planning what I would say if Will asked me not to do it. Henry was an earl. I was no one, only half a noblewoman.

There was no way I could refuse him.

Everyone pushed their masks up on their foreheads as they sat at the tables, and I realised I wouldn't be able to eat. Nor could I sit at the prominent table where Henry and Will did. There was a tall man with a stiff air about him, in a dark mask and cloak, whose solemn bearing and gestures reminded me of Graves. He can't be here, I told myself. He's only a servant. But I kept seeing him everywhere, jumping at shadows. I excused myself and sat in the most remote corner of the most remote table, where a guttering candle wasn't quite doing its work, refusing course after course. Wafer cakes and suckets, tarts and baked pears, roasted swan and goose. How I wanted to eat them!

Finally, I gave in, surreptitiously blowing out the candle at my table and removing my mask to eat the baked pears soaked in cream and gulp my mead before a servant came to relight it. When the servants brought away the final course, Lord Burghley held up his goblet. "To my lovely niece and the Veres, who are so gracious as to bless us with their company today—"

The countess stood. "To the Veres!"

On the other side of the room from where I sat, I could just barely see Elizabeth straightening in her seat, smiling demurely. She mirrored the gesture reluctantly, as if she were embarrassed at all the attention.

Several more pledges went round, and then the masque began. A true spectacle. A musical reenactment of the Persephone myth beginning with her abduction by Hades, followed by her ingestion of the pomegranate seeds, and ending with her escape from the underworld. An extravagant set, elaborate guises, a cast of as many women as men. Women played all the goddesses, and Demeter, Hecate, and Persephone had such extensive speaking roles that I wondered if the script had been written by a woman. The fact that women are allowed to perform in private masques but not in professional plays has always nettled me.

I was particularly taken with the woman who played Hecate. She was beautiful, fair-haired, dressed in flowing black robes. She wore a mask with a face on either side of her own, making her three-faced like the goddess, and she held real torches. The way she danced—the subtle movements of her hips—reminded me of Cecely. I felt my friend's absence, suddenly, the hole that had yawned within me while Will was gone opening back up.

I blew out my candle again and tried to fill the emptiness with mead.

When the performance ended, I checked to make sure my mask was straight and approached Will, who was staring into his drink with a thoughtful expression. Henry made his way toward us. "What did you think?"

Will cleared his throat, meeting the earl's eyes with a slight bow.

"There was much to admire. Hades's part was masterful. Do you know who wrote the script?"

"Her ladyship will not say," Henry said, referring to his mother with mocking deference.

He led us up a grand staircase, two grooms hurrying out after us with harried expressions. Henry called for someone named Trixie—a servant, I thought, until the cat appeared, trotting after us the way Hughe followed me.

All the mead had gone to my head. I found it difficult to walk, tottering on my heels. The attention to detail on the balustrade, the filigrees, the candleholders, everything about the décor was dizzying. There were paintings and statues, murals and tapestries. Henry seemed oblivious to all of it, and Will walked beside him as if he knew exactly where we were going.

The groom posted at Henry's chambers let us in. Henry called to a servant. "Bring drink!" Then he gestured to a small table with a chess set, directing a servant to take it away. I spread out my notebook and instruments and pushed my mask up on my forehead to drink from my goblet, my caution disappearing as I savoured the moment. We were in private now. The earl could be trusted, couldn't he? Richard and he couldn't be close. Richard would *hate* him. I wanted to celebrate the beauty of my lavish surroundings, the feast, the masquerade, the fact that I was sitting in a mansion. The fact that an earl was paying me to cast a horoscope.

Trixie jumped into Henry's lap as soon as he sat.

Will straddled his chair, resting his head on his hands. His eyes clouded, darker than usual, brooding.

Pretending not to notice, I asked Henry to tell me when he was born—the eighteenth hour on the sixth of October in 1573, Sussex—and I cast his nativity. When neither man was looking, I closed my eyes and murmured a quick prayer for insight into Henry's nature. *Regina Caeli—*

His chart made sense. The sun and Mercury were in Libra,

explaining his airy charm. Taurus was rising, explaining his love of beauty, sensuality, the arts, theatre, music. But Venus was afflicted by Saturn in his seventh house, indicating frustration with love and marriage.

He listened as I shared this, rapt, lifting his eyebrows. Will glared at me over his brandywine, his expression growing darker by the minute.

Henry rolled his eyes. "Don't tell me you're on their side, Will."

"Your mother is paying me to be, your lordship. I am contracted to persuade you to accept the betrothal."

"I'll acquit you."

"You could not acquit the damage to my reputation if I fail."

"Nor could you acquit the contract that would bind me if you succeed."

Will shook his head, chuckling despite himself. "An impasse."

Henry's grin lit up the room. I could see why Will said he was charming. "Continue," he said to me, resting his chin on his hand.

I consulted my ephemeris to remind myself of the current influences, explaining what I was doing as I filled in the current positions of the planets beside the houses of his nativity. Will scowled, tapping his boot against the floor beneath the table, impatient.

While I was working, Henry caught Will's eye. "I cannot marry her," he said with such intense feeling that my heart went out to him. "I told you. It will wreck me."

Will nodded as if he understood, but he was obviously agitated. He smiled stiffly, adjusting his earring. The gold glinted in the candlelight, then disappeared beneath his dark hair. He rose, walked to the window, and stared out at the stars as if he found meaning in them.

While his back was turned, Henry searched out my eyes with a pained look. "Mistress Notte," he whispered, his voice desperate, pleading, as if he were drowning and only I could save him.

"I heard you praying in Latin earlier. I will do *anything* to stop this wedding."

Sympathy swelled in my chest. The fact that I'd given him a false name, deceived him, suddenly seemed wrong. "There are things I can do," I whispered. "Not here—"

He searched my eyes, then nodded, satisfied with whatever he found there. He cleared his throat, raising his voice loud enough for Will to hear. "What advice do you have for me?"

"Saturn is in Cancer now and will be for almost two years." I thought about this placement further. "While Saturn passes through Cancer, he teaches us about boundaries, activates our defences around our feelings. You're feeling those effects in your desire to separate yourself from your guardian's and mother's wishes. If you show it, they're like to put even more pressure on you to marry. You would do well to hide your feelings."

Will turned from the window, his eyes narrowed.

"For someone whose Venus is afflicted by Saturn," I went on, ignoring him, "in Scorpio, no less, this will be a difficult time. Try not to overreact to the matchmaking attempts. Remember, betrothals are not sealed until you accept the dowry."

Henry looked thoughtful, then clapped for a servant to bring his purse. He pulled out a handful of sovereigns, thanked me, and put them in my hand without even counting them.

Will glared at me, his pretty lips pressed together tight, his eyes flashing with barely concealed jealousy. "I'm tired," he said stiffly.

He turned to go, and I curtsied to the earl, who met my eyes. *Come back tomorrow*, he mouthed.

I blinked, hesitant to accept his invitation. Will had done much for me. I needed the steady income that composing for his plays would bring. My commission from the Henry play had been considerable, and he was hard at work on the sequel. I didn't want to anger him further. But the earl was so wealthy, so free with his money. To hell with it, I thought, and nodded.

Will was silent as we left Southampton House, the only sound the thud of his boots on the cobblestones outside the mansion. When he didn't offer his arm, I knew how angry he must be. It was nearly midnight by then, the street dark.

There were no lights outside, no carriage drivers holding up lanterns to look for passengers. The only brightness came from the whites of Will's eyes as he searched the street for a carriage. "There," he said in a hard voice.

It took a moment for my eyes to adjust to the darkness, to see that he was looking at a carriage turning onto the street. From this distance, the lantern the driver held looked like a will-o'-the-wisp. I could just barely make out the faint drone of carriage wheels against the stones, the echo of the horse's hooves. So shadowy, so faint, it seemed almost spectral.

The carriage drew close, and the driver held up his lantern in greeting. "Ho," he said. "Where to?"

"Shoreditch," Will said coldly. "Then Bishopsgate-within."

We would go our separate ways that night.

The driver nodded. Will hesitated when he should've offered an arm to help me into the carriage, as if I had been inside a plague house. In the lantern light I could see the grim set of his jaw, the fury he was barely keeping in check for the driver's benefit. I took off the delicate heels that made climbing difficult and pulled myself up by the rail without help.

Behind me, he swore under his breath, insulted.

As he spoke with the driver, I arranged myself on the seat of the shadowy carriage. I left my mask on, grateful that it would hide my fury. I needed money. I didn't have the luxury to refuse the earl. Will wasn't seeing this from my perspective. I straightened my bodice, smoothed the wrinkles of my gown, and slipped my heels back onto my feet. I couldn't find a natural position for my hands on my lap.

Will was silent as he climbed into the carriage. He sat across from me, kicking my billowing skirts out of the way with his foot. The carriage lurched into motion. I watched him through my mask's eyeholes.

"Take that off," he said, gesturing at my mask.

I glared at him but did so reluctantly.

"I cannot believe you did that," he said under his breath, the words coming out in a barely controlled hiss. "It's one thing to play the astromancer, but that was good advice you gave him."

"What does it matter?"

"I'll be more likely to receive another commission from the countess—or Lord Burghley, or another royal—if I succeed. I asked you here to offer your services to the *countess*. You're working against me."

"Sonnets don't change minds."

"Don't be obtuse. The countess asked me to work on him personally as well."

"You don't even believe in astrology. Why do you think you can convince him to marry?"

"The yoke comes for all of us."

All of us, I thought, first person, himself included. I remembered his response when I told him I married unwilling—*a forgivable offence*. I studied him. The brightest part of the light from the driver's lantern shone over only one side of his face, leaving the other in partial shadow. The effect was almost eerie. He was watching me, waiting for me to react. He wanted to hurt me.

"You too."

"Yes."

"Married."

"A family in Stratford-upon-Avon. A house, a wife, children, all of it. Why the devil do you think I need more commissions?"

I blinked at him, unsettled at the intensity of his ire, the sudden tension in my chest. I couldn't tell if I was uneasy that he had a wife, or angry that he hadn't mentioned her.

He sighed. "If not for me, Rose, then have a care for yourself. It's not only the countess you're working against. It's Burghley too. *The queen's advisor*, the most powerful man in England. The betrothal was his idea. Elizabeth is his niece, Henry his ward. What sort of game do you think you are playing?"

Not triumph, I thought morosely. The carriage rocked, the wheels groaning over the dirt road that led back into the city. Out the window the stars dotted the night only faintly, so dim, so interrupted by buildings and clouds I could not discern any constellations. I thought about what he was saying, remembering my promise to myself not to be reckless. I closed my eyes, suddenly sick of the rocking of the carriage. *He's right*, the nightbird tittered. *He's right*—

"Let me think about it."

I agonized over my choice for the rest of that night—as Mary helped me undress, in bed as I stared sightless into the darkness. The nightbird whispered its ugly whispers. It occurred to me that if my mother were witching me, I *should* detect the scent of roses, but I didn't. Could she be invoking a power other than the queen of heaven, I wondered, some obscure daemon whose scent was less noticeable? I smelled nothing.

I wondered if I was too furious anymore, too lost, to sense such subtleties, or if she'd cast a spell that had stolen my ability to sense them. I resolved to check her spell book as soon as I could, to see if she had written down whatever she had cast.

The only shadows I had seen lately were those of the steward lingering in doorways. He seemed to be everywhere in Underhill House now: pacing the hall outside my room, peering into the library to ask if I needed anything.

I needed to leave Underhill House and soon. There was no way

I could reject Henry's offer, no matter what Will thought. I needed the money.

As the grey light of morning began to spread from the horizon, I found myself thinking of Cecely, wondering where she was now. Had her cousin let her help with the brewery? Was she lying with someone else already? The thought scalded me. I withdrew from it as quickly as one would withdraw one's hand from a pot of boiling water.

Later that morning, weighing the bag of coins in my hand, I went downstairs to my mother's chamber. I stood outside the door for a long time. I was still furious with her for witching me, for—in all likelihood, I thought—selling the ring. I wanted to confront her again, but it was pointless; I knew she would deny it. And yet the sad truth of the matter was I had no one else to confide in. I drew a deep breath and knocked, trying to still the fury that I felt in my very bones.

"Mother. I need to talk to you."

There was a long silence. "Come in," I heard finally. Opening the door, I found her on the bed in her nightgown, looking at me expectantly. Her patient expression—kind, almost *maternal*—infuriated me. She was a consummate actor.

Swallowing my ire, I explained the chance Will had given me to compose for an audience, the betrothal and everyone behind it, Henry's intense opposition to the arrangement. Her countenance darkened at first, but when I showed her the sovereigns, she lifted her eyebrows.

"May I?" she asked, holding out her hand.

I let her hold the bag, feel the weight of it in her hand, pull out a coin with the reverence of a pauper. It occurred to me that once she saw how lucrative my astrology could be, she might tell me where she sold the ring so I could buy it back.

"He handed it to me like it was nothing."

She gave it back reluctantly. "Did you speak to the countess?"

I shook my head. "Nor did I give my real name. Will introduced me as Mistress Ravenna Notte. I'm being careful. A residence can't cost more than a few sovereigns a month."

She glowered at me.

"With clients like the earl, we could live quite comfortably."

"Life would be simpler if we stayed here."

"We could lease a respectable farmhouse in Waltham Forest. Edmund and Hughe would have room to run."

Mother rolled her eyes. Her lack of appreciation for how strategic I had been hurt. A knot rose in my throat, ridiculous, sullen. She should be proud of me.

"You're sleeping with the dramatist. That's where you go at night."

I took a deep breath and nodded. "Lord Wriothesley told me to come back tomorrow. I told him there are things that can be done to forestall his marriage."

Her eyes widened. "How old is he?"

"Eighteen. He'll be nineteen in October."

An uneasy silence settled between us. She watched me, that old familiar look on her face that I knew from watching her play chess with my father. It could go either way. She could advise me or threaten me. I closed my eyes, making my voice as sweet, as imploring as I could manage. "Mother," I said. "This would be a better life for all of us. For once in your life, will you please trust me?"

Her expression was cold at first, impassive. But after a moment she met my eyes and nodded reluctantly. "Very well. Let's try it your way."

I blinked at her, stunned. I had convinced her, finally, persuaded my intractable mother. I couldn't remember ever succeeding at such a thing. After everything she'd done—forced two betrothals, witched me, stolen the ring—a childish pride coursed through me that *I* had finally convinced *her* to do something.

"Send a messenger," she sighed. "Invite the earl here. Explain that you need to be discreet. Use the initials of your false name, transposed. Do not tell your lover what you're doing lest you make an enemy of him. Avoid him as much as you can without alarming him."

"That won't be too difficult. We had an argument."

"Convenient." She smiled tightly, then heaved such a deep sigh, I believed she had well and truly changed her mind. "I will grant you this," she said. "Edmund would be happier in the country."

She so rarely allowed that I had been right about something, my spirit soared, my anger at her all but forgotten. I almost wanted to hug her. I imagined myself in an expensive gown in a country cottage, sitting before a table, reading a chart for a well-dressed woman. Let me make this true, I prayed, please, *Regina Caeli fiat fiat.*

When I opened my eyes, Mother was watching me, uneasy, as if she were already second-guessing her decision.

"You won't regret this," I said quickly. "I'll send for the errand boy to bring the message. Help me decide what to tell the earl when he comes."

She nodded slowly.

As she helped me dress, we went through the story I would tell Henry. How I came to be in London, why we were staying at Underhill House. She acted reluctant at first, resigned, but as we developed the plan, she seemed more committed. I instructed Mary to watch for my "cousin" and intercept him. When I told her he would ask for Ravenna, she lifted a brow but said nothing.

Once dressed, I could do nothing but wait for Henry, pacing my chambers. I couldn't compose, couldn't even still my thoughts with claret. I was afraid I would miss him if I left the house to walk Hughe, so I tossed the ball for him in the courtyard, revisiting all the possible implications of the horoscopes I had cast for Henry.

It was late afternoon before Mary announced that my "cousin" was waiting for me in the parlour. I found the earl seated in the best chair, his long hair braided and hidden beneath a hat and a simple but well-made grey cape, the only sign of his extensive wealth the fur ruffs on his sleeves. He had taken my plea not to attract attention seriously.

I entreated him to follow me into the drawing room, the only place in the house with any opportunity for privacy. Inside, we sat at the table beside the window that looked out into the courtyard. Embarrassed by its condition, I found myself confiding in him that I was only a guest.

"How is it that you come to stay here?"

"The Underhills needed my services. They're alchemists."

"I see. Speaking of magic—"

I nodded encouragingly.

He smiled, restrained and regal, straightening a stray thread in the embroidery above his cuffs, then met my eyes, his gaze solemn and almost helpless. He cleared his throat. "You said there are things that can be done. I want to sabotage my betrothal. Or prolong it, at least, until my twenty-first birthday. However long it takes me to have charge of my estate and obtain the authority to reject it."

I laughed, unable to control my glee, a great smile spreading across my face. If there was any area in which I could offer advice, it was that. "Forgive me," I said. "This task is perfect for me."

He grinned. "Good. I have no care for the expense or the method. Astromancy, scrying, what you will. I'll pay you handsomely."

I nodded, went to the door, and sent for my mother.

After I explained what Henry wanted, Mother asked him to retrieve a lock of hair from himself and Elizabeth. He plucked one of his own and promised to come back the following day with one of hers. Apparently, he was being subjected to frequent visits from Elizabeth at Cecil House; Lord Burghley kept inviting her to watch his fencing practice.

My anxiety grew as I waited for him to come back, making

me restless. I paced the house. Both Richard and the doctor were scheduled to return next week. There was very little time left. I was terrified that Richard would come back early, but we couldn't afford the sort of place my mother would agree to until Henry paid us again.

Will did not come to see me perform that night, and I did not go to him.

When Henry returned with the lock of hair, we took him into the drawing room, closed the door, and posted Mary at its exterior to tell anyone who came that we were taking care of a family matter. Mother went to work twining the hairs together immediately. Then she began casting the spell, invoking the queen of heaven. The ritual involved a beeswax candle circled with dried roses and yew berries, fed one by one into the fire while the hairs were untwined.

Afterward Henry asked questions about the proceedings. She had rushed through the invocation; what spirit did the spell call upon? *A little-known saint*, Mother lied. The meaning of the hair and rose petals was obvious, but why the yew berries? *To poison the betrothal; did you see how they sizzled?*

When he was satisfied, Mother nodded. "Ravenna can advise you on the politics of sabotaging your match as well, my lord. She has already wrecked two matches of her own. She's an expert!"

"Really," Henry said. "What would you recommend?"

I thought. Will would be angry with me if the advice I gave didn't consider his needs as well as mine. "Pretend," I said, smiling.

The earl looked puzzled. "I'm not sure I understand."

"They'll be more likely to postpone the wedding if you appear to accept the betrothal. Swoon over Will's sonnets, spend time with him, appear to listen. Let your mother think he swayed you. The spell will take care of the rest."

Henry's eyes danced, his pretty lips turning downward in an appreciative smirk. "That's brilliant."

Relief poured through me. Will would appreciate my efforts on his behalf. The only thing that could go wrong was if Lord Burghley or the countess found out I was involved. "Our consultation must be confidential, my lord."

He nodded, listening. "I will not tell a soul."

"I have nowhere near your mother's stature or your guardian's. I could be imprisoned or executed."

"My lips are sealed."

Henry was so impressed with the proceedings, he gave us another pouch full of sovereigns, explaining that he would send word if he needed additional advice. My mother let out a little yip as soon as we heard him exit the front door. "Brava!"

When I turned to smile at her, she was watching me, her expression thoughtful. Like a jeweller who looks upon a gemstone and thinks, *This has value.*

I am embarrassed by how much this moved me.

<hr />

The next morning, Mary woke me to tell me that she'd just seen an old man leaving Underhill House, and the steward was at his desk writing Richard a letter. As I got out of bed, I felt a subtle tightness in my chest, an irrational certainty that Graves had seen through my deception. Surely the old man wasn't the physician, come to my room to examine me covertly while I slept. Mary couldn't say whether he was the doctor, only that he was wearing a hood and robes.

I hurried downstairs, pretending to be on my way to take Hughe into the courtyard. My heels clicked on the steps. I slipped out of my shoes, pausing at the foot of the staircase. The steward was indeed at his desk, deeply involved in his writing.

I could see only part of his face, but a lantern burned brightly on the far side of his desk. There was an alarming urgency in his rigid

posture, in the set of his jaw. Hughe followed my gaze, letting out
the softest of growls. "Hush," I whispered.

Graves's pen scratched the paper.

I tiptoed closer, ready to slip on my shoes and pretend I was on
my way to take Hughe outside. On the desk beside the letter was
a sheet of thick parchment, letterlocked and sealed with wax. The
seal was imprinted with a glyph like the ones I'd imagined I saw in
Mother's book. I froze, shaken to see one in reality.

Graves sniffed, setting down his pen to wipe his nose with his
handkerchief. Over his shoulder, I could decipher only a few words
on the page he was writing: *Doctor Dee, warning, false angel.* My
chest tightened. Was that who had been here, John Dee? An old
man in a hood and robes. Had Richard written him?

The steward's handwriting was ornate, difficult to read at a distance. Holding my breath, I crept another step closer and tried
again:

> *Dee says the enclosed incantation should conjure the aerial
> spirit he spoke of before, who has knowledge of the occult prop-
> erties of metals. The physician is due to return in three days,
> so we shall have news regarding Mistress Underhill when you
> return . . .*

I must have gasped. Graves straightened and turned to look at
me. I sprung into action, slipping on my shoes, pretending to have
been on my way toward the courtyard door. "Hughe," I said in a
stern tone, as if the dog had done something wrong. "I told you.
You must do that outside—"

Hughe lowered his head and slunk toward the door with such
remorse, I felt guilty. Following him, I nodded at the steward, who
was now shielding the letter from view.

He eyed me suspiciously but said nothing.

Outside, I comforted Hughe, trying to act calm, though my

heart was pounding. *Three days?* The physician wasn't supposed to return until mid-April. He had moved up his visit. We could delay no longer.

That afternoon, Mother and I pretended we were going to market but instead went to look at a retreat in Waltham Forest whose annual rent we could afford. I made her walk on foot for almost a mile before we hired a carriage—outside the city wall, to make sure we weren't being followed. On the way, I tried to talk to her about where she sold the ring, but she continued to deny that she had taken it. Her stubbornness was infuriating.

Swan House, the cottage was called, for the crafty flock of wild swans that kept nesting in the pond in a nearby clearing, no matter what the swan collectors did. It was remote enough that Richard wouldn't easily find us, but not so distant that it would discourage wealthy London clients.

The landlord's steward met us at the road where a dirt lane turned into a thicket of oaks and birch. Closer to the house, there were lime trees; the floral fragrance as you approached was energising. I took my time walking down the lane, taking it all in, imagining what our life there would be like. There would be no worries about our clients being spotted by neighbours.

The house was an old stone cottage with a walled courtyard edged with sweet-blossomed lime trees. Mother would have room for a garden and beehives. A service-tree guarded the door just like the one at Cecely's. The observation brought a pang.

Behind it stretched a tiny pasture—room for Edmund and Hughe to run, a cow, some chickens—a tiny barn, a pond. The steward said the swans from which the farm took its name would return to the pond in a few weeks to breed. The garden courtyard was almost overgrown with thyme, dianthus, rosemary, crocuses, and other blooms already buzzing with bees. A shock of the forget-me-nots my father loved grew beside the gate.

Mother caught my eyes with a pleading look.

I turned to the landlord's steward. "We'll take it."

I thought I would feel relieved when I finally found another place to stay. Instead, I suffered from a nagging unease, the sense that the accomplishment was hollow. At first I thought avoiding Will might be affecting my mood, but it had been only a few days, and I hadn't been particularly tempted to go to him.

The next day, Mary caught us packing and asked where we were going. "To see a cousin," I told her.

She eyed my portmantle, which was stuffed to the brim with everything I had brought to London and all the dresses I had bought since. My virginal sat on the trunk beside it. "Nay, but tell me the truth, miss."

"Why do you ask?"

"Is it too far to travel to St. Helen's on Sundays?"

I searched her face. "It would be a very long walk."

"Graves is making things difficult for me." She met my gaze, her warm brown eyes worried. "He gives me so many tasks on Saturday that I struggle to finish them before church. He resents my desire to be christened. He says I should stop acting like an Englishwoman, that no matter how hard I try, I'll never be one. If you would have me, madam, I would go with you."

A pit formed in my stomach. It would be a risk to take her, but I couldn't live with myself if I left her behind. "You must promise never to tell anyone in the Underhill household where we've gone."

She nodded, agreeing without argument.

9

The next morning, Mother informed Graves that we were leaving to see family and asked him to send a groomsman with us to help move our luggage onto the boat. The decision was less about convenience than it was about ensuring that the steward knew that we left the city. Graves glared down his nose at us with apprehension. I knew from his letter what was bothering him: that I would miss the physician's visit. "Master Underhill left strict instructions about the prospect of you travelling, Mistress Rose," he sniffed. "You are not to leave the city."

"I doubt he would uphold those instructions if he knew why we were leaving," Mother said, her indignance matching his. "We just received word that my sister-in-law has succumbed to an ague. She may not survive, and she's the only family member who remains on good terms with us. We simply must see her."

Her speech was so convincing, I felt a brief pang of concern for Aunt Margery before I remembered my mother was lying. Her falsehood was impressive. A death in the family was probably the only thing that would've convinced the steward to let us go under the circumstances, and she had also planted a seed that would mislead Richard about where to look for us without naming our destination. She was so cunning.

Graves opened his mouth to speak but sputtered. "Well," he sighed. "I suppose—"

In a moment he'd sent for a carriage to take us to the wherry. The last thing I did before I left Underhill House was write a note and leave it in the top drawer of Richard's desk in his study. *Richard,* it read. *My suspicions were right about my condition. I have gone to stay with family. Do not look for me.* I signed it *Rose*, praying he would forget his obsession with me and have our marriage annulled. Or at least never look for me in Waltham Forest.

I placed my marriage ring atop it.

On the carriage ride to the docks, Hughe stared out the window, concerned, and Edmund kept asking who we were going to visit. "Your cousin Lorenzo," Mother answered loud enough for the groomsman to hear. "He lives deep in the marshlands. You've not seen him since you were a baby."

There was no such cousin.

We told the boatsmen to let us off at the next town, then stopped to eat dinner at an inn before we hired a coach to bring us to Swan House. We took a table in the back, Mary seated beside me, and Mother and Edmund across from us. Hughe crept under the table with an eager look in his eyes. When the servant came to see what we wanted, Mother beamed, ordering everything they were serving that day without concern for the cost.

The servant curtsied. "Yes, madam."

As soon as she went away, Edmund launched into a series of rapid-fire questions about his cousin: how old was Lorenzo, where did he live, did he have horses or a dog or children—?

"Jesu Christo," she burst out. "There is no Lorenzo. We're going to our new house in the forest!"

"It's a farm," I added before he could get upset. "Just like we used to have. We'll have chickens and a garden."

"Geese?" Edmund asked hopefully.

The maid returned with our mead.

Mother watched the maid pour. "Better. Swans."

The coach ride to Waltham Forest took the rest of the afternoon.

Swan House was even more beautiful at dusk than it had been the day we visited, idyllic. The ancient trees that shaded the lane, the stone cottage, the lime blossoms buzzing with bees. It was twilight, the sky alight with a purple glow, the air full of the odour of leaves and blooms and loam. As I got out of the coach, I saw the barn and—in the distance—a single swan gliding over the pond. I couldn't help but think of the farmhouse where I grew up.

The thought of our old home brought back memories. My father on his sickbed, telling me about his decision, his eyes full of regret, enlarged by his spectacles. Cecely and I, laughing on our way to Gravesend to buy perry. Something rose in my throat as I surveyed our new residence, a grief as wide as the sea. I stood beside the coach, trying to master it before I followed my mother and Edmund inside. I touched the place where my father's ring should have been with a sudden thought. I had been blaming myself for everything that had happened, but none of it would've happened without my mother's maddening need to find me a husband.

I stood there, fists clenched, rooted to the spot for a quarter of an hour. I went inside only when Edmund called me. "Rose! Come see!"

The landlord's steward had left a note for us on the door. *Several deliveries today.*

Inside we found beds occupying the three bedrooms. In the kitchen, a large table with two sturdy benches. There were curule chairs in the parlour, finer than I had ever owned, stretched with brocade. Behind them, on the wall before a fancy table, was a gold-embroidered, rich black tapestry, showing stars and planets in their ecliptics. I shivered at the sight of it, feeling as if it was something I would've bought for myself.

A sealed note sat upon the table. I tore it open. *Mistress—All's well, will call soon, with gratitude—WH.* Henry. I had sent him a sealed message when we found Swan House, letting him know we had procured a "summer house" and asking him to keep the address secret.

My excitement at our new lodgings quickly dissipated, my unease returning. I had a nagging sense of emptiness, as if changing houses had accomplished nothing. On my first morning there, I woke disoriented. The bedcurtains Henry sent were thick; my bed was dark. In the moment between sleeping and waking, I thought I was lying beside Cecely at Underhill House. When I realised where I was, I felt a powerful sense of *wrongness*.

I decided to write her a letter.

Outside the bedcurtains, my room was still. The house was quiet; no one was yet awake. The room was suffused with a soft grey light. I tied my wrapping gown tight about me and went to the parlour with my quill pen, ink, and paper. But when I sat at the desk to write, the blank page stared back at me, unwritten upon, defiant. I wanted to right the *wrongness* between me and Cecely, but I didn't know how. I couldn't be too specific; Cecely would have to ask someone to read it to her. It took me an hour and four attempts to write a draft I was happy with.

By the time I was finished, the room was bright with morning sun. I put on a heavy cape and hood, despite the spring weather, and walked through the forest to the nearest post house, jumping at every sound I heard. With Richard home so soon, I needed to ensure I wasn't seen. If he heard I was still living near London, he would be much more likely to pursue me.

I had to take a deep breath before I entered the post house, my heart pounding at the idea of sending the letter. It was stilted, inauthentic. There was so much it didn't say. But the sense of wrongness I had felt that morning haunted me. Pulling my hood down to shade my face, I made myself go in and post it. The draft I sent went something like this:

Good Cecely Weaver,

With regret at the way our last meeting ended, I am writing to inform you that we have changed house. Should you need to find me, we

*are renting a place in Waltham Forest. All's well—well enough that
I would be delighted if you travelled west to visit. Please let me hear
from you. And so I bid you farewell. From Swan House, Great Monk
Wood.*

Your assured friend while I draw breath,

R

As I walked out of the post house, the sun seemed too bright,
and my heart was heavy.

I should have been proud of everything I'd accomplished. I was
free of Richard. I had my own home, an income. The music I had
composed for the Henry play had been performed for thousands of
playgoers. It had run for half a dozen nights in two different theatres;
my share of the subsequent nights' ticket sales would be considerable. I'd found a generous patron in the earl, an accomplishment
regardless of how dangerous Will claimed that alliance was.

The real danger was that Richard was coming home, and I had
no idea how he would take the note I had left him. The boy I'd
known growing up was too proud, too righteous, too proper to
marry a girl like me. Even if it were true that he fancied me as a
boy, he would've sought an annulment as soon as he read my letter. But the new Richard was unpredictable. I feared that the spell,
or my sabotage of it, had raised an unnatural anger in him. I felt as
if I didn't know him at all: openly affectionate, possessed with his
father's contract, desperate enough to consult *non-angelical* spirits.
Who in the world was this person?

At least Mother had seen to it that if Richard tried to find me,
he would look elsewhere first, but there was no telling where he'd
look once he realised we weren't with the Rushes. As much as I
loved performing, I decided it would be best to stop playing at
the brothel until we knew how he would react to my departure.
On the next day I was supposed to perform, I sent a cryptic note

without a return address apologising to Luce and went, cloaked, into the nearest village to post it.

I knew I couldn't put off seeing Will much longer. My anger at him was fading, but his anger at me would grow beyond recovery if I stayed away too long. Our relationship was like a loose thread. If pulled, it too could unravel the whole of my plans. A few days after we arrived at Swan House, my longing finally outpaced my anger. I told myself I needed to ensure that he understood that Henry's apparent change of heart was my doing, but the truth was, I wanted to see him.

I asked Mary to help me change into my clothes, my heart fluttering with anticipation, though whenever I thought about his disapproval of my work for the earl, a subtle, cold sensation travelled through my chest.

The late-afternoon sun shone through the window, sending an uneasy raft of light over the southern part of my room. I checked my reflection in the mirror, then hurried downstairs. I told Mother I had unfinished business with the dramatist, pulling down my hood on the way out to prevent anyone from recognising me, then hiring a coach in the village.

My stomach grew more and more unsettled as the coach approached the boardinghouse. When I finally arrived at the door, I could hear the landlady and her husband bickering from outside; the husband kept yelling the phrase *a whole sovereign* over and over. The landlady opened the door, waving me upstairs without a word. No sooner had I set foot on the staircase than they went back to arguing.

The noise unsettled me. My progression up the stairs was slow, as I thought about how much depended upon Will being happy with me, how miserable I'd been lately.

He didn't answer my knock at first. For a moment, I thought I would have to talk myself into coming back another time. I was turning to go when I heard footsteps inside; he was pacing. I had to force myself to face the door again. "*Will?*" I called, knocking more loudly.

The pacing stopped.

"It's Rose. I need to talk to you."

The door opened. Will was wearing a half-tucked tunic and breeches. The tunic was loose, half-buttoned. I could see the compact muscles of his chest. He glared at me, his gaze as distant, aloof, as it had been when we first met. A traitorous urge to make him look at me worshipfully again swept through me, followed by a wave of disgust with myself.

"What do you want?" he said crossly, pulling a small clump of wool from each of his ears. "I'm trying to write."

"May I come in?"

"That depends on why you've come."

"It's about the earl."

He eyed me sceptically, then opened the door. He cleared his desk of papers quickly before I could read them, moved the stack to the table beside the bed, and motioned for me to sit at the desk. Then he lit the candle in a nearby wall sconce and sat in the only other chair, leaning against one of its arms to watch me with a cynical expression.

"The sequel?" I asked, nodding at the papers he'd moved, hoping to get him talking about his work because it improved his mood.

"Something else," he said in a dismissive tone. "Say what you came here to say."

I searched out his eyes, my expression apologetic. "Henry came to see me, Will. I couldn't refuse him."

Will glared at me, his eyes narrowing to angry slits.

"Not like that!" I held up a hand. "I advised him to pretend to agree to the betrothal. To swoon over your sonnets to his mother, to appear to be swayed by them."

Will blinked. This was clearly not what he thought I would say. "Why would you do that?"

"It serves all three of us. I get a new client. You appear to be successful. Henry gets goodwill from Burghley and his mother, so he can postpone the wedding until he's old enough to refuse it."

Will raised his eyebrows. "And he agreed? That would ensure my success. Who thought of this?"

I smirked, shaking my head. "I did."

"I've never known a woman so shrewd."

I searched his face, wondering if he was being facetious. His eyes were wide, his surprise genuine. It took all my willpower not to roll my eyes. He had met women as shrewd as I was, no doubt. He just didn't see it because he didn't expect to. "You should meet my mother. Katarina Rushe would confound you."

He blinked—once, twice—as if he were trying to decide how to react to my snappishness. Finally, he laughed. "Give me a moment." He walked over to the desk and wet his quill pen, jotting something down. The nib scratched the paper. He blew on the ink to dry it, then read over it.

"Does this settle our disagreement?"

"Peace," he said, holding up a hand.

I watched his expression—a subtle smirk—as he finally set the page with the others, thinking again of everything I could lose if he turned on me. My freedom from Richard, Henry's confidence. He could even turn Lord Burghley and the countess against me if he wanted.

Would he do such a thing? He guarded his true nature close. He was complicated, contradictory. Both flatterer and peacock, manipulator and people-pleaser. He had a sullen streak; beneath his arrogance was a dark insecurity, which I had seen in flashes in the bedroom. And beneath that, so buried he might not even be aware of it, a deep need to be loved.

That was probably the most dangerous thing about him.

"You are much like me," he said finally, interrupting my thoughts.

I blinked at him, realising with horror that he was right. Every conclusion I'd just drawn about him was also true about myself. I hated him for the insight.

He watched me, an inscrutable smile playing at his lips. Something had come over him. His voice was taunting. "I couldn't have met my double in a woman."

His statement was less a compliment than it was a challenge. Defiance surged through me, the urge to prove to him that it was possible. I felt a sudden flush of warmth as I remembered the pleasure we took in one another.

"Will," I began, but for perhaps the first time in my life I didn't know what to say next, torn between my resentment and my desire to kiss him.

"Rose," he said, that smile still pulling at his lips. His amusement had spread into his eyes. "Have you gone mute?"

"No," I managed to say. My chair was hard beneath my thighs, and I couldn't help but think how soft the featherbed would be beneath us.

"Come, come," he said, smirking. "We both know where this ends."

He held out his hand.

I wish I could say that I refused him, or that I went to him because I calculated that it would be wise to do so. But the truth, the embarrassing truth, is that I went to him because I wanted to.

We saw each other almost nightly after that. It was a long ride to Shoreditch, but I never invited him to come to me. Sometimes we met at his boardinghouse, sometimes at an inn near the halfway point between our two homes. He brought mead. I wore a hood so I wouldn't be recognised. The danger was thrilling. Our encounters were delicious enough that I forgot my unease.

Henry visited again on the first of May, by which time I knew

Richard must have come home. I was becoming worried about how he'd reacted to my note, whether he would search for me and how relentlessly. But we had prepared for this. Of my acquaintances in London, only the earl knew my address, and he had sworn not to tell anyone.

The earl looked out of place in his embroidery-studded navy brocade doublet, his high lace collar, his voluminous breeches, and his supple knee-high boots. At the door he asked if he could see the room he had furnished for me to see clients.

I led him into the small chamber, where my instruments lay on the table beside my atlas and my calculating notebook.

The tapestry dominated the room with its shining goldwork and celestial patterns. One window looked out over the courtyard. Through the other, we could see a single swan swimming in the pond, and the wood beyond it.

"I like what you've done with the place."

I laughed. There was no furniture but the things he'd sent over.

"I wanted to thank you in person. Your suggestions worked beautifully. My mother and Lord Burghley were happy to postpone the wedding for a few years. There's someone else to whom I'd like to recommend your services if you agree."

"Of course, please do," I said, amazed at how quickly what we'd hoped for was happening—until I was struck with a sudden fear that my name would spread to the wrong person.

Mother must've had the same thought. She cleared her throat from the doorway. "Can you rely on this person to be discreet? It would be risky for anyone who doesn't approve of the full scope of our work to know of it."

"It's John Dee's wife, Jane. I heard her tell her husband that she wishes she could speak to a woman occultist." He cleared his throat. "I need a favour from her."

I swallowed. Richard knew John Dee well enough to ask him for advice. Were they close enough for Richard to know Jane too?

Mother glanced at me, a hungry look in her eyes.

I knew what she was thinking. The Dees were extremely well connected. If we could become known to them as astrologers for women, we would soon have an excess of clients.

Mother smiled. "She wouldn't tell your mother or Burghley?"

He shook his head. "John has been accused of witchcraft himself. Jane understands the need for discretion."

"She is welcome," I said quickly, as it occurred to me there was another benefit of saying yes. Jane might know something of the glyph I'd seen on her husband's letter.

The following evening, a middle-aged woman arrived on our doorstep in a bonnet and a lovely but faded blue gown, her skirt supported by a ridiculously large Spanish farthingale.

"Good day," she said with a brisk nod, clasping a pale blue purse with embroidered strings in her gloved hands. "Mistress Notte, I presume? How do you do?"

"Quite well. Mistress Dee?"

She nodded. "Jane, please. Born Fromond."

"Good day. Welcome."

She stepped through the doorway. Before I shut it, I looked out at the beautiful lane and breathed in the heady floral scent of the flowers, the loam, the green scent of all those trees. The setting sun was shining through their branches, casting a beautiful net of shadow and light over the lane. I was in the best mood I'd been in for days; the previous night had been especially delightful.

As I closed the door, I noticed that the wrinkles around Jane's pretty blue eyes crooked down in a permanently harried—or perhaps pained—expression.

"Forgive me for coming so soon," she said, pulling off her gloves. "We return to Mortlake tomorrow."

"It's no trouble. We're honoured to have you."

"What a charming home. Lord Southampton said you are new to the area?"

"Indeed." I smiled. "Come this way."

I led Jane into the parlour and gestured for her to sit in the curule chair on the other side of my desk. I sat across the table from her.

I had seen my mother speak with clients so many times over the course of my childhood that I had no trouble setting the atmosphere for the session. I lit the candles I had placed in sconces behind my desk, then made a steeple with my hands and smiled at her, unblinking. Fully aware of the black dress I had chosen, the kohl with which I'd lined my eyes, the cascade of voluminous black curls that fell to my shoulders.

Jane would no doubt understand that I was cultivating a mystique. But at the same time I suspected she would not be immune to the effect.

She drew herself up. "I've never had a session with anyone but John, so forgive me if this is a bit wayward. A friend once urged me to go to Simon Foreman, but I didn't like him." She met my eyes. "I get feelings about people. Senses. Like a watery vapour they carry with them. His was dark, putrid, and corrupt, like a fetid swamp. I left before he could do the reading."

The description was so similar to my own experience, I froze. "Putrid. Did it have a scent?"

"Like a blacksmith's shop during a thunderstorm: iron and fire, lightning in the air."

Mars and Saturn. I wondered if the malefics were strong influences in his chart.

"Can you sense mine?"

"Fire and roses. Copper and iron."

"Intriguing," I said, thinking of the location of Venus in my chart and my sun sign—Aries. In many ways the combination ruled me. I wondered if the auras I had smelled were something similar. Then I remembered my task, pulling my notebook toward me. "Tell me the time and place of your birth."

"April 22, 1555. The ninth hour after dawn, Cheyham."

"Both the moon and the sun in Taurus. I can see why you're with your husband. A spiritual person would be perfect for you." I filled in the rest of the chart, explaining how her influences affected her, mostly to prove myself since I knew her husband would've cast her chart before. "Mars in Virgo. You probably run an orderly household. You'll feel most fulfilled when you're serving others. Saturn in Aries. You will suffer from a conflict between action and self-doubt, constantly worrying that you are deficient. Your twelfth house, the house of intuition and inner life, is Cancer. That's probably why you're so sensitive to others' feelings. Does any of this resonate?"

She lifted her eyebrows, impressed. "Very much."

"Good. Tell me what you want to know."

She sniffed, shaking her head, convulsing suddenly with an involuntary shiver. As she opened her mouth to speak, the downward lines at the edges of her eyes grew deeper. "Henry said you would be discreet. What I am about to say must remain confidential."

"Of course. All I ask is the same discretion from you."

She nodded. "This is mortifying, so I'll have out with it quickly. I can't even speak to the parson about it, I'm so embarrassed."

I nodded, giving her a sympathetic look. "Don't be."

She took a deep breath, then fixed her eyes somewhere on the wall over my shoulder. She spoke in an automatic voice, the words tumbling out. "When we were in Trebona, my husband's scryer deceived him into believing that he spoke with an angel in his mirror who ordered them to share everything, including their *wives*—"

There she paused, her eyes flitting briefly to meet mine, liquid and ashamed. Then she hurried to say the rest of what she had to say, clearly wishing the conversation would be over quickly.

"We left Edward in Trebona, God be praised. I should have said at the outset that I *hated* him from the moment I met him. The vapour he emanated was worse than Foreman's. Polluted, treacherous. John attributed it to the melancholy disposition that he seeks out in his scryers, but I've never met anyone this ungodly. It made my skin crawl just to be in the same room with him. You can imagine how horrible it was to—" She stopped, shuddering. "This was four years ago. My son Theodore—"

My heart broke for her.

Jane cleared her throat, fighting to blink back tears. I couldn't believe the ordeal this woman had endured—with her husband's blessing! How could he think an angel would sanction an unwilling coupling?

"My own vapour has shifted since then. Become darker. As if some bit of whatever force taints him entered me that night. I need to exorcise it or forget the night altogether. And stop imagining *Edward's* wife with *John*. Joan was blameless in all of it, like me. We had no choice. We have since learned without a doubt that Edward was lying. But at the time I tried to tell John, he was so deeply under Edward's influence that he wouldn't listen. Edward has a way of convincing people of things."

That was when it hit me that she was talking about Edward Kelley, the same man Richard and Humphrie had gone to see in Bohemia. Of course. *False angel*, Graves's letter had said, *warning*. I thought of everything I knew about Richard, how desperate he was to complete his father's work, how unpredictable he'd become since my mother witched him. How far would he go to complete his father's contract? Would Kelley take advantage of him?

I blinked, forcing myself back into the present moment.

"Please don't judge me," she was saying. "I am an otherwise chaste woman."

"Mistress Dee—"

"Please. Call me Jane. I have just told you my darkest secret."

"Jane, then. There is nothing to judge. You and your husband were duped."

"John is not blameless. Edward was only able to dupe him because of his pride."

"I understand. I didn't want to implicate him—"

She shook her head. "I do. He shouldn't have pressured me. Can you help?"

My heart went out to her. I closed my eyes and sent up a quick prayer for the queen of heaven to guide me. The room around us was still except for the flickering candles, which were wholly responsible for the movement of the shadows in the corner. The room felt empty.

"Yes." I drew myself up. "Saturn is in Cancer right now. He will be for the next two years. This is the season for learning lessons about the boundaries between yourself and others. Yours are porous. The mist you sense, the way you've carried that piece of Edward around inside you. I'm afraid for your own well-being you need to cast it out, then wall yourself up, set up boundaries between yourselves and others."

She nodded, her expression fierce, determined.

I thought about the rituals I'd read in my mother's book. There was one that was supposed to be for addressing this problem, though she had always sent me away so she could cast it in private. *For releasing hurt,* it was called. "My mother has a ritual for this. If you don't mind, I'd like to call her in. I won't tell her the details, but—"

Jane nodded.

I related some of what Jane had told me to my mother, who confirmed that she had a ritual for this circumstance. I showed her Jane's nativity, the instincts that comprised her temperament. Mother seemed grateful for something to do.

When we first arrived at Swan House, she had seemed the most relaxed I'd ever seen her. She had spent hours watching the swans, drinking mead, enjoying herself. But as the days passed, she had become restless, as if she didn't know what to do with herself. As I explained what Jane needed, I could see the purpose that animated her when she was with clients returning.

Mother warned Jane that the ritual she had to use for this was hard on the subject. It made things worse before it made things better. Jane thought about this and nodded once, the pained lines at the edges of her eyes turning hopeful.

Mother left the room and returned quickly with a brazier and wolfsbane and a pair of long black gloves. It took her only a moment to set up, lighting the candle, picking the wolfsbane into tiny shreds so we could burn it. Then she handed the gloves to Jane. "Put these on."

Jane complied, eager. "Now what?"

"Hold out your palm." She put the pile of shredded wolfsbane in Jane's hand. "Now close your fist around them. Good. We're going to connect the wolfsbane to your memories of Edward. The worst ones, the ones you can't stop thinking about. You're going to visualize them one by one, then burn them."

Jane's grip tightened. A determined glint appeared in her blue eyes, or perhaps it was only the candle flame's reflection.

"Are you ready?"

She nodded.

"Open your hand. Stare into the fire. Watch the flames, feel their power. Fire cleanses. Good. Now take the first piece of wolfsbane. Imagine the worst memory you have of that man, the whole thing, walk through it. Then drop the wolfsbane into the fire, repeating these words. *Regina Caeli, roudos! Transeat a me dolor iste.*"

Jane was silent for a long moment, her eyelids moving the way they move in sleep. Her expression turned sour, then angry; she looked like she was going to cry.

As I watched her, I felt a sympathetic despair, an uncomfortable compassion for whatever she imagined. For a moment, I thought I saw it: Jane, following a shadowy man into a bedchamber, reluctant.

Terrible candlelight. Jane's fingers wrapped tight around the stem of a blood red glass of claret. Then it was gone, and I shook the image from my head, unsettled. It had been too easy to imagine.

Jane squared her shoulders and opened her eyes, pinching a shred of wolfsbane with gloved fingers and dropping it into the flames.

It sizzled, releasing a foul-smelling, putrid smoke. Dark and ominous. After a moment, the wolfsbane scent cleared. I could not help but note I smelled nothing but the spell ingredients.

Jane was crying. Her expression was so vulnerable, tears sprung to my eyes. I hoped this would work for her.

"You did it," Mother said in a gentle voice. "It always feels worse before it feels better."

I had never seen her be so compassionate with anyone but Edmund. I thought of all the times she had looked at me with disapproval and hatred. A bizarre despair clutched at my throat, so strong I had to suppress a sob.

"Now think of the next worst memory that bothers you."

The orange flames flashed in Jane's eyes. She had picked up another shred of wolfsbane eagerly. "It feels so good to watch it burn."

Mother nodded. "That means it's working."

We walked her through the process three more times until the hand with which Jane held the wolfsbane began to tremble. She looked up at my mother, shaking her head, her lips curving downward, trembling. "I don't think I can do this anymore. It's becoming too painful."

"Sometimes it takes two or three sessions."

Jane searched my mother's face, her expression pleading. "May I come back another time?"

"I was going to suggest just that. There's no rush," Mother said softly, taking Jane's hand and squeezing it. I watched her, feeling as if she had been replaced by some kind of double-walker. Who was this compassionate woman? It hit me then, how complex the human temperament is, how even someone as choleric as my mother could show watery instincts.

It stung that she had never done so for me.

Jane broke into a grateful smile. "Thank you. How much do I owe you for today?" she asked, reaching for her purse.

Mother looked at her faded gown, the pain in her expression, then shook her head. "However much you can afford."

My mouth fell open. I had never heard her say this before.

"What?" Jane said, fumbling in her purse. The coins inside it jingled. "Don't be ridiculous. You can't—"

"The person who taught me that ritual made me promise never to withhold it from anyone who needed it. It's—special. Sacred, if you will."

Jane pulled an angel, a noble, and a crown from her purse. The gold glinted in the candlelight. "Here is what I brought. Please. Take it."

Mother took the coins. "Jane. The mind has a way of burying unpleasant memories. This ritual, the remembering, stirs them up. Other memories may become vivid over the next few days, memories connected to the hurts you released today. Come back as soon as you feel ready, and we'll work on releasing the rest of them."

Jane nodded. "I will."

I walked her out. "Jane," I said softly, remembering the glyph I had seen on her husband's letter.

She paused in the doorway, wrinkles crinkling around the edges of her eyes—painful memories.

"Is it true your husband speaks to spirits? Or was Kelley only duping him?"

She drew a deep breath. "He does—or did when Kelley was here. They spoke *through* Kelley, so it was difficult to tell what was true and what wasn't."

I paused, trying to think of a subtle way to ask what I wanted to know. "Did they use a special language to summon them?"

"Yes. Kelley claimed to have learned it from an angel."

"Have you seen it written?"

"No." Her voice cracked with such pain that I regretted prying.

I touched her hand. "I'm sorry. I hope what we did today helps."

She nodded, squared her shoulders, then stepped into the night. For night it was, nearly midnight. The stars were out, and the moon was rising.

Returning to the parlour, I found my mother standing at the window, looking out. The sight of her stirred up my jealousy over how gentle she'd been to Jane. I searched her face, wanting to ask her where she'd been hiding that compassion, that soothing voice, when I was a girl. Why hadn't she offered me the same kindness that she showed Jane, that she showed my brothers? I wanted to ask, but when I opened my mouth, I couldn't find the words. A pit formed in my stomach. "Is what you said about not withholding that ritual true?"

"Yes," Mother said. "But also, the more satisfied she is with her session, the better for us."

Her answer comforted me in a selfish way; here was the mother I had come to expect. Another question occurred to me, a safer one that didn't require me to be vulnerable. "Who taught you that ritual?"

Mother took a deep breath, her black eyes gleaming with an eerie sort of knowledge. I wasn't certain if she would tell me, but I thought there was a chance. Finally, she shook her head, closed her eyes, and answered.

"My mother."

⁓

In bed that night, I couldn't stop thinking about what Kelley might have whispered in Richard's ear when Richard talked about me. For Richard was very like to confide in Kelley, unless my mother's spell had faded with distance. Unease filled my breast, fear, a desperate need to be comforted. The unloved feeling that my mother's behaviour to Jane had stirred in me was unbearable. I felt like a child again, alone, rejected, watching my mother ruffle the first Edmund's hair from the doorway.

I tossed and turned in the beautiful bed the earl had sent, my emotions swinging between hurt and anger like a pendulum. The soft sheets, the warm coverlet, the beautiful embroidered bedcurtains did nothing to soothe me.

I kept thinking of Cecely, the maternal way she ran her hand through my hair. How the gesture unravelled me. The memory of kindness in her black eyes, the desperate way we clung to one another before she left. I pressed my eyes tight and imagined her beside me, the nightgown that always slipped off her shoulder, the pink curve of her hip beneath it.

The longer I lay there, the more uncomfortable I became. The more fulsome, the more lonely. I told myself I would send another letter to Cecely through her aunt in the morning. It had been three weeks since I sent my first and she had not replied. It must've been too vague to entice her to visit. I hadn't even told her that we changed house because I had left Richard. If I apologised more clearly, explained the situation, and begged her to come, I truly believed she might. But the thought did nothing to soothe my present loneliness. In the dark, in my nightgown, now, I wanted—*needed*—someone to hold me.

Taking a deep breath, I sat up in bed. I pulled on my gown, trying without success to lace my bodice myself. I needed to leave before I changed my mind. It was a terrible idea to go to Will when I felt this broken. I knew it was. But that didn't stop me.

Soon the candle I lit woke Mary, who sat up in the truckle bed, rubbing her eyes. "Where are you going at this hour, madam?"

It was probably four in the morning. I felt a flush of heat in my cheeks, my own shame rushing up to meet the judgement I expected. "I have business with the dramatist that can't wait," I said in a weak voice.

She looked at me with such a startled expression that I felt a pang of guilt. She helped me dress. As she fastened the last hook, she said formally, "There you are, madam. Is there anything else I can do?"

I shook my head. "No. I'm sorry to wake you."

I grabbed my coat and slunk out of the cottage.

The sun was turning the sky above the cottage a vague sort of grey; the lane glowed with the shadowy alertness of the night before dawn. The woods on either side of it were still dark. The air was chilly, and there was dew on the grass. I carried the decision to confide in Will down the lane, guarding it carefully, the way you shield a candle with your hand. Already, I could feel my pride—or was it caution?—threatening to extinguish it.

The scent of the lime blossoms was less prominent so late at night, or so early, perhaps because the blooms were closed. I hurried down the lane, heels growing muddy with the dew that frosted the earth. By the time I reached the village, it was not so difficult to hire a horse.

I didn't knock on the door of the boardinghouse. I simply opened it and let myself in. I stood on the landing outside Will's room for a long moment, gathering my courage. But as I stood there, I thought I heard movement inside. Footsteps, a murmuring sound. He was awake, pacing, talking to himself with a rhythm that sounded almost like an incantation.

"Will?" I whispered. The footsteps and murmuring stopped. The door creaked open.

"What are you doing here?" he snapped with a distraction that indicated I had disturbed his writing. His eyes burned like a madman's.

"I couldn't sleep," I said, my decision to confide in him faltering. He was too absorbed in his work to comfort me. The only thing I could talk to him about when he was like this was whatever he was writing. I sighed, resigning myself to another sort of encounter than the one I wanted.

"Come in. I want your thoughts on something."

The sonnets he read to me that night were the strangest and most beautiful things I had ever seen him write up to that point. His plays were collaborations between him and his company, but these poems were all his own, written in a fit of inspiration. There were half a dozen of them, and I had no idea what to make of them at first. They had nothing to do with his commission.

The first compared Henry to a summer's day, his face to the eye of heaven, and claimed to make him immortal with its lines. Another spoke of the way his thoughts kept returning to the earl when he tried to sleep. They were beautiful, so intimate, they made me jealous.

I sat on the bed, uneasy, my respect for him as a poet growing. Here was the inspiration that proved itself in scattered fragments of his plays sustained for the duration of fourteen lines. Even their music was original, dispensing with the Italian structure and using another that turned only at the end. The effect of the final couplet was a rhetorical whiplash.

"What do you think?" he asked when he was finished reading the last poem. His eyes were hopeful, burning with an almost boyish excitement.

"They're brilliant," I said quietly, and I meant it.

He broke into a boyish grin. "Aren't they?"

"Will. You should use that structure to revise the others. Are these for the commission?"

"No," he said helplessly. "I'm still not satisfied with those. I don't know what these are. They came fully formed."

I understood what he meant, reminded of the furious melody I had heard on the way back from Gravesend. "Sometimes the music just comes."

He smiled at me, held out a hand.

I hesitated, wanting to take it, but knowing that if I did, I would cry. I was too in need of comfort. I closed my eyes, trying to swallow my fear. *I want*, my heart said. *I need. I can't be alone any longer.* When I opened my eyes, he was watching me, his brow raised in surprise. The coldness in his eyes had faded, replaced by a cautious warmth.

I took his hand, letting him pull me to him, the tears already coming.

10

I woke hours later in Will's bed, uneasy at the sight of him beside me. I hadn't managed to hold anything back at all. I had sobbed to him about how much I missed my father, how cold and manipulative my mother was. How I had ruined everything with Cecely, my dearest friend. At one point, he had listened so closely, I suspected he was storing the information away for a play. I felt naked, used, in more ways than one.

When Will opened his eyes and bade me a bleary good morning, my embarrassment came rushing back.

He must've read my face. "We don't have to talk about it ever again," he said easily, squeezing my hand, then changed the subject. "Come with me to Southampton House tonight. Henry wants to hear the sonnets. Help me pick one or two to read."

Once it was clear that no one else would be there, I agreed to go with him. We chose the best two poems, reading them aloud, revising them, counting feet until they kept time perfectly. I watched over his shoulder as he copied them in his florid handwriting. Then I left, hiring a carriage to bring me as close as I dared to home, too undone to send my letter to Cecely.

At Swan House, I took a long bath infused with lavender, then slept, hoping to recover the pieces of my shredded pride, but I still felt off balance when I left for Shoreditch. My thoughts whirled for the entirety of the carriage ride, chaotic.

When Will climbed into the carriage beside me, he was kind enough—or self-absorbed enough—to pretend nothing had changed. He left me to my own thoughts. I was grateful at first for the privacy, then puzzled, then irrationally hurt that he hadn't asked about the feelings I was hiding.

I cursed my inner clinginess, worried I'd made a mistake by opening my heart to him—or anyone. I was not designed for emotional involvement. Nor was he, it seemed. As we approached Southampton House, I couldn't help but wonder what configuration of stars had conspired to make a man so like me.

The mansion rose before us like a high tomb against the black sky. The only lights were the torches burning along the walkway that led to the door of the mansion. The night was gloomy, a mist settling down over the streets.

Will became more and more agitated as the residence loomed, tapping his foot against the floor of the carriage rapidly, his hand on the satchel full of papers at his hip. He peered out the window, eyes wide, as if our carriage was galloping at top speed toward a cliff.

"Do you really think these sonnets are ready to show him?" Will asked, his gold-flecked eyes pensive. "He's had access to court, tutors. I've heard him tear other poets apart."

I stared at him, understanding his anxiety, but mildly irritated. The second poem he was going to read was *brilliant*. I had told him a dozen times last night already. Why did he need to be praised so constantly?

His wife must know, I thought suddenly. There was no way Will could be anywhere long without finding someone to feed his self-affection. There would have been another woman before me.

"Rose?"

I sighed. Too irritated to praise the poems again, I took a different tack. "You needn't worry about him being too harsh," I said begrudgingly. "His lordship worships you."

Will nodded, but his restlessness didn't ease. As the carriage rocked to a halt, his muscles tensed and he leapt out as soon as it stopped. The torches glittered, bright orange.

The steward opened the door. "Good Shakespeare," he said formally, blinking as I climbed out after him. "And good, er—"

"Mistress Ravenna Notte."

The steward bowed. He led us inside, up the grand staircase, and into the anteroom outside Henry's chamber. "The earl is sitting for a portrait," he said, then called through the door. "My lord, Shakespeare is here with a Mistress Notte."

"Send them in!" Henry called back.

The steward opened the door and disappeared. Will leaned toward me. "The artist is very famous. He keeps asking to work earlier in the day when the light is better, but Henry refuses to get up before four in the afternoon." His tone was amused, indulgent, the way my father had once spoken of me. *That's Henry for you*, his eyes said. *Passing dissolute, but what can you do?* A notable shift from before when he made jokes about Henry and Narcissus.

The artist hurried out, a middle-aged man with a slick brown moustache. An apprentice clutching his box of paints scurried out after him with an affrighted expression, as if he felt lucky to be escaping with his life. "Have at him," the painter said to us in a vaguely French accent, with a mocking lift of his eyebrow.

"Will! Ravenna!"

We found Henry standing beside a table, where a glass of brandy-wine or perhaps claret sat. In the corner, an easel stood covered with a tarp. As we entered, the earl interlaced his fingers and stretched his arms to the ceiling, his black velvet doublet riding up to show his tapered waist. He yawned, rolling his shoulders. "Forgive me. I've been sitting for that damned portrait for *hours*." He reached for his drink, turning to Will with a mischievous smile. "Did you bring the sonnets?"

Will smiled. "I did."

Henry rang the bell and a servant appeared in the doorway. "Your lordship?"

Henry held up his glass. "Bring two more of these, claret, and something from the kitchen."

The servant bowed and vanished.

Will walked over to the painting and lifted the tarp. Beneath it, a rough image of Henry looked out, unfinished, a sketch of his face awash with only a single layer of colour. Peach skin, golden curls of long hair, flat geometries of white and blue in the shape of a lace collar. Unnoteworthy in its current form despite the artist's fame: the rough foundation for a painting.

"I haven't given him much time. He insists on leaving when the light changes."

The servant returned with refreshments. Claret in wineglasses made of sugar-plate, tartlets smeared with damson and apple cheese, which made my mouth water. One bite of the tartlets, and I was in heaven.

"Marvellous, aren't they? Our cook does astonishing things with fruit. And the sugar-plate adds such a lovely sweetness to the wine, don't you think?"

When I agreed, he nodded to Will, raising his eyebrows ironically. "Let's hear how you're going to convince me."

Will opened his bag and brought out the pages we had selected together. Then he cleared his throat, and, summoning the full force of his charm, launched into the first poem we'd chosen with far more confidence than he had shown that morning.

"*From fairest creatures we desire increase...*" Will's voice was a melodic tenor capable of a wide range of emotion. Flattering, when he called Henry *the world's fresh ornament* and *only herald to the gaudy spring*. Sardonic, when he scolded the earl on behalf of his mother. "*Thou, contracted to thine own bright eyes...*"

Impressions flitted across the earl's face like shadows on glass: satisfaction, mischief, amusement. When Will read the final couplet, the earl laughed and shook his head. "Quite a trick," he said, shaking his head disdainfully. "Mother will love it. What's this other one? Is it on the same theme?"

"No. It was written for your lordship."

"I see," Henry said, intrigued, sending Will that rakish smile again. He looked so eager to hear the sonnet that he seemed a boy performing the role of the young Earl of Southampton instead of the earl himself. "Let's hear it."

Will gave him a smile that was almost shy, the confidence with which he'd read the first poem faltering. He closed his eyes for a moment, then launched into the second sonnet we'd picked, the best of the poems he'd written the previous night in a fury. His voice as he read the first line was hesitant. "*Shall I compare thee to a summer's day?*" he murmured, meeting the earl's eyes, as if he were asking permission in earnest.

Henry nodded, and Will went on a bit more easily. As the argument progressed, the earl's expression turned solemn and astonished. He set down his glass of claret, rising slightly in his seat. "Read it again," he said as soon as Will had finished.

Will blinked—once, twice—a faint blush colouring his cheeks. Then he started over at the beginning of the poem, confidence returning. This time, he read more fluidly, his eyes flitting up to meet Henry's as he finished each line. By the second quatrain, their eyes had locked, and Will was reciting from memory. "*Sometime too hot the eye of heaven shines, and often is his gold complexion dimm'd . . .*"

Henry swallowed, his expression turning solemn as Will read the third quatrain. His fingers so tight around his glass of claret, I thought he might break it. "*But thy eternal summer shall not fade, nor lose possession of that fair thou ow'st . . .*"

By the ending couplet, Henry looked like he had stopped breathing. "Let me see that."

Will handed him the page. The earl's eyes darted over it. "*So long as men can breathe or eyes can see, so long lives this, and this gives life to thee.* Will—" Henry met his gaze, his pale blue eyes overcome with feeling. "This is beautiful."

"Thank you, your lordship."

"Simply marvellous—that volta! You must write more in this

vein," he said, handing the paper back. "I would like to offer you a commission, Will, to begin as soon as you finish my mother's. You can jot those last few poems off soon, can't you?" Will nodded. "Why don't both of you come back tomorrow evening for supper? I have invited a few other guests. A small gathering. Jane will be there, Ravenna. She wants to speak with you about a potential client."

"I would love to," Will said.

I hesitated to accept. There was no way to tell what someone like Henry meant when he said "a small gathering," and this time, there would be no guises. Richard or someone he knew could be there. But it would be evening: dark, candlelit. I could lurk about on the edge of things and wear a veil that shaded my face. If a potential client was there, we could put the money toward next year's lease. My heart pounded.

I took a deep breath and nodded. "I'll come."

On the ride home from Southampton House, Will was in such a celebratory mood, he half undressed me in the carriage. Certain of himself, kissing me hard on the neck, the shoulder, and lower. When the driver stopped in front of his boardinghouse, he covered my loosened bodice with his coat and pulled me upstairs. A delicious shiver shook me as I anticipated what was to come.

The intimacy we had shared the night before was still present. Will was confident, magnetic, commanding, as temporarily sure of himself as he had been after the play. But after he lit the candle and pressed me to the bed, his expression became distracted. He tried to fight it, but it was too strong. When he apologised and went to his desk, I realised he had been writing a poem in his head.

I watched him from the bed, clutching the bedsheets to my breast, more than a little miffed. The candle sputtered.

"Just a moment, I have to get this down."

I closed my eyes, embarrassed. The momentum of our time in the carriage was quickly dissipating. I could hear his quill pen scratching the paper. My thoughts wandered to the second letter I had meant to send to Cecely. I had gotten so caught up with Will and Henry that I had let another day pass without sending it.

The scratching stopped. Will put away his quill pen, then came back to bed, apologising with a series of kisses along my neck.

It took me ages to get back into the mood, but I managed.

The following morning, when I told my mother about the earl's invitation, she was nervous about my decision to go. "Unmasked? Are you sure?" She bombarded me so forcefully with counsel that I had to send her out.

I was grateful for the solitude of my bath, but my mother's anxiety exacerbated my own. After dinner, I selected the black confection I had worn to the masquerade with a different black overskirt that was almost funereal and a black cape. Mary pinned my hair into a black coif with a spray of dark lace that cast my face in shadow. The only splash of brightness in the whole ensemble were tiny seed pearls that shone against the black lace like stars.

The ride to Southampton House was long enough for my stomach to become completely unsettled. When I finally got there, Will was waiting for me outside with an impatient expression. When he hurried in, my knees locked, and I felt rooted to the spot where I stood. *Tranquilla sum*, I thought. *Tranquilla ero*—

Stepping inside, I was relieved to see a single long table in the hall. It was lit with a candelabra, garlands of spring flowers. There were only a dozen place settings. A huge sugar sculpture glistened on the table. I scanned the hall for the Underhills. When I saw that neither of them was there, I breathed a sigh of relief.

On the far side of the room, however, I saw Lord Burghley, Henry's mother, and Jane Dee clustered together, talking. My chest tightened at the sight of the man who stood beside Jane. He was unmistakably her husband with his grey beard, long black robes, and white hat. Henry hadn't mentioned that John Dee would be here.

Remembering what he and Kelley had done, I felt a stab of anger. I wanted to confront him, to ask how he could do such a thing to his wife. Then I remembered the aerial spirit he'd advised Richard to consult, the language he knew, the glyph. But I was so angry, I didn't trust myself to ask him about it. Besides, how would I explain why I was asking? I couldn't exactly tell the truth. *I read a letter Richard Underhill's steward was writing without his knowledge before I fled the household—*

It would be a disaster.

On the other side of the room, Kit, the dramatist from the tavern, was smoking his pipe in a corner with Henry; the two men were drinking and speaking animatedly. When Will saw them, his eyes widened and he pulled me over to join them, grumbling, "Kit Marlowe, you sycophantic prick—"

As we were making our way over, Burghley invited everyone to be seated. Kit and Henry began making their way to the table, deep in conversation. As soon as it seemed Henry had chosen a chair, Will smiled at Henry, slipping into the single available seat beside him before Kit could.

"Will! Ravenna!" Henry said, his blue eyes brightening. "I was beginning to wonder if you were coming."

For a moment, Kit stood beside the chair Will had taken from him, as if he were startled by Will's rudeness. Then he lifted his eyebrows at Will as if to acknowledge that he'd been bested, and found a seat beside a beautiful gentleman with shining black hair.

From the opposite end of the table, Jane sent me a helpless look as she sat beside her husband. He was speaking to several guests I didn't recognise, gesturing in a grandiose fashion that made me roll my eyes. Seeing my expression, Jane smirked, bringing her hand to her mouth to suppress a titter.

There was an amusement in her eyes, a condescension, which told me she was having at least some small measure of success with distancing herself from her overweening husband. Good for her, I thought. She deserved all the distance she could manage.

I hoped she would speak to me alone, but after dinner, I saw both Dees approaching the corner where I was conversing with Henry and Will. A cold sensation travelled through my chest at the prospect of speaking to this man. I wanted nothing to do with him. Henry saw him coming, rolled his eyes, and pulled Will away to find a drink. They were halfway across the room by the time Jane addressed me.

"Mistress Ravenna," she said with a curtsy and a smile that implied I was going to like what she was going to say. "How good it is to see you again."

The conjurer nodded in the dignified manner for which he was famous, then took in my hair, my eyes, my clothes. I had to suppress my urge to glare at him; the best I could manage was to nod at him stiffly.

"Mistress Notte. A forbidding name for a forbidding woman," John said, lifting his eyebrows. "Jane, you neglected to tell me she was so beautiful."

His appreciation made me stomach-qualmed.

"Forgive me," Jane said with a subtle roll of her eyes.

John pretended to kiss my hand. I had to force myself to curtsy politely. He knows Richard, I reminded myself. Don't be too memorable.

He leaned toward me, looked around to make sure no one was eavesdropping, and lowered his voice. "Jane tells me you are something of an astromancer."

My chest tightened. I glanced at Jane, hurt. She had promised not to tell anyone. She shook her head with a look that suggested I should listen to what her husband wanted to tell me. "So it is said."

John watched me steadily, his brown eyes sad, almost gentle. "I wanted to thank you for what you did for Jane. She will not say what you did, only that it brought her mind to much-needed rest."

My throat tightened. Was the damage already done? I closed my eyes, taking a deep breath, startled to find such softness beneath John's grandiose exterior, a love for his wife that I hadn't expected to see. Perhaps Edward really did dupe him, I thought. But of course Jane was right too; without the doctor's surplus of self-affection, his ridiculous need to *prove* himself, he would not have been susceptible to Edward's lies.

I wondered about their dynamic. John's grandiosity, Jane's self-doubt and eagerness to serve. It would be difficult for her to overcome. I drew a deep breath, irritated with the ridiculous convolutions of the male temperament. Beneath the confident persona of every man, it seemed, was an insecure little boy.

"I was happy to help."

"There is a woman I have been unable to counsel. Her stars are thwarting, and she wasn't comfortable stating her query to me. Jane believes she would be more candid with a woman."

Jane caught my eye. "She's a noblewoman with extensive resources."

I raised my eyebrows. So this was why she had brought him over. The client was his recommendation. "Go on."

John went on. "She has always paid well for my services. That said, I suspect she would want to see you anonymously. Would you be open to that?"

"Of course," I said hurriedly, eager to secure this client if her patronage would be as lucrative as Jane implied. "There is no reason for me to know a person's identity to cast their chart. I only need know the details of their birth."

"I'll ask her," John said, promising to send a messenger when he had her answer. "Don't tell anyone about this."

"Of course. Discretion is as important to me."

John nodded sagely, his eyes full of sympathy.

My memory of the rest of the revel is a blur. I kept to myself, avoiding the other guests, speaking only to Will and Henry. I was silent, enjoying the mead the servants kept pouring, but triumphant, wondering who the noblewoman would be. A baroness? Perhaps even a duchess? If this client was as lucrative as Jane implied, we might save enough to buy Swan House outright.

I may have celebrated a bit too zealously. I started with mead, but Henry kept sending for claret, then brandywine, until Will was more intoxicated than I had ever seen him, and I felt as if I were floating.

Hours later, when all the other guests had left and the servants had long ago finished cleaning the hall, Henry invited Will and me to follow him upstairs.

The upper stories of the mansion were completely dark. We stumbled up the grand staircase. I had to take off my heels so I wouldn't trip on the steps. The servants had gone to bed, except for the steward, who woke reluctantly when Henry rang the bell. Henry sent him to find claret and sugar-plate glasses. He asked for music too, but the steward apologised with a stern expression that the musicians had gone home.

The three of us laughed at how judgemental he was, though when I look back on that night now, I pity him. Forced to serve three entitled merrymakers who had no consideration of how tired he must have been. After he brought us drink, we retired to the balcony behind Henry's bedchamber, which looked over an extravagant courtyard. The steward, his task completed, disappeared.

We sat beside one another at the corner of the balcony. Henry, then Will, then me. Will put his head on my shoulder, his expression dizzied. Beside him, Henry kept touching Will's arm to get his attention. I remember being shocked at how *close* they seemed. How familiar the earl was being with both of us.

It was starry outside, and there were flowery vines blooming on the trellis. I drank so much, my memory is shadowy. I could not tell you what the flowers were. Only that they were large, fragrant, sweet, and white.

It was the turning point between night and morning: when the sky's ghost-grey and you feel awe that you're awake at all. The air was unseasonably cool.

Henry sat reclining against the wall, his legs outstretched, one knee bent to the sky. Trixie found us not long after we ventured outside, circling his ankle, pressing her body against it. The earl petted her absent-mindedly.

I removed my heels and veil. Will was still leaning against me, his legs tucked beneath him, running his finger around the top of the cup the way Luce once had.

The thought of Luce brought back thoughts of Cecely, who had been with me when I saw her make the gesture. My emotions were so wild, so uncontrolled from all the drink, I was suddenly certain that I would never hear from her again.

I managed to turn my sob into a stifled sort of moan. Will met my eyes, a question. *Are you well?* I held up a hand, lifting my drink to my mouth. *I will be.* Will nodded, turning his attention back to Henry, who was watching the two of us with interest.

"How long have you two been lying together?"

I blinked at him, shocked. Despite my own penchant for bluntness, I was surprised at how direct the earl was. I had never met someone daring enough to flout the conventions of polite society quite so flagrantly. I would have respected it, I think, had the bluntness not been directed at my private matters.

"Since February," Will said offhandedly, as if he were unbothered by Henry's prying.

The earl met both our eyes, setting down his sugar-plate glass, still half-full of claret. His pale blue eyes sparkled with the pleasure of provocation. "Is it serious?"

"He's married."

"Serious enough," said Will.

Henry picked the sugar-plate goblet back up, inspecting it as if it were a jewel or a painting, as if he were looking for cracks. *What is the value of this thing*, he seemed to be thinking. *What is it worth?* Then something passed over his face, some hidden resentment or great boredom. With a violent flick of his wrist, he cracked the goblet against the railing like an egg.

The sugar-plate shattered. Claret began to leak out, a thin trickle of red, so much like blood I shivered.

The earl watched it drip, stain the floor of the balcony with an expression that was only mildly interested.

In the same way that he had looked like a boy playing a young man earlier, now he looked like a much older man trapped in a youth's body. Trixie approached the pool of wine and sniffed it, then walked away, tail up, disinterested.

Neither Will nor I spoke.

"Kiss," the earl said in a thin voice, setting down his glass, meeting each of our eyes in turn. "I want to watch."

The surprise of his request, following the sudden violence of his gesture, knocked every conscious thought from my head. I sputtered, making a series of startled vowel sounds that didn't quite succeed in forming words. Suddenly I felt completely sober.

Will cleared his throat. "Pardon, your lordship?"

He met each of our eyes again, his pupils liquid with a sudden, intense sorrow. "You're going to do it later."

I shook my head, disconcerted by the sudden shift in his demeanour. His emotions were as changeable as the weather. "Are you in earnest, your lordship?"

"Quite."

I shivered, stricken with a sudden frisson. He's accustomed to making outrageous requests, I realised, accustomed to having them fulfilled. His expression reminded me of what—in my inebriation and shock—I had forgotten. Both of us were dependent upon

Henry for income, and he knew too much for us to risk embarrassing him.

Henry met my gaze, a strange look on his face. "Indulge me," he said in a tight voice, his eyes crinkling with what I thought was a trace of desperation. I searched his face, trying to understand what made him want this. Whatever it was, it possessed him completely. "It's only a kiss."

Will shook his head at me, chuckling with a thin and somewhat forced amusement. *That Henry*, his eyes said again. *Passing dissolute, but what can you do?* I thought I saw apology there too, and traces of a prurient interest that, searching my own spirit, I realised I shared.

Will pulled me onto his lap. Something fluttered in my belly, and lower, a tingle, a warmth. An anticipation of the pleasure that I had come to know when I met Will's controlling persona in bed—of being relieved of responsibility for my actions. But instead of cupping my chin to turn my mouth toward him, Will was watching Henry. He stared at the earl, and Henry at him, for a long moment. Then Will shifted his gaze to mine, full of a surprising want.

His kiss was harder than any he had pressed upon me before, more desperate. I had drunk so much mead. I kissed him back, very aware of the fact that Henry was watching. I could feel Will's desire for me pressing my thigh. I pushed into him and he gasped. Henry made a small sound beside us.

I opened my eyes, glancing up at him over Will's shoulder.

Henry had the strangest expression on his face. His eyes were liquid, dazed with want, incredibly blue and pale and sad. There were pained lines at their edges, and his lips were parted slightly with a tortured expectancy. I didn't understand it at first, his sorrow, that ache. And then, suddenly, I did, remembering what Will had said before I met the earl. Henry was so powerful, so rich, he could do anything he wanted. I closed my eyes tight. I had seen something I wasn't supposed to.

Henry wanted Will.

I feigned illness as soon as I could without being obvious, leaving the two of them to continue drinking on the balcony. I was in such a rush to leave, I forgot my heels.

It must have been almost five by then, and no carriages were out. No coaches, and all the groomsmen were asleep. I would have to walk all the way from Southampton House to Waltham Forest, wary of shadows and cutpurses, anyone who might disturb a well-dressed woman's walk. I tripped along as best I could in stockinged feet, wishing I had brought Hughe. Too inebriated to run very quickly—or notice if anyone saw me.

The walk was long and cold. I pulled my cape tight about me to ward off the chill, alternately dizzy and nauseated. My thoughts turned to the way Will's gaze had lingered on Henry before we kissed, the difficulty Will was having with the commissioned sonnets, the passion with which he was writing new ones, the way he'd paused during our last encounter to jot some lines down. I felt a rush of jealousy, but it was soon tinged with concern. Will and Henry didn't live together like Cecely and I had. People would talk. They were already far too intimate in public. Henry was so rich, so well connected, he would never face charges. But Will, a merchant's son, a poet—

As I thought on it, my head began to ache.

It was only after I passed through Shoreditch that I thought to pull down the hood of my cape.

By the time I reached Waltham Forest, it was morning, and my throat was parched. The leaves rustled. I could hear deer in the woods, twigs breaking beneath their hooves. I stuck to the middle of the road, watching my step, trying not to tear my stockings, though I knew the attempt would fail.

As I neared Swan House, my hurt feelings transformed into a disconcerting combination of anger and shame. I felt sick over the performance we had put on for Henry, what it might have meant to *both* of them—although I was fairly certain Will was unaware of how he felt.

I needed to confront Will and tell him that things couldn't continue the way they had been going. I thought of Will's wife, his children. I had tried to convince myself that if not me, it would've been someone else, and I was obviously right. But thinking of that woman in Stratford-upon-Avon, raising his children and waiting for him to come home, I knew I couldn't continue seeing him.

The realisation hurt. I knew I would long for him still, no matter how he felt about Henry or how I felt about his wife. Our desire was like a sickness.

By the time I reached Swan House, my stockings were shredded, and I was weak with the excesses of the night before. My skin crawled and I felt filthy.

Mary offered to draw me a bath. She was kind enough to suspend the pity and judgement with which she usually looked at me when I came home like this, and which today I wouldn't have been able to bear. I lowered myself into the hot water, closing my eyes, wishing the heat could scald away the subtle queasiness that nagged at me, the unease, but of course it couldn't.

Then I slept. Long, deep. I woke in the evening, dusk filtering through the open window like a beautiful plague. When the usual time came for me to go to Will's house, I did not go. Nor did I go the next day, or the next. My desire for Will became difficult to ignore, especially at night, but I knew it was too unhealthy to indulge further.

Henry sent gifts. A tapestry embroidered with an image of purple hyacinths, a design signifying apology, regret. An invitation to pay for me to sit for Nicholas Hilliard, the queen's favourite artist, who could perhaps paint my likeness on a pendant or locket. A bribe, I thought, not to tell anyone.

Will must've persuaded Henry somehow to give him my address, because a note from him came every day:

R— Where are you? It has been too long. Come as soon as you can. —W

R— One more night alone, and I shall have to be confined. I am frantic-mad for you. I went to the Abbey to see you perform, but Luce said you no longer played. Pity me and come as soon as you are well. —W

R— Desire is death. My fever will not abate, and there is no physic but you. Is it safe for me to come to you? If I do not hear from you, I shall. —W

I answered none of them until the last, to which I replied with only three words, *Do not come.*

Dee sent word that our new client would send for me the following night. The carriage would bring me to an undisclosed location where the session would take place. I was to bring my instruments with me.

I spent the rest of that day preparing. I planned my attire, packed my instruments, and sent Mary out to purchase a new quill pen with which I could draw horoscopes. That night, weary, anxious, I found myself thinking of Will's ignorance about his desire for the earl. The way his body responded when the earl asked us to kiss. All the signs that he shared the earl's interest, which he refused to acknowledge.

How could he be so unaware of his own feelings?

The thought startled me. I blinked, suddenly wide awake, a familiar thought—uncertain, hesitant—struggling to emerge like the memory of a dream. This time, I let it come. My breath caught. How like him I was. How foolish I was not to see it. I had told myself I was incapable of love, prickly, walled up, but my encounters with Cecely had been soft, beautiful, intimate, with none of the *fraughtness*, the struggle, of my encounters with Will. Something bound me to her, the celestial opposition of our signs, her air to my fire. She fed me.

I got out of bed, uncertain what to do or say. This insight had been so long in coming, it might be too late to do anything about it. Cecely could already be betrothed to someone in Norwich. I needed to find her, ask if she shared my feelings, and—if she did—stop her from making a mistake. But how would I find her? She was so angry when last we spoke. Would her aunt even tell me her address?

Should I go to Gravesend and beg for it? My current situation was fragile. My business with Will unfinished, Henry sending me bribes, the size of my new client's purse unknown. I closed my eyes, my resolve faltering.

Perhaps I should wait to find her until after I saw our new client and had settled things with Will. He would be angry with me for ending our affair. He was so insecure, so dependent upon me for praise—and criticism—so desperate to continue our affair and superstitious about our arrangement. Perhaps I could blame my desire to end things on his marriage or help him acknowledge his feelings for the earl. If he accepted that *he* had caused our parting, perhaps he would be less likely to lash out at me.

I thought on this and got into bed, drawing the bedcurtains, then lay back down to try to sleep. I needed to be well rested when I saw our new client.

⁓

The next night when the knock on the door came, I took a deep breath, trying to master myself. I hadn't slept well, and I was far more anxious than I would've liked. I opened the door to find a fine black carriage glowing dimly in the torchlight. A middle-aged man stood beside it in a flat cap, his beard trimmed and his moustache oiled.

"Right this way, mistress," the driver said, holding up his torch.

I climbed into the carriage, astronomical instruments rattling in my bag, painfully aware of how much depended upon this excursion.

My farthingale made it difficult to sit inside the carriage, but I managed, its black skirt arcing foolishly over my lap. I was so preoccupied with the damned thing, I didn't pay attention to which way the carriage turned at the end of the lane. When I finally tried to look out the window to see where we were going, I realised the shutters were bolted shut.

Soon the clop of the horses' hooves turned to thuds. All I could tell was that the carriage had turned north in the opposite direction from London. The ride was surprisingly long; it felt like hours before the carriage took several sharp turns and finally stopped. Stomach fluttering, I thought of Cecely as I slid toward the carriage door, the money I would need to convince her to come back to London.

The carriage driver, opening the door, handed me a pair of pattens to protect my shoes from the muck. The carriage had stopped in a wood so dark that, despite the driver's lantern, I could barely see my feet to strap them on. The ground was sludge, muddied from a recent rain; our progress was slow going. It was a quarter of an hour before we approached a clearing with a shadowy structure.

The driver held up his lantern. A flickering circle of light brightened the clearing. At its centre stood an extravagant hunting lodge. Stone walls, stained-glass windows, a garden. There were two guards at the door. I heard something in the shadows beyond the treeline and felt a chill. I hurried toward the door, handed the driver my pattens, and stepped inside.

The lodge was lit with wall sconces. They flickered, casting a foreboding web of shadow over the floor. The hall in which I stood was full of ancient-looking furniture, well-made, polished. There were furs on the floor, gorgeous tapestries on the walls. At the back of the residence, another guard stood stationed at the doorway to a dim room.

Inside, a woman was sitting at a table. From the doorway I could see only her silhouette. Behind her, a small fire burned in a brazier to chase away the night's chill. There were candles on all four of the walls and a lantern at the table where she sat. She was tall, and her dress was capacious, grey, and nondescript, but well-made; a voluminous hood cast her face in shadow. She looked up as I walked in, meeting my gaze, the whites of her dark eyes bright. Though she was wearing only a few rings and no other jewellery, I knew by her regal—almost piercing—gaze that she was a baroness at least, maybe even a duchess.

"Mistress Notte," she said slowly, taking care to enunciate every word. "It is a pleasure to make your acquaintance."

I hesitated to approach her, wondering how to greet her. She was the wife of a knight at the very least. I curtsied, bowing my head and averting my eyes. "The honour is mine, your ladyship. May I sit?"

She nodded. Beneath her hood, her face was gaunt and covered in subtle pocks. There were large gaps between her teeth that betrayed a lifetime of eating sweets. Her dark eyes were troubled. She looked as if she was in her late fifties, and apparently, like me, she eschewed face paint. Her features bespoke a former handsomeness—a symmetrical bone structure, well-defined lips— and her dark eyes were as watchful and aloof as Will's.

"The information I give you today must not go farther than this room. You are not here. Nor am I. This lodge is empty. "

"I require discretion as well, your ladyship."

"Good. I have powerful friends."

I saw the comment for what it was: a threat. "I would be your ladyship's friend too if she will do me the honour, though I cannot boast much power except divination."

A soft chuckle echoed in her throat. "Well said. To the point. I want you to cast the nativity of a man who is courting a woman's favour and interpret it. I need to know his proclivities when it comes to—" Her lips curved slightly downward in a prim smirk. "Matters of love, as well as his trustworthiness with money. I am hoping for good tidings, but I fear already they will be ill. When we are finished, you will destroy the horoscope in that fire."

I bowed my head, arranging my instruments on the table between us. "Tell me the hour and place of his birth, your ladyship."

She waited for me to have my quill pen at the ready. When I met her eyes, she spoke. "November 10, 1567, the third hour after dawn." She paused, clearing her throat. "Bromyard."

I began the calculations, wondering about her situation as I filled in the chart. Judging by the air with which she commanded the guards, the way her presence filled the room, I thought she must be a widow in charge of her own household. The man courting her favour must be a suitor she didn't know if she could trust, but he was only a few years older than me. I wondered if he might be a suitor for her daughter. As I completed the horoscope, she shifted uneasily.

"Mmm," I said when I had finished, sending up a quick prayer to the queen of heaven for guidance. "A conjunction of the moon and Mars in Cancer in the eighth house," I said quietly, a note of disappointment creeping into my voice. I had hoped to have good news for her. "The eighth house is the house of sex, death, and other people's possessions. This man will seek relationships with people for material reasons. He will tend toward reckless action and spend others' money without thinking."

She winced. "And if his love had Venus and the sun in *her* eighth house, the synastry?"

I blinked at her, doing my best to hide my curiosity over whether *she* was the love. "Without the rest of the other chart, I cannot say for sure, your ladyship, but given such a configuration, the attraction between the two would be almost impossible to resist."

She shook her head with a laugh that despite her best efforts sounded pained. "What is your opinion, then, on how she should proceed with him?"

I paused, uncertain whether to be honest with her. Based on the details I had, the conclusion was plain. This man would be a terrible choice for a husband—all that aggression in the house of desire, his reckless nature, his spending. Any partnership with him was like to end in disaster. It was possible the answer would be more positive if I cast the other chart and looked at the synastry, but it was clear she wanted to keep that information secret.

It took me longer than I would have liked to decide. I needed her to be happy with my reading so she would pay me well. But I had never lied to anyone about a chart, and it felt wrong to do so. "I suspect this is not what you want to hear, your ladyship, but a relationship with this man would be risky for anyone. He is like to act rashly, to be profligate. If he doesn't struggle mightily against his influences, the consequences of developing any sort of dependence on him could be disastrous."

She cleared her throat, her hand going to her clavicle, her eyes closing with a barely concealed disappointment. "Very well," she said in a tight voice. "I appreciate your honesty. Everything you said has the ring of truth."

Her expression was tired, resigned. I stood, bowed very deep, and turned to go.

"Mistress Notte," she said as I opened the door.

"Yes?"

"The fire."

I remembered her directions. I went back to the table and threw the paper into the flames. It made a crackling sound as it blackened.

"The guard at the door has your payment. I cannot emphasize

enough the need for discretion." It took me a moment to parse what she said next, it was so at odds with her tone. She spoke as calmly as if she were speaking of the weather. "If you speak of this meeting to anyone, I will see you hanged."

I bowed, bending my head to stare at the thick rug on the floor. The firelight in the room made it appear to be a dim brown the colour of dried blood. As I stared at it, I wondered if her payment would be large enough to compensate for this risk. Perhaps she would be so concerned about guaranteeing my confidence that she could afford to pay me as well as Henry. "I will not tell a soul."

"I appreciate your advice. If I am ever in need of divination again, I shall contact you."

The pouch the guard handed me at the door was heavy; the coins clinked with the deep notes of gold, not the tinkle of silver. I was dying to open it and look inside, to see what manner of coins were within, but I knew better to wait until I was alone.

I fingered them in the carriage. It was too dark to tell, but I hoped they were sovereigns. There were at least forty. It wasn't until I lit a candle at Swan House to inspect them that I saw what they were. Fine sovereigns, each worth half again as much as the coins Henry had given me. Enough, with what we had already saved, to purchase Swan House outright.

"Who was it?" my mother breathed, rushing downstairs. "Where did they take you?"

I shook my head, slipping past her. "Even if I did know, I couldn't tell you."

In the morning, the first thing I did was reach up to check the pouch that I had worn around my neck, thinking about how I could use it to convince Cecely to come back to London. I thought my best chance was to go to Gravesend myself and prove how successful we'd become, how independent. If she wasn't there yet, I would convince her aunt to tell me where to find her in Norwich. It wouldn't be too long a journey by coach.

I hid the pouch under a floorboard beneath the trunk in my room. It made me anxious to have so much money hidden in the house, but I had to settle things with Will before I spent it.

His eyes widened when I showed up outside his rooms later that day, and a complicated series of expressions flitted across his face. Relief, then anger, a flash of wounded pride. When he spoke, his voice was tight, controlled. "It's been almost a week."

"May I come in? We need to talk."

He met my gaze, nodded, and opened the door wide.

Inside, the lanterns on the wall were burning and the window-less room was as light as it got, day or night. I sat in the chair across from the bed. Will raised his eyebrows—usually one of us sat on the bed—then turned the chair of his desk around and straddled it, watching me warily. Stretching his fingers, gripping the rail of the chair, then letting it go, over and over. "Out with it."

"I have been thinking of your wife and your children."

He closed his eyes. "Have you."

I thought of his jealousy, the way he always fought me for control in bed. I thought of the brutal treatment of Lavinia I had heard about in *Titus*.

"I am not without compassion."

He let go of the chair, inspecting the back of his hand idly. Then his eyes travelled back up to meet mine, perfectly cold, expression-less. Catlike, golden. I had the uncanny sensation that he could see into my soul, and I felt suddenly naked. I closed my eyes, struggling to find a way to approach the subject of our parting that would position *me*, not him, as the victim.

"My wife is aware that when I'm in London, I am my own man." He searched out my eyes. "I'm gone too long for her to expect otherwise. I send back a great deal of money."

"The thought of her nags at me."

"And your husband? Does the thought of *him* nag at you?"

The truth was it did not. I thought of Richard only with regard to my fears of being discovered. "It's not the same. We have no children. We have never even shared a bed."

"I have difficulty believing that."

"You haven't met him."

His lip quivered with amusement, despite everything. He never failed to laugh when I mocked Richard: the nobleman whose wife he'd stolen.

"I—" I closed my eyes, taking a deep breath. My courage was faltering. Then I thought of Cecely, sweet Cecely, and I reminded myself of how Will put off our lovemaking to write the earl a poem, the way he'd looked at Henry before he kissed me. End things, I told myself. Be done with him. "There's another reason we may wish to stop seeing one another. One that will perhaps be more important to you."

He rolled his eyes. "What's that?"

"Henry worships you."

Will blinked—once, twice—his expression confused. "Of course he does. You said this before. He wishes he could write, but nothing comes to him."

I shook my head. "His affection for you runs deeper than that. When we kissed, his expression was *tortured*."

He stared at me blankly, then realised what I was saying. His eyes flashed. "It's *you* he likes. Don't pretend you don't know it."

"Will—"

He stood, shaking his head furiously, and began to pace the chamber. "That low-cut bodice, your mournful eyes. The other night, you looked like some dark Venus fallen to Earth. He's been sending you gifts, he told me. A bed! A goldwork tapestry! I never should have introduced you—"

"Will. Look at me."

The soft sound of my voice startled him. His anger abated slightly, and he stopped pacing, met my eyes. I let the moment stretch out as long as I could, giving him time to consider what I had said. Silence does far more to change opinions than speech.

"Have you ever seen him look at a woman with interest?"

Will began to shake his head rapidly. "Don't be ridiculous."

"I have heard the way you speak of him. You are very fond. Indulgent of his foibles."

"I am seeking his favour," he breathed, biting the words off.

I didn't answer, waiting.

He stood perfectly still, his eyes closed, all the muscles in his body tight. "Get out," he growled.

There it was. Good. Let him think this was his idea.

"I'm no fool," he said in a voice trembling with quiet rage. "I see what you're doing. It wounds me that you chose to slander me and my friend rather than *say* you wanted an end."

My stomach dropped. He knew me better than I thought he did.

"And Henry. Henry—" His voice shook with fury. He glared at me. "To accuse an *earl*, a feckless youth, the Lord Burghley's charge, of such things to his beneficiary. From your position! It's reckless, like everything you do. You are a walking curse."

His criticism was like a slap in the face. "I curse the day I met you."

"Get out. Now." His eyes glittered with a furious condescension. "Good luck with your astromancy. I hope it's lucrative enough to compensate for the commissions you won't be getting from me."

I narrowed my eyes. "It already has been."

11

On the way home, I thought about what had happened and what the consequences might be. The more I reflected, the more certain I was that I'd acted wisely. No matter how popular Will's plays became, he would have far less influence than the Dees and Henry, and if Will decided to *tell* Henry what I'd said, it would likely have the opposite effect from what he wanted.

Henry's request to see us kiss, I was almost certain, was an opening move in a chess game that he wanted to end with him and Will in bed. I had planted a seed in Will's thoughts and gotten myself out of the way. I had done the earl a favour.

As soon as I arrived at Swan House, I retrieved the pouch and set about purchasing everything I needed for my trip to Gravesend. It took the rest of that day and part of the next, but soon everything was ready.

Hughe wouldn't let me leave without him; he jumped into the new coach before I got in myself. The driver's whip cracked and the horses—black shining beasts—galloped along the road. The seats were comfortable, the windows decorated. A coach fit for a lady, a show of wealth like the gown I had chosen, my black cap, my veil, my shoes, the pendant set with rubies that I had purchased from a well-known jeweller. *I can provide for you*, these things said. *I'm safe, I'm successful, I'm stable. See? The life we want* is *possible.*

The pouch still contained enough money to purchase Swan House from its owners.

The ride to Gravesend seemed endless. Thank goodness for Hughe, calming me, nestling at my feet. I stroked his head, terrified Cecely wouldn't be at her aunt's, that she might already have married.

I was so ill at ease, I must've smoothed my dress a thousand times. There was a spot of dirt on my overskirt that I kept trying to rub off with my handkerchief. Hughe kept changing positions, reflecting my anxiety.

By the time the coach arrived in Gravesend, it was the golden hour between afternoon and night. The sky was a bright bliss of pink; the evening star was shining. My pulse fluttered as the driver stopped in front of Cecely's aunt's house. I said a quick prayer for the queen of heaven to bless me, then got out of the coach. The kitchen shutters were open. I could hear voices rising and falling.

One of them was Cecely's. My heart leapt.

"For the last time, there's no altering it," she was saying in a tight voice. Even angry, her voice made me tear up, filling me with a rush of relief so dizzying, I teetered on my heels.

Hughe whimpered, his eyes darting toward the kitchen.

"I'll be right back, boy," I told him. "I'm going to get her."

He went quiet, panting happily.

The pink sky felt too close as I turned to walk toward the door. Time seemed to slow. Everything depended on this moment. It wasn't until I drew near the house that it occurred to me to wonder how long she had been here, why she hadn't responded to my letter. A blue tit landed on a branch of the tree that grew beside the door, scolding me with a loud *churr*. I paused, thinking of the nightbird. But the only voice that perched on my shoulder now was my own. *Go to her*, it said. *Tell her you love her*.

The word *love* stopped me in my tracks. I closed my eyes beneath the service-tree, wavering with a sudden indecision. I had two choices: knock on the door or go home. The first terrified me, but the second would mean a life of regret. The tit churred again, hopping this way and that, protecting her nest.

I thought of Will and the aloof persona he protected himself with, his refusal to acknowledge how he felt about Henry. We were so alike.

I opened my eyes, took a deep breath, and made myself knock on the door. Opening it, Cecely's aunt blinked at my fine clothes and the coach behind me. "*Cecely!*" she shouted in a tone that made it clear that she'd been involved in whatever argument they were having.

Cecely rushed to the door. "*Get inside*," she said, her eyes flitting from my dress to the coach behind me, the horses. "You know Geoffraie's cousin lives next door!"

I stepped into the parlour. She shut the door quickly behind me. I took a deep breath, terrified to say what I had come here to say. But if I wanted her love, I needed to learn to let myself be vulnerable with her.

"I assume Richard is back?"

"I don't know."

Her brows furrowed. "But—the coach. Your gown. Your—" She saw the expensive pendant at my breast and raised her chin, her voice trembling with jealous pride. "Who bought that for you?"

I let the moment stretch out. "I did."

"*What?*"

"I perform at the brothel, and we started an astrology business. The Earl of Southampton is one of my clients. For a time, I was composing music for Will Shakespeare's plays, but you were right about him. He's not trustworthy."

She shook her head, blinking furiously. "Rose—"

"I'm renting a place in Waltham Forest. Didn't you get my letter?"

"I thought Richard moved with you."

She was glaring at me, her black eyes glittering with mistrust. But her eyebrows were slightly raised, as if beneath her suspicion was a hidden well of hope.

I drew myself up, gathering my courage. *Say it*, I told myself.

Trust her. I lowered my voice, looking around to make sure no one was eavesdropping. "I want you to come home with me."

Cecely's lips parted slightly, a softness coming over her face. Then her eyes crinkled with pain, as if the suggestion hurt. "Just like that."

"What do you mean?"

"No word from you for three months—no message, no apology— and you think you can just say the word and I'll come?"

"I sent a letter."

"A notification that your address had changed?!"

Shame coursed through me. "I'm sorry. I—"

"You were seeing Will, weren't you."

"Yes, but I ended it."

Her eyes flashed. "I haven't been exactly chaste either. That's why everyone is so damned tense around here."

The revelation stung. I felt as if she had slapped me in the face, but the truth was she owed me nothing. I had held myself back from her, tried to keep her without offering what she needed in return. I made myself meet her eyes—so black, so furious—trying to master my jealousy, my wounded pride.

"I can give you everything Geoffraie could. A stable roof over your head, fine clothes. You'll never have to worry about whether you'll have enough to eat."

"That's not all I want—"

"*I know.* You want to be mistress of your own house. I'm offering you the chance to live in a house without a master."

She froze, going pale. When she spoke, her voice trembled. "Don't mock me, Rose." She searched my face. "What are you saying?"

For the first time, I let myself see all the feeling beneath the surface of her words—all the pain, the ache that had made her cry at the wedding. She cares for me, I thought, understanding finally what I should've known all along. I took a deep breath, my throat yawning with so much longing I could scarcely speak. *Say it*, I told myself. *Say it.*

"I love you."

She blinked at me, and her face crumpled. "Rose—" Her voice broke. Her hand went to her mouth. Her eyes glistened with tears. There was disbelief and hurt all over her face.

"I love you," I whispered again, my own eyes wet. "I'm sorry I didn't see it before. I've been obtuse."

"Rose," she said, shaking her head, as if she were coming out of a reverie. "No. You can't—"

"What? I'm—" She stiffened, braced herself, as if I were hurting her. "I'm being genuine."

Her answer came out in a rush. "I know you are. You believe every word that comes out of your mouth, even when you're making grand proclamations that you can't possibly fulfil. That's what makes them so seductive."

"This is different. I've wanted you for years."

She glared at me, but I could tell she was wavering. "I'm such a fool," she said through her teeth. "I can't say no to you."

"Then say yes," I whispered, reaching out to wipe the tear from her cheek. "Please. Let me take care of you."

Her face crumpled again. "Do you know how long I've wanted to hear you say that?"

I held out my arms. When we embraced, my skin bloomed with chills, and I was crying again. But I was smiling too, and she was smiling, and my heart felt like it was about to burst with relief and joy. I squeezed her tight, reluctant to let the moment pass. "Cecely," I whispered. "My best friend, my bedmate, my love. Come back with me to London."

Cecely went downstairs to tell her family she was going to leave with me. The conversation went more quickly than I had expected. Their voices stayed low, but I heard enough of what was said to guess what had happened in Norwich. Her mother said *Good*, and her father said *Don't ruin this too*. When she came back upstairs to pack her things, her hands were shaking.

She opened her portmantle and started packing, throwing in her heels, a brush, and a bodice with so much force they made a slapping sound against the leather.

I put my hand on her shoulder. "It doesn't matter what they think."

She froze, taking a deep breath.

"It doesn't matter what *anyone* thinks anymore."

She stiffened. "Those are the words of a madwoman, Rose. It matters. You can't just—*will* the world into something it isn't."

"We're going to live like Luce and Lisabetta. Outside the city, outside the rules. I have wealthy clients, the earl to protect me."

She let out a shaky breath. I took her hands in mine and squeezed them. She searched my face, as if she wanted to absorb whatever confidence she could from me. After a moment, her expression turned defiant, her beautiful black eyes flashing with determination. "If anyone can do this, I suppose it's you."

We carried her things downstairs. She stood in the doorway to her aunt's kitchen for a long moment, silent.

"Goodbye," I heard her father say. Her mother said nothing.

Outside, the evening star glowed, faint and shimmering in the fast-fading twilight. Apart from that, the sky was empty and black. I sent up a quick prayer of gratitude to the queen of heaven. For the first time in a long time, I felt whole. The night seemed to shiver with joy.

The driver smiled at our obvious good cheer, then opened the door for us to get in. Hughe leapt out, bounded toward Cecely, and stood up on his hind legs to lick her face, his tail wagging so hard the back of his body shook. "My goodness," she laughed, patting his side. "I'm happy to see you too."

We clambered up the steps, the dog behind us. Inside the

shadowy coach, I took Cecely's hand and squeezed it. As the wheels lurched into motion, she met my eyes with relief. I felt myself tearing up again. So many times in a single day had to be a record. It was as if the emotions I'd buried in some deep inner dungeon had escaped and were now rioting through the streets.

"How did you do it?" Cecely asked.

I told her the full story, hiding nothing.

She leaned back into her seat, pulling away when I told her about my affair with Will and how it ended. "He's the most dangerous loose end in all of it, I think. He knows too much, and he's a precarious combination of arrogant and insecure."

"That was the feeling I got. Do you think he'll turn on you?"

I explained to her why I thought I was safe: my alliances with Henry and Jane, the earl's feelings for Will, my mystery client.

She shook her head, clearing her throat, impressed. "You would make a good lord. You're so good at strategy."

The words struck a strange chord in me. It was something I had often thought about my mother. "I learned from the best," I said, realising that it was true.

Cecely's brow furrowed. Then she caught my drift. "Yes. I suppose you did." She sighed. "I'm sorry about what I said, Rose. You are no more cruel than I am."

She bit her lips, meeting my eyes, her expression turning so serious and solemn. I knew she wanted me to kiss her.

I closed the panel between the coach and the driver, then the shutters on both sets of windows, so no one could see in. She was still beside me—watching, I presumed, though her face was almost completely in shadow.

When our privacy was assured, I turned to her, putting my hand on her knee. "I've missed you."

"I've missed you too."

"I've never felt safe with anyone else. Not like this."

"Nor have I."

"I was miserable without you. Looking for anything and everything to distract myself." My voice, so heavy with feeling it couldn't support its own weight, broke. "Promise me you'll stay with me."

"I promise," she whispered.

The words were like an aphrodisiac. The shadows seemed to dance, swirling subtly around us, as if they shared my joy. The coach rocked over the bumpy road. Something yawned in my throat. Desire, pure and simple.

My feelings for her were so plain to me now, it was difficult to believe I had ever denied them.

I put my hand behind her neck and leaned in toward her. She parted her lips, wrapped her arms around me, and a shiver shook my shoulders, my arms. A lightheaded giddiness filled me, and I felt myself tearing up again, letting go. There was no fear associated with the sensation, only a feeling of falling, a surrender.

"Rose—" she murmured, pressing herself to me, and I felt a quickening of my breath, my heartbeat. With her so close, I could smell notes of a faint, familiar scent that I can describe only as her. I slipped my hand down her side to unfasten the hooks of her bodice.

As she melted into me, her bodice came away in my hand. She shivered when I slid my palm over her bare skin, leaning in to breathe in the scent of her hair, kissing her neck. The feel of her skin beneath mine, the sound of her breath catching in my ear was sublime.

A dizzy feeling—delicious, dark—descended over me like a shroud, as soft and as smooth as velvet. I lost myself in our kiss. I couldn't tell where she ended and I began. I had been so miserable without her, but now—

"I love you," I whispered. "I love you."

"And I you."

Our voices were the only thing in that shadowy, silvery world. I wished I could look into her eyes. I wanted to know every inch of her heart, every aspect of her temperament, her secrets.

How strange it was to feel so vulnerable and not want to run.

The first morning I awakened beside her in our new chamber—a corner room with more privacy than we had in Underhill House— my heart swelled with an indescribable joy. We had left the bed-curtains open, and a raft of pale sunshine was slanting across the room to light her face. Her expression was peaceful, soft, and there was the faintest trace of a smile at her lips, as if even in sleep she knew contentment.

Jane Dee must have spread the word about what my mother and I did for her, because that night a prostitute named Maggie came to us on horseback, saying she had heard from a maid-servant that we could soothe painful memories. Could I do this for her, she wanted to know, even though she couldn't pay very well? There was a pained expression in her green eyes, an endur-ing sorrow, which caused me to wonder what her life must've been like.

"Yes," I said immediately, remembering what my mother had said about that ritual. "But you must be discreet."

When she nodded, we called for Mother and started the cer-emony right away. It was rewarding to see the smile pulling at Maggie's eyes after her last session, when she finally had achieved a small amount of peace.

Perhaps my mystery client spread the word about our astro-mancy too, because Maggie was not the only client to show up at Swan House that week. We saw a gentlewoman who wanted us to cast a synastry chart for her and her husband, whom she suspected was lying with one of her maids. A pregnant lady wanted us to cast a chart for the date the child was due, which she feared was unlucky; she wondered if she should take herbs to bring about her labour early. We saw a young baroness who was trying to decide the most auspicious month to conceive an heir.

Without prompting, Mother made conversation with our clients while they waited, feigning an interest in gossip to tease out news of the Underhills. She found out when they had returned from Bohemia—the fifteenth of April—and that they had an argument with John Dee when they returned, though we couldn't find out about what. When Mother brought me this information, the expression on her face was solicitous. I didn't realise it then, but I understand now she was trying to apologise for what she'd done, though she was too proud to say it.

On the nineteenth or twentieth of May, not long after I advised the baroness on a conception date, we heard a knock on the door. Outside stood a man bearing a thick envelope whose wax seal was stamped with a simple ring, no noble crest. "My employer told me to hand this to you personally and wait to make sure you read it, madam." He bowed reverently. "Its contents are private and urgent."

I slipped my finger under the seal, breaking it, assuming that the note was related to our astrology work—the duchess, perhaps, sending for me again.

Several sheets of paper fell out. They fluttered to the yard outside Swan House, drifting hither and thither in the breeze. The messenger picked up the others, while I unfolded the only sheet of paper I hadn't dropped.

It was a letter. I scanned it first, recognising Henry's handwriting, the omission of my name, his initials transposed to hide his identity just as we had done before:

Mistress—

It is with deep regret that I write to inform you of some potentially disastrous news. Your decision to stop seeing W— infuriated him. He missed an appointment with me, an uncommon occurrence. When he finally answered my summons, he strutted and paced, ranting about you. On and on he went about how you wronged him. He tried to turn me against you, but of course we have no quarrel.

When W— realised he couldn't convince me, he asked if I was seeing you without his knowledge. I assured him that was as preposterous as we both know it is, and he stormed out. We did not speak for a week, and it seems during that period he apparently wrote some rather unkind sonnets about you. In truth, I should be plain and call them what they are. They are not only unkind. They are ferocious, vicious . . .

The trouble is, some of these poems are quite good and he knows it. He had copies made and circulated them among his poet friends. There is one about you playing the virginal, another that calls your eyes "raven" black, and several references to night, punning obviously on your name. Together with the physical descriptions that appear in others, anyone who knows you would recognise you. I have enclosed the copies I recovered so you may see the extent of his malice, but I should warn you again that in moments they can be quite vicious. If you're willing to act on my word alone, you may wish to forgo reading them.

One of them insinuates you are a witch. Do with this information what you will, but the poems are becoming notorious in certain circles. When these came to my attention this morning, I confronted him and learned that you have enemies who may be looking for you. I was so furious on your behalf that we had an argument. I am working to recover the copies for you, but I have only been able to find this set thus far. There are four others, as I understand. I fear the damage may already be done.

I would advise you to be very discreet until we recover the copies and find out who has read them, lest your fame spread even more widely. There are already whispers. I have sent this with my best servant, whom I would trust with my life. Please burn everything within when you are finished reading, for both our sakes.

Yours in friendship,
W— H—

The letter trembled in my hands, making a quiet rippling sound. A fire ignited inside me, forging a red-hot hatred. How could Will do this? It was cruel, shortsighted, and selfish. Tears burned my eyes.

Loathing the idea of crying in front of a stranger, I breathed deep—once, twice—my breath rattling in my throat. *Tranquilla sum*, I thought. *Tranquilla ero.* Then I put out my hand. The messenger handed me the rest of the papers. The poems. I felt a curdling dread at the idea of reading them but needed to know how much danger I was in.

Tyrannous, the first called me, accusing me of black deeds. Another described our encounters as *th' expense of spirit in a waste of shame*, a sinful sort of heaven that led to an inner hell. Another seemed to insinuate that I consorted with the devil: *Oh from what power hast thou this powerful might?* The one that described my playing was complimentary—it revolved around his desire for me to touch him like my keys—but it was full of phrases he'd borrowed from the song I sang the first time he saw me perform at the brothel.

Henry was right, the reference to my virginal combined with the pun on my stage name and others' descriptions of my features was damning. *My mistress' eyes are raven black . . . If snow be white, why then her breasts are dun . . .* One poem had a line about my eyes seeming like mourners, so *becoming of their woe, that every tongue says beauty should look so.*

No, I thought, remembering the compliment Richard had given me on our wedding night. *I have never seen grief look so beautiful.*

My chest went tight. I could barely speak to dismiss the messenger.

I remembered the long walk home from Southampton House, how I hadn't remembered to put on my hood until I was well on my way here. I could've been seen walking north.

If Richard had read these, we were in danger.

Cecely found me standing before a brazier, trying without success to understand how these poems came out of the relationship I remembered. I didn't even hear her at first. Deep in thought, staring into the flames, watching a sonnet burn: the one about my music.

I was bewildered by the intensity of the other poems, their proclamations of passion, the deep sense of betrayal that ran beneath the surface. My plan was to burn them all, except for the one that compared me to a goddess, which I had tucked into my pouch to read again later. *My mistress' eyes are nothing like the sun* . . . I couldn't tell if Will was inventing a relationship for us that subverted courtly conventions, or if he was simply layering insult upon insult. The more I thought about it, the more I suspected the latter. My rejection had hurt his feelings, and what I said about the earl had transformed his resentment into self-righteous fury.

"Rose?" Cecely was saying. "What happened?"

I read her the letter, the sonnet about our shameful encounters, the ones accusing me of tyranny and bargaining with the devil. Her eyes widened. "I didn't know things were so serious between you."

"Nor did I. Our encounters were passionate, but never intimate," I said, a sinking sensation in my stomach. As soon as the words were out, I knew they weren't true.

Cecely frowned. "I was in Norwich, Rose. It's not my concern. You were your own woman."

"He's married and in love with the earl. We were nothing to one another, I assure you—"

She shook her head, her lips turning downward in an expression of bemusement. "Who are you trying to convince?"

The flames crackled. The scent of burning paper tickled my nostrils. I had never been so disgusted with myself. I threw another sonnet into the fire. *Th' expense of spirit in a waste of shame—*

"What are you going to do?"

"What the earl suggests, I suppose. I wish I'd listened to you about Will. He's the most infuriating man I've ever met."

She met my eyes. Though she was kind enough not to say it, I knew what she was thinking: *I told you he would undo you.* After a moment, she sighed, and her expression turned pensive. "Don't you think it's unlikely Richard will read these? He doesn't travel in literary circles. And even if he does, the poems only implicate Ravenna. Didn't you tell him you were leaving London?"

"Yes, but I could've been seen leaving Southampton House or Will's. I've been to a masquerade, some plays."

Her eyes widened.

"Richard has become unpredictable. I was worried about how he would react to my note, but this—" I exhaled sharply. "He could do anything."

"We need to convince your mother to undo her spell on him."

I blinked. Why hadn't I thought of that? As ever, when I lost hope, she was able to remain clear-eyed. My mother and I weren't the only ones who were good at strategy.

We found Mother standing in the garden, pruning a rosebush. I stood there for a long time, silent, reluctant to tell her. I was certain she would be angry with me, intolerably haughty about the fact that she was right.

"Mother," I said.

When she looked up and saw our expressions, her eyes glittered with a perverse interest. "What is it?"

I told her about everything that had happened, waiting for her to scold me, but she only listened intently. When I told her she needed to undo her spell, she drew herself up.

"I'm going to tell you something, and I need you to believe me." She set down her shears, waiting for me to nod my agreement. I felt uneasy as I waited for her to go on. Her eyes glowed with a desperate sincerity. "I did not take the ring."

I rolled my eyes. "We've been over this—"

"Upon my life, Rose, I have said. *I didn't take it.* Someone else did. Your father called the ring lucky because he thought it made him more..." Mother frowned, struggling to find the right word, finally settling on a music metaphor. "*Attuned* to the stars' influence. John Dee's mentor, Gemma Frisius, made it. Your father believed it strengthened his connection to astral forces. I don't know for certain because he never let me near the damned thing, but I believe it will amplify the power of spells that invoke the queen of heaven. If we want to restore Richard to himself, we need it."

I stared at her, disbelieving, a wild laugh rising in my throat. Here was the reason she'd been trying to get the ring from me all this time. Not to sell it, but to increase her power. I thought about my dream of the house on fire, my vision of myself on the staircase, the ghost roses. I had been wearing the ring for all of it, and my abilities had faded as soon as I stopped wearing it. "So that's why you wanted it."

"I only wanted to *borrow* it. Father and I agreed that you should have it, given how much we were asking you to give up."

I searched her face. What she was saying sounded so *reasonable*, so compassionate, so completely unlike her. But her eyes were full of sympathy, as if she believed what she was saying. Could she have been telling the truth all this time? I knew Mary hadn't taken the ring. If it strengthened the wearer's connection to astral forces—

"Are you in earnest?"

"Upon my life."

I remembered how much Master Underhill wanted the ring, how preoccupied Richard seemed sometimes when he kissed my hand. He had always seemed rather incapable of deception, but he had changed these last months, and his father's work was so important to him. "Pluto and hell." I turned and called out. *"Mary?"*

The maidservant found us quickly. "Yes, madam?"

"Do you trust anyone who still works at Underhill House?"

She nodded. "I was close with another maid."

"The ring you thought was misplaced. I suspect Richard took it. Do you think she might be able to get it back? He would guard it closely. Wear it, or keep it locked in his workshop."

"Your husband was meticulous about who had access to his workshop. Graves was the only servant who did. But I can ask my friend if he's wearing the ring. She's like to be at the market if I hurry."

I nodded, grateful. "I also need to know if Richard is looking for me, but I need her to be discreet about finding out. I'll reward her handsomely. And you—"

Mary nodded, hurrying away to find her friend, and I breathed a sigh of relief.

I closed my eyes, trying to gather my wits, dimly aware of my mother beside me. She met my eyes, a rueful expression clouding her eyes. I waited for her to say *I told you so*, but she only shook her head and turned to go inside.

As I watched her go, black hair shining in the sun, I was haunted by a feeling so subtle I couldn't name it. A vague regret, perhaps, or guilt. She had been telling the truth about the ring all this time. I had been so angry at her.

Cecely took my hand. I tried to relax, filling my lungs with the fragrance of the myrtle blossoms that suffused the air. But the thought of losing the life we had worked so hard for devastated me. My thoughts kept returning to the ring. It was *mine*, a gift from my late father. Even if it had been a powerless ornament, I would've wanted it back.

Mary must've taken a carriage, because it was still light out when she found me in the parlour, an apologetic expression clouding her dark eyes.

"I'm sorry, madam. She hadn't seen him wear the ring, and she had no advice about how to get it. She agrees it's like to be in his workshop."

"Is he looking for me?"

"She didn't know that either. All she was able to tell me is that since he and Humphrie returned, they only leave the workshop to sleep."

I rose from the table, reaching into my skirts for the coin pouch I kept full of coins to pay for minor purchases and vails. "For both of your troubles."

She took the money and curtsied. "Thank you." She drew a deep breath, lowering her eyes.

"If I may speak with you about another matter...?"

Her expression was urgent. "What's wrong?"

"Seeing my friend reminded me of something that has been bothering me since we changed house. I haven't been going to mass at St. Helen's because I've been afraid of being seen; everyone at Underhill House knows I left with you. The cook attends services, and so do others. I can't avoid church forever."

I blinked at her. Why hadn't I thought of this? If Richard was looking for me and had someone follow her home, she would lead them straight to us. "You can't attend another church?"

"I don't feel welcome at the church here," she said. "Everyone stares at me. Mistress Underhill introduced me to everyone at St. Helen's. They know me. I fear I'm putting you in danger by working for you. I'm not exactly inconspicuous."

She stopped, waiting for me to understand. She wanted to go to work elsewhere.

"Cornelia says the Montefiores don't have an opening. If there's anywhere you can recommend me—"

I sighed reluctantly. I didn't want to find her a new employer, but if she wanted to leave, I couldn't stop her. Was there anywhere I could recommend her? The brothel was an impossibility for obvious reasons.

"What about Henry?" Cecely asked.

I let out a deep breath. "Southampton House. Yes. That's an excellent idea." Henry had a hundred servants. The Southamptons were powerful, well-respected. Henry would be eager to do me a favour. "After we get the ring, I'll ask him."

Cecely and I decided we would try to get the ring back that very night. Mary had never relinquished her key to the servants' entrance, so we had a way into Underhill House as long as no one had changed the lock. The only question was how we would get into the workshop. I imagined both Richard and Graves kept their keys close. Acquiring either one would be risky.

I decided to ask my mother if she had seen where Richard or the steward kept their keys. It was the sort of detail she might've noticed. I told her everything we had decided. "The servants say he isn't wearing the ring, so I suspect he keeps it in the cellar."

She shook her head. "I have no idea where the key is, but I can cast a spell to help keep you hidden while you find it. Why don't you ready yourselves to go? Put on your darkest clothes. Anoint yourselves with rose oil. We can start as soon as the evening star rises."

Cecely and I dressed in dark cloaks, anointed ourselves, and hurried into the garden. By then, twilight had fallen and the evening star shone in the sky. Mother lit twelve black candles in a circle, strewn with twelve roses, one for each house of the zodiac, and a sprig of myrtle. She opened her spell book to a page in the back. Then she told us to bow our heads while she fingered the beads of her myrtlewood rosary—which I realised, suddenly, was not a simple rosary at all. "*Regina Caeli, roudos, nox enmortos*—" she murmured. "*Fiat obumbratio!*"

The shadows seemed to start moving around us in a circle, like they had around her in the kitchen months ago. As she repeated the blessing, the shadows deepened, surrounding the pool of candlelight, and I could feel a subtle rush of wind. By the fifth or sixth time she repeated the blessing, I could see shadowy shapes in the air, as if a flock of birds were circling us. The night darkened outside the candle's penumbra, becoming a perfect black. I shivered, preternaturally chilled, as if it were the dead of winter instead of May. The candles flickered. I felt no magic, though I could see the spell working.

By the time Mother repeated the blessing for the twelfth time, Cecely and I were trembling with cold. Even the candlelight seemed dim. The beads rattled in my mother's hand. "*Regina Caeli,*" she sang. "*Fiat fiat!*"

The night seemed to explode. The candles went out, and I heard a loud snap. The world went black. Mother gasped for air, stumbling. Cecely and I fumbled to catch her, it had become so dark. As we helped her stand, I could hear the myrtlewood beads rolling over the stones of the courtyard. The thread upon which they were strung had snapped.

"There," Mother said, struggling to catch her breath, her voice so weak it was barely audible. "You're ready. While you're there, find something of Richard's that he recently touched, something meaningful. We'll need it to undo the spell."

I nodded. "Is it safe to leave you like this?" I couldn't see her, but I suspected the ritual had weakened her, the way potent spells sometimes did.

"I need sleep, that's all. I'll recover. Go. The shadows will follow."

We hurried on foot down the road that led through Waltham Forest. It would be too risky to take a carriage, and besides, the noise would call attention to the shadows that were following us. By the time we reached Underhill House, it was nearly midnight. The night was blessedly dark.

The house towered before us, a dim monstrosity. The gables

curved, shadowy and solemn. The angels glared down at us in stony judgement.

We hurried to the servants' entrance and tried the key Mary had given us. It was slender, a simple bar with a cross-shaped prong. I breathed a sigh of relief when the lock turned. We opened the door a crack and peered inside. The servants' hall was empty. We took off our shoes.

Pulling the door closed behind us, we crept inside in our stockinged feet, pressing ourselves—and our shadows—against the north wall. As we passed through the servants' kitchen, my chest tightened with anger. Why did Richard think he had the right to take this ring? Had he always been this entitled, or had my mother's spell twisted him?

Cecely met my eyes and nodded, then crept toward the servants' staircase. She led me up several flights of steps to the topmost floor, where the upper servants slept. The shadows crept with us, so dark, I was confident they would obscure us from the sight of anyone who wasn't looking directly at us. I shivered, feeling a rush of defiance and determination to find the key to the workshop.

We had decided to try Graves first, since he slept alone, unlike Richard, whose manservant slept in his truckle bed. As we approached the steward's room, we could hear the soft sound of his snores. His door was slightly ajar. Cecely pushed it open so we could peer in.

It was difficult to see inside. Very little light came in through the window. I could see only dim shapes. The bed, solid, square. A form tangled up in its blankets. The shadows that followed us were both a curse and a blessing. If Graves awakened, he would see only a preternatural darkness in his room. But that meant we couldn't see anything either.

We slipped inside. Everything was fine until I heard a loud creak beneath my feet, then the rustling of sheets on the featherbed. I froze. Graves stirred, the whites of his eyes flashing as he turned in the direction of the sound.

"Fraunces?" he murmured grumpily. He peered into the darkness, his voice uncharacteristically affectionate. "I told you not to come tonight."

My eyes widened. Beside me, Cecely stiffened. It was shocking that the steward was capable of affection for anyone.

When Fraunces didn't reply, he shook his head, pulling the sheets over his face.

I held my breath, waiting to hear the soft sound of his snoring before I approached. Remembering how cruel he had been to Mary and Cecely, I wondered if we could make it look like *he'd* taken the ring, so Richard wouldn't suspect *we* had. But how would we do that?

On the table beside the bed, I could barely make out a formless white shape. The shadows were so deep, I would have to touch it to know what it was. I tiptoed closer and picked up something soft. The handkerchief Graves always carried with him. The handkerchief embroidered *with his initials*. I slipped it into my pouch.

Beside where the handkerchief had sat, I traced the shape of a curved bar forming a U—the pendant the steward always wore. Beside it was a ring with three keys. One was shaped like the key Mary had given us, the key to the servants' entrance. The second matched the one I was given when I lived here, the key to the front door. The third was unfamiliar to me, engraved with filigrees and pretty stones. I felt a rush of hope, until I put it in Cecely's hand. She put it back, and I understood that she knew it wasn't the key to the workshop.

I followed her back toward the door, waiting for her to explain. As we slipped up the servants' stairs, she whispered, "Wine cellar."

My chest felt hollow as we slipped through the chambers to Richard's rooms. The floor didn't creak. Nothing moved. The shadows flowed.

Before we opened the door to Richard's bedchamber, I closed

my eyes, praying that the shadows would hide us if he or his servant woke.

Richard's room was almost completely dark already. It took me a moment to make out any shapes at all in the chamber. Even then, the figures I saw were dim, barely perceptible. But after a moment, I could see the shadowy shape of Richard's manservant on the truckle bed. He was snoring softly. I held my breath, listening for the sound of Richard breathing behind the bedcurtains.

There. I breathed a deep sigh of relief. He was here and not in his workshop. I scanned the surfaces of the tables and desks, looking for evidence of the key, but it was too dark to tell. I pressed the palm of my hand against Cecely's arm, the meaning clear—*stay here*—and tiptoed inside.

On the table beside his bed where the heavy curtain was open just a crack, I thought I saw something. I crept closer, holding my breath. I had the strangest sensation that I wasn't moving, perhaps because of the way the shadows were moving with me. The object on the bedside table was palm-sized. I tiptoed toward it. But when I reached out to take it, it skittered on the wood, and Richard stirred. I yanked back my hand, pressing myself against the wall as the bedcurtains rustled.

I could see the whites of his eyes. I froze, holding my breath. He seemed to be staring straight at me.

My pulse raced, and I could feel a cold sweat on my brow. My hands trembled.

"*Who's there?*" he said aggressively. I could hear him fiddling with the tinderbox. A candle flickered to life, and I saw his face: black hair falling into narrowed green eyes, jaw clenched. He held out the candle, methodically sweeping the room with its light. When he reached the wall where I was hiding, his eyes seemed almost to meet mine, and everything slowed—time, the shadows, the night itself.

Finally, he shook his head subtly, sweeping the candle around to check the rest of the room. I let myself relax against the wall, suppressing the urge to sigh in relief. The doorway was pitch black. I couldn't see Cecely at all.

When Richard finished scanning the room, his brow furrowed. He drew a deep breath, then held out the candle so its light fell upon the bedside table right beside me, where something glinted.

He nodded slightly, then rolled back over in bed. I waited until his breathing became regular to see what the object was. Minutes passed. Five, perhaps ten. Only when he began to snore did I tiptoe closer, holding my breath. Very carefully, I closed my fingers around the object. It was the emerald pendant that belonged to his father. Why was he worried someone would take it?

Something nagged at me. Graves had kept his pendant beside the bed too.

God-a-mercy, I thought, feeling foolish. The pendant *is* the key. I had heard of such things—puzzle rings, secret keys that could be kept close. It was just the sort of thing Master Underhill would own.

I wrapped my fingers around the pendant and slipped back toward the door, a triumphant smile spreading across my face, sending shivers of rebellious pleasure down my cheeks and neck. Cecely followed me out.

"You found it?" she whispered when we were several chambers away.

"It's the pendant."

I heard her soft exhalation of breath, the same surprise and foolishness I had felt when I realised it myself. As we crept toward the staircase, we heard a creak behind us. I couldn't be certain if it was the house or someone following us.

"Hurry," I whispered.

Our feet made no noise as we hurried downstairs. The shadows moved with us, enveloping us in an unseasonable chill. As

I reached the landing, I remembered my vision of myself on the staircase, drinking claret. How free I felt now in comparison.

Downstairs, Cecely led me into a dark hall. I had no idea where we were going. I had never been in this part of the cellar.

Then I heard a hinge creak, the sound of flint scraping steel. A flame leapt to life right next to where I stood. Cecely had used a tinderbox to light a candle from a holder. "There," she said breathlessly, setting the tinderbox back in an indentation in the wall.

The flame danced, chasing back the shadows that surrounded us so that they flew *outside* the immediate pool of light cast by the candle. In a moment we could see an ancient wooden door upon the wall. Something about the door felt heavy, absolute. Its lock was strangely shaped, its aperture a narrow vertical slit that reminded me of a mouth.

I swallowed, feeling ridiculous about how frightened I was, then pulled out the pendant to inspect it. The emeralds spelling the letter U glittered in the candlelight. It was a handsome piece of metalworking.

I ran my fingertips over the stones, searching for a loose part or aperture. The front of the pendant seemed solid and smooth. I turned it over, my heart pounding.

On the back of the pendant was a tiny metal button. When I pressed it, the pendant opened. It was a locket. Inside was a smaller golden U that fit inside the outer shell. At the curve on the bottom of the letter was a handle. I pulled it out by the grip and pressed the prongs of the letter into the lock. It clicked.

I drew a deep breath, listening for the sound of movement on the floor above. Perhaps I had imagined the creak upstairs. We were almost finished. If we hurried, we might well get out without being seen. "Ready?" I asked Cecely.

She nodded, shading the candle with her hand. We slipped inside, the shadows closing around us, swallowing the light from our candle so that it cast no penumbra.

There was something unnatural about this effect, but it felt somehow holy too. The shadows were like the blackness of the night sky between the stars, vast and eerie and beautiful.

Cecely held up the candle, using it to light a lantern on the wall. The chamber leapt to life. The flames reflected in the many containers of a glass apparatus that dominated the largest table, creating the illusion that it was on fire. Alembics, cucurbits, and bulbous tubes. There were books everywhere, strange metal devices. A furnace, a cauldron, bellows, ceramic pots of every colour and shape and size.

Then, in the farthest corner, I saw it. A table with a glittering crystal ball. The candlelight flickered in the glass. Something glinted in the centre of the desk. Something *gold*.

"There," I breathed, taking the candle and hurrying toward it, my heart rushing into my throat. The shadows travelled with me, making the workshop very dark outside the circle of candlelight, but when I reached the desk, I saw it: the ring, fanned out into the shape of the heavens.

Richard *had* taken it.

I swallowed my fury, closing its hoops, then slipped it onto my left hand, anxious to feel the presence I felt the first time I put it on. As the metal encircled the base of my finger, the shadows that had followed us into the workshop granulated, shivering. I smelled the ghost roses, stronger than ever before—a gorgeous, heady scent— as if someone wearing strong perfume had just left the workshop.

The queen of heaven, I thought. Had she been here? Was she the "aerial spirit" Richard had been trying to summon? Tears burned my eyes. Had he actually *succeeded* in summoning her? I had heard of magicians summoning spirits and daemons and forcing them to do their bidding—John Dee was supposed to have such powers— but surely no one could enslave the queen of heaven. Could they?

I was so caught up, I almost didn't notice the seal upon which the ring had been sitting. When I did, I gasped. It was a map of

the heavens, inscribed with alchemical symbols and strange letters. The signs of the zodiac, the moon, the stars. Around the edge
of the circle was a string of eight repeating symbols. The glyphs I
had seen in my mother's spell book and on the seal of Dee's letter.

Eight glyphs. The same word, inscribed over and over. My heart
dropped. Was I looking at the name of the queen of heaven?

A strange feeling washed through me, a heady combination of
sacrosanct awe and fear. My knees felt weak. I stared at the glyphs—
which seemed to shiver and granulate—trying to memorise their
curves, wishing desperately that I knew how to read them.

The scent of roses filled the room. She *had* been here. She had.
Did Kelley teach them how to trap her, make her do his bidding?
It seemed *wrong* to ask her for advice on turning base metals into
gold. Unholy.

"Rose—"

Cecely's voice seemed so far away, I didn't register it.

"Rose—" Her tone was frantic, full of dread.

I blinked, coming out of my reverie. She was clutching a sheet of
paper. "Look!" She held it out.

My heart plummeted when I saw what was written upon it. A
familiar handwriting: florid, proud. Fourteen lines.

It was a sonnet.

12

There were five other sonnets on the desk where Cecely had found that one. Richard had a copy of every poem Henry had sent me. On a slip of paper beside them was a list: *The Stallion*, the first line read. *The Hen House. The Goose. The Abbey.*

Panic shot through me. Cecely and I exchanged a glance. We put everything except for the ring back where we had found it. Then I pulled Graves's handkerchief from my pouch.

Cecely's eyes widened, and despite everything, her lips curved downward into a smirk. "You aren't."

"I am."

I dropped it to the floor beneath the table where the ring had been, feeling rather pleased with myself.

Cecely insisted she be the one to put the pendant back where we'd found it, while I looked for something of Richard's that we could use for the counterspell. I agreed reluctantly. I knew him better than she did. It had to be something meaningful, something he recently touched. Most of the items on the tables were alchemical ingredients or tools. Beads of copper, bars of lead, ceramic jars full of mysterious ingredients. There were dusty books, but he would miss those. Finally, my eye fell upon the desk, where a quill pen sat beside the list of brothels. I hurried over to inspect it; the point was stained with ink.

I slipped it into my pouch, then pulled another quill from the box on the edge of the table and placed it where the first one had been. Then I hurried upstairs and into the alley to wait for Cecely, my heart pounding in my ears.

When she opened the door, relief washed through me. We rushed up Bishopsgate Street, knowing we needed to get home before daylight.

By the time we arrived at Swan House, it was almost dawn. The house was utterly silent until I called out, "Mother!"

It was a moment before I heard footsteps. As soon as she stepped into the room, still weak, supporting herself on the wall, she checked my finger. "You found it. Thank goodness."

I nodded, relaying the rest of what had transpired. Cecely added details where I forgot them, breathless, overcome. Mother's eyes narrowed when I told her about the seal, the glyphs, my sense that the queen of heaven had been in the workshop.

"He's using her against us?"

"No." I shook my head, horrified at the idea. "At least, I don't think so. From what I understand, he was seeking alchemical advice."

She pressed her lips together. "Are you certain? She can be ruthless. If he summoned her—"

"Whatever he did is already done. We have the ring now. We should cast the counterspell. I brought back one of his quills—" I broke off, fumbling in my pouch for the utensil, unable to find it. There were the coins, the sonnet I had meant to reread. The quill wasn't there. My breath caught. Had it fallen out?

Mother shut her eyes, rubbing her temples. When she spoke, her voice was hard. "The safest thing to do is start over somewhere else."

"Madam Rushe," Cecely said. "Forgive me for being so bold, but—" Her eyes shone, glittering and black, impassioned. "We can't let him ruin us."

I felt a buoyant sensation in my chest, a lightening. Cecely reached for my hand and squeezed it, her eyes glistening with feeling. "We have to do something," I told Mother.

We glared at her, unified.

Mother stiffened, her gaze travelling down to our hands, her eyes widening only slightly. When she raised her eyes up to meet mine, I glared at her, feeling defiant, waiting for the reproach I thought was coming. The insults, the berating, the slurs. But Mother only rolled her eyes. "If you think this is news to me—" she muttered.

"What?"

"My room was next door."

I blinked at her. Cecely swallowed a giggle.

Mother shook her head, changing the subject. "I've been thinking. I'm not certain undoing the spell will achieve anything. I doubt Richard is searching for you out of love. I suspect his motivations have more to do with jealousy and pride."

My heart sank. She had a point. I tried to think of another option. "Could we cast a spell to prevent him from finding us? I have seen you cast spells to *find* things many times."

Mother looked thoughtful, then left the fast-brightening kitchen. "Let me see what ingredients we have. For now, you should both sleep. We can't cast any spell until this evening."

As soon as she was out of earshot, I asked Cecely if she would mind going into the village to send a letterlocked note to Luce. *Beware*, I wrote. *My husband is looking for me in the brothels. I pray you tell him I no longer work there, that I am gone, that I have left England. Forgive me for causing trouble. Destroy this note once you have read it.* I hesitated to include my address in case the letter was intercepted, closing the letter with more cryptic instructions on how to find me: *WH knows where I am.*

After Cecely left with the note, I fell into bed, too exhausted to forgo sleep another moment.

I didn't awaken until just after sunset when I heard the sharp echo of a *woof* at my feet, the skitter of Hughe's claws as he rushed out of my room toward the door. Blinking away sleep, I pushed back the bedcurtains, getting out of bed as carefully as I could so I wouldn't wake Cecely. Wrapping my gown about me, I heard a sharp rap from the back of the house, a muffled voice, another bark, the creak of stairs beneath Mother's feet. Someone was here.

Alarm coursed through me. I slid my feet into my slippers and arrived downstairs as Mother was opening the back door.

She froze when she saw who was outside. Luce and Lisabetta. Behind them, a black carriage. "Rose." Luce addressed me over my mother's shoulder.

Lisabetta smiled at me tightly, avoiding my mother's eyes.

"What are you doing here?" I said hurriedly, slipping past my mother to speak with her.

"Richard checked the Abbey last week, but I didn't know how to find you. It's not only Richard who is checking the brothels. A constable is involved."

All the breath went out of my chest. The stairs creaked behind me. Cecely, coming down, bleary-eyed.

"Your husband accused you of fornication, lewdness, and witchcraft," Luce said. "He used your married name, Rose Underhill. The writ accuses you of murder."

Murder? I froze. I couldn't think, couldn't speak, shocked that Richard would go so far. Even now, it seemed beyond what he was capable of.

Mother turned to me, standing as stiffly as one of the statues in Underhill House. "What are *they* doing here?" she hissed.

"I was working at the brothel," I said flatly. "As a performer. Before Will started circulating the sonnets."

"How did you find them?"

"Does it really matter, Kat?" Lisabetta said in an icy voice. "Are you still so intent on controlling everyone around you?"

Mother took a deep breath, all the rage, the concern on her face disappearing. In a moment her expression was completely neutral. "No," she said in a disturbingly quiet voice. "I see you haven't changed, sister."

Lisabetta glared at her.

"They're searching everywhere," Luce said to me. "How many clients have you seen here?"

"Is there any way you could've been seen coming or going?" Lisabetta asked.

I thought of the night I had walked home from Southampton House. Drunken, confused, careless. Hood down. I thought of Will, who hated me and apparently had my address.

"We have to go," I said, my voice catching in my throat. I closed my eyes, taking a deep breath. I didn't want to sacrifice everything we'd worked so hard for.

"Agreed," Mother said.

Beside me, Cecely reached for my hand.

My thoughts raced. Richard had already checked the Abbey. I met Luce's eyes. "The cottage in the woods. How far back from the brothel is it? Do you think it would be a good hiding place while we figure out what to do? You said no one goes back there..."

Luce looked thoughtful. "It's quite a ways back."

My aunt closed her eyes. "In the devil's name—"

Mother was watching me carefully, her mouth as pinched as if she'd just swallowed a lemon. I searched her face. Although she had been perfectly willing to *leave* London, I could tell she didn't want to go anywhere near the brothel.

"All right," Lisabetta sighed, finally, folding her arms.

Mother pressed her lips together tight. Luce's expression was strained.

"Thank you," I said. "We should hurry."

⁓

We hitched a cart to the back of the coach. Mother brought her witching trunk, of course, and the black candles we'd used for the shadow spell. I brought the notebook in which I did my calculations. She gathered the myrtle sprigs and roses from the shadow spell, so we could use them in a ritual to protect the cottage. I didn't want to be parted from the tapestry Henry had bought me, nor did I want to leave behind my father's ephemeris or my better dresses, but we were in a hurry.

The four of us crowded into the coach with Hughe. Luce and Lisabetta sat up front, driving the horses. Mother seethed, Edmund sleeping in her lap. I stared out the window, holding Cecely's hand tightly, hoping that we were doing the right thing.

Luce rushed the horses. The carriage rocked down the lane. The ride to Clerkenwell seemed to take ages, but soon we were creeping into the woods that obscured the cottage from the road. There was a path about fifty yards back from the brothel, well hidden from the street. We had to duck beneath the low-growing boughs of a hawthorn tree to find it.

The cottage was a quarter hour's walk into the woods. A ramshackle place, stone. Through the trees, in the shadows, it looked almost idyllic. The stars cast a dim glow over the thatched roof. There was a creek somewhere, a faint melodic trickle—runoff from the river.

As we drew closer, the holes in the roof became clear. The rot in the boards, the cracks in the shutters. On the side of the cottage, I saw a gravestone beneath a hawthorn tree. I waited for Mother to see it, wondering if it was her mother's resting place.

When her gaze finally chanced upon it as we climbed out, a strained look passed over her face. She crossed herself, repeating some Latin prayer under her breath, too low for me to make out the words. After a moment she turned to her sister, who was climbing out of the front.

"When did she die?" Her words were so tight, they hummed.

Lisabetta froze. "You know when."

"In truth, I do not."

"Right after you left."

Mother drew a slow breath, her shoulders rising and falling.

"You deserted her—"

Mother closed her eyes. Lisabetta watched her, waiting for her to reply. Neither sister spoke.

"She was not without blame," Mother said finally.

"I see repentance is still beyond you."

Mother drew a deep breath and left, weakly picking her way through the underbrush toward the grave. Edmund followed her.

I turned to my aunt. "What happened?"

Lisabetta blinked, surprised, as if she'd forgotten I was even there. As she met my gaze, her eyes were resigned, almost haunted. Her grief over her mother's death was still raw, even all these years later.

I made my voice gentle. "Please, tell me."

My aunt didn't respond. Edmund fell into the underbrush, perhaps scratching his hand on some thorn, and Hughe let out a great breathy *woof* at my mother. She turned, doubled back, and placed her son on her hip, comforting him, before they set back off toward the stone and hawthorn.

Lisabetta sighed. "She refused to let your mother marry Secundus. Your mother witched her, then disappeared when the spell went wrong. My mother went mad."

The night seemed to grow darker, closer. I shivered, recalling how reluctant my mother was to undo the spell on Richard, how worried she'd been about me when I reacted poorly to her spell. "Why would my grandmother refuse to let her marry my father?"

"She hated gentry. Kat was her favourite, and she knew what would happen when your father took your mother home—" She let out a dark chuckle. "She was right, wasn't she? Here you are, cast out. They set your house on fire."

I turned toward the stone, the hawthorn. Mother was standing in front of it. She had set Edmund down. He was leaning against Hughe, who was sitting beside her.

"What was my grandmother like?"

"A strong woman, like you, fiery, independent. When our father died, we were very small. She began renting rooms in our house to women. A few years later, we moved here. She—" My aunt paused, searching my face. "She taught your mother everything she knows."

Her eyes were full of grief.

I lowered my voice, speaking softly. "About witchcraft?"

"That's why what she did was so difficult to stomach. She used my mother's lessons against her."

"Did your mother teach you too?" She nodded. "Do you know anything about the queen of heaven? My mother won't even tell me her name."

My aunt blinked at me, her forehead wrinkling with a mixture of surprise and fear. She shook her head, her voice so low I could barely hear it. "I don't know if anyone knows it. My mother believed she was another aspect of the Mother of God—all the sex, the power, the shadow that was forgotten in favour of the Virgin's chaste light. She dedicated the Abbey to her."

I remembered the shadows I sensed the first time I visited the brothel, the roses. I told my aunt what I found in Richard's workshop, how I suspected he was trying to summon her and ask her about alchemy. "They call her an 'aerial spirit.' Mother was afraid he was using her against us. Do you think that's possible?"

My aunt's expression clouded. "Men often dismiss what they do not understand. Your husband may be able to summon her, but I doubt he can make her do his bidding. She rules over the night and the world of the dead. Your husband is foolish. I don't meddle with her, and I wouldn't recommend you do either."

A rustle, from the underbrush. Mother was picking her way back toward me, a strange look on her face.

Seeing her, Lisabetta withdrew and went back to Luce.

"We need to perform the ritual as soon as they leave," Mother said under her breath. "To prevent the constable from finding us."

When I went to tell Luce and Lisabetta goodbye, they explained that they would send Maggie with a basket of food in the morning, then hurried back down the path.

Mother put Edmund to bed inside, then hurried back out. "All right," she said grimly. "Let's call the shadows."

I volunteered to cast the spell this time, since she hadn't recovered, and I didn't want to let her borrow the ring. Mother warned me that the spell was potent. It would drain me. I summoned my courage as she arranged the candles in a circle. When she nodded, I spoke the incantation as she had directed—I was supposed to chant it for as long as it took Mother and Cecely to ring the cottage with roses.

"*Regina Caeli, nox enmortos, roudos! Fiat circulus umbrarum.*"

With each repetition, the spell summoned a strange energy from deep within me, a hum so low I soon found myself trembling. It had been so long since I felt a spell working, the sensation startled me. The scent of roses grew stronger as I chanted, as my mother and Cecely ringed the cottage with myrtle sprigs and roses. Each time I repeated the prayer, the shadows around me seemed to deepen, the night granulating, vibrating with power. My body hummed. The prayer beads, restrung, held together this time, but Mother and Cecely seemed to take an eternity to return.

I couldn't think, I couldn't breathe. The night rolled, shivering and trembling like marbles in a bowl. I thought my own temperament would burst into pieces and scatter. Soon I could feel a flock of shadows circling the cottage like shadowy birds.

I could hold the spell's energy only until I saw Mother and Cecely rushing toward me. Then I let it go, a great wind rushing from my throat, and everything went black.

For three days, I slept, disturbed only by a faint voice from somewhere deep inside me. Not the nightbird this time, but something louder, deeper, true. *Sleep*, it whispered, *sleep*. The words comforted me, as if my inner mother was singing me a lullaby.

The spell had weakened me. I was shivering. That first day, I kept losing consciousness. My body had lost the ability to warm itself. But the spell seemed to be effective. The cottage remained undisturbed. The voice in my head was reassuring.

When I woke, we discussed what we would do when I was well enough to travel. Mother wanted to start over elsewhere, and Cecely agreed. They said the earl or the Dees could recommend us to new clients. They were right, I knew they were right, but everything in me fought against it. Although I was bone-tired, the fact that no one had come after us made me hopeful that our plan might work. If Richard believed that Graves took the ring, and we were able to hide for long enough, Richard might believe that we had gone. He was a stubborn man, but if he thought I'd left England, surely he would petition for an annulment and move on.

While I was recuperating, I asked Maggie to post a discreet letter to Henry to see if he had any extra space in his home for a servant. The earl replied, saying one of his mother's chambermaids had just resigned, which I thought was perfect. Henry's mother was known to be extremely gracious and traditional. She was a better candidate for Mary's employer than I ever was.

The next day, we said our reluctant goodbyes. I felt a pang to see her go, though I knew she would be happier with access to St. Helen's.

Despite the season, I could not seem to get warm. The shadows would not leave me alone, gathering in the corners, drawing close when no one else was in the room. Yet the effect was not as frightening as it might sound. Instead, it was almost lulling, like Cecely's hand in my hair. My memory of that maternal lullaby stayed with me.

Before the sun rose each morning, Maggie smuggled us food, leaving a basket of cheese and bread and fruit at the door, a cloth folded tightly around it, smeared with crushed mint to repel ants. I spoke with her the fourth morning we were there, finally recovered enough to answer her knock on the door, supporting myself with the wall.

She told me that Luce had been in contact with many of the other brothel owners, and she had some hopeful news. Luce had asked whether anyone had seen the constable lately, pretending she was concerned he would interfere with her operations. "No one has seen him in days."

My spirits soared. "Richard has given up?"

"Perhaps. He's stopped searching the city, in any case." She smiled. "I wish you a good day."

As soon as it was bright enough to see the forest floor, but—I hoped—too early for anyone else to be about, I walked the ring and checked to make sure the rose petals were still there. A few had drifted this way or that, but the circle around the cottage was largely undisturbed. I put the stray petals back, speaking the incantation under my breath. Although it was slow going, the walk was peaceful. The woods were quiet.

I thought I felt a presence wherever I walked, dark and protective, eerily sacrosanct. The shadows followed me. In the grey sky, through the skeletal branches, I could see the morning star. Venus.

My sense that we were protected, my hope, swelled.

That afternoon, Cecely went out to wash her clothes in the stream. I had told Mother about the drifting petals, and we were arguing over whether we needed to redo the spell. The witching trunk and the spell book were spread out on the table. Mother was rereading the spell. "I think you're right. We should redo it tonight to be safe."

As she closed the book, we heard a faint, sharp sound from the direction of the brothel. Hughe, barking. Next came the neighing of a horse. Men's shouts. "The boy! Look!"

"They must be back there."

Horror swept through me. No, I thought, no. This cannot be. But of course it was. Edmund must've been exploring the pasture beside the brothel. We should have paid more attention to what he was doing.

"Grab him!"

Mother's eyes went wide. We ran from the cottage toward the shouts, our fear of discovery forgotten. She shot out faster than I could. I had to stop and support myself on a tree while I caught my breath, halfway there.

"Edmund!" my mother shouted.

"Mama!" Edmund's scream was piercing.

I rushed toward the sound more quickly than I should've, cursing my decision to stay here. It had been selfish, I realised. Why hadn't it occurred to me that Edmund might be the one to suffer for it?

A deep voice. *"Get him off me!"*

At the edge of the woods, Hughe had jumped on a man who was holding my little brother, biting his leg. Edmund was crying and squirming. My heart stopped, and panic cut through me.

"Edmund!" Mother screamed.

Another man was readying a caliver.

"Hughe!" I shouted. "Drop it. Down!"

The dog obeyed. The man lowered his caliver, and the man who was bitten turned toward me, sneering. *"There* she is."

The bitten man—a constable, I realised—spoke to the others. "Get the trot too, and the dog, for the trial."

My heart dropped. Hughe growled, baring his teeth.

"Strike that. Shoot it!"

"Run, boy!" I screamed. "Go!"

Hughe hesitated, uncertain, his instinct to protect us warring with his training. Then another man raised his caliver. Time seemed to slow as the groomsman braced and aimed it, but the dog had seen my father shoot at foxes. By the time the flash went off, he'd already bolted.

Deeper into the woods toward the creek where Cecely had gone to wash our clothing, I thought I saw a flash of bright black fur. There was no yelp, no whimper, to indicate he was injured. Relief washed through me.

I prayed that he would find Cecely and alert her to what was happening before she too was taken. My throat constricted. I couldn't believe this had happened. Why hadn't we kept closer watch over Edmund?

"Mistress Rose Underhill, Mistress Katarina Rushe, you have been accused of witchcraft," the constable said. "You are to be examined at the Tower."

As they apprehended me, grabbing my arms so hard I knew they would bruise, I remembered how we had left the cottage. All the evidence of our occultist work on the table. All the money we'd worked so hard to collect, our future! A sob leapt from my throat. What would happen to Edmund if we were convicted?

He was still struggling, crying now, tears streaming down his chubby cheeks. "Mama! Rose! Help!"

The constable snarled at him to "Be still!" in such a loud voice that Edmund went quiet, his face ashen.

As they pushed us into a carriage, I thought of the ring. Perhaps there was something I could do to stop this. I fingered its inscription. SUPERIORA DE INFERIORIBUS, INFERIORA DE SUPERIORIBUS. I reached out with my spirit, searching desperately for some sort of metaphysical presence in the air around me, but sensed nothing.

Regina Caeli, I prayed, help us—

Nothing happened. No ghost roses, no whiff of copper, except the shadows seemed to shiver, and I felt even colder than before as the guards slammed the doors.

My throat constricted as I turned to my mother. "Did you grab the money?"

She shook her head. My throat constricted.

"We left everything on the table. Everything."

From my side of the carriage we could just barely hear the guards arguing. "The boy is too young to know anything. Why would they separate them?"

"You heard the constable. Orders are orders."

My heart felt like it was being wrenched from my throat. Why in the world would they take Edmund away? I thought of the dungeon I had seen advertised in pamphlets. The rack, the manacles, the terrible, filthy conditions.

Edmund whimpered from my mother's lap, where he was clutching her tightly. "Don't let them take me," he said.

"I won't, Edmund," Mother said in a gentle voice, petting his hair, pressing her cheek to his like we did when he had trouble sleeping. She met my gaze over his shoulder, her expression the most vulnerable I had ever seen, her eyes brimming with a wild despair. Her lips trembled with the effort to keep from sobbing.

It occurred to me how alike we were. Perhaps she only let herself feel so strongly for my brothers because they were safe objects for her affection. It was the same way I felt about little Edmund and Hughe myself. They couldn't hurt me. For a moment, I wondered if she had loved me like that when I was little, if I simply didn't *remember* her affection before the first Edmund was born.

Somehow, I doubted it.

As we rode, I shivered in the dim carriage, eyes closed, cape wrapped tight about me. I prayed that Hughe had found Cecely, that she had figured out what happened and went to Luce. If she heard the caliver fire and Hughe came running, surely she would've. I hoped she hadn't been captured separately.

The carriage rocked, making me queasy. I couldn't stop thinking about how reckless I'd been—again, again—the damage I'd done. My contrition soon mixed with anger at Will. This never would have happened if he hadn't circulated his stupid poems. I was furious with Richard too. Murder! The accusation endangered my very life, and my mother's. If we were imprisoned, or worse, who would care for Edmund?

When the carriage finally stopped, I could see a vast grey stone wall through the window bars. The groomsmen dismounted and began speaking to a pair of guards in a low voice. One of them waved us in, and we lurched back into motion to the sound of metal machinery creaking. The Tower gates.

Inside, the late-afternoon air was heavy with the pungent scent of the famous menagerie, the sour smell of animal urine and excrement. There were lions, supposedly, tigers, a great white bear. From the same direction, I could hear the crowd whom I'd heard paid for their admission with a stray cat or dog for the lions. The same horrible people, no doubt, who enjoyed dogfights or bear-baiting.

The carriage rattled through a courtyard toward whatever building they were going to hold us in. As we clacked to a stop, I heard a piercing shriek that sounded human. I tried to convince myself it was a monkey, though I couldn't help but think of the stories of torture.

I thought we had reached our destination, but a woman came to the carriage instead. She was older than my mother, grey-haired, dressed in the well-made but modest clothes of a merchant's wife or upper servant. The guards flanked her, opening the bolted door. When I realised what was happening, my stomach dropped.

"No!" Mother breathed, as if the word were being torn from her throat.

Edmund, realising what was happening, clung to her. "Mama!"

The guards had to pry his fingers from her neck. I heard what the governess said to him under her breath. "Your mother will be going away for a while, but *you* get to come with *me* to see the menagerie!" The words weren't cruel, but something about the way she spoke them chilled me. Her emphasis on the word *me*, the greedy undercurrent to her tone. Mother must've heard it too, despair flashing across her face.

"I don't want to!"

Mother took a deep breath, obviously forcing herself to stay calm. I knew what she must be thinking: The kindest thing she could do for him now was to allow him the distraction. "Edmund," she said in a soothing voice. "Go with the governess. I have business elsewhere. You get to see the lions!"

Edmund sniffled, meeting her eyes, recovering somewhat.

"You'll come back later?"

Mother hesitated only a moment before she nodded.

"Lions," the woman continued. "A panther—completely black, sleek, wait until you see—and monkeys! Then we'll get a special treat from the kitchen. Tell me, do you like sugar?"

He nodded solemnly, reaching out his arms.

It was heartbreaking to watch the woman take him away. My mother closed her eyes, her hands shaking, her mouth crumpling with grief. I was shaking too, as they led us up a spiralling flight of stone stairs, wiping the tears from my cheeks.

The cell they locked us in was private and clean but smaller than the room in which Edmund slept at Swan House. The only light was a single torch on the wall. A simple wooden bench large enough to serve as a bed, a writing table—though we had no quill pen or ink—a simple chair. The walls seemed too close, especially because of the shadows in the corners, which seemed to be dancing.

I slipped off the ring, overwhelmed. The shadows stilled somewhat, but I felt unprotected without the ring on my finger, uncomfortably alone, so I slipped it back on.

I thought of Edmund, how upset he would be to sleep apart. Through the bars, the acrid scent of the menagerie wafted in. I felt a sudden rush of sympathy for the animals.

When the guards left, Mother and I sat on the bench or bed, whichever it was, without speaking. I couldn't stop wondering how

Edmund was doing, whether Cecely had been captured separately. By the time we heard footsteps on the stairs, I was in torment.

We couldn't see the guard who unlocked the door. "Your husband is here to see you."

The words summoned an anger so strong, I felt sick. But I stood and prepared to go.

My mother stopped me on the way out. "The ring," she whispered, holding out her hand. "You don't want him to see you with it."

I froze. What a disaster that would've been. "Thank you," I said in a tight voice, slipping it into my pouch.

Without it on my finger, I felt unsafe, but there was nothing I could do. Richard would take it from me if he saw it, and who knew what he would use it to do?

The guard led me downstairs to another locked room. As I descended, reluctantly letting him support me, I thought of everything Richard knew that I didn't. The name of the queen of heaven. What evidence he was going to bring against me in court.

I cursed the power he had over me, even still, worrying I wouldn't be able to convince him to tell me either. The evidence would have to be my first priority.

The guard's keys jingled as he fit one into the lock. Inside was a well-furnished room with a fireplace, several curule chairs, and an ornate table. It was set with a candelabra, a fresh bouquet of red roses, and a familiar-looking hawthorn crown dotted with red berries.

Richard stood in the corner.

Eyes flashing with that unnatural anger, he looked as furious as I imagined the lions felt in their cages. I thought of something my mother used to tell her clients. *Hurt is the mother of hatred.* I remembered the way Uncle Primus had lashed out at us when I embarrassed him, the way Will had lashed out at me when I did the same. Had my mother's spell amplified Richard's affection for me so much that my betrayal had maddened him?

"I don't even know where to begin," Richard said furiously, his eyes flashing with indignation. I saw how they flitted, briefly, to my naked ring finger.

Anger braced me. "Why don't you start by telling me what you're accusing me of?" I said, deciding to get right to the point.

"You deceived me about your pregnancy, not to mention the physician," he said, his voice trembling. "The cook said you were intentionally asking for foods that cause the belly to swell. Barley bread, oatcakes, *horseradish*. All sorts of suspicious things—"

I blinked at him, straightening one of the rose blooms in the bouquet on the table mock-nervously. I put on a sorrowful face, though I knew my chances of deceiving him at this point were slim. "I was having cravings."

He scoffed. "You said you were staying with family."

"We—" I couldn't keep the steel out of my voice. I lowered my eyes, trying to swallow it, but I was too angry, too resentful. I plucked a petal from a rose and began to shred it without thinking, anxious. "We found another way to survive."

"Performing in a *brothel*? Casting horoscopes for harlots? Lying with that poet? You have brought shame onto our house—"

"I wasn't using your name."

"You are my wife," he said, each syllable an accusation. A vein in his temple bulged, and his face reddened. His reaction shocked me. I had never seen him this angry. I remembered how hot I'd felt after I burned the rose. By the gods, had that act amplified some suppressed fire in him? Had *I* done this?

Something in me snapped. My disgust with myself. The grief over losing Edmund, my father, Underhill. The inhuman shrieks, the smell, it was all too much.

"I never wanted to be your wife," I snapped. "I had no choice. I only wanted what your father promised before mine died: a place to stay until I could support myself!"

The words hung in the air. Richard blinked, then straightened, his face white. He crossed himself. When he spoke, his voice dripped with condescension. "I had hoped I could sway you, but I see now you are too far gone. My trip to Bohemia was useless. The angel that Kelley summoned was false, and the spirit Dee told us to consult won't submit. She taunts us."

Won't submit. Taunts us. The urge to laugh was so strong, I coughed, unable to suppress a smirk. They didn't know what they were dealing with.

"Does that amuse you?"

I closed my eyes, pressing my lips together tight.

"You are too much in league with the devil, I see, to change your mind. I suppose I shall have to let my accusations stand. It will be easy to prove your transgressions. I have the sonnets, your spell book full of all sorts of devilish things. Your letter to me. Everyone has seen that dog following you around. He came out of the woods a few hours after my men found you, and they caught him. Your *familiar.*"

My heart stopped. First Edmund, now Hughe. Would he take away everyone I loved?

I closed my eyes, fighting the hopelessness off. I couldn't succumb to it, couldn't give up. "You know well he is just a sheepdog, Richard, and a fine one at that. A loyal pet."

Richard shook his head, as if he were sorry to say what he said next, as if he had no choice in any of this. "I wish you would confess and repent. Your case will be heard at the Old Bailey before the courts close. If they convict you, and you don't renounce the devil's influence, you could hang."

A cold feeling spread through my chest, though Luce had warned us his writ accused me of murder. It made no sense. For a witch to be hanged, her spells had to cause someone's death, and I had caused no such thing.

My hands trembled. I thought of Edmund, off with that governess. Cecely, wherever she was. Richard's proof sounded damning, but it wasn't without weakness. The dog and the letter could be explained away. If I could convince Will and Henry to testify on my behalf and find some way to explain my mother's spell book, perhaps we would be safe. Richard hadn't mentioned the witching trunk. Had Mother hidden it before we rushed out?

"You would let Edmund lose his mother."

"Better a ward of the court than a ward of a witch."

"Richard," I pleaded, my voice catching with fear and grief, hoping to appeal to the kinder, if insufferable, man that I hoped was still inside him. "How could you do this to him? No matter how much I wronged you, he is innocent."

The lanterns flickered. His hands, for the first time since I entered the chamber, went still. He sat across from the table in a curule chair in the corner and folded his hands in his lap. His eyes laughed with a cold mirth. Then he spoke in the sort of offhand voice he used to comment on the weather.

"If you come home with me, I will drop the charges."

I should have seen this offer coming—the roses, the hawthorn crown, his demeanour—but the truth was, it knocked the breath from my chest. It didn't make sense. My reputation was ruined at this point. The Richard I had known all my life would have petitioned the bishop for an annulment the moment he read my letter, if not sooner. This *had* to be the spell, warping his feelings for me, unless—had Graves convinced him he hadn't taken the ring? Did he know I had it?

I wanted to scream. I was already so angry at him, at everyone else who had contributed to trapping me in this hell. Will, my meddling mother. I drew a deep breath, glaring at the table between us. *Tranquilla sum*, I thought. *Tranquilla ero*. I cannot let my fire rule me.

My gaze fell on the pool of blood red petals I'd shredded on the table between us—roses, ruined, dead—and the bouquet from which they came.

He had touched them. Brought them here, for me.

It took everything in me to suppress my triumphant smile. I pulled a rose from the bouquet, making myself look sorrowful instead. "Who is the governess who has him?"

"She's one of Burghley's."

I took another bloom casually. "She'll be kind to him?"

He had the audacity to look hurt. "I'm not a monster."

A third bloom. I set them on the table before me. Then I picked up a hawthorn berry, rolling it idly beneath my finger, and dropped it surreptitiously into my pouch. I picked up another, meeting his eyes.

There was no way I could go back to Underhill House now, even if I could swallow my pride and agree to it. I met his eyes and said the most honest thing I had ever said to him. "I'm sorry I misled you. I will see you at trial."

On the way out of the chamber, I slipped the roses into my sleeve and one of the candles from the table into my pocket, praying that no one would notice. The hawthorn berries I'd taken rattled in my pouch, and the rose thorns pricked my wrists, but no one spoke of my extra-voluminous cape as I carried it all back to our cell. As I stepped into the room, I fumbled for the ring in my pouch and slipped it on. The shadows shivered to life.

"What did he want?" Mother asked once the wardens were gone.

"To change my mind," I said in a voice so cheerful she looked concerned. I set the roses on the table and sat across from her.

Mother lifted her eyebrows. "What did you tell him?"

"The truth. Deception would only resurrect our marriage or postpone the trial. I don't want to prolong Edmund's ordeal if there's a chance—" My voice caught as I thought of Edmund, alone and without family for the first time in his life. I hoped the governess stuffed him full of sugar and cake, that he enjoyed the menagerie, that he had no idea anything was amiss. But even if he was able to fall asleep, I knew he would wake up in the middle of the night and cry for Mother like he did when we first arrived at Underhill House.

Across the table my mother winced, no doubt performing the same mental calculus.

"Richard said he had my calculating notebook, my instruments, and your spell book. Did you hide the witching trunk before we left?"

She shook her head, looking puzzled. "His men couldn't have missed them. Perhaps he is being strategic, not telling us everything he has against us."

"Perhaps." I pulled the hawthorn berries and the candle from my pockets, nodding at the roses on the table. "Can we cast the counterspell with these? He brought them for me. The berries came from the crown I wore at our wedding."

The smile that spread across her face was wide. "How fortunate," she said, raising an eyebrow appreciatively. "The counterspell would take more energy to cast than the shadow circle. It will deplete you utterly. How do you feel?"

"Well, at the moment." I laughed bitterly. "I think my rage sustains me."

"Casting two powerful spells in a row would be dangerous, but I don't see another option to—" She left the rest of her thought unspoken, and I knew she was thinking of my brother. "Unless you want to give me the ring."

I closed my eyes, swallowing the anger that was rising in my chest. We didn't have time to argue. "Richard said my case would be heard at the Old Bailey before the spring courts close. That means we only have a few days. We need a ritual we can perform tonight, so I'll have time to recover."

Mother nodded, closed her eyes, thinking.

It was an effort to be still, not to get up from the table and pace, but I knew I needed to conserve my energy. As I waited for my mother to finish strategizing, I cursed the entitlement my sabotage had awakened in Richard, the same impulse that had driven Will to write those poems.

A gust of wind blew into the cell from outside the Tower, making the flames of the torch on the wall gutter. Shadows flocked around me, pulling me down, stretching my awareness thin. I wasn't sure if they were calling me or if I had called them. As the fire leapt back to life, the room brightened, and the whites of Mother's eyes reflected it.

When she looked up, her eyes flashed with resolve. She listened for a moment to make sure no one was on the stairs, then took the candle to the torch and lit it. She set it on the table between us, where it flickered and danced, its pale light shivering around it.

"Gather the roses," she said. "Think on Richard's passion. Call it out of *you* into *them*. I've never been able to do this myself, but perhaps the ring will help you."

"Now?"

She nodded. "While his touch is fresh. Repeat after me," she said. "*Regina Caeli . . .*"

I closed my eyes, reciting what she said, hoping this attempt to use the ring would be more successful than my last, now that I had her guidance and the roses and berries. I reached for the blooms, hoping that they would help me get inside Richard's head. I tried to *see* him on his way home to Underhill House. Nothing happened, just as before. The shadows didn't even shiver. My hope, already fragile, faltered; I worried our fate was sealed.

No, I told myself. Be still. I took a deep breath, trying to think through the problem.

The ring connected me to the queen of heaven, who connected the stars with all of us. I tried to reach through her into him, casting about in the shadows. Still nothing.

Perhaps I'd touched the roses with the wrong hand. I tried using my left hand to finger a petal. Nothing again. Then it hit me. I was reaching out. Mother had told me to call it *out of me* into them.

I focused my intent inward. *There.* Almost immediately, I felt a thrum. I saw him on the backs of my eyelids, as clearly as if I were sitting in the carriage with him. He was furious, staring out the window into the dark, seething with a resentment that was tangled up in his desperate need to complete his father's work. His mind was a jumble of incoherent images. Of Humphrie sitting before his crystal ball in his workshop, staring fruitlessly into it. Of me, doing the same. Me? I almost lost control of the spell, I was so shocked at the image. Why in the world would Richard imagine me at his crystal ball, unless—?

He wants me to be his scryer, I realised, remembering how much he wanted me to accompany him on his trip, how he'd seemed to want something from me the night he confided his difficulties with his work. When had this idea occurred to him? After I sabotaged the spell, or earlier, when I first arrived at Underhill House? Had I misjudged Richard Underhill entirely?

I sent my will deeper into his mind to see what impulses lay beneath his resentment. There was entitlement, whirling with a passion so strong it felt unnatural. Eternal, dark, suffused with a mephitic love. And barely perceptible, beneath that, his natural affection for me, the infatuation he felt as a boy—it was real—and even more buried, our friendship.

I tried to separate the natural feeling from the unnatural, calling only the dark passion and everything above it into the roses. If the natural affection stayed with him, perhaps he would behave toward me with more compassion. But tendrils of the dark passion had reached down into the natural feeling, and the outrage had mingled with it. It was all tangled together, inseparable, an unpredictable mixture of love and lust and anger. There was betrayal there too, entitlement and wounded pride. I had no choice but to try to call *all* of it into the roses, unwilling. It was like trying to turn a wild river in its bed. The current turned only slowly, tumbling and rolling back on itself each time I tried to redirect it.

"Rose?"

"Wait—" I breathed.

And then it was done. The effort knocked the wind out of me. The roses were red-hot. I dropped them. They seemed to have absorbed all my heat.

Cold sliced through me. My teeth began to chatter. It had taken all my remaining power to imbue the blooms with that feeling. I could still see Richard in my mind's eye. I thought his expression seemed softer, as if what I was doing was already working.

"Now feed the petals to the flame one by one," Mother said. "*Regina Caeli, roudos. Ignis comedat passionem. Fiat consumptus!*"

I did as she said, voice quiet and trembling, my hands shaking more violently with each petal I burned. The scent of burning petals—an odd odour, charred but cloying—filled our cell. Beneath it, a scent that reminded me of the blacksmith shop. When I withdrew my hand from the flame, I felt freezing cold. I pulled my cape tight, shivering, relieved to be finished.

"Now the berries," Mother said.

My heart sank. I had forgotten there was more to do. The haws sat on the table before me: tiny, round, bright red. They were only berries, but I glared at them, irrationally infuriated by their existence. With difficulty, I made myself pick them up, one by one, and drop them into my palm.

"Eat them."

"*What?*"

She nodded. "Put them in your mouth."

"Why?"

"They represent your marriage with Richard. You're going to consume it, take control."

That was all she had to say. I placed them on my tongue eagerly, improvising my own prayer. *"Regina Caeli, roudos. Ignis comedat mat-rimonium. Fiat consumptus!"*

"Rose, no—" Mother tried to stop me, horrified.

The scent of roses filled the air.

The last thing I remember before I lost consciousness is the taste of the haws on my tongue. They were so hard, so dry, I expected them to have almost no flavour. But when I bit into them, they burst with a fiery sweetness. It spread from my tongue to my cheeks, my throat, warming me from the inside. At first the sensation was curious, almost pleasant, until my throat began to burn. Then I realised why my mother had tried to stop me. The berries were burning, or rather, the fire in me was burning *them*. Soon there were three searing balls of fire in my throat, so intense I was afraid I might never speak again.

The flames seemed to burn forever.

When the heat finally receded, my throat still felt like it was on fire. I had no energy left. I couldn't move a finger. The night began to granulate. Shifting around me, rolling, liquid, the shadows rising, until the world of the senses evaporated. I could feel something pulling me down, caressing me.

Then I lost myself, becoming one with the darkness.

13

When I woke, I felt as if my spirit was slowly emerging from some inner night. I had the uncanny impression that I had not yet fully left it. I could feel it turning within me, my stars imprinted upon some inner sky. They clung to me like a sparkling shroud, making our cell seem distant, bright, and mystical.

My head ached. I pressed my eyes shut, wondering how long I had been unconscious. The boundary between my outer and inner worlds was still too thin.

I tried to open my eyes again, more slowly, squinting, dizzied by the misty stars that glimmered in our cell. Mother was hovering over me with a watchful expression. There was a bitter taste in my mouth.

More than a night had passed. I could see it on her face. It had been several days, though I wasn't hungry. Apparently, the hawthorn berries had been more sustaining than one might expect. Who would have thought a mock marriage would be so nourishing, I thought, a bitter laugh rising in my throat.

"Don't—" Mother said quickly.

Pain seared my throat. Scalding, as if I'd swallowed boiling water. I almost choked.

Mother brought a cup to my lips. Water, infused with a faint hint of ginger and thyme, a touch of mint. The cold liquid soothed my throat. I wondered how she had convinced the guards to bring it, then laughed. She wouldn't need magic for that. I gulped the drink, grateful for the connection between my body and this world—the sensation was like a tether, keeping me above water.

"Go back to sleep," Mother said in a steady voice. Her control over her emotions, for once, was comforting. "The trial isn't for three days yet. I'll ask the guards to bring more of this."

How long was I out? I mouthed with effort.

"Three whole days. Your wording was unfortunate. I don't know how long it will take for you to be able to speak. The justice came to examine us, but we couldn't rouse you until they found me rhodiola." She nodded at a vial on the table beside the bed. "I answered some questions on your behalf. I denied everything, but they're sending a jury of women and a churchman to examine us." She bit her lip. "I'm not certain if the justice will come back himself."

Dread prickled the back of my neck, cold and numb. I wouldn't even get to defend myself? The idea that I might still be mute by the trial startled me, and I succumbed for a moment to my vertigo. Down, down, I slipped into a strange not-sleep. Our chamber spun in a slow-moving gyre, and I had to fight my way back up to squint at my mother. Seeing the strain on her face, I thought suddenly of poor Edmund, wondering if he would be at the trial, if Richard would involve him in whatever spectacle he was about to put us through. My throat constricted, and I was stricken with the sudden urge to cry. *Edmund?* I mouthed.

Mother's gaze faltered. She shook her head, tight-lipped. "Scared to death, I'm sure. He's never been away from us this long."

The thought of him crying for us, waiting for us to come back for him, was too painful to dwell on for long.

I thought of Hughe, next, another sweet creature who depended upon us. I hoped whoever had him was feeding him, giving him walks, but I doubted it. He was probably locked in a cage with the other animals in this godforsaken place. The notion that he would be missing me, possibly even refusing to eat, the way he did after he lost my father, was too much. I had to choke down a sob, barely able to suppress the sound.

The knife that sliced my throat was agony.

"Sleep," Mother said. "When you've healed enough to speak, we'll discuss our strategy for the trial."

It was all I needed to hear. I was exhausted, in pain. The urge to fall into myself was strong. It was the last thing I heard her say before I let myself succumb. I had the sensation of falling, of being pulled under by shadows. Soft, inviting hands, a thousand of them, enfolding me, caressing me in some dark aether. Nothing upon nothing upon nothing.

The next thing I knew, the chamber was dim. Someone was shaking me awake, a calloused hand gripping my arm. A woman I'd never seen before. She frowned down at me, her expression pinched and disapproving, her blue eyes angry. Her grey hair was pulled back into a tight white coif. "Mistress Underhill," she said in a clipped voice. "You are avowed to come with me."

Mother stood in the doorway, another matron gripping her arm tight. Behind them stood three guards.

"*Where—?*" I started to ask, but the single syllable caused the pain to come back as bad as before, red-hot, and I gagged.

"Don't speak," Mother murmured as they led us from the room. "It's only been a few hours."

They tried to escort me down the stairs behind my mother, but my knees buckled underneath me so frequently that a guard called out. "What's wrong with her? Is she always like this?"

"No," Mother snapped. "She's ill."

The guard, a muscled man of nearly six feet in height, grabbed me and carried me the rest of the way downstairs. I struggled, fighting him off until he held my wrists. They brought us to a shadowy chamber without furniture. Stone walls, a window, nothing more. There were no tapestries, no rugs upon the floor. Not even a chair. "Send the minister in," the woman said to the guards, who nodded and left.

They returned with a young man with a full head of pale hair and grey eyes who looked upon us with pity. He cleared his throat when he saw me slumped on the floor. "Would you like to confess and repent?"

My mother glared at him. "We have done nothing wrong."

"What about you?" The minister's gaze was cool, deeply condescending.

I shook my head vehemently. Even if I had wanted to speak to the man, it would be too painful.

"Very well. May God have mercy upon your souls. Send for me if you change your mind." He rapped on the door, and the guards let him out. I heard him murmuring something to them I couldn't quite make out.

In a moment the guards reappeared with three matrons in simple clothes. Two of them were carrying bags full of fruit, which they set down on the floor. The third was carrying a basket of eggs, which she set beside the fruit. The guards must have pulled them off the street. We could hear the key twisting in the lock behind him. I felt so weak I thought I might faint.

"Take off your clothes," the grey-haired matron said flatly.

I stared at her, indignant. I had heard of the marks that had been found on the Essex women, supposedly proving that they suckled familiars and contracted themselves to the devil. But I didn't believe for a second that such marks were anything but an invention of their captors.

This would be a mockery of a trial. Infuriated, forgetting the pain it would cause, I began to protest. "I will do no such—" I started, but the unbearable searing pain in my throat made me stop. I had to support myself on the wall, shaken by a terrible cough, unable to still myself.

"Help her!" Mother called to one of the women who had been carrying fruit.

She narrowed her eyes at me, pulling me back up onto my feet but shaking her head with a disgusted expression, as if my struggle was somehow proof that I was in league with the devil.

The fruit women set to me, one of them holding me up, the other yanking and pulling at the laces of my bodice. Every bone in my body balked, and I couldn't help it. I shoved at them. Pain sliced through me. The guards stepped in, pulling my arms back so tight I could no longer move. The egg woman got to work on my mother, who said nothing at first, shoulders squared, glaring at the stone wall as hatefully as if she were staring down my grandmother.

By the time they had undressed us to our shifts and bare feet, my stomach was roiling with fury and embarrassment. My heart pumped so hard, I was shaking. I jerked my arm away from the woman who'd been supporting me, wishing I knew how to free my spirit from my body. I didn't know how I would endure this.

"Take off your shift, afore God," one of the women sneered at me. "I would prefer not to touch the likes of you."

I glared at her, filled with a torturous urge to scream, to call her out on her treachery. *Tranquilla sum*, I told myself, *tranquilla ero*, deciding if she wanted to inspect me, she would have to peel my clothing off herself.

Her expression soured.

Beside me, Mother clenched her fists, closed her eyes, and began speaking furiously in Italian, cursing the woman who had set to her loudly in a dozen different ways, calling her *puttana* and *traditrice*.

The woman whose job it was to inspect me reached for the seam of my shift and tugged on it until it ripped, making a loud tearing sound. In a moment, she was holding the cloth in her hand, and I was naked, heart pounding in my throat, toes curled against the freezing cold of the stone floor. Another woman would've covered her breasts and hidden the dark fur between her legs with her hands, ashamed.

"Cover yourself," the woman said. "You foul thing."

I glared at her.

She instructed the other women to hold me still as she touched my stomach, and I flinched. She began to circle me, inspecting the visible portions of my body, squinting. There was nothing to see, nothing to say, for an endless moment. Then she saw the mole near my left hip just above my groin. A simple birthmark, nothing, a small unremarkable black circle as round as the moon. Ordinary, even pretty. During our first nights together, Cecely had fallen into the habit of kissing it. But the woman inspecting me paused, calling the matron in charge of me over to inspect it.

"Ahh," the matron murmured in a perverse and satisfied tone. "There it is."

Anger poured through me, so powerful, it exhausted what remained of my caution. "It's a birthmark!" I screamed at the top of my lungs, and the pain that coursed through my throat scorched like fire. The last thing I remember is the pain of my knees on the stones and my vision going black as I fainted.

The next time I woke, it was Cecely—sweet Cecely!—who was leaning over me. At first, I thought I was dreaming, concocting a fantasy to replace the farce that my life had become. But when I blinked, she was still there. The relief I felt was indescribable. "Cecely—" I said without thinking, then winced, waiting for the pain. My throat was raw, but it was nothing like the searing sensation I'd felt the last time I made a sound. How many days had passed? Was it evening? Early morning? Our cell still seemed shrouded in shadow.

"Rose," she said, her eyes seeming to brighten. It was difficult for my eyes to focus; her face seemed hazy and blurry.

"She doesn't have long," Mother informed me.

"I'm supposed to be here to see the menagerie," Cecely explained. "I bribed a guard."

"*How did you . . . ?*" I couldn't finish the question. My voice was a gasp, a parody of what it had formerly been. Each syllable I spoke scratched my throat, which still burned as if it had been the site of a terrible fire, my siren song replaced by a pathetic little gust of wind.

"Hughe ran to me while I was washing clothes," Cecely said. "He kept nipping my ankles and pointing in the direction of the commotion. When I realised what was happening, I ran back to the house and grabbed the witching trunk. I thought the spell book was in it, but it wasn't. I've been staying at the Abbey. What's wrong with your voice?"

I pressed my lips together, looking to my mother to answer.

"It's the spell I told you about," she said. She nodded at the things on the desk: an array of herbs, the pouch in which she kept poisons. Our face paints, a mirror. "Cecely brought gifts."

"The face paint is to counter the description of your complexion," Cecely said.

I couldn't help but grin at her cunning. *Thank you*, I mouthed, overwhelmed with a rush of love and gratitude. I wanted to kiss her, but I was too weak.

"The guard said I only have a few minutes. Is there anything I can do to help with the trial?"

I thought this over. A difficult task, considering how dazed I felt. I closed my eyes, trying to focus, fighting the vertiginous sensation of the stars moving with my every thought. I waved my hand at the ephemeris.

Cecely handed it to me. Mother turned to the page with today's date. I scanned it, visioning the stars that turned in the sky above us. Saturn in Cancer, I thought. "Find Southampton—" I croaked, swallowing the pain, but I had to mouth the rest of the directions. *Ask him to visit us with Will.*

Cecely nodded. "Anything else?"

If I could talk Will into denying I was the subject of his sonnets before the court, perhaps Cecely could manage to discredit the other piece of evidence that would cause us the most trouble. *The spell book?* I mouthed.

Mother and Cecely met one another's eyes, their brows furrowed. "Where do you think it will be?"

The Old Bailey. I motioned for a pen, then wrote. *Mary's brother is bound to a judge there. He may not mind tampering with evidence.*

Cecely took a deep breath, then nodded. "I'll talk to her."

A sob rushed into my throat, and I was overwhelmed by another surge of gratitude. I had never felt such uninhibited feeling. My eyes watered, and the stars glittered wetly, obscuring my vision.

She was watching me, her eyes hopeful, waiting for me to respond to her idea. I nodded eagerly, yes yes yes, a thousand times yes, then mouthed, *I love you.* If Mother didn't approve, the devil take her.

Mother averted her eyes.

"I'll send word if I'm successful," Cecely said aloud, a complicated smile on her face, pulling her lips downward in a mixture of sadness and joy. *I love you too,* she mouthed, squeezing my hand, her eyes watering, before she pulled me into an embrace, whispering in my ear. "I love you, I love you, I love you."

After Cecely left, the shadows enveloped me again. I could feel dark hands caressing me, gently pulling me down. My connection to the queen of heaven was strengthening. She called to me, singing my name like a dark lullaby, *Rose Rose Rose.* My eyelids were heavy, fluttering, helpless against the strange vicissitudes of her power.

Mother saw me struggling to keep my eyelids open. *"Rose!"* Her eyes clouded with horror, and she shook me. "Don't let her take you!"

But the light was fading. I thought I heard a tinkling music— soothing, orderly, perfect. A voice, not the nightbird, not some inner doubt, but her. *Come,* she called, her voice so lulling, so comforting, I forgot to be afraid.

As I fell, faint points of light emerged from the dark. The scent of roses surrounded me. I thought I saw constellations—the Dove, the Lion—drifting in an infinite night. More and more stars appeared, until there was an endless sea of constellations and symbols. I heard a rush of whispers in a thousand languages—an incoherent noise—and for an instant, I knew all the names of the queen of heaven across time and space.

I am the nothing, she sang, *from which they all sprung. The mistress of the night. The aether.*

I should have been terrified, but I wasn't.

Whoever she was, she was made of both light and darkness. I understood, now, why different people perceived her differently. She showed you what you expected to see. She showed you a mirror.

I don't know how long it took me to finish my journey down, hours or days. It felt like weeks. I was conscious only of that dark voice calling me. When I stopped falling, I found myself suspended in darkness, surrounded by a familiar pattern of starlight. My nativity, hung in that inner sky. Mercury and Venus and the sun in Aries—glittering, holy, bright—in the eighth house, the house of sex. Jupiter and the moon in Aquarius, the ninth house. Saturn in Libra.

The template that made me, me.

There is a heaven in each of us, a holy geometry, a map. Some of the aspects we may have forgotten, swallowed, allowing them to be overcome—empty houses overshadowed by more powerful aspects. I was gazing at Saturn in Libra, thinking about this phenomenon, when the voice spoke again, echoing from the space between the stars. *Look*, it whispered. *Learn*—

The heavens fell away. Where the stars had been, a ghostly courtroom at the Old Bailey manifested like mist. Shadow-judges and jury, witnesses gathered at the benches all around me. I was sitting beside my mother at the dock. On the balcony, outside the immediate area of the proceedings, was an audience of deeply unsympathetic, largely noble spectators. The judge stared down at us, the jurors looking on with a finality that implied the results of the trial were obvious.

I felt a familiar doubleness, the sense that I was seeing something that would come to pass. The jurors smirked, their expressions so condescending and judgemental, a creeping horror filled me.

Mama! a familiar voice screamed from the seats where the witnesses sat. Poor Edmund was trying to climb out of the governess's lap. Hughe sat in a cage in the corner, barking loudly. Behind them, the women who had examined my mother and me for witch's marks. In the nearest balcony, I saw Luce, her arms around Cecely and Lisabetta, their faces heartbroken. Henry, brows knitted. Beside him, Will's expression was stony, devoid of sympathy.

I understood suddenly that he had none for me.

Richard and Humphrie smirked from nearby witness seats, smiling and congratulating one another. A creeping horror filled me. We would be convicted, then, imprisoned or hanged. Edmund would grow up without us. Hughe would probably be—

I couldn't even think it.

Guilty! the judge cried out. His voice echoed and echoed—

We were being manacled. The guards' armour clinked, their boots pounding my despair. Beside me, Mother was sobbing Edmund's name.

Although the courtroom around us was full, I had an inexplicable feeling that someone was missing. Someone else is supposed to be at the trial, I understood, but I had no idea who. I tried to ask, but my lips wouldn't move. When I reached up to touch my face, I didn't have a mouth. *Who?* I tried to scream but couldn't.

The courtroom granulated, dissolving into a million grains of light. They shivered and faded until there was nothing left but the night itself. For a moment, I knew nothing, saw nothing, was nothing. The world went completely black. Then a disturbance rippled the darkness, a sound so strange I didn't recognise it at first as laughter.

The duchess—

The next time I woke, my hands and feet were numb and I was groggy. The scent of roses suffused the air, so strong it made my head ache. I couldn't move, there were pins and needles all over my skin, I couldn't see, I couldn't even feel my body. It was as if I had left some part of myself behind in the dreamworld beneath the surface of my thoughts—as if the queen of heaven wasn't ready to release me. It took a while for me to recognise the bitter taste of rhodiola in my mouth. Slowly, the shadows of the chamber took shape around me, and I realised Mother was massaging my hands, my arms. That was what was causing the pins-and-needles sensation.

As my awareness slowly surfaced, I thought about my vision. It seemed too strange, too eerie to be real. Had I communed with an ancient goddess or intuited what I should do myself? Was there a difference? Why did it feel as if I had awakened before I was supposed to?

"The trial is tomorrow," Mother said, but her voice was like an echo, as if it were coming from far away. I could barely hear her. Behind her, I could see the golden pink light of dusk through the barred window, casting a lovely glow over our prison. "You've been asleep too long. We need to talk. Will hasn't come. Can you speak?"

"Let's see—" I tried. My voice was a shell of its former self, like a scratchy gust of wind, oddly separate from my awareness. But the pain seemed to have receded somewhat.

I told her what the queen of heaven had shown me, a revelation that startled and impressed her. "We need to cast a sympathy spell on Will, or he won't help us. And I must find a way to ensure that my mystery client attends the trial."

"Lemon balm, lemon balm," Mother muttered, rummaging through the herbs Cecely had brought. "*There.* The wolfsbane will be in the poison pouch. We only have time for a single casting, but perhaps it will help. As for your client, we don't even know who she is. Let's take care of the dramatist, then discuss her later. You don't happen to have anything that he touched with you, do you?"

I blinked at her, once, twice. Then I reached into my pouch and pulled out the poem. Her eyes widened as she read it. "By the gods, Rose, this is good."

"I know," I groaned. "That's why he was passing them around."

She set to work, preparing to cast the sympathy spell herself. She said if I drew on the queen of heaven, I would fall so far into myself, I might never come out.

When she spoke the incantation, the shadows drew closer and I smelled the scent of roses. Suddenly my eyelids felt too heavy to keep open. I could feel the voice inside me, calling, as if she had something else to say. I wanted to give in. Seeing my expression, Mother let go of my hand, moving to the other side of the room to finish.

Afterward, we talked, trying to plan for all the possible avenues the trial might take, but we had so little information. We did come up with one way to summon my client, but it would work only if Henry came. I could stay awake for only about an hour before sleep overtook me again.

I woke to the sound of a key turning the lock. The cell was pitch black until an elderly guard opened the door and peered in, holding a candle. "Mistress Underhill has more visitors than Mary Stuart at Fotheringhay," he mocked me, his white eyebrows arcing like caterpillars. "And so late at night. If *her majesty* will come with me..."

I rolled my eyes. The ominous implications of his comparison—

the queen's treason, her execution—weren't lost on me, but I was hopeful that Henry and Will had come.

Mother helped me from the bed so I could take the guard's arm. My limbs trembled. As we made our way downstairs, I cursed the fact that Will might see me like this. I had already been far too vulnerable with him.

As the guard led me downstairs toward the room where I had seen Richard, my legs shook beneath me, and I could not fill my lungs with breath. My awareness kept slipping in and out. I couldn't shake the sense that the queen of heaven was calling me. One moment I was in the Tower, and the next I was falling into myself, away from the world of the senses. I had to be half carried downstairs.

When we finally arrived, the door to the room was open. The hawthorn crown was gone, but the roses and candles still adorned the table, now several days past their prime.

Henry and Will stood, backs half-turned, by the fireplace. As the guard helped me into the chair, Henry touched Will's arm, laughing at something he said. The amused tone of Will's reply, too low for me to parse, seemed genuine, but his posture was hesitant.

Once I was settled enough to appear as if nothing was wrong, I cleared my throat. When they turned, I caught a brief glimpse of the longing in Henry's eyes, before he mastered it and shot me a debonair smile. He withdrew his hand from Will's arm and bowed. "Mistress Notte," he said in greeting, then added, "or should I say *Underhill?*"

"Or Rushe—" Will said coldly. The man who had written those sonnets in a feverish fit of anger was nowhere to be seen. Here was the aloof man I'd met in the tavern. The subtle narrowing of his gold-flecked eyes was the only sign that he felt anything at all about me. "You have so many names, I've forgotten which one we're supposed to use."

I was surprised at how little work the sympathy spell appeared to have done, or else how intense Will's scorn for me had been before we cast it. "What's in a name?" I rasped.

Will lifted an eyebrow. "You sound criminal."

I couldn't tell if he was referring to the substance of my speech or the ruined voice in which I was speaking. From the gloating lift of his eyebrow, I assumed it was both. I sat up straight, trying to hide how incapacitated I truly was.

"How fitting," I said hoarsely, with mock enthusiasm. "My husband wants to see me hang."

He rolled his eyes. "You're the noble wife of a royal alchemist, not some hag from an almshouse. You'll be pilloried at worst."

His scorn betrayed a startling lack of empathy. "I've been committed for murder by witchcraft. You realise witches aren't even allowed lawyers."

"I know how it works," Will grumbled.

"She's right, Will," Henry said. "Your poems endangered her."

"Richard has my mother's spell book. One of your poems implies I'm a witch. Have mercy, Will. I need your help."

His brow furrowed subtly. "Her spell book?"

"The trial is tomorrow. Please."

He shook his head, unmoved. He was obviously still angry with me for my insights, my escape from his influence, or both. "I didn't intend for this to happen, but I won't pretend there isn't a part of me that enjoys it, Rose. You slandered me."

"In private," I breathed.

Henry met my eyes quizzically. "Slander?"

"It's nothing," Will said quickly.

"But you just said—"

"I apologise, your lordship. I misspoke."

Henry was still looking at me. Beside him, Will shook his head, his gold-flecked eyes flashing with desperation. He's afraid I'll sabotage the earl's patronage, I realised, afraid I'm right about his feelings and the earl will see it. I doubted Henry would be angry if he knew what I said; he appeared to know himself far better than Will did.

I met Will's eyes, thinking of Edmund, allowing my defences to temporarily crumble. "They took my little brother," I said hoarsely, my voice catching with genuine heartbreak.

Will blinked at me, startled. The fear in his eyes faded, replaced with something so like pity I thought it might be sincere. The spell. Perhaps this was the way it would work. I should've thought to appeal to his fatherly instincts earlier.

"If we're hanged, he'll be a ward of the court. His name is Edmund. He's only five."

Will closed his eyes for so long, I thought he wouldn't reply.

"He lost his father last year."

Will met my gaze, his eyes tight with resignation. When he spoke, his voice was strained. "How can I help?"

"Tell the court I'm not the subject of your poems."

He heaved a sigh. In the distance, through the window, one of the animals shrieked its discontent. "Very well."

The earl still looked concerned. "It may not be enough if they have your mother's book."

"I know." My voice was almost completely gone. "Do you think you could get a message to Jane Dee for me, your lordship?"

"Of course."

"Tell her I need all my allies at the trial. *All of them.*"

Henry's lips curved downward with a subtle mirth. Looking thoughtful, he walked to the window where we could still hear the creature shrieking, too high-pitched to be a lion or tiger. A monkey, perhaps, or some sort of owl.

While the earl's back was turned, Will caught my gaze, his eyes pleading. "Do not repeat your slander," he murmured. "To anyone. I beg you."

"It was not slander," I hissed. "Why do you think it made you hate me? Why do you think you enjoyed kissing in front of him so much?"

He stared at me for long enough that I knew I had struck a chord. "That's not true," he said, his voice trembling. "I was—we only—"

"Think of the sonnets you wrote to him, the speed with which they came, the flashes of inspiration."

His eyes flashed with a final, extravagant burst of denial before the impulse finally fizzled. He blinked, once, twice. Then his gaze travelled to the earl at the window. He stared at Henry for a long moment, his indignant expression faltering. His mouth opened, then closed, then opened again. He shut his eyes, going very still, then his eyes darted back to meet mine. "You are mad," he said, but his voice trembled.

"If you defend me, I'll never speak of this while you live."

He watched me quietly, his expression cold and thoughtful. Then he nodded, his eyes burning with a sudden anger. He was still looking at me that way when the earl turned from the window.

Seeing Will's face, Henry lifted his eyebrows, shaking his head. "Leave her be," he said. "By the gods, Will, *you* are the one who slandered *her*."

The conversation exhausted me. Once Will and Henry left, the guard had to help me upstairs. Although part of me was relieved that I'd convinced Will to defend me, there were still too many other factors that could go wrong. We hadn't heard from Cecely, so we had no way of knowing whether Mary's brother had stolen back the spell book.

Mother was thrilled when I relayed the assurances I had extracted from Will and Henry. Keeping my promise, I did not tell her how I convinced the dramatist. Our conversation soon turned to the task of discrediting her spell book and the question of what the altered counterspell might have done to Richard.

By the time we were finished strategizing, my voice was gone. I felt like I would fall asleep at any moment. The border between my waking will and my inner night had grown too porous. With no reason to resist the queen of heaven's call, I let my awareness slip down, down, anxious to hear what she had to tell me. As I fell, I saw Edmund, tossing and turning in some unfamiliar bed, a nurse begging him to eat. Richard and Humphrie, trying desperately to summon their "aerial spirit" in that crystal ball. I slipped deeper, listening, waiting.

The next thing I remember is the faint pressure of someone's hand on my arm, shaking me awake. The taste of rhodiola. *"Rose, Rose—"* My mother's voice. "You must wake up. The trial—"

I didn't want to open my eyes, I wasn't finished, my eyelids were too heavy. There was a shroud between me and the outer world. The pressure of my mother's hand on my arm felt muted, the hardness of the wood beneath me vague, almost fuzzy. I tried to move my hand but couldn't lift a finger. Mother began to curse in Italian. "Rose, are you awake? Squeeze my hand."

I could do no such thing. The vague sensation of pressure travelled from my arm to my right hand, until it crawled suddenly with pins and needles. She was massaging my fingers. "There," she said. "Can you move now?"

All I could manage was a half-hearted pulse, with a stab of regret that my ordinary awareness was returning.

"Good, Rose, stay with me." She called for the guards, massaging my other hand until it crawled too. "We need the rhodiola tincture again! She must be awake for the proceedings."

The numbness spread as she massaged my arms, shoulders, neck, and temples. After the guards brought the tincture, I could open my eyes wide enough to see my mother. Her eyes were wet, and she was watching me with such a worried expression that I was moved.

It felt like days before I was properly inhabiting my body again, but perhaps it was only an hour or two. By the time I could sit up in bed and move well enough for my mother to help me dress, it was nearly noon. In the mirror, I saw she had painted my face while I slept.

I looked nothing like myself. Even though Cecely had brought the face paints, the fact that Mother had done it while I slept irritated me.

She slipped a flask into my hand. "Lemon balm draught," she whispered. "I made it last night. It will soothe your throat and sweeten your speech. I took a draught this morning."

I tucked the flask into my pouch.

The guards escorted us downstairs to an enclosed carriage in the courtyard. Mother got in first, and the tallest guard tried to help me inside. I jerked away, irritated, summoning the strength to do it myself before I settled on the seat beside Mother.

As soon as they closed the door, she nodded at my left hand. "Give me the ring."

"What?" I blinked at her. "Why would I do that?"

She frowned, as if the answer were obvious. "She's pulling you under."

The carriage rocked into motion.

I scoffed, my sour mood amplifying my lifelong mistrust of her. I couldn't tell if her concern was genuine. The child who needed her to love me wanted desperately to believe it was. Out of habit, I pushed that feeling down, focusing on my scepticism out of self-preservation. The effort made me angry. "The queen of heaven isn't as dangerous as you think she is. You don't see her benevolent aspects because you see *yourself* in her."

Complicated wrinkles appeared at the edges of her eyes. "I'm not entirely cruel."

"Everything is a transaction for you. You only show kindness when it benefits you."

"That's not true."

"You're kind to Edmund," I allowed. "But he is useful. A boy has the power to take you into his household if you need help. But a girl, well, unless you arrange her marriage yourself…"

She took a deep breath, her dark eyes full of rue. "You see the worst in me."

I watched her coolly. "I think the reason Father never took the ring off was that it checked you."

Her brow furrowed. "Checked me how?"

I didn't answer. Let her wonder, I thought. She deserves to wonder for the rest of her life.

"Checked me how, Rose?"

I drew a deep breath, then spoke through gritted teeth. "I know everything you did at Underhill House. The scheming, the spells. I could sense them. I heard a bird tittering in Italian, trying to convince me to do your bidding. Calling me reckless, a whore. I thought I was going mad."

Mother froze.

"How could you cast spells on me without my permission?" My voice caught, trembling like the string of an instrument deprived of its consort. "Me, your daughter? You must've known the effect it would have on me."

Her eyes widened, and she looked as if she might be close to tears. The show of feeling surprised me, though it occurred to me she might be allowing herself to show her pain, amplifying it to draw my sympathy. But when she spoke, her voice was shaking. "I thought there was a part of you that *wanted* to live in London. I thought in time you would be able to enjoy life with Richard, the fine clothes, the feasts, the gowns, the revels. Richard was educated and handsome. He was your friend until you sabotaged my spell. You're just too stubborn to see it."

She met my eyes, her expression so frustrated I realised she thought she was being genuine. I couldn't help but laugh. This was just like her. She had been so caught up in the opportunity she saw at Underhill House, she'd convinced herself that I wanted what she wanted. "There isn't a bone in my body that wants him. You should've trusted me. You're deluding yourself." I met her eyes, desperate for her to understand what she'd done. "Look what he did. Look what your spell made him do."

She searched my eyes, pressing her lips tight. After a moment, her face crumpled. She looked tired, older than her years. When she spoke, her voice was thin. "I was trying to help. I made a mistake."

The words echoed through the carriage. I had never heard her say them. I blinked at her—once, twice—uncertain how to respond.

"I shouldn't have cast a spell on you unwilling." She started to say something, then paused, biting her lip. "I'm sorry."

I watched her, shocked, a traitorous feeling rising in my throat. A childlike desire to accept her apology, to fix things between us. But the desire sent warning bells ringing throughout my being. *Don't trust her*, a small voice in me cried. *She's lying! It's not safe!*

It took me a long time to decide what to say. Even then, the words came out soft, overly cautious. "Thank you?"

Mother straightened in her seat, looking at me with a strange expression. Puzzlement, surprise, a hesitant tenderness. She did not take my hand or thank me. She didn't say she loved me. But she nodded, and something subtle changed between us. The air in the carriage suddenly wasn't as tense.

We didn't have long to enjoy our truce—a moment or two—before we arrived at our destination.

As the guards escorted us inside Justice Hall, I removed the ring and slipped it into my pouch. Immediately, I felt unmoored, unsafe, but I couldn't risk Richard seeing it.

I was sick to see that the room was just as it had been in my vision. The same judge, the same jury, the same sea of dispassionate spectators in the stands. I had hoped I'd done enough to change the whole scene. But as the guards settled us in the dock where I had stood in my dream, I saw Luce and Lisabetta and Cecely, watching anxiously from the balcony where they had sat in my dream. Richard and Humphrie sat steely-eyed on the witness benches in the exact same positions where they had sat. And there were poor Edmund and his governess in the second row; in the corner was the cage with Hughe curled up in an innocent ball.

The sight of my brother and the dog made my heart leap from my throat, and I sobbed. But my despair lasted only a moment before I was filled with a rage so violent, it fortified me. My fists clenched.

A grim determination filled me, a steely inner fire. I surveyed the courtroom, looking for some hint as to which strategy we should use to best increase our chances. The only difference I noticed between what I had seen and what was happening was Will's expression, concerned instead of stony. Thank the gods. Perhaps my actions had accomplished something after all.

"*Mama! Rose!*" a small voice called. Edmund had seen us walking in and had jumped from his seat to run toward us as fast as he could. The governess rushed after him, grabbing the tail of his shirt.

He struggled and called out in a terrified voice. *"Let me go!"*

Hughe barked furiously, jumping against the bars of his cage.

The governess carried my little brother out of the courtroom. The judge slammed his fist on the counter before him. "Silence!" he boomed. "Order! Someone quiet the dog!"

A boy scurried out from the side of the court to offer Hughe dried meat, but he refused it, too focused on us to care. Without thinking, I caught his eye and moved my hand in a signal for Hughe to hush. He quieted, but I saw one juror's eyes widen, and he began whispering to the man beside him.

"Mistress Rose Underhill. Mistress Katarina Rushe. How do you plead?"

"Not guilty," we said.

The same dread I felt during my dream filled me, and I prayed that we had done enough to change the events I'd foreseen. I closed my eyes, dizzied, a frantic heaviness weighing me down. Something nagged at me, but I was afraid to focus on it. I couldn't afford to lose consciousness now, but I couldn't shake the sense that the queen of heaven still had something to tell me.

The judge rose, calling the court to order, and announced that the trial would begin. A puritanical fellow in a staid black button-up doublet stood, the ruff of his collar so tight it looked like it was trying to eat his face. He nodded at the witnesses and jury and cleared his throat dramatically. The prosecutor, I realised.

He read the date, then pushed his spectacles up on his nose and declared the proceedings open. His voice was dry until he began reading the indictments, when his tone turned brazenly theatrical.

"The court hereby indicts Mistress Rose Underhill, wife of Master Richard Underhill, for the royal offence of witchcraft and murder by sorcery. The accusations are as follows. That, lacking the fear of God in her heart, she succumbed to the devil and fornicated with another man while her husband was abroad. That, shaming her husband's name further, she performed lewd and sinful acts in public. And that, under the delusion that this would free her from the God-fearing rule of her Christian husband, she lied to him that she was pregnant and cursed the ship on which he attempted to return to England so that it capsized, causing the deaths of three passengers."

The crowd gasped. I blinked, an icy sensation in my core. Never would I have imagined Richard would go so far. This was absurd, sensationalist. How could anyone believe such a thing of me? But the crowd was riveted. Mother blanched, meeting my eyes. On the balcony, Cecely let out a terrified sob.

Fury rushed through me, bubbling up. I gripped the dock where they had put us, my knuckles white. It was strange to be so simultaneously furious and exhausted. I felt like a fire in a blizzard whose heat was constantly being depleted.

"Furthermore," the prosecutor continued in his nasal voice, "Mistress Underhill, working in diabolical consort with her mother, Madam Katarina Rushe, widow of Master Secundus Rushe late of Kent, routinely performed acts of diabolical witchcraft so numerous that only a small proportion will be proved today for brevity's sake." He sniffed, looking up at the jury, his mouth turned down in a wry smile as if he were enjoying himself, then turned to the witnesses and nodded. "The first evidence will be brought by Master Richard Underhill himself."

Richard walked to the front of the courtroom, his expression grave. As he passed the dock, he met my eyes, smiling tightly. His eyes flashed with a callous hatred.

When he arrived at the stand, the prosecutor handed him several envelopes. From one he pulled out a sheaf of loose papers: the sonnets and my letter, no doubt. From another, he retrieved the notebook in which I calculated horoscopes. And from a third—my stomach dropped at the sight—he pulled my mother's spell book.

14

Fear yawned in my throat. I had the terrifying impression that our fates were sealed. It seemed as if the life I'd worked so hard to create was flickering, on the verge of extinguishing forever like a guttering candle. My music, my astrology, the life I could've lived with Cecely. Why had I been so foolish? I had wasted so much time denying what I should've known from the beginning. I had put Edmund in danger.

The eyes of every single spectator were on Richard. An expectant energy filled the room, making the air heavy and tight like the air before a storm. It reminded me of the energy in a theatre before a play. Richard, for his part, was playing the wounded husband. His brow was furrowed, his eyes sorrowful. It was impossible to tell how much of his feelings were natural. There were many ways for my fire to consume our marriage.

"I address this court today with a heavy heart. I do not bring these charges against my wife to hurt her so much as to *tame* her. I trust that God will bring a just conclusion to these proceedings. I love my wife a great deal, and I regret that the devil seduced her while I was away. In retrospect, I see that perhaps I shouldn't have left her alone so long. Her mother is a known practitioner of witchcraft, and her spirit is clearly weak—"

I straightened, gritting my teeth.

"Unhappily, I had business abroad that was crucial to my alchemical contract with Lord Burghley," he went on, proud, as usual, to mention the Lord High Treasurer. My fists clenched. At least half of the jurors were nodding, impressed by his connections to court. "Rose has always had an *overactive* mind. She cannot sit still, and her thoughts are restless. You know the sort of woman. Shrewish. Speaks too quickly, too much fire, choleric. My physician was treating her for it: wet foods, rest, the like. But as soon as I left, she went back to composing music, reading widely, practising astrology. While I was abroad, she covertly changed house in order to do the devil's bidding without alerting my steward."

Here he paused, a note of sadness creeping into his voice, as he gazed into the stands where Cecely sat, shaking his head.

"After that, all was lost. She became unruly, performing in a house of commerce, infecting men's hearts with lust, casting horoscopes for clients of all sorts—and I do mean all sorts. A prostitute, I am told. This astrological notebook and ephemeris should provide ample proof of those endeavours."

He gestured at the evidence on the table before him. The boy who had tried to calm Hughe retrieved it to bring it to the jury. The first juror flipped through the books and nodded imperiously, then passed it to the juror on his left.

"I share this not to denigrate the natural art of divining the stars' influence, but to illustrate the interest my wife has in the occult. In recent weeks I have become aware of an unnatural power she may have over the weather. At our wedding, the sky grew dark and lightning struck at the very moment that she set foot in the hall. I thought nothing of it then, nor did I blame her for the capsizing of our ship on rough seas on our way back to England. But now, when I look back on both incidents, how suddenly those storms overtook us, I fear it was her doing."

The crowd went silent for a moment, then a murmur rose from the stands. I could make out a few of the comments from the nearest spectators. *"Demonic ... shameful ... wicked—"* And a lone detractor. *"But that could be circumstance!"*

"I have also brought the letter she wrote to me deceiving me about her condition." He read it aloud. "We know from her landlord that she never went to stay with family, and as you can see, she has no symptoms of current or recent pregnancy. The women who examined her confirmed this…"

Everyone in the jury looked at me.

"The accused will stand," the judge said.

I gritted my teeth, paralysed with fury, and pulled myself up. I could barely support myself. My mother rushed to brace me. Everyone stared at me as if I were a sow for sale at market. A low murmur passed through the courtroom.

"You may sit."

I did, barely managing to keep my expression still.

Richard went on. "I am loath to waste this court's time with the surfeit of evidence we have, so I have chosen only the most damning to share. That sheaf of sonnets, circulated by one William Shakes-beard, speaks of their adulterous affair—" He gestured at a small stack of pages sitting on the table. "The jurors will note the sundry allusions to ravens and night, the poem about her playing the virginal. I am told her 'stage name' at a certain house of commerce was Ravenna Notte, that she played the virginal there, her favourite instrument." He spoke quickly, shaking his head, as if this entire ordeal embarrassed him, like a father whose child misbehaved at the market. "Over there is her familiar—" He pointed at Hughe, then held up my mother's spell book. "And this is her grimoire."

The crowd gasped. I gripped the railing of the dock.

"There are diverse charms in it, a number with malicious intent, obviously diabolical. You may look to the back of the book for those if you are staunch of heart," he intoned dryly, addressing the jurors. The boy brought them the evidence, and Richard addressed them, his expression disdainful. "With all due respect, I believe this is all you need. But I understand there is additional evidence against her. I trust God will guide this court in ascertaining the truth."

The prosecutor nodded. "Thank you, Master Underhill. That will be all."

Richard began making his way back to his seat.

The first juror examined the letter, nodding, then turned his attention to the spell book. When he opened it, his brow furrowed and he held up a finger. "Sir?"

The prosecutor turned.

"But this is blank."

Richard froze, bringing his hand to his breast, blinking. My spirits soared. Mary had not only succeeded in convincing her brother to steal the book but replaced it with another, so Richard wouldn't realise it was gone. I thanked Mary inwardly, sweet Mary, rejoicing at her cleverness and that of her brother. That is, until Richard turned to my mother, his expression so dark I nearly jumped out of my skin. *"What sorcery is this?"*

There was an uproar from the stands, and the jurors began passing the book around, astonished. No, I thought. No—

"Enough," the judge called. "Quiet!"

The courtroom went silent, and my thoughts raced.

"Call the next witness."

The prosecutor stood, scanning the papers before him. "The next witnesses will be goodwives Edwina Pursglove, Susanna Mason, and Wynne Smith."

The three matrons the guards had pulled off the street to find my birthmark stood, making their way to the bench. Their lips were pursed, and their eyes were hard. One of them bowed her head in prayer. I swallowed, fury burning inside me, thinking of Edmund. This was a travesty.

"I understand you inspected the person of this woman?" the prosecutor asked them.

All three nodded.

"Pray tell, what did you find?"

I was so angry, I could barely listen as the eldest woman said,

"Your Honour, members of the jury, we do confirm that when we modestly and reluctantly inspected her person, we did indeed find no evidence of pregnancy. Further, we observed a mark—" She sniffed and looked at the others. They nodded, their expressions expectant. The youngest woman nudged her. Finally, she cleared her throat and spoke. "A devil's teat, for that black dog to suckle her blood, in a place too delicate for good churchgoing women like us to mention—"

The courtroom went wild. Richard blinked, horrified. I raised my eyes, looking for Cecely. Her eyes were wet.

I stared balefully at the women, the word *traitor* echoing weakly through my head. *How could you?* I wanted to cry out, but I knew it would be detrimental to my case.

The prosecutor stood. "Thank you, my good women."

They curtsied and returned to their seats.

"The next witness the prosecution wishes to call is William Shakes-beard, the author of the poems and Mistress Underhill's alleged lover."

There was a murmur from the stands, an excited rush of talk. I closed my eyes for an instant, praying Will would keep his promise.

Will stood, wearing even more excellent attire than he had been the last time I saw him. A black velvet doublet with pretty brass buttons, matching breeches edged in white lace. The golden flecks in his eyes flashed as he met the clerk's gaze. He looked irritated. "It's Shake*speare*," he muttered to no one in particular, obviously frustrated, as if this happened all the time.

The prosecutor gestured for the boy to approach him. "The witness will speak to the subject and authorship of these sonnets. Do you confirm that they are your work?"

Will nodded. "I do."

"Do you confirm that the woman being indicted today is their subject?" He nodded at the boy, who fetched the sheaf of papers from the jury. The prosecutor rifled through them, reading snippets.

"Whose hair is 'black...' whose eyes are 'mournful...' whose soul is as 'tyrannous...as black as night'?"

Will didn't react at first, his expression completely neutral. He blinked, his gaze flitting to me for an instant as if to remind me about my promise. Then he returned his attention to the clerk and muttered, "I do not."

"Pardon?" the prosecutor sputtered.

"I have said. This woman is not their subject."

Relief rushed through me, and I said an inward prayer of thanks. I crossed myself and mouthed *praise God* for the jury's benefit. Beside me, my mother did the same, raising her eyes to the heavens. There was a murmur from the crowd and jury, who were looking at one another with quizzical expressions.

"Silence!" the judge said. He turned to Will. "Explain yourself."

"Mistress Underhill is an associate of mine, Your Honour. I know her through the theatre. She wrote the music for one of my plays. I am a married man with a family in Stratford-upon-Avon. A poet, Your Honour. The woman in these sonnets does in fact resemble Mistress Underhill physically, but she is a character of my own invention. An answer, if you will, to the fair mistress in the tired Italian sonnets that are now so ridiculously beloved."

The prosecutor stared at him, sputtering like a frog.

The judge obviously didn't believe Will either. "You swear this before the court," he interjected. "Before God."

Will didn't miss a beat. Looking irritated, he crossed himself. "Aye."

"Very well." The judge looked to the clerk.

The prosecutor lifted his eyebrows, then shook his head in disgust at Will. "That will be all."

Will stood, rolled his eyes, and returned to his seat.

"The final witness the prosecution calls is the son and brother, respectively, of the accused, Master Edmund Rushe."

My heart clenched.

The errand boy hurried from the side of the courtroom through the door to retrieve my little brother. As we waited for him to return, my throat constricted. The crowd whispered, and I felt a terrible throng of emotions in my breast. Fear, anger, pity, a great inner noise, unruly. I blinked, trying to quiet it. Then the errand boy returned with the governess, carrying Edmund at her hip, whispering something in his ear.

His eyes were red, his expression solemn, but as they walked in, he sniffed and stopped crying. Dread rushed through me. I knew— I *knew*—what she must have told him.

The woman set him down. He stared up at us solemnly, wide-eyed, his breath still hitching. The prosecutor looked to the governess, who nodded at him. "Go on. Tell the jury what you told me. The truth about your mother and sister."

Edmund burst into sobs. My heart broke for him, and my mother reached for my hand. She was sobbing silently, her shoulders shaking. Seeing her so upset made my throat constrict and my eyes grow wet with tears. I knew what they were doing, and it was unfathomably cruel. To force Edmund to testify against her, to tell him he was speaking on our behalf so he could reunite with us.

The governess knelt before him and hugged him, whispering in his ear again. Edmund drew himself up, summoning all the strength he had. "They're *helpers*," he said finally, his small voice difficult to hear in the echoing courtroom. "When people lose something, they help them find it. When people are upset, they make them feel better. They heal those who are sick."

"And how do they do this?"

Edmund's face brightened. "With flowers and candles and prayers. Sometimes herbs."

The crowd was silent. The jurors watched, leaning forward in their seats so they wouldn't miss anything he said.

"Witchcraft," the woman said quietly, her expression carefully neutral.

Edmund shook his head furiously. Mother had been telling him ever since he learned to speak never to admit this. "No. Or yes, but—" Edmund looked at the governess, who nodded carefully.

"Good now. Say it."

His eyes were as wide as moons. "They're good witches. Godly. They *help* people—"

"Thank you," the governess told Edmund.

The judge nodded. She picked him up and began to carry him out.

"Let me go!" he screamed, squirming to see us, eyes wild. "You told me I could go if I told the truth. *Let me go!* I want to go with *them!*"

I felt an ache in my throat, a sob pressing its way up. I pressed my eyes tightly shut, wishing there were something I could do.

When the sound of his terrified cries faded, the prosecutor stood, a grave expression on his face. "Your Honour—"

The judge nodded.

"Clearly the boy has a—" He cleared his throat. "*Childlike* impression of what his mother and sister do. They hid the full scope of their craft from him. And with all due respect, Master Shakespeare is not the honest man he claims to be. He says what he says to guard his reputation. May I remind the court that he writes stories for a living and works as a professional actor?"

The judge nodded. The prosecutor sat, his expression triumphant.

My heart sank. We're doomed, I thought. There's no way to come back from this. I closed my eyes, reaching deep inside myself for strength. *Regina Caeli*, I prayed, *benedic nos—*

A steely fury filled me—determined, hard—as the clerk called my mother, the first of the accused, next. She rose from beside me, her expression completely neutral. All those years of practice controlling her demeanour were on full display. She stood at the front of the court, curtsying to the jury, the judge, the prosecutor, nodding at the audience. I made a note to do the same when they called me. The more submissive I appeared, the more likely they were to acquit me.

"Madam Katarina Rushe," the prosecutor said. "How long is it since you made the acquaintance of the devil?"

Mother glared at him proudly. "I have never."

"Then how did you erase the contents of your spell book?"

"I did no such thing. I have never seen that book before in my life. It is a fabrication, which Master Underhill tried to use against us." She raised her chin high, then sniffed. "Perhaps he wrote the spells he claims were in it himself, and the Lord God, taking pity on my daughter and me, erased them."

A faint ripple of laughter echoed through the crowd.

"What have you to say of your son's claims that you are a witch?"

She looked at the prosecutor and spoke in an even voice. "I am a spiritual healer, sir, a finder of lost things like he said. I am guided by prayer, the saints, and the holy spirit. I burn candles, yes, and I'm a gardener with knowledge of herbs, but many wives use prayer and medicine to keep their family well and cure their sickness. Would you try all of them? I have never cast a spell with malice."

She said this so convincingly, I wondered if she actually believed it. She seemed to. Perhaps it was true to some degree. There was the ritual she had performed for Jane and Maggie, the spells I had seen her cast at home. Even the spell she cast on Richard and me had not technically been cast with malice. She had seen it as finding me a husband, procuring her family safety. Though my mother was determined and cold, manipulative, shrewd, I would not call her evil.

"If I may add—" she went on, looking for permission from the judge, who nodded slowly. "My son is the light of my life. Conceived after many years of prayer with my late husband, God rest his soul, who died only last Queen Elizabeth's Day. Our first son died seven years ago, and I had many miscarriages before Edmund was born," she said, a note of real pain in her voice. Her eyes glistened with tears. The effect was so powerful that I found myself tearing up too, thinking of the first Edmund and my late father. A wave of powerful grief overtook me, and my hands began to shake with anger at everything we had been forced to endure.

"Edmund is all I have left of my husband," she went on, deeply distraught, her voice shaking violently. "I would like to remind the court that my son is only five years old. To imprison me, or, God forbid, to hang me and my daughter, would deprive him of the only family he has left."

She pressed her lips together as if trying to master herself, though I knew it was the opposite. She was *allowing* herself to show her feelings.

Several members of the jury looked distraught. Others were shaking their heads. She was good. So good. Would it be enough to acquit herself and ensure that Edmund would be returned to her? I prayed that it would, though it occurred to me that her attempt to recover Edmund probably wouldn't help my case.

The jurors looked at one another, whispering. The crowd did the same. The judge let this go on for some time, his expression thoughtful. Then he nodded at the prosecutor.

Even he looked as if his sympathy had been aroused. He tugged at his ruff. "Thank you, Madam Rushe," he said just loudly enough for the court to hear. "You may be seated. The final testimony will be from Mistress Rose Underhill, herself."

I drew a deep breath, trying to still the wild admixture of emotions in my breast. It was as if my heart was exploding with every emotion I had ever felt. A chaos of feeling: grief and fury, sadness, love, a tempest of hope.

I stood, slowly making my way toward the front of the court-room. Sweating. My heart was beating so hard that walking was not as difficult an effort as it otherwise would've been, but my legs still felt shaky, and my movement was so slow I was ashamed at how weak I must look.

Until, that is, I realised it would be a boon. To appear helpless would only arouse more sympathy in the jurors. Perhaps I should faint, I thought wryly. Or pretend to—

I stopped trying to hide my difficulty, allowing myself to wobble on my heels. I took a handkerchief from my pocket and wiped my dewy brow. The clerk nodded at the boy who came to my aid, giving me his arm, which I took gladly. When I drew near Hughe's cage, the dog pushed his muzzle against the bars, making a whining sound for me to free him. I looked at him, allowing my face to crumple with genuine sympathy. I crossed myself, unable to staunch my tears, though I wasn't certain displaying my affection for him would help my case.

"Good now. Someone will let you out soon," I said softly, with a wild stab of hope that I would be acquitted so it would be me.

He stopped for a moment, but he began to whimper again as the boy brought me a chair. "Thank you," I said loudly to ensure that my gratitude would be heard by everyone. I made myself curtsy, as much as I could from a seated position. Three times, as my mother had done—for the judge, the jury, and the audience—trying for once to look as ladylike as possible. The crowd looked back at me, their faces swimming.

As I scanned the stands, I noticed two spectators who had not been there before, two spectators who had not been there in my vision. Jane Dee was sitting beside Will and Henry. And at the back of the courtroom, a shadowy figure stood in the doorway, hands clasped before her. I could see only her silhouette because of the way the light shone behind her.

The skirt of her gown was so wide that no one could stand

anywhere near her. A quartet of guards stood before her, just inside the doorway, with several more behind her in the hall. She took a step forward, and one of the torches on the wall lit her face. It was pale, brightly painted with spirits of Saturn. Her cheeks blushed with cerise circles. Her hair was a pale russet, streaked with white. She wore a golden crown.

Queen Elizabeth.

She searched the crowd with an imperious expression. Her gaze lingered for a moment on Jane, who met her eyes and stood, bowing deeply. Henry followed her gaze and saw the queen, then jumped to his feet and did the same. Soon the other members of the audience—the jury, the prosecutor, and the judge—were rushing to bow as well. I followed suit, waiting to straighten until everyone else had already done so, my thoughts racing. Why in the world would the queen attend these proceedings? Had she wandered into the wrong room?

"Your Majesty—" the prosecutor said uncertainly.

The queen shook her head firmly, making a turning gesture with her hand; she wanted him to continue as if she weren't there.

He took a deep breath and drew himself up, stammering, anxious to please her. "Mistress—" he said to me, clearing his throat, as if he had forgotten my name. He rifled through his papers as if the text on one of them might remind him. "Mistress Underhill," he said finally, relieved. "What have you to say in answer to these accusations? Let us begin with the fact that you left your husband's household and performed in a house of commerce."

I blinked, trying to still the wild rhythm of my heart. Mother and I had discussed several ways to explain my actions depending upon which way the trial went, but it had never even occurred to us that the queen might be here. I felt as flustered as the prosecutor must've been, though I was no doubt better at hiding it. I could think of only one thing left to try. Beneath my voluminous sleeve, I slipped the ring on my finger, praying for insight, remembering my sense that the queen of heaven had something else to tell me. *Regina Caeli*, I thought, speak to me—

What happened next took only an instant. I blinked, feeling a powerful undertow from the dreamworld inside me. When I surrendered, my awareness sank faster than it ever had before—so quickly, the reverie wouldn't have been perceptible to anyone but me. The response to my prayer came immediately. Two words, so clear, each one seemed a burst of light from the deepest shadow.

Be true. A solemn voice—so natural, so familiar—I couldn't tell if it had come from within or without me.

My eyes filled with tears. *Superiora de inferioribus, inferiora de superioribus.* Above, below. Without, within. They were one and the same. I blinked, trying to reorient myself in my surroundings. By the time I could see again, the crowd was murmuring.

The prosecutor was watching me expectantly, as were the spectators, the jury. Across the courtroom, the queen was doing the same. Something about the look in her eyes distracted me. She seemed familiar, as if I had met her before, though I knew I hadn't. Unless—those dark brown eyes, piercing, hard—her regal gaze. The way her hands were clasped in front of her.

God-a-mercy, I thought. My client. She had hidden her identity masterfully. I was so stunned, my emotion must've shown on my face. Across the room, the queen lifted an eyebrow, and her lips curved faintly downward. Fear rose in my breast. The change in her mien was so subtle, so brief, if I had blinked, I would have missed it.

I swallowed, terrified, remembering her threat that she would see me hanged if I betrayed her. No wonder. I prayed she wouldn't punish me for what she now knew I knew. I remembered my voice. The flask Mother had given me. My rasp might reinforce the notion that I was cursed by the devil.

I felt in my pocket. The flask was cold, heavy. I pulled it out, wondering what Mother had made, and took a deep draught. It was a syrup sweetened by honey with hints of cinnamon, anise, and lemon balm.

"Mistress Underhill?" the judge said. "Answer the question."

Be true, I thought, *be true*—

"Forgive me," I began, relieved to find that the lemon balm draught had done its work. My voice had come out soft but sweet, like music. I saw expressions change as soon as I said the words—a tilt of a juror's head, the judge's eyes widening, the queen leaning forward. I cleared my throat again, hoping I could make it loud enough for the queen to hear. "Before God and this court, I will speak plainly. I am a musician, Your Honour. A singer. I play the virginal, the lute, the psaltery, and the viol. I came to London to audition for a position at court. When my request for an audition was rejected, I was desperate to perform." I allowed my voice to tremble. "What Master Underhill says about me is true. I am restless when I do not play."

The queen listened impassively. The prosecutor was wearing a quizzical expression. The jurors too.

"In a house of commerce, though. Surely you could find some other place—"

"I had no other options, sir. As a woman acting without permission of her husband, my choices were limited."

"Your pregnancy?"

"I lost it."

"Your astromancy. The prostitute. Is what your husband said true?"

"It is. She was suffering. My mother and I wanted to help her."

"Your familiar?"

"A beloved pet, nothing more. His name is Hughe. He belonged to my late father, God rest him. A sheepdog from our farmhouse in Kent." My voice cracked authentically, and I realised my hoarseness was returning. I drank the rest of my mother's syrup.

"The shipwreck?"

I closed my eyes, summoning every last bit of my very real horror at that particular accusation, allowing a genuine tremor to creep into my voice.

"I had no awareness of it until this day, when the charges against me were read in this court. My powers are limited to divination and healing, blessings and prayers for sympathy, upon my life. They are quite minor, I assure you." I bit my lip, turning to meet the eyes of the judge and jury in turn. "I admit that I am an imperfect creature, Your Honour, with desires and foibles like all of God's children. But upon my life, I have never met the devil. My only sin is a wish to live apart from a man I was forced to marry—and I do mean forced. It was the only way I saw to provide for my brother after my father died and his family turned on us."

The judge shook his head, letting out a deep sigh of consternation. The men of the jury were sitting up straight. There was a low murmur from the stands. Women especially looked at one another, whispering.

"I would seek an annulment, Your Honour. Our marriage remains unconsummated. I pray you, have mercy upon me. And if you have no mercy, Your Honour, then consider how miserable Master Underhill would be with me for a wife."

There was a titter from the audience. I bit my lip, cursing my inability to let the opportunity for wit pass.

"May I say a word, Your Honour?" a familiar voice said from the crowd: an educated accent, a proud tenor. When I looked up, Henry had stood to address the court. The judge nodded, and he went on. "Mistress Underhill is known to me. I would vouch for her character and good works. As would my friend here, Mistress Dee, wife of John, with whom the court may be familiar."

The judge lifted his eyebrows.

Jane stood. "May I speak as well?"

He watched her steadily, thinking, then nodded.

Jane cleared her throat, straightening the lace ruffs at her wrists.

Then she cleared her throat, setting her chin high. "With all due respect, Your Honour, this trial is unjust. These women do God's work. They helped heal my heart when I was suffering."

A rush of gratitude poured through me. I allowed myself to look at Jane only for an instant. She nodded subtly.

"I have said," she sniffed, and sat with a huff.

The prosecutor sighed, drawing himself up. "We have no further witnesses, Your Honour."

From the back of the courtroom, the queen retreated.

The jury deliberated for several hours. We waited in a dim, hot room lit with lanterns, windowless but not empty. There were chairs, a draw table, a shadowy painting of Lady Justice with her scales. She stood at the front of a crowd of tiny ancients, who were looking up at her reverently. It occurred to me that she must be powerless now given what a mockery her sphere of influence was these days.

Mother asked me why the queen had come, but I kept my promise not to name my client, saying that I thought perhaps she had stopped by the court on her way elsewhere. But from the way my mother watched me, eyes narrowed, I suspected she knew.

The wait seemed interminably long. Apart from our conversation about the queen, we did not speak at all. I think my mother's superstitious streak prevented her from making any predictions. I wished I had my ephemeris, so I could consult the stars, but all I could do was consult my intuition. It occurred to me that perhaps that would be enough. The stars, after all, hung inside me. But every time I closed my eyes, I was shaken with such a mixture of hope and dread, I got vertigo.

By the time the judge finally summoned us for our sentencing, I was a wreck, my heart beating like a ridiculous drum. Mother was tight-lipped, her expression hard, her shoulders squared like a soldier on the way to a battle. The courtroom was as packed as it had been before. Richard and Humphrie looked cross from where they sat, arms folded, legs folded one over the other. Richard's eyes were narrowed and his lips were pursed distastefully, as if he had swallowed a lemon.

Luce and Lisabetta were there, and Cecely. Henry and Will. Edmund was nowhere to be seen. The queen had not returned. Hughe's cage had been moved elsewhere. I hoped someone had taken him outside.

Mother crossed herself as we sat. I followed suit.

Most of the jurors were watching us with neutral expressions, but a few of the men looked irritated, reluctant, as if they weren't quite satisfied with whatever had been decided. I prayed it was what we wanted to hear.

"Madam Katarina Rushe, you may rise for sentencing."

Mother took a deep breath and stood.

"The jury has decided that the widow Katarina Rushe is—" Here he paused. "*Not guilty* of all indictments. We petition the court to return her son to her as soon as possible."

I felt a rush of relief. Edmund was safe. They would live a happy life. With her reputation as a wise woman secured publicly, she could probably provide for him.

Mother beamed—her eyes sparkling, triumphant—but only for a moment. Then she bowed her head, ever eager to reap the social benefits of outward prayer, as if she truly believed that it was God who'd cleared her name.

Richard cleared his throat impatiently, changing which leg rested on top of the other. The judge nodded at my mother, and she sat. The crowd murmured.

"Mistress Underhill, you may rise." He paused, waiting. The moment seemed to stretch out, long enough for me to curse the fickleness of time.

I stood, looking around the courtroom. As everyone turned to look at me, I felt a wild and desperate stab of hope.

"The jury finds you not guilty of all indictments *except* the accusation of leaving your husband's house and shaming him, to which you freely admit. The court commands that you return to him according to his wishes, cease playing music, and cease offering your services as an astrologer."

My heart dropped, plummeting to the great black depths within me. My inner heaven spun. From the stands I heard the sound of Cecely's heart breaking. I began to sob, deep great heaves, in front of everyone.

"Your Honour," I said, not caring if I was perceived as insolent or weak. My voice heaved. "I pray you. I would speak on my behalf."

"This is most irregular."

I sniffed, a rush of pride surging through me. "Your Honour, I am an irregular woman."

Another ripple of laughter echoed throughout the courtroom.

The judge blanched. "You may not. The court's decision is final. Your brother is safe. Even your dog will be returned. Be satisfied with the mercy the court has shown you."

My hands began to shake. I felt dizzied by the too-quick turnabout from hope to despair. I felt as if I were going to faint. My mother reached for my hand. "Rose," she said. "*Rose*, stay with me—"

I balked, feeling a wave of grief so intense I felt powerless against it. If my father had not died, none of this would've happened. How I wished my mother had been able to heal him.

A boy rushed in with a scroll in his hand, a page, in clothes finer than I had ever seen a boy his age wear. A velvet doublet with slashed sleeves, a matching flat cap, slashed breeches. He was only twelve or thirteen. "Your Honour—" he called in a changing voice. It cracked on the second word. He cringed.

The judge swivelled his gaze to look at him. "Yes?"

"A message for you." He held up the scroll, running toward the bench. It was closed with a thick beeswax seal.

The judge took the scroll. He froze when he saw the seal. My heart leapt. I felt a strange twinge in my belly. It couldn't be. It couldn't—

The judge widened his eyes, shook his head, slipped his finger beneath the seal and broke it. His eyes scanned the document. Its message must have been brief. The judge cleared his throat, shaking his head in disbelief. "It is Her Majesty's will," he said in an incredulous voice, "that you be cleared of all charges. Your request for an annulment must flow through the proper channels, but it has her blessing. She has heard of your skill with music and would engage your services as a musician."

I blinked, unable to believe what I was hearing. From the stands, Cecely cried out with joy. I met her eyes, breaking into a smile so wide it hurt my cheeks. Chills bloomed all over my face. I felt so light, suddenly, that it seemed I might fly away.

Out of the corner of my eye, I saw Richard's jaw drop. My heart burst with triumph. The twinge in my belly solidified into three searing points. The berries.

This can't be real, I thought, but a small voice inside me shouted—crystal clear, each syllable a burst of light—*it is, it is!*

All because I was true.

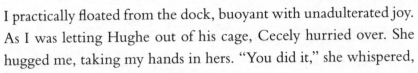

I practically floated from the dock, buoyant with unadulterated joy. As I was letting Hughe out of his cage, Cecely hurried over. She hugged me, taking my hands in hers. "You did it," she whispered, meeting my eyes. "You're safe."

"*We* did it." I hugged her, tears streaming down my cheeks.

We led Hughe away just as Mother returned with red-faced Edmund, his round face covered in snot and happy tears. We followed them out of the Old Bailey, gripping one another's hands.

As we were scanning the street for a carriage to take us home, I heard a familiar voice behind us. "Rose—"

Turning, I saw Will. Dark hair, golden-brown eyes, the flash of earring. The fine black velvet doublet and lace-edged breeches. When he saw my expression, he winced. He pulled down his doublet absently so that it flattered his narrow waist. "May I speak to you for a moment? I won't keep you."

His eyes went to Cecely, and I realised he wanted to speak to me alone. At my feet, Hughe growled, showing his teeth. Will paled. I didn't bother to suppress my smile.

Cecely met my gaze, a question. I lifted my eyebrows and shrugged. She nodded, moving to stand with Mother and Edmund, bringing Hughe with her.

I folded my arms. "What?"

"I didn't mean for this to happen."

"I am well aware of your motivations. You were hurt by what you perceived as my betrayal. You wanted to impress people. Your tenth house must be full of stars. It's the single most controlling influence in your temperament."

He scoffed. But years later, when Henry told me his birth date, I would find out I was right. It was all there. Mars, Saturn, and Jupiter in the house of status. The Crab. Ambition, perseverance, desire for fame, sensitivity.

"I denied it. Doesn't that count for something?" He searched my eyes, and his voice broke. "I *helped* you."

"Not exactly out of the goodness of your heart. You're afraid of what I might say about you."

"That's true, it is." His eyes gleamed with a desperate need for me to understand. "But I also wanted to help. Both things can be true."

"Say what you came here to say."

"I already did. Except—" He lowered his voice. "Did you read them?"

It was my turn to scoff.

"What did you think?"

I groaned. He was so damned predictable. "What do you want me to say? They're good, Will, so good everyone was talking about them. They'll launch your career, make you famous. *Congratulations!* You've immortalised me. I'm the bitch of the century!"

He stared back at me, horrified, his eyes widening.

Cecely touched my shoulder. "Let's go, Rose. You probably shouldn't be seen with him at all."

Pluto and hell, I thought. She's right.

I sent Will a withering look and walked out of his life.

But that is not where my story ends.

Playing at court was everything I thought it would be. Suffice it to say that I played my heart out, that I wore the absolute *gaudiest* of clothes. Singing, the lute, the virginal, whatever the queen wished. Once I'd played for her long enough that she knew I would not use that information against her, I made the only request I would ever make of her. Soon Cecely had a position as a dancer, and we were both performing for the queen in her privy chambers. At masquerades, at balls, at feasts with fizzy sweet mead, delicious cakes, elaborate sugar sculptures.

This went on for over a decade.

Occasionally, we performed an act we wrote together at the brothel: an exotic song for lute that evoked the granulating shadows and a dance of Cecely's own invention. There were no lyrics. The melody shifted in and out of a minor key, slow and sensual, then faster, as Cecely danced a scandalous dance.

The crowd was always enthralled, knocked into a sort of stupor. Men and women alike forgot their drinks, hands limp, a rapt expression overtaking almost everyone's faces: lips slightly parted, eyes dreamy and half-lidded. When it was over, everyone blinked and applauded with startled expressions, looking around as if they had forgotten where they were. They drained their cups and the tables emptied quickly, making their way hand in hand toward the stairs.

What else will you want to know? Let me think. I did not need an annulment after all. Richard died that summer—God rest him, I suppose—though most days, it is difficult for me to wish him well. My feelings about him are conflicted. I have never been able to parse how much of what he did was his own free will. Death was not kind to him. Mary's friend at Underhill House said that he shook, just like his father, that he had difficulty breathing. His decline was as fast as his father's. I couldn't help but think if their deaths had something to do with their work.

Not long after Richard died, we bought Swan House. I became known for casting horoscopes. We cast love charms too, though we did so less often after Mother died. Our most important work of that nature is the ritual to release hurt, which we still cast for anyone who says they need it. When I cast that spell wearing the ring, I can sense the malefic influence, a metallic aura, pouring out of them. When my mother fell ill, Lisabetta asked me to cast it for her, and so their rift was mended.

Hughe lived to the ripe old age of twelve. I bought him sheep to chase around. We learned to shear them and sold the wool each spring. He was loyal until the end, dying at the foot of my bed in his sleep.

Edmund became a barrister and married a gentlewoman. They have eight children. I'm glad for him, though if I had to live his life, I think I might want to jump off London Bridge.

Mary became one of Henry's mother's favourite maids. She was christened that summer. She still works for the Southamptons. After Henry's mother died, she went on to work for his wife.

Henry died too. You may have heard. Rather recently, while commanding troops in the Low Countries, of a fever. He managed to put off marriage for five years before the yoke, as Will put it, came for him. It all happened just as John Dee predicted, unfortunately. Marriage, the fever, a brief imprisonment in the Tower all those years ago—in rather finer chambers than the room we were given, I might add. He was even allowed to bring his cat. I visited.

A few weeks after the trial, I invited him to a revel we held at Swan House to celebrate my acquittal. It took us that long to restore the farmhouse to its former condition. After our release, we found it in shambles. Whoever searched it had been thorough. But by Midsummer, we had cleaned their mess, planted a kitchen garden, and trimmed the rosebushes and vines in the pleasure garden.

The forget-me-nots that had brightened the gate when we first arrived were dead, but there were summer blossoms everywhere—dianthus, lavender, rue.

For the revel, I hired the sisters from the brothel to sing, and a fiddler Luce had recommended to accompany them. The fiddler, it turned out, was one of the men who played at the feast Richard had arranged to announce our betrothal. He smirked when he saw me, shaking his head with a small whimper of mirth. "Good day to *you*, madam!"

We had bought mead from a beekeeper the Montefiores recommended. My mother had started a batch of her own, but it wasn't ready. Everyone was serving themselves, pouring mead into simple cups. The atmosphere was becoming giddy. Hughe and Edmund were running around, wreaking havoc, being generally terrible and amusing.

Night was falling, and the bonfire was bright. The sky was purpling, and there was a bright pink line at the horizon. The rosebushes and hawthorn cast a thick web of shadows. We had hung garlands along the garden wall, which flickered with pretty lanterns that cast large circles of light.

The musicians were playing a spritely folk song. My spirits were high. I had lost count of the number of cups of mead I'd drank. Luce and Cecely were teaching the brawle to me, Jane Dee, and

Lisabetta. We had kicked off our shoes and hiked up our petticoats and were enjoying ourselves immensely. Mother watched disdainfully, but to her credit, she said nothing. She never did manage to shed her preoccupation with modesty.

"Mistress Ravenna!" a bright tenor called out. When we looked up, we saw Henry, waving, sending Cecely and me a rakish smile. He wore a white doublet and breeches with thin stockings, and his blond hair fell in waves over his shoulders. His icy eyes danced as he drew close, pretending to kiss my hand, then turned to my friend. "And you are...?"

"Cecely Weaver," I said, smiling.

His eyes flitted from me to her and back with a flash of understanding. He smiled at Cecely, bowing much more deeply than he should've. "It's an honour to meet you, Cecely. Any friend of Rose's is a friend of mine. But surely you are closer than that. Cousins, perhaps? Sisters?" He smirked with his usual pleasure at hinting at what no one else dared talk about.

"Something like that," I said, amused at the sudden rush of affection I felt for him. This had been happening more often. I felt things all the time now. Affection not only for Edmund and Hughe, but for Cecely, my mother, strangers, as if I had become a different flower altogether. Thornless. Or at least in control of her prickles.

Henry hadn't even finished his first cup of mead before he congratulated us. "Good for you," he said, "making this life for yourselves."

Beside me, Cecely smiled at him, leaning her cheek against my shoulder. I nodded, a great lightness in my heart that I could only partially attribute to the mead. "It's everything we ever wanted. How are you and Will?" I asked reluctantly.

His eyes sparkled. A grin spread across his face, his lips twitching. "I think he's coming around. The other day he wrote me a sonnet calling me the master-mistress of his passion."

"Really."

Cecely raised her eyebrows.

"He thinks of you with something like affection, although it is admixed with bitterness. He wrote another poem mocking astrology, saying he plucks his judgement from my eyes." That grin again. "I'll mention how you're doing. Perhaps it will inspire him."

We sat for hours at one of the benches my mother and I had pushed around the bonfire, watching the flames dance, drinking mead, talking about everything that had happened.

"This is quite good," he said just before he left, holding up his cup, "though it would be better from sugar-plate."

"Not everyone can afford such indulgences, your lordship."

He chuckled. "I'll have some sent over. The other night Will told me that he regretted distributing the poems he wrote about you."

"How now?"

"He asked me to tell you he was reckless."

Reckless. Was that an intentional acknowledgement that he shared my flaw, or coincidence? Knowing him, it was probably the latter. I wondered what influences created his conflict between arrogance and insecurity, if he would ever set aside his need to be liked and accept his true nature.

The flames danced, their heat spreading through my hands, filling me with a pleasurable warmth. My forehead was dewy. I closed my eyes, feeling the world granulate subtly around me. That was happening more often too. The boundary between my inner and outer selves had become permanently porous.

"He asked me to tell you he wishes you well."

I blinked, startled by a rush of disbelief and bitterness. I thought Henry was mocking me until I saw his expression. Liquid, hesitant; he believed that Will's well-wishing was in earnest. I remembered the first night the history play was performed, the way Will tried to be vulnerable with me, and wondered if it had been sincere. "He did?"

Henry nodded. "He asked me to tell you he's sorry."

I balked at that. The stars glittered furiously. The sun had just moved out of two-faced Gemini into emotional Cancer. Henry waited for me to respond, but I shook my head fiercely.

"There an end," Cecely said quietly, leaning in. "She doesn't want to hear it."

The earl nodded, understanding, then stood and bade us good night. As he waved goodbye, my pulse raced. I sipped my mead, staring angrily into the fire as Cecely took my hand. Who did Will think he was?

I am not breaking my promise to him by telling his secret. I only vowed to keep it while he lived. He died a few years ago, in Stratford-upon-Avon with his family at his side, I hear, of some sort of fever. We never spoke again.

He must've thought about me off and on. There were references to me in plays, lines glorifying or arguing with things we said to one another. He added a few sonnets praising me before the sequence was published and slipped a few weak attempts at apology into his plays—that line in *Romeo and Juliet* about roses smelling sweet regardless, Rosalind's joke about Orlando's poems having too many feet—as if he thought I attended every play, hanging on to his words.

I did not, although I will admit I saw more of them once he started giving further thought to the way he portrayed women. I don't know what happened. Perhaps he showed his plays to another mistress. Or perhaps he finally learned to care less what people thought of him.

But it wasn't enough. It was never enough. If I were less talented with rhetoric, if we hadn't used the full extent of our powers, my brother would be an orphan.

No, a pox on that man. A secondhand apology. Some throw-away lines, some poems.

It was never enough for me to forgive him.

AUTHOR'S NOTE

Will Shakespeare's life is famously shrouded in mystery. We know the dates of his christening and wedding, the dates his children were born. We have his testimony in a London court case, the day he died, the hex he put on his gravestone: *Cursed be he that moves my bones.* I've always suspected that his sonnets tell us more.

These 154 love poems, which began circulating among Shakespeare's friends during the 1590s, have invited speculation since they were dedicated to a mysterious "Mr. W.H." in 1609. The speaker addresses two characters: a beautiful Fair Youth and a mysterious Dark Lady. There is a centuries-long debate over whether these characters are fictional or inspired by historical people from Shakespeare's life. Most critics are adamant that the Fair Youth and Dark Lady are constructs of Shakespeare's imagination, responses to the fair mistress who was idealized in the popular love poetry of his time. But the speaker has much in common with Shakespeare: He characterizes himself as a poet, referring to the actual sonnets he's writing and a rival poet who vies for the Fair Youth's attention. The dedication, too, hints that the poems might be autobiographical. I'm not alone in wondering about the story behind them.

Over the centuries, there have been theories that the Dark Lady was a brothel owner named Luce Morgan or the poet Aemilia Bassano Lanier. It's been suggested that the Fair Youth was Henry Wriothesley or William Herbert. The truth is we'll never know.

All we have is the story the sonnets tell. The first seventeen encourage a fair young man to marry and produce an heir, a theme so different from the poems that follow, critics wonder if they were written on commission. Something changes at sonnet eighteen: Shakespeare sets the young man's refusal to procreate aside and starts writing him love poems. The next hundred or so sonnets are so passionate, beautiful, jealous, and full of longing for the young man that I find it infuriating when people try to claim the speaker isn't in love with him. Who lies awake at night, staring into the darkness, unable to stop seeing a friend's image? Who calls a friend the "master-mistress of my passion"?

The twenty-six sonnets that follow the Fair Youth poems paint the picture of a troubled affair with another, quite different individual. Some of the poems addressed to Shakespeare's infamous mistress praise her dark beauty and declare his love for her, but others are more ambiguous, and many have a deep vein of misogyny running through them. I've always been put off by how scathingly Shakespeare condemns the Dark Lady's morality and the way he bemoans his lust for her, describing their encounters as the "expense of spirit in a waste of shame" and succumbing to a self-loathing so intense, it makes my skin crawl. The speaker blames his mistress for stealing the young man away from him, implies that she gave them venereal disease, and even insinuates that she might have made a pact with the devil...

This novel was born of my fascination with the woman who inspired those lines. I've always wondered what story she would tell. How would *she* feel if she read these poems? What would they have done to her reputation if her identity was discovered? What if she had a friend-turned-lover of her own?

The details of Rose's life come straight from the sonnets. She plays the virginal; she has dark eyes and hair; she's married before their affair starts. She's briefly involved with the Fair Youth, or so Will thinks. She's strong, sensual, independent. She has powers of her own.

I chose my favorite historical candidate for the Fair Youth, the famously beautiful Henry Wriothesley, 3rd Earl of Southampton,

Shakespeare's known patron. I'm partial to the theory that Henry's mother commissioned the procreation sonnets and Shakespeare fell in love with him and wrote the rest on his own. Henry's character is utterly fictional, of course, but I drew details from the sonnets, a 1922 biography by Charlotte Carmichael Stopes, and period portraits—including one John de Critz painted of him in the Tower of London with his cat Trixie.

The magic in the novel is inspired by the complicated mélange of faiths that existed in sixteenth-century England: legally mandated Anglicanism, suppressed Catholicism, and the ancient belief in magic that was mingling with both. I wanted to explore the Elizabethan obsession with astrology and alchemy, the natural witchcraft embraced by Christian folk healers, the spirit-summoning spells that circulated in secret grimoires like *The Sworn Book of Honorius*. I wanted to write John Dee, the royal astrologer who was famed for his alchemical experiments and conversations with angels, and dramatize the less-examined life of his wife Jane. I wanted to explore the reasons women were accused of witchcraft, which echo the reasons Shakespeare's Dark Lady was maligned.

Rose's readings of horoscopes are drawn from my own interpretations of period star charts and historical characters' horoscopes. The Queen of Heaven was an epithet that referred to several ancient goddesses who were associated with the night sky, love, sex, war, and the evening star.

Since the truth can only be guessed, I chose the order of Shakespeare's early plays that best suited this story, but the order I chose *is* possible. There are theories that *Titus* was inspired by *Tamburlaine* or the result of a collaboration between Shakespeare and Kit Marlowe. The ledger of Philip Henslowe, owner of the Rose Theatre, records that a play called "harey vj" was performed sixteen times during the spring of 1592. The notorious pamphlet published that fall, *Greene's Groats-worth of Witte*, alludes to the play Will Shakespeare is writing when he and Rose break up.

I invented young Will Shakespeare's character from what we know of his biography, the sonnets, the bawdiness of his plays, and his startling insights into characters like Petruchio and Richard III. I've always imagined him as an insightful man capable of great empathy and feeling, who was simultaneously arrogant, self-absorbed, and deeply insecure. In 1602, John Manningham recorded a secondhand account in his diary in which Shakespeare overheard Richard Burbage arranging a tryst with a woman who was beguiled by his performance as Richard III. Shakespeare went to the woman's home first and was already with her when Burbage arrived, at which point he sent down the teasing message that *"William the Conqueror was before Richard III."*

I really do wonder if he was this way.

ACKNOWLEDGMENTS

To Sam Farkas, Brit Hvide, and Angelica Chong, thank you for brilliant editorial advice. I am extremely fortunate to work with each of you. To Ellen Wright, Lisa Marie Pompilio, Amy J. Schneider, Bryn A. McDonald, and the rest of the team at Orbit, thank you for everything you have done to help me bring this novel into the world. To Wendy Muruli at Tessera Editorial, thank you for invaluable cultural accuracy feedback. To Ronlyn Domingue, Allison Epstein, Kaytie Lee, Olesya Salnikova Gilmore, Connor Chauveaux, and Fox Henry Frazier, thank you for reading. Additional thanks are due to Kaytie for reconnaissance work in London, and to Allison for so generously answering my last-minute plea for assistance. I am in your debt. My love and gratitude go to David, for years of unwavering support, Alix—my first and best reader, always—and Dylan, for being so quiet while I tapped away at the keyboard, sometimes even when "Greensleeves" *wasn't* playing.

I am grateful to historian Dr. Robin Hermann at the University of Louisiana for patiently answering my questions about the period and recommending books. Thank you to Dr. Jordi Alonso at Louisiana State University for help with Latin. All mistakes are my own. Thank you to Dr. Susannah Monta, my undergraduate early Shakespeare professor, for inspiring my interest in Shakespeare's early plays.

I am grateful to the authors of the following books, which were especially helpful among the many I read to try to do this story justice: Don Paterson's *Reading Shakespeare's Sonnets*; Helen Vendler's *The Art of Shakespeare's Sonnets*; Liza Picard's *Elizabeth's*

London; Charlotte Carmichael Stopes's *The Life of Henry, Third Earl of Southampton, Shakespeare's Patron*; Valerie Traub's *The Renaissance of Lesbianism in Early Modern England*; Laura Gowing's *Common Bodies*; Peter Parolin's *Women Players in England, 1500–1660*; Duncan Salkeld's *Shakespeare Among the Courtesans*; Bill Bryson's *Shakespeare*; Onyeka's *Blackamoores*; Miranda Kaufmann's *Black Tudors*; Imtiaz Habib's *Black Lives in the English Archives, 1500–1677*; Wallace Notestein's *A History of Witchcraft in England from 1558 to 1718*; Anne Llewellyn Barstow's *Witchcraze*; Barbara Rosen's *Witchcraft in England, 1558–1618*; Keith Thomas's *Religion and the Decline of Magic*; Deborah E. Harkness's *John Dee's Conversations with Angels*; James Orchard Halliwell's edition of *The Private Diary of Dr. John Dee*; Joseph H. Peterson's edition of *The Sworn Book of Honorius*; Frank Klaassen's *Making Magic in Elizabethan England*; and Alexander Boxer's *A Scheme of Heaven*.

To the Atlanta Shakespeare Company at the Shakespeare Tavern Playhouse for the productions that inspired me as I finished the novel; to my former students for the opportunities to return to the sonnets; and to you, dear reader, for picking up Rose's story—

Thanks, and thanks; and ever thanks.

MEET THE AUTHOR

David S. Bennett

MARY MCMYNE is a novelist, poet, and former English professor who is fascinated with the stories behind stories and the portrayal of women in history, folklore, and literature. She is the author of *The Book of Gothel* and a poetry chapbook, *Wolf Skin*, which won the Elgin Chapbook Award. A graduate of the New York University MFA program, she has won the William Faulkner–William Wisdom Award for a Novel-in-Progress and has received a grant from the Sustainable Arts Foundation, among other honors. She is the poetry editor for *Enchanted Living*.

if you enjoyed
A ROSE BY ANY OTHER NAME

look out for

THE BOOK OF GOTHEL

by

Mary McMyne

Germany, 1156. *Shunned by her village for her unusual
fainting spells and black eyes, young Haelewise's only solace lies
in her mother's stories of witches, magic wolf-skins, and ancient
mist-cloaked towers. When her mother dies, she sets off through
the woods for the mysterious tower of fable: Gothel. There,
Haelewise discovers a haven, a safe refuge for women like her
and for those who have lost their way in the harsh world of
men. A place where magic lives and where the fairy tales of her
mother's stories have more truth than she'd ever imagined.*

DECLARATION

This is a true account of my life.

Mother Gothel, they call me. I have become known by the name of this tower. A vine-covered spire stretching into the trees, cobbled together from stone. I have become known for the child I stole, little girl, my pretty. Rapunzel—I named her for her mother's favorite herb. My garden is legendary: row after row of hellebore and hemlock, yarrow and bloodwort. I have read many a speculum on the natural properties of plants and stones, and I know them all by heart. I know what to do with belladonna, with lungwort and cinquefoil.

I learned the healing arts from a wise woman, the spinning of tales from my mother. I learned nothing from my father, a no-name fisherman. My mother was a midwife. I learned that from her too. Women come to me from all over to hear my stories, to make use of my knowledge of plants. Traipsing in their boots and lonely skirts through the wood, they come, one by one, with their secret sorrows, over the river, across the hills, to the wise woman they hope can heal their ails. After I give them what they seek and take my fee, I spin my stories, sifting through my memories, polishing the facts of my life until they shine like stones. Sometimes they bring my stories back to me, changed by retelling. In this book, under lock and key, I will set down the truth.

In this, the seventy-eighth year of my earthly course, I write my story. A faithful account of my life—heretical though it may be—a chronicle of facts that have since been altered, to correct the lies being repeated as truth. This will be my book of deeds, written from the famous tower of Gothel, where a high wall encloses the florae and herbs.

—*Haelewise, daughter-of-Hedda*
The Year of Our Lord 1219

1

What a boon it is to have a mother who loves you. A mother who comes to life when you walk into the room, who tells stories at bedtime, who teaches you the names of plants that grow wild in the wood. But it is possible for a mother to love too much, for love to take over her heart like a weed does a garden, to spread its roots and proliferate until nothing else grows. My mother was watchful in the extreme. She suffered three stillbirths before I was born, and she didn't want to lose me. She tied a keeping string around my wrist when we went to market, and she never let me roam.

There were dangers for me in the market, no doubt. I was born with eyes the color of ravens—no color, no light in my irises—and by the time I was five, I suffered strange fainting spells that made others fear I was possessed. As if that wasn't enough, when I was old enough to attend births with my mother, rumors spread about my unnatural skill with midwifery. Long before I became her apprentice, I could pinpoint the exact moment when a baby was ready to be born.

To keep me close, my mother told me the *kindefresser* haunted the market: a she-demon who lured children from the city to drink their blood. Mother said she was a shapeshifter who took the forms of people children knew to trick them into going away with her.

This was before the bishop built the city wall, when travelers still passed freely, selling charms to ward off fevers, arguing about the ills of the Church. The market square was bustling then. You could find men and women in strange robes with skin of every color, selling ivory bangles and gowns made of silk. Mother allowed me to admire their wares, holding my hand tightly. "Stay close," she said, her eyes searching the stalls. "Don't let the *kindefresser* snatch you away!"

The bishop built the wall when I was ten to protect the city from the mist that blew off the forest. The priests called it an "unholy fog" that carried evil and disease. After the wall was built, only holy men and peddlers were allowed to pass through the city gate: monks on pilgrimage, traders of linen and silk, merchants with ox-carts full of dried fish. Mother and I had to stop gathering herbs and hunting in the forest. Father cut down the elms behind our house, so we had room to grow a kitchen garden. I helped Mother plant the seeds and weave a wicker coop for chickens. Father purchased stones, and the three of us built a wall around the plot to keep dogs out.

Even though the town was enclosed, Mother still wouldn't let me wander without her, especially around the new moon, when my spells most often plagued me. Whenever I saw children running errands or playing knucklebones behind the minster, an uneasy bitterness filled me. Everyone thought I was younger than I was, because of my small stature and the way my mother coddled me. I suspected the *kindefresser* was one of her many stories, invented to scare me into staying close. I loved my mother deeply, but I longed to wander. She treated me as if I was one of her poppets, a fragile thing of beads and linen to be sat on a shelf.

Not long after the wall was built, the tailor's son Matthäus knocked on our door, dark hair shining in the sun, his eyes flashing with merriment. "I brought arrows," he said. "Can you come out to the grove, teach me to shoot?"

Our mothers had become friends due to my mother's constant need for scraps of cloth. She made poppets to sell during the cold season, and the two women had spent many an afternoon sorting scraps and gossiping in the tailor's shop as we played. The week before, Matthäus and I had found an orange kitten. Father would've drowned him in a sack, but Matthäus wanted to give him milk. As we sneaked the kitten upstairs to his room, I had racked my brain for something to offer him so we could play again. Mother had taught me everything she knew about how to use a bow. Shooting was one of the few things I was good at.

"Please please please," I begged my mother.

She looked at me, tight-lipped, and shook her head.

"Mother," I said. "I need a friend."

She blinked, sympathetic. "What if you have a spell?"

"We'll take the back streets. The moon is almost full."

Mother took a deep breath, emotions warring on her face. "All right," she sighed finally. "Let me tie back your hair."

I yelped with joy, though I hated the way she pulled my curls, which in general refused to be tamed and which I had inherited from her. "Thank you!" I said when she was finished, grabbing my quiver and bow and my favorite poppet.

Ten was an odd age for me. I could shoot as well as a grown man but had yet to give up childish things. I still brought the poppet called Gütel that Mother made for me everywhere. A poppet with black hair just like mine, tied back with ribbons. She wore a dress of linen scraps dyed my favorite color, madder-red. Her eyes were two shining black beads.

I was a quizzical child, a show-me child—a wild thing who had to be dragged to Mass—but I saw a sort of magic in Mother's poppet-making. Nothing unnatural, mind you. The sort of thing everyone does, like set out food for the Fates or choose a wedding date for good luck. The time she took choosing the right scraps, the words she murmured as she sewed, made that doll alive to me.

On our way out, Mother reminded me to watch for the *kinde-fresser*. "Amber eyes, no matter what shape she takes, remember." She lowered her voice. "You'll want to warn that boy about your spells."

I nodded, cheeks flushing with shame, though Matthäus was too polite to ask what my mother had said under her breath. We hurried toward the north gate, past the docks and the other fishermen's huts. I pulled my hood over my head so the sun wouldn't bother my eyes. They were sensitive in addition to being black as night. Bright light made my head ache.

The leaves of the linden trees were turning yellow and beginning to fall to the ground. As we stepped into the grove, ravens scattered. The grove was full of beasts the carpenters had trapped when the wall was built. It was common to see a family of hares hopping beneath the lindens. If you were foolish enough to open your hand, a raven would swoop down and steal a *pfennic* from your palm.

Matthäus showed me the straw-stuffed bird atop a pole that everyone used for archery practice. I sat Gütel at the base of a tree trunk, reaching down to straighten her cloak. My heart soared as I reached for my bow. Here I was, finally outside the hut without Mother. I felt normal, almost. I felt free.

"Did you hear about the queen?" Matthäus asked, pulling his bow back to let the arrow fly. It went wild, missing the trunk to stray into the sunny clearing.

"No," I called, squinting and shading my eyes as I watched him go after it. Even with the shadow of my hand, looking directly at the sunlight hurt.

He reappeared with the arrow. "King Frederick banished her."

"How do you know?"

"A courtier told my father while he was getting fitted."

"Why would the king banish his wife?"

Matthäus shrugged as he handed me the arrow. "The man said she asked too many guests into her garden."

I squinted at him. "How is that grounds for banishment?" I didn't understand, then, what the courtier meant.

He shrugged. "You know how harsh they say King Frederick is."

I nodded. Since his coronation that spring, everyone called him "King Red-Beard" because his chin-hair was supposed to be stained with the blood of his enemies. Even as young as ten, I understood that men make up reasons to get rid of women they find disagreeable. "I bet it's because she hasn't given him a son."

He thought about this. "You're probably right."

I strung my bow, deep in thought. After the coronation, the now-banished queen had visited with the princess, and Mother had taken me to see the parade. I remembered the pale, black-haired girl who sat with her mother on a white horse, still a child, though her brave expression made her seem older. Her eyes were a pretty hazel with golden flecks. "Did the queen take Princess Frederika with her?"

Matthäus shook his head. "King Frederick wouldn't let her."

I imagined how awful it would be to have my mother banished from my home. Where my mother was protective, my father was cold and controlling. A house without Mother would be a house without love.

I forced myself to concentrate on my shot.

When the arrow pierced the trunk, Matthäus sucked in his breath. At first I thought he was reacting to my aim. Then I saw he was looking at the tree where Gütel sat. A giant raven with bright black hackles was bent over her.

I charged at the bird. "Shoo! Get away from her!"

The bird ignored me until I was right beside it, when it looked up at me with amber eyes. *Kraek*, it said, shaking its head, as it dropped Gütel on the ground. It kept something in its beak, something glittering and black, which flashed as it took off.

On the left side of Gütel's face, the thread was loose. The wool had come out. The raven had plucked out her eye.

A cry leapt from my throat. I fled from the grove, clutching Gütel to my chest. The market square blurred as I ran past. The tanner called out: "Haelewise, what's wrong?"

I wanted my mother and no one else.

The crooked door of our hut was open. Mother stood in the entryway, sewing, a needle between her lips. She had been waiting for me to come home.

"Look!" I shouted, rushing toward her, holding my poppet up.

Mother set down the poppet she was sewing. "What happened?"

As I raged about what the bird had done, Father walked up, smelling of the day's catch. He listened for a while without speaking, his face stern, then went inside. We followed him to the table. "Its eyes," I sobbed, sliding onto the bench. "They were amber, like the *kindefresser*—"

My parents' eyes met, and something passed between them I didn't understand.

Overcome by a telltale shiver, I braced myself, knowing what would happen next. Twice a month or so—if I was unlucky, more—I had one of my fainting spells. They always started the same way. Chills bloomed all over my skin, and the air went taut. I felt a pull from the next world—

The room swayed. My heart raced. I grasped the tabletop, afraid I would hit my head when I fell. And then I was gone. Not my body, but my soul, my ability to watch the world.

The next thing I knew, I was lying on the floor. Head aching, hands and feet numb. My mouth tasted of blood. Shame filled me, the awful not-knowing that always plagued me after a swoon.

My parents were arguing. "You haven't been to see her," Father was saying.

"No," Mother hissed. "I gave you my word!"

What were they talking about? "See who?" I asked.

"You're awake," Mother said with a tight smile, a panicked edge to her voice. At the time, I thought she was upset about my swoon. My spells always rattled her.

My father stared me down. "One of her clients is a heretic. I told your mother to stop seeing her."

My gut told me he was lying, but contradicting him never went well. "How long was I out?"

"A minute," Father said. "Maybe two."

"My hands are still numb," I said, unable to keep the fear out of my voice. The feeling usually came back to my extremities by this point.

Mother pulled me close, shushing me. I breathed in her smell, the soothing scent of anise and earth.

"Damn it, Hedda," Father said. "We've done this your way long enough."

Mother stiffened. As far back as I could remember, she had been in charge of finding a cure for my spells. Father had wanted to take me to the abbey for years, but Mother outright refused. Her goddess dwelt in things, in the hidden powers of root and leaf, she told me when Father was out. Mother had brought home a hundred remedies for my spells: bubbling elixirs, occult powders wrapped in bitter leaves, thick brews that burned my throat.

The story went that my grandmother, whom I hardly remembered, suffered the same swoons. Supposedly, hers were so bad that she bit off the tip of her tongue as a child, but she found a cure for them late in life. Unfortunately, Mother had no idea what that cure was, because my grandmother died before I suffered my first swoon. Mother had been searching for that cure ever since. As a midwife she knew all the local herbalists. Before the wall was built, we had seen wise women and wortcunners, sorceresses who spoke in ancient tongues, the alchemist who sought to turn lead into gold. The remedies tasted terrible, but they sometimes kept my spells away for a month. We had never tried holy healers before.

I hated the emptiness I felt in my father's church when he dragged me to Mass, while my mother's secret offerings actually made me *feel* something. But that day, as my parents argued, it occurred to me that the learned men in the abbey might be able to provide relief that Mother's healers couldn't.

My parents fought that night for hours, their white-hot words rising loud enough for me to hear. Father kept going on about the demon he thought possessed me, the threat it meant to our liveli-hood, the stoning I would face if I got blamed for the wrong thing. Mother said these spells ran in her family, and how could he say I was possessed? She said he'd promised, after everything she gave up, to leave her in charge of this *one* thing.

The next morning, Mother woke me, defeated. We were going to the abbey. My eagerness to try something new felt like a betrayal. I tried to hide it for her sake.

It was barely light out as we walked to the dock behind our hut. As we pushed our boat into the lake, the guard in the bay tower recognized my father and waved us through the pike wall. Our boat rocked on the water, and Father sang a sailing hymn:

> *"Lord God, ruler of all, keep safe*
> *this wreck of wood on the waves."*

He rowed us across the lake, giving a wide berth to the northern shoreline, where the mist the priests called "unholy" cloaked the trees. "God's teeth," Mother said. "How many times do I have to tell you? The mist won't hurt us. I grew up in those woods!"

She never agreed with the priests about anything.

Pulling our boat ashore an hour later, we approached the stone wall that surrounded the abbey. Elderly and thin with a long white beard and mustache, a kind-looking monk unlocked the gate. He stood between us and the monastery, scratching at the neckline of his tunic, as Father explained why we had come. I couldn't help but notice the fleas he kept squelching beneath his fingers as he listened to my father describe my spells. Why didn't he scatter horsemint over the floor, I wondered, or coat his flesh with rue?

Mother must have wondered the same. "Don't you have an herb garden?"

The monk shook his head, explaining that their gardener died last winter, nodding for Father to finish his description of my spells.

"Something unnatural settles over her," he told the monk, his voice rising. "Then she falls into a kind of trance."

The monk watched me closely, his gaze lingering on my eyes. "Do you suspect a demon?"

Father nodded.

"Our abbot could cast it out," the monk offered. "For a fee."

Something fluttered in my heart. How I wanted this to work.

Father offered the monk a handful of *holpfennige*. The monk counted them and let us in, shutting the heavy gate behind us.

Mother frowned as we followed the monk across the grounds. "Don't be afraid," she whispered to me. "There is no demon in you."

Through a huge wooden door, the monk led us into the main chamber of the minster, a long room with an altar on the far end. Along the aisle, candles flickered below murals. Our footsteps echoed. When we reached the baptismal font, the monk told me to take off my clothes.

Father reached for my hand and squeezed it. He met my eyes, his expression kind. My heart almost burst. It'd been so long since he looked at me that way. For years, he'd seemed to blame me for the demon he thought possessed me, as if some weakness, some flaw in my character had invited it in. If this works, I thought, he'll look at me that way all the time. I'll be able to play knucklebones with the other children.

I stripped off my boots and dress. Soon enough I was barefoot in my shift, hopping from foot to foot on the freezing stones. Six feet wide, the basin was huge with graven images of St. Mary and the apostles. I bent over the edge and saw my reflection in the holy water: my pale skin, the vague dark holes of my eyes, the wild black curls that had come loose from my braids as we sailed. The basin was deep enough that the water would rise to my chest, the water perfectly clear.

When the abbot arrived, he laid his hands on me and said something in the language of clergymen. My heart soared with a desperate hope. The abbot wet his hand and smeared the sign of the cross on my forehead. His finger was ice cold. When nothing happened, the abbot repeated the words again, making the sign of the cross in the air. I held my breath, waiting for something to happen, but there was only the chilly air of the minster, the cold stones under my toes.

The holy water glittered, calling me. I couldn't wait any longer. I wriggled out from under the monk's hands and climbed into the basin.

"*Haelewise!*" my father bellowed.

The cold water stung my legs, my belly, my arms. As I plunged underwater, it occurred to me that if there was a demon inside me, it might hurt to cast it out. The silence of the church was replaced by the roar of water on my eardrums. The water was like liquid ice. Holy of holies, I thought, opening my mouth in a soundless scream. How could the spirit of God live in water so cold?

When I burst out, gasping, the abbot was speaking in the language of priests.

"What do you think you're doing?" my father yelled.

Finishing his prayer, the abbot tried to calm him. "The Holy Spirit compelled her—"

I clambered out of the basin, wondering if the abbot was right. Water rolled down my face in an icy sheet. Hair streamed down my back. I stood up, flinging water all over the floor. My teeth chattered. Mother fluttered around me, helping me wring out my hair and shift, trying to dry me with her skirt.

Father watched while I shivered and pulled on my dress. He looked at the abbot, then Mother, his brow furrowed. "How do you feel?"

I made myself still, considering. Wet and cold, I thought, but no different. Either there had been no demon, or I couldn't tell that it had left. The realization stung. I thought of all the remedies we'd tried so far, the foul-tasting potions, the sour meatcakes and bitter herbs. Who knew what they'd try next?

I met their eyes, making my own grow wide. Then I knelt in my puddle on the stones, making the sign of the cross. "Blessed Mother of God," I said. "I am cured."